Praise for *Meet Me at the Starlight*

"Hauck pulls out all the stops in this heartwarming novel of perseverance and family, with her trademark dual-era nostalgia and mysterious, heaven-sent character."

—*Library Journal* starred review

"*Meet Me at the Starlight* is a delightful multigenerational novel. I was fully invested in these memorable characters who are as colorful as the iconic Starlight's neon sign. This story will have you flipping pages well past midnight as the community fights for their local treasure, and the ending will renew your faith as good prevails."

—Nancy Naigle, author of *The Shell Collector*

"In a charming story set across three generations, Hauck introduces readers to a delightful town, Hollywood stars, a royal mystery, and the Starlight skating rink at the heart of it all. While *Meet Me at the Starlight* wraps you in a twentieth-century fairy tale, its themes of forgiveness, trust, second chances, acceptance, and love carry the day and will leave you grinning at the last page."

—Katherine Reay, bestselling author of *Dear Mr. Knightley* and *The Printed Letter Bookshop*

Praise for *The Best Summer of Our Lives*

"Hauck's exploration of friendship, second chances, and faith is tender and often emotionally nuanced. It's an undeniable heart-warmer."

—*Publishers Weekly*

"Bestselling, Christy–winning Hauck presents a powerful inspirational tale of friendship that touches on two horrific real crimes of the 1970s and charts a rocky path to redemption and love."

—*Booklist*

"Themes about the endurance of friendship and the ability to come home give readers plenty to think about, and those nostalgic for childhood summers will enjoy this novel."

—*Library Journal*

"In true Rachel Hauck fashion, *The Best Summer of Our Lives* blends faith and hope into a story about the seasons of life, the seasons of friendship, and the seasons of love. A journey that will warm your heart and make you yearn to reconnect with old friends."

—Lisa Wingate, *New York Times* bestselling author of
The Book of Lost Friends

"Rachel Hauck sets the gold standard in inspirational fiction. *The Best Summer of Our Lives* is a nostalgic novel of friendship, romance, and the choices that define a life."

—Brenda Novak, *New York Times* and
USA Today bestselling author

THE SANDS OF
SEA BLUE BEACH

Bethany House Books by Rachel Hauck

The Best Summer of Our Lives
Meet Me at the Starlight
The Sands of Sea Blue Beach

THE SANDS OF SEA BLUE BEACH

RACHEL HAUCK

BETHANYHOUSE

a division of Baker Publishing Group
Minneapolis, Minnesota

© 2025 by Rachel Hauck

Published by Bethany House Publishers
Minneapolis, Minnesota
BethanyHouse.com

Bethany House Publishers is a division of
Baker Publishing Group, Grand Rapids, Michigan

Printed in the United States of America

Library of Congress Cataloging-in-Publication Data
Names: Hauck, Rachel, author.
Title: The Sands of Sea Blue Beach / Rachel Hauck.
Description: Minneapolis, Minnesota : Bethany House Publishers, a division of Baker Publishing Group, 2025.
Identifiers: LCCN 2024054645 | ISBN 9780764240997 (paper) | ISBN 9780764245053 (casebound) | ISBN 9781493450824 (ebook)
Subjects: LCGFT: Christian fiction. | Romance fiction. | Novels.
Classification: LCC PS3608.A866 S26 2025 | DDC 813/.6—dc23/eng/20241122
LC record available at https://lccn.loc.gov/2024054645CIP info]

Emojis are from the open-source library OpenMoji (https://openmoji.org/) under the Creative Commons license CC BY-SA 4.0 (https://creativecommons.org/licenses/by-sa/4.0/legalcode).

Cover design by Faceout Studio, Molly von Borstel

Baker Publishing Group publications use paper produced from sustainable forestry practices and postconsumer waste whenever possible.

25 26 27 28 29 30 31   7 6 5 4 3 2 1

To Sally Longoria

1

EMERY

Now ...
New Year's Eve

Well, she did not see this coming. A midnight proposal with all the family around. Yet it was the way of James Gelovani. And he wasn't proposing to her. He was proposing to Ava. Her sister. Two words that she still struggled to reckon with after fifteen years.

Down on one knee, Jamie professed in honeyed tones, "Ava Quinn, beautiful Ava, I never thought I'd find a girl like you. Will you marry me?"

Emery smiled and raised her glass of champagne as the weepy—and beautiful—Ava bent to give her man a kiss and softly answered, "Yes, I'll marry you." Then she shouted, "I'm getting married!"

Emery applauded along with the family—Dad, Joanna, Elianna, and Blakely—then congratulated the happy couple. After all, she'd played a part in their romance by inviting Jamie to the Quinn Family Memorial Day weekend.

Friends since their Ohio State days, Emery went on to become a journalist at the renowned sixty-year-old *Cleveland Free Voice*, while Jamie conquered the world of law. They lost touch, then reconnected at a Buckeye alumni meeting eight months ago.

The *Free Voice* had just closed down, and she was trying to hustle up another job. Jamie, on the other hand, regaled a crowd of curious Buckeyes about his work on a landmark Bitcoin case. At the end of the night, he and Emery walked to the parking lot together, reminiscing about Saturdays in the Shoe when he'd said, *"I could use a break from this case."* So she'd invited him to Dad's big M-Day bash.

Somewhere between the Saturday afternoon cookout by the pool, the Sunday Funday at Cedar Point, and the Monday night Cleveland Guardians game, Jamie fell in love with Ava.

He claimed it was when she walked out to the pool deck in front of nearly thirty friends and family—every one a diehard Buckeye alum—wearing head-to-toe Michigan gear and singing their fight song on a dare from a Michigan colleague. Blakely recorded it all on her phone.

Ava had taken her life in her hands wearing *that* getup, singing *that* song, among *those* Buckeye faithful. Yet Jamie, who bled scarlet and gray, thought the move was hysterically gutsy.

"Em, that's Ava? The sister you talked about at school? She's awesome. Why don't you like her?"

Who said she didn't like her? She liked her. Loved her, even. But things were complicated in the Quinns' blended household.

As the clock in the hall chimed midnight, Dad passed out champagne. "Happy New Year," he said, raising his glass. "To the Quinn family, and to the soon-to-be new family, Jamie and Ava."

"To the Quinn family. And the future Gelovanis." Jamie gazed at his fiancée as if she were the only woman on earth, and for a moment, Emery felt that flash of yearning for a man to look at her that way.

"Happy New Year to all of us." Joanna, Dad's wife, smiled and glanced about the circle, her joy visible. Her oldest daughter was getting married.

Dad married Joanna, a widow with two young daughters, a year after Mom died. In a single day, Emery's world went from just the two of them to a stepmother and two pesky little sisters whom Dad adopted right after he said, "I do." The effervescent Blakely arrived a year later as the "whole" meant to bond the "halves."

Dad caught Emery's attention and tipped his head gently toward Ava, who was showing off her ring to Elianna and Blakely. *Go on, get in there with your sisters.*

Over the years, she'd come to understand how desperately he wanted her to feel a part of the family he'd created with Joanna. As a busy high school senior when they married, then a college freshman when Blakely arrived, she'd always felt more like the guest who tagged along with the new husband and father.

In the early days of blending two families, Joanna invited Emery to call her Mom, to which she replied, *"I have a mom. I'll stick with Joanna, if you don't mind."* Or even better, *my dad's wife.* But she didn't go quite that far.

Couldn't they all see? Emery alone carried the legacy of Rosie Quinn, and she'd not let anyone or anything replace her.

"Happy New Year, Emery." Elianna was the affectionate sister, a peacemaker, and a brilliant businesswoman. At twenty-two, she'd taken over her mother's three coffee shops, and in two years, turned red ink into black.

"Guess who will have a list of maid-of-honor duties by tomorrow night?" Emery said, sipping her champagne.

"You?" Elianna said.

Emery laughed. "Guess again. And fifty bucks says she picks pink as her color palette. I don't do pink."

"Happy New Year, big sis." Blakely threw her arms around

Emery. She was the jovial athlete, fourteen going on forty, who knew nothing about stepmothers and moms who died too young.

"Happy New Year, Blake. I have a feeling pink is in your future."

Blakely glanced toward her glowing sister. "I don't mind. It's for Ava."

Feeling put in her place by her wise little sister, Emery crossed over to hug Ava. "Your new year is off to a good start."

"I owe it all to you." Ava lingered in their embrace. "You invited him home."

"What choice did I have? He looked like a lost puppy working that bitcoin case. His parents lived all the way down in Portsmouth. I felt sorry for him." She made a face at Jamie, and he laughed.

"Happy New Year, Em," Jamie said. "Free legal advice for life. You introduced me to my future wife."

"Whoa, wait until you're married a few years. I may not want any credit for this."

"Let's hope we never need legal help." Dad had a look that said *Let's all follow the law* as he poured another round of champagne and gathered everyone for his traditional New Year's toast. "Here's to finally getting some additional manpower around here. Welcome to the family, Jamie."

"To my wedding," Ava said with a quick glance at her fiancé. "I mean, *our* wedding." She fell against him, and he buried his face in her hair.

"To a good basketball season," Blakely said. She was a star freshman on and off the court at an exclusive all-girls high school.

"To Mom and me finding a location for our next Sophisticated Sips café," Elianna said.

"What Elianna said." Joanna clinked their glasses.

"Emery?" Dad drew everyone's attention to her. "What are your plans for the new year?"

She smiled through her embarrassment over being the older, unemployed sister, thirty-two with zero prospects in career or love. Except one. And she was hesitant to accept it.

"To something new and exciting," she said with too much umph as she raised her glass. "Don't ask what because I don't know."

This year had to be better than the last. Her beloved *Cleveland's Free Voice* folded. Her boss and mentor, Lou Lennon, the paper's founder, had refused to sell any assets to the corporate fat cats he'd exposed for sixty years. Then the lease on her downtown loft expired and she had no choice but to move home. Most of her friends were married, having children, buying houses. She'd not been on a date since, well, was it the Governor's Ball . . . ? No, she went with Tonya, so it had to be the art gallery opening in . . . ? Good grief. Five years. She'd not been on a date in five years?

But she hadn't cared then. Her professional life had been in full swing, running the *Free Voice* under Lou's tutelage. When he closed the doors, she'd not felt so lost since Mom died.

She'd scoured the internet for jobs, called all of her contacts from J-school and beyond, managed to land articles in *Marie Claire* and *Glamour*, wrote a piece on the new downtown development for *The Plain Dealer*, and published a four-part political series for an online outlet.

But full-time employment evaded her.

Until this past month. A friend of Lou's, a man named Elliot Kirby, called her with an editor-in-chief position. But saying yes was unthinkable. A yes meant going back to the saddest place and time in her life. She felt like a square peg facing a round hole.

Yet refusing the job seemed like holing up and hiding.

Elianna snuggled next to Emery. "I think Ava will ask you to be maid of honor."

"Me? Naw, it'll be you. And it should. You're her sister."

"And you're her sister too." Elianna's voice had a slight edge. "I mean, you didn't kill her when she spilled purple nail polish all over your shoes just as you were heading out to prom. If that's not sisterly love, I don't know what is."

Emery laughed. "I still think she broke a law of physics when that happened."

Over the years, she'd warmed to Ava, Elianna, and especially Blakely—who looked just like Dad—but the older two felt more like cousins than siblings.

"Dad," Ava's said, "in six or seven months, you'll be walking me down the aisle." She planted a kiss on his cheek. "Your first trip."

"I'll be crying the whole time." Dad hugged her close with a side glance at Emery. She knew he felt caught in the middle sometimes, between his only daughter for seventeen years and his new daughters for the last fifteen.

She nodded. *It's okay.*

"You know she'll ask to borrow your pearls," Elianna whispered.

"Not again. She knows better."

"Since we're talking about walking down the aisle . . ." Joanna held up the calendar she pinned to the kitchen wall every year. "Let's talk dates. Ava, Jamie, summer or fall?"

"As soon as possible?" Jamie made a goofy, eager face, and Ava blushed.

So the Quinn family started the new year with the joy of a wedding. While Joanna and the sisters debated the best seasons to get married—Jamie couldn't get a word in edgewise—Emery left the warmth of the crackling fireplace for the crisp, clean chill on the second-level deck, where a New Year's snow had started to fall. The icy gusts sent flakes skating over the green pool cover.

"Why don't we take a walk?" Dad stood beside her with her coat in hand. "We've not done that in a long time."

"Are you sure you want to leave the party?" Emery slipped on her coat.

"They won't miss us," he said, heading down the deck stairs and around the side of the house. "And about what Ava said, she—"

"Forget it, Dad." She tugged on her hat and gloves, then wrapped up in Mom's old plaid wool scarf. "She's not wrong."

Through the glow of the neighbor's lights and the streetlamps, she caught a hint of sadness in his smile, as if he was afraid to say what he felt.

I wanted it to be you.

It wasn't a regular conversation when she was a girl, but every now and then he'd say, *"Don't be in a hurry. I want to walk you down the aisle to the right man."* In those days, she was his one and only daughter. Then death changed their story.

Dad slipped his arm through hers. "So, what about the job in Sea Blue Beach?"

"Still there. Elliot Kirby texted me tonight."

"And?"

"He asked me to take the job. I'm afraid Lou talked me up a bit too much."

"I don't know, Em. You *were* everything to the *Free Voice* when Lou struggled with his health. You kept it going for him."

"Okay, fine, I can be an editor-in-chief and do it well. But you know it's not about the job."

"It's about the location."

"How can it not be? Dad, it's Sea Blue Beach. I haven't been there since *that* summer." Emery's foot slipped on a dusting of snow, and Dad steadied her as they made their way down the sidewalk.

Tonight, their pretty, suburban Cleveland neighborhood was

quiet under the falling snow and twinkling Christmas lights. Somehow, the atmosphere seemed to respect their conversation.

"If the job was in any other city, would you say yes?" Dad, a Case Western Reserve professor, appealed to her sense of reason.

"I'd be packed and head out tomorrow morning," Emery said.

The *Sea Blue Beach Gazette* was a historic family newspaper—a unicorn these days—in beautiful Sea Blue Beach, the gem of the north Florida coast. Its focus was mostly microlocal journalism, which Emery loved. News about *you*, literally. About the citizens, local businesses, the schools, and government. The press run was semiweekly, which meant she'd have time to develop a vision for growth.

"Elliot lives in Atlanta, so he won't be popping in every other day, and I'll have complete reign."

"Sounds perfect. Is the pay good?"

"Define *good*."

Dad's laugh crackled against the cold. "Can you survive?"

"I can." She smiled as Southerly Park came into view. Of course he led her here. "I was thinking, if I did go, I'd stay at the Sands Motor Motel." Emery glanced up at him. "In Cottage 7."

"I see. You'd prefer that to a house or an apartment? As I recall, the cottages were small and a bit out of date."

"I'd have two bedrooms. And it'll only be me unless visitors come. If it's out of date"—meaning if it looked like the cottage she'd shared with Mom during her last summer—"I wouldn't mind."

As they crossed the street into the park's light, Dad said, "Remember that big red sled you got for Christmas when you were ten?"

"How could I forget? It snowed all day, and we rode down every little hill we could find."

"Mom's favorite was the golf course."

"She crashed into the ditch shouting 'Fore!'" Emery said. "I didn't even know what it meant."

"You shouted back 'Five!'" Dad laughed. "She broke through the ice trying to climb out. Her feet were soaked."

"But she wanted one more hill," Emery said.

Mom conquered all of her hills. Except the last one. Cancer.

"Sledding that Christmas is one of my favorite memories." Dad's voice carried a reminiscent tone that made Emery well up. "We finally convinced Mom to go home, dry off, build a big fire, drink hot chocolate, and eat grilled cheese." Dad squeezed her arm. "You fell asleep on the floor watching *White Christmas*."

"I miss her," Emery whispered. "Sometimes when I'm working, I look up, expecting to see her standing in my office."

"Hard to believe it's been sixteen years. You know Joanna reminds me of her birthday every year, asks if I want to talk about her. She's not afraid of my love for your mom, Em. I'm not intimidated by her love for her first husband. The mystery of the human heart is its ability to love so wide and deep."

"That was very poetic, Dad."

"Old age setting in." They arrived at a bench under a streetlamp. He brushed away the snow and motioned for Emery to sit. Mom always swore he was a snowman on the inside. "I want you to be okay with me walking Ava down the aisle first, but I can't demand it or even really ask."

"Do I seem that shallow?" Was this the fruit of her resistance to becoming a full-fledged member of the family? "It's not like Ava did it on purpose. I'm happy for her and Jamie. Compared to the girls he dated in college, Ava is pure gold studded with diamonds."

Meanwhile, Emery was still waiting for her man to crawl out from under some moss-covered rock. Did every woman in her early thirties who was floundering in her career wonder if love would find her?

"You should take the job, Emery," Dad said, low and soft but with conviction. "I'll miss you. We'll all miss you. But go to Sea Blue Beach. Maybe you'll find something there you left behind."

Walking back home through the swirling, thickening snow, Emery considered Dad's advice, sorry she made any sort of deal out of Ava being the first daughter down the aisle. She was just frustrated with her career and the pace of her life.

At home, the house had quieted, with Jamie and Ava cuddled on the couch, watching a movie. Blakely was curled on the floor under a heavy blanket, sleeping, and Elianna had gone to bed since she started work at six a.m.

In the kitchen, Joanna loaded the dishwasher. Dad refilled their champagne glasses and kissed his wife, whispering words only husbands and wives share.

"Oh, Emery." Ava slipped out from under Jamie's arm and met her by the stairs as she said good night. "You'll be a bridesmaid, won't you?"

"As long as we don't wear pink or puffy sleeves."

"Define *pink*. And one hundred percent no to the puffy sleeves."

"Pink as in pink."

"We'll talk."

Emery laughed. "Any shade of pink, Aves."

"Fine, but, Emery—" Ava glanced up at her. "We looked at a couple of wedding dresses online, just to see, and there was one—"

Emery leaned against the banister, waiting.

"—with pearls. It was so stunning and classic. It was all Lauren Bacall in *How to Marry a Millionaire*. I was wondering—"

"No."

"Elianna forewarned you, didn't she?"

"You need a new playbook, Ava."

"Okay, fine, but I don't understand why—"

"That's the problem, Ava. You don't understand. You can wear pearls with the Lauren Bacall gown, just not mine." How many times had they had this conversation? Four? Five? In person. Over text. Ava being fixated on Mom's pearls made zero sense. "Dad and Joanna can give you a set for a bridal gift."

"But—"

Emery pointed to Ava's hand. "Your ring is beautiful. Jamie has good taste."

"He knew what I wanted before I did," Ava said. "Hey, Em, I'm sorry. Are you mad?"

"I'm not mad. And honestly, I'm really happy for you guys. Good night."

In her room, she stared out the window, where snow layered the bare tree limbs, and tried to imagine the sun and sand of Sea Blue Beach. She pictured the cute cottages of the Sands Motor Motel, the old brick street going through the east end of town, the Blue Plate Diner, and the semi-famous Starlight skating rink.

She'd become a part of the town as the editor-in-chief of the *Sea Blue Beach Gazette*.

Sun, sand, cute cottage, being her own boss, developing a newspaper like Lou did back in the sixties and seventies? Check, check, check, and check.

Emery snatched up her phone before fear walked in with a list of cons.

> Elliot, Happy New Year. Sorry to respond so late, but yes, I'll take the job. Thank you so much.

As her decision settled in, Elliot pinged a reply.

Excellent. We'll talk tomorrow. Or rather, later
today.

Emery readied for bed, then slipped under the covers, clicking off the bedside lamp. She'd finally hammered her square-peg self into that round hole.

2

CALEB

Starting over wasn't supposed to be this hard. He was an experienced architect with a degree from Cornell. Nationally certified. Working on innovative sustainable designs. He was a man with a plan.

Then Mom called.

"Nothing to worry about. Just a small bit of cancer."

Small bit of cancer? Was there such a thing? In a singular moment, he was sixteen again, bursting through the back door after football practice into Mom's fragrant kitchen, into her loving embrace. To his surprise, he wanted to go home. Go to ground. The sandy ground of Sea Blue Beach.

His partner understood, bought Caleb's half of the business, along with his Belltown loft. Now he lived in a renovated craftsman one street from his parents with an office under the staircase. Six months ago, he hung out his shingle for Ransom Architecture, ran an ad in the *Gazette*, then twiddled his thumbs.

Not really, but that's what it felt like. Caleb's experience was in restoration and refurbishment, but he wanted the challenge of a new build.

He landed some consulting work with clients back in Seattle. For three months he worked on a renovation plan for one of the old downtown buildings, a former haberdashery turned vintage shop turned into a yet-to-be business. Two months later he hit a hard stop when the bank foreclosed on the building.

He'd tried to get meetings with some of the prominent developers, but nothing materialized. He bid on Sea Blue Beach projects—all in the West End—but lost to the favorite son, Tommy Lake at JIL Architects. Tommy's sister was married to town councilman Bobby Brockton, but let's pretend that had nothing to do with JIL winning every bid.

The East End of Sea Blue Beach had declined since he left for college. Only home for holidays and a week in the summer, he never noticed.

Then last week, the owner of the historic Alderman's Pharmacy, one of the first businesses in Sea Blue Beach besides the sawmill and roller-skating rink, contracted him to inspect the place and lay out a plan for restoration. Jenny Finch, a digital creator with eight million followers on social media, planned to reopen Alderman's Pharmacy with the same name, functioning as a lunch counter and soda fountain, just like a hundred years ago. Minus the pharmacy. Everyone filled prescriptions in the West End.

This morning, Mayor Simon Caster knocked on his door with a dozen canisters, all with drawings of the rotting Org. Homestead neighborhood homes. Org., short for *original*, was where Sea Blue Beach founders, a royal prince from the North Sea island of Lauchtenland and a freed slave, built the first homes. Prince Blue had the money. Malachi Nickle had the skill.

"Can you inspect these?" Simon said. "See what it will take to repair and restore those homes? I'd like to make them affordable housing for young families, or even for seniors on a fixed income."

The bank had foreclosed on ten of the twelve houses years ago. There'd been talk of bulldozing the area for new development. When the East End folks protested, talk changed to restoration. But there'd been no effort until now.

"We have discretionary funds to dole out," Simon said, "if I can find buyers. If the West End town council members don't put up a fuss. They think two-thirds of all money should go to their side."

"They do bring in most of the tax money," Caleb said.

Over the past forty years, hotels, shopping centers, large beach homes and condos, along with every kind of tourist attraction, popped up on the western side of Sea Blue Beach, attracting spring breakers, families, conferences, businesses, and pro sports like golf and tennis.

"Yep, and they never let us forget it." Simon held up one of the canisters. "Let me know what you think it will take to bring the homes up to code. Then we can look at funds, negotiate with the bank on sale prices. I can't imagine a hundred-and-forty-year-old dilapidated home is worth more than thirty or forty grand."

"You're looking at the condition of the homes, Simon. The bank is looking at location: on the edge of the West End, two blocks from the beach. Prime property."

Simon sighed. "Yeah, I know, but a man can dream."

Caleb pulled a plan from one of the canisters and unrolled it on his drafting table. It was beautifully drawn by a man hovering over a drafting table with different-grade pencils, erasers, T and set squares, a protractor and compass.

"I'll inspect a couple of them." The address was 2 Port Fressa Avenue.

"I'll pay you, of course," Simon said.

"Okay, but, Simon, what's going on? These houses have been foreclosed on for years."

Caleb worked for Simon at the Starlight during high school, and besides his dad, there wasn't a man he respected more.

"Rumblings," Simon said. "During a Chamber of Commerce meeting, I overheard Mac Diamond was talking to the bank about buying the whole thing."

Mac was a golf course developer with big ideas and the newest member of the Sea Blue Beach town council.

"Dad says Mac ran for town council to have sway with property rights and taxes." Caleb returned the plan to the canister.

"Based on how Mac talks and votes, your dad is right." Simon glanced out the window toward Sea Blue Way and the visible corner of the Starlight. "When I was a teenager, Mayor Harry Smith got bamboozled by a slick development company named Murdock. They convinced him that if Sea Blue Beach didn't modernize and build, build, build, we'd limp into the twenty-first century, losing tourism and business to places like Niceville or Destin. And it all started with invoking eminent domain on the Starlight. Smash it with a wrecking ball and put up a parking lot."

"Then a movie star fell in love with a supermodel and saved the day." Everyone in Sea Blue Beach knew the story of Matt Knight, hometown boy turned Hollywood star, saving the iconic skating rink alongside supermodel Harlow Hayes.

"It was Booker Nickle, a descendant of Malachi's, who saved the day. Remembered the Starlight didn't sit on Sea Blue Beach land but ground that belonged to Lauchtenland, the old royal kingdom." Simon smiled. "It was glorious. Even Harry was relieved. No one wanted to destroy the Starlight. But no one wanted to be stuck in the past either."

"The West End is booming, Simon. No one can say we're stuck in the past. It's like Oz over there. The East End may be like a Kansas farm with Sea Blue Way as the yellow brick road, but we have purpose too."

"We're seen as dead weight. Can't offer anything new." Simon looked slightly defeated. "I don't want to be the mayor who lets progress bulldoze everything our founders worked to build. We just need to get folks to see the beauty in the East End. Polish it up, get families in these old cottages. Fix up Doyle's Auto Shop and some of the other places." He pointed to the canisters. "Starting with the Org. Homestead should inspire everyone."

"I'll do what I can, Simon. But I've only been back for six months. I'm still figuring out how things work around here, how to commission new jobs."

"I'd put my finger on the scale for some of the city contracts, but I've been calling out the West End council members for throwing everything at JIL. However, I'll support you all I can." Simon headed for the door. "Send me a contract for looking over those drawings and developing a restoration plan. Don't be cheap." He grinned. "The West End doesn't have to know every dollar the mayor's office spends. I have some prerogative."

When Simon had gone, Caleb unrolled another of the Org. Homestead drawings. One of the canisters came with a set of grainy, black-and-white photographs.

Most of the houses were the classic Florida Cracker, built entirely of lumber with a slanted roof and wide porch. Several had a subtle European appearance, probably the influence of the prince from Lauchtenland.

Spreading each one on his drawing table, he felt a bit emotional. One photo had an African-American family on the front porch. Another had a white family with their dog and goat. These were his people. The ones who fought to make a life by the sands of Sea Blue Beach so that others, like Caleb's great-grandparents, could also plant their flag.

He came back because of Mom, but maybe there was a deeper purpose.

The front door opened again, and Simon poked his head inside. "There is *one* more thing. Sea Blue Beach has never had a preservation society, but I've been doing some research, and I think forming some kind of Main Street initiative would go over well with our western brothers and sisters. Sounds more modern and business-forward. This could help to fix up the East End. What do you think about taking the lead on that?"

"I don't know, I'm trying to—" .

"Caleb, you're a hometown boy—smart, educated, experienced. Frankly, you're the future, which is way more palatable to the West End. And according to my wife—and I don't take it personal—you're very good-looking and charming."

Caleb laughed. "Okay, well, tell Nadine thanks, I guess."

"I might as well tell you the rest of what she said. She wonders if there's a girl in your life." Simon leaned against the doorframe, more relaxed than fifteen minutes ago. "I should warn you, if you say no, she's going to try to set you up."

"Then, yes, I have a girl in my life. Mom's a girl, right?"

"Done. If she asks who, I'll tell her you said it was none of my business."

Caleb liked Nadine, an artist who used to come to the rink thirty minutes before the last session ended and tie on a pair of skates, saying she had to work out the kinks.

Grabbing a sandwich, Caleb spent the afternoon researching Florida's Main Street initiatives, made a few calls to neighboring Main Street cities, then scanned the Org. Homestead drawings into his Revit system. He appreciated the historical drawings, but he'd work on updates the modern way.

When the afternoon sunlight faded from his office windows, he packed up to meet Jenny Finch at Alderman's. She'd flown in from Miami to go over his proposal..

He'd just gotten into his truck when Mom called.

"You busy?" she said, rushed and stern, intoning the voice of her boss, a West End lawyer. She claimed it got clients to take her seriously.

"Heading out to meet the woman who's restoring Alderman's."

"Can you come to the house?"

"Sure, after I meet Jenny." Caleb climbed behind the wheel. "Want me to pick up Tony's Pizza or—"

"No, come now."

Caleb heard Dad talking with someone in the background. "I've got a meeting, Mom. What's going on?"

It wasn't like either of them to be home at four forty-five in the afternoon. Dad's job as a logistics supervisor for an outfit that shipped products all over the world required long hours. Mom often worked overtime. She called it vacation money.

"You'll understand when you get here."

Caleb glanced through the truck's windshield toward his parents' backyard. He couldn't make out much through the ancient shady oak, but he could see Mom pacing past the kitchen window.

He left his driveway to park at the side of the house and entered through the kitchen. Was Mom's cancer back? It'd been a bit more than a little thing. After surgery to remove her thyroid, and a round of radiation, Mom had been declared cancer free but . . .

"Mom? Dad?" Caleb shot Jenny a quick text that he was on his way as he walked into the living room. "What's so urgent?"

"Uncle Caleb." His eleven-year-old nephew Bentley flew across the room.

"Hey, buddy, what are you doing here?" Caleb hoisted him up for a big, I-missed-you hug.

"Mom said I could stay with you. Can I?"

"Your mom said what?"

"Hey, little brother." Cassidy emerged from the powder room, drying her hands down the side of her shredded jeans. "Miss me?" She wore a tight T-shirt under a beaded, fringe vest, and feathers in her braided wavy blond hair. She looked like Jenny from *Forrest Gump*.

Speaking of Jenny . . . He looked to see if his client had texted him back.

"Cass, what are you doing here?" Caleb asked.

Mom tugged Bentley toward the kitchen promising milk and molasses cookies. Dad situated himself between Caleb and Cassidy in his BarcaLounger. "What's this about Bentley staying with me?"

His big sister by eleven and a half months made him restless. Made him want to yell. Scream. Say things he'd regret. No matter how much time had passed or how she claimed to have changed—very little—he could not, would not trust her.

"It's good to see you too." She plopped down on the couch and patted the cushion next to her. "Come, sit. Let's catch up."

"I'd love to, but I'm late for a meeting." Classic Cassidy. Shows up and interrupts. "Why does Bent think he's living with me?"

"Will you please sit down?" Cassidy slapped the cushion. "I don't want to talk looking up to you. I promise I'll be done in time for your precious meeting."

"I'm already late."

"Give her sixty seconds." Dad tipped his head toward the couch. "I'll watch the time for you."

"Thanks, Daddy. Glad to know you're on my side." Cassidy spoke fluent sarcasm. "Okay, Caleb." She perched on the edge of the cushion. "Things are going great for me. My Etsy store is killing it. I'm selling these beaded vests and these feathers"—she pointed to the black one in her hair—"like crazy. I'm starting to sell some of my art too. And I've met someone." She flashed her winning smile. The one Dad and Mom bought with two years of braces. "He's amazing. Arturo Mooney. He runs a trucking company in Louisiana, and he's got this great big house on the bayou with a pool and big, modern kitchen, five bedrooms, four baths, a media room. Wait till you see it."

"Sounds like Bentley would love to live there."

"See, that's the thing." Cassidy lowered her voice and inched closer to Caleb. "Arturo's not big into kids. He's never had any of his own, so it's—"

"But you do, Cass. Why are you with a guy who doesn't like kids?"

"I never said he doesn't *like* kids. I said he's not into them." Cassidy squeezed his arm. "I need some time for him to get used to the idea. We also need time for us as a couple, you know, to get used to living together and all."

"Any marriage plans?" Dad said. "Any thought to letting us meet him before you move in?"

Cassidy had never introduced the family to her boyfriends. They'd never been to any of the places she'd lived. They'd never met Bentley's father.

"Dad, this is my life and my decision. I don't need you to meet him. But for your information, yes, there are plans to marry. Eventually." She turned back to Caleb. "I'd like Bentley to live with you. Please? Wouldn't it be cool for him to attend Valparaiso Middle School like we did? You really want that big ol' house all to yourself?"

"It's a dollhouse compared to what you described. Are you saying you want me to keep Bentley for the rest of middle school?" At eleven, he was a young sixth grader with two and a half more years ahead of him.

"What? No. Maybe. At least for the rest of this school year." Cassidy smiled as Bentley came in the room, offering everyone a cookie. When he begged Grandpa to play the old Wii system in the upstairs library, Dad stood and called time for Caleb. "It's actually been two minutes."

29

Now he was really late. Caleb scooted closer to Cassidy and leaned in. "What are you doing? You wreck our family, and now you want to wreck Bentley? Dropping him off to live with his single uncle while you shack up with God-knows-who?"

"Wreck the family . . . ha! Judgmental much? I thought you'd have grown up living in Seattle, but I guess I was wrong."

"Don't make this about me. This is all you."

"Are you ever going to let go of what happened back then? Huh? I've raised a pretty darn good kid on my own and—"

"That kid is a testament to his own tenacity and spirit. And Mom's prayers. Now, I have to go. I can't lose this commission."

"All right, look. I know things haven't been easy between us. Y'all didn't even tell me about Mom's cancer. But I'm asking this one *little* favor. I've stopped drinking, stopped getting high. Arturo is good for me. He wants to help me with my business. I know he loves me, and he's going to love Bentley." Caleb detected just enough sincerity in her voice. "I can't leave Bentley with Mom. She doesn't look like she has the energy for an eleven-year-old boy. Besides, you remember what it was like growing up here. I didn't like it, so why—"

"I did."

"—would I subject Bentley to it?"

Caleb scoffed. "Really? You loved living here until you went rogue. All of our friends wanted to live here." He glanced at his phone. Jenny had texted a question mark, followed by *Did I get the time wrong?*

"I have to go." He faced his sister. "If I take him, it's on my terms. I get him for the rest of the school year. I'll determine his spring break and his routine. You can't just come in here and yank him out for some wild adventure you saw on TikTok."

Cassidy's expression darkened, but she held her rebuff. "Fine. For the school year." She relaxed into a smile. "We packed a couple of suitcases, so he's set for a few weeks. I'll send the rest of his things when I get home. And some money."

"Just send his things. I'll take care of the rest. Now I really do have to go."

On the short drive down Sea Blue Way to Alderman's Pharmacy, Caleb wrestled with those not-so-buried, not-so-decayed memories and emotions from his teens.

She'd been bouncing in and out of their parents' life for sixteen years. She'd even showed up in Seattle once. She'd determined that the family owed her something beyond their love and support. None of which she returned.

But Bentley? Caleb loved that kid. The first time he held him in his arms, he knew he'd give his life for him. Today, Cassidy tugged on that secret pledge. Today, Caleb kept his word.

Mom. The Org. Homestead. Bentley. Maybe all of them combined made up why he returned to Sea Blue Beach.

THE GAZETTE
Telling Stories from the Sands of Sea Blue Beach
Established 1902

Gazette Editorial

Sunday January 5th

By Elliot Kirby

I grew up running around these shores when my family visited my aunt and uncle, Alvin and Rachel Kirby. Every summer, Uncle Alvin took us to the printing plant to watch a press run of Aunt Rachel's beloved *Gazette*.

Every summer, we spent days in the newsroom, watching a

true newswoman in action. There was always the thrill of telling a story under deadline. In many ways, the *Gazette* is a citizen of Sea Blue Beach.

Aunt Rachel hoped my sister or I would take her place as editor-in-chief one day. But life had other plans for us.

Yet our affection and belief in this newspaper remains unwavering. Since Aunt Rachel's death two years ago, we've made every effort to keep the paper going. Uncle Alvin's printing plant sold years ago, and the *Gazette* moved production to Panama City.

Keeping a print paper alive in the internet age has not been easy. Many small-town newspapers have not survived. For the *Gazette*, we reduced our print days to Sunday and Wednesday.

Yet Sea Blue Beach remains special because you *all* love print news. The Kirby family remains committed to the stories of Sea Blue Beach. In that vein, please welcome our new editor-in-chief, Emery Quinn.

A native of Ohio and graduate of Ohio State University's School of Journalism, she spent eight years on staff at the *Cleveland Free Voice*, eventually rising to the title of associate editor-in-chief. We have every confidence in her abilities to take the *Gazette* into the next decade as a microlocal news source. Please give her a warm SBB welcome.

From: Momof2@gmail.com
To: editorial@SBBGazette.com
Re: New editor

How can someone who didn't grow up here love the *Gazette* and our town as much as one of us?

From: GolfisLife@aol.com
To: editorial@SBBGazette.com
Re: New editor

Welcome, Emery Quinn. I think you'll bring a fresh perspective.

From: admin@hiltonhotel.com
To: editorial@SBBGazette.com
Re: New editor

I don't care who is editor. Are y'all going to fix the missing ad problem?

3

EMERY

She'd only doubted her decision to pack up her Honda Accord and drive nine hundred miles south to the north Florida coast a few times. Maybe a thousand times. But she kept her foot on the gas anyway.

The Quinn family had given her a lovely send-off, inviting her friends and former colleagues from the *Free Voice*. Lou caught her before the end of the night to give her a boost of confidence.

"I'm proud of you, Emery Quinn."

"You think I can do it, Lou?"

"Would I have recommended you to Elliot if I didn't think you could? The *Free Voice* only survived those final years because of you."

"That's because I knew you were right there if I needed you."

He gave her a soft chuck on the chin. "I'm still here if you need me. But you won't. You'll do a good job there, and in a couple of years, you'll write your ticket to any major metropolitan paper."

"Thank you." Was that her goal? To land at a major metropolitan paper? She'd not thought about much beyond this next year. Mom's death taught her how uncertain life could be.

Dad and Joanna gave her a piggy bank of cash. Ava gave Emery her choice of possible pinks for the bridesmaids' gowns—all of them in the bubble gum, Pepto-Bismol family. When Emery picked the brightest and loudest pink, Ava caved.

"It was a joke. I hate every last one of them."

Elianna gifted her a used coffee machine from the café, still in good working order, and a large canister of freshly ground coffee beans. "I'll send more when you run out."

Blakely wrapped up a framed picture of the four of them from last Christmas. It was a rare shot, and it was almost as if Blakely was reminding Emery *you're one of us.*

She packed two suitcases, a box of books, and her laptop. The next morning, she headed out at five a.m. with a baggie of cinnamon scones from the café and cooler of snacks and water.

She spent the night in Nashville with a friend and, by midafternoon the next day, drove down Highway 98 into the East End of Sea Blue Beach. Emery rolled down the windows so the cool, dewy January air filled the car. Filled her. When her tires burped over the worn brick of Sea Blue Way, it was as if she'd driven back in time to her last innocent summer.

Eager to see the town, she drove past her turn on Avenue C toward the Sands Motor Motel. Was it like she remembered? How much of the East End had changed?

The Blue Plate Diner looked busy, as usual. The bakery, Sweet Conversations, had a crowd at the counter, and several young people exited the coffee shop, One More Cup.

The iconic skating rink, the Starlight, remained a beacon on the north shore. The sight of it made Emery feel welcomed. In her mind, it was like a pushpin in the sand, holding the east and west ends of town together.

The food trucks still lined the Beachwalk, with its Victorian lamps and row of wrought-iron benches. The Midnight Theater advertised a film from last year. And the old shopping center with the Starlight Museum, a yarn shop, and a small art gallery had a couple of storefronts available for rent. Circling the roundabout, Emery headed back east and toward the *Gazette* office and the Sands Motor Motel.

The parking lot of Tony's Pizza was active, and Biggs Grocery Store had shoppers coming and going. Alderman's Pharmacy still advertised the "best soda fountain in town," but the place looked dark and abandoned. What was going on there?

At the stop sign, Emery looked left up a slight hill toward Rachel Kirby Lane and the *Gazette*. Elliot was driving down from Atlanta to meet with her later today.

Circling around, she made her way back to Avenue C and the motor motel. Parking in the sand-and-shell lot, she saw the old courtyard and seven cottages for the first time in sixteen years.

The cottages sat under overhanging roofs to shade from the sun and protect from the rain. The stucco exterior was painted the same seashell pink with coral trim. Several Adirondacks circled the stone fire pit. Grass sprouted between the edges of the stone pavers, and an American flag still waved over Cottage 1. A string of white lights swung from cottage to cottage, and the old grill Dad always fired up sat nestled between Cottage 3 and 4.

The owner, Delilah, waited for her by Cottage 7.

"Shew," Emery whispered. "Here we go."

"Welcome back." Delilah handed her the key to Cottage 7, then held Emery's shoulders for a good once-over. "You grew up mighty fine. I knew you would."

"I'm not sure how I feel being back here." Emery unlocked the door, then peered inside without moving. "Dad thought I'd be happier in an apartment or house, but . . ."

"This place has memories of your mother." Delilah wrapped her arm around Emery as if she'd done so a hundred times. "I'm sorry I've not kept in touch."

"It's fine, Delilah. It wasn't expected." Emery stepped over the threshold with her suitcases and set her laptop on the round dinette table. "You knew, didn't you?" She turned to Delilah. "About the cancer?"

"I did, yes. She told me shortly after we met that summer." In her mid-to-late eighties, Delilah was tall and slender, refined-looking with wisdom lines on her otherwise smooth skin. She was also somewhat of an urban legend.

What happened to Delilah Mead?

She'd been a music sensation in the late sixties and early seventies as part of the dynamic folk duo Samson Delilah. Until she walked away and never looked back.

"You can stay as long as you want. I'm still in Cottage 1. My door is always open for you."

"Thank you, Delilah. I mean it."

"I'll let you get settled. When you have time, let me know how it feels to be back."

So far, sentimental and melancholy. She almost expected to see Mom on the settee under the southern jalousie window, reading a book, then falling asleep, waking up when Emery bounded in for dinner.

"How was your day, my sun-tanned girl?"

If only Emery had known then what she knew now, from the get-go. She'd have spent more time with Mom.

But she'd spent sixteen years making peace with the past. This moment was like being able to reach back and touch buried feelings and images, maybe solve the mystery of why she felt she'd left something behind.

Emery also half expected to see Dad standing at the stove,

making pancakes or marinating steaks for the grill, oldies playing on the radio.

"How're you doing, sweetie?"

It was hard to reckon this place as one of the happiest yet saddest of her life. On the drive down, she decided to focus on the present. On the job she'd been hired to do.

In the meantime, Cottage 7 had not changed much. The hard pine floors still creaked and needed a good buffing. The walls remained a white shiplap, though freshly painted, and a narrow, golden beadboard covered the ceiling. An old, wood-burning fireplace sat dark and quiet in the corner.

In the kitchen, a seventies-style scalloped edge trimmed the white kitchen cabinets, but Delilah had updated the appliances. The furniture was the same—eclectic 1950s estate sale—with a few new pieces added. The room still smelled of sea spray and coconut suntan oil.

Dragging her things down the short hall, Emery settled into the bedroom where she'd stayed *that* summer. The one with the beach-facing window. The one Caleb Ransom knocked on late at night.

They'd lost touch once Emery returned to Cleveland and Mom went on hospice. She wondered what he was doing these days. Were his parents still around? His sister? Probably not.

In the closet, Delilah stacked plenty of clean towels and sheets, and a plethora of hangers. After unpacking, Emery was inspecting the kitchen for groceries and supplies when Dad called.

"You're there?"

"I'm here. And not much has changed. Delilah doesn't seem to have aged."

"Tell her hi for me."

"The place is still quaint and cozy, like walking into a 1950s movie, only with Wi-fi."

He was silent for a moment. "Are you all right being there? I worry about you."

"I know, and I love you for it. You and Mom did a great job raising me, if I say so myself. I thought a lot about it on the way down, about what you said on New Year's Eve, and I feel like there is something for me here. Something I'd forgotten. Maybe even need."

"Then I know you'll find it." There was affection in his tone. "Is the weather beautiful?"

"Fifty-five degrees and stunning. But I won't go on about it." She smiled at Dad's laugh. "The East End looks run-down. I kind of feel sorry for it."

"Well, Miss Editor-in-Chief, write about it."

"If there's a story, I will. But I want to tread lightly at first. Get a feel for things."

They talked for a few more minutes, then said their good-byes. Emery made a shopping run and set up her kitchen and bathroom. Then she walked the beach, trying to remember it was January, not June.

A little before five, she borrowed one of the Sands' guest bikes and started up Avenue C to meet Elliot. She could get used to living in a town where she rode a bike or walked to work.

With each pedal, Emery felt a little more confident in her decision. She didn't know what the future held, but for now, this place under a southern winter sun would do.

Taking the long way to Rachel Kirby Lane, she headed up Sea Blue Way, passing Alderman's Pharmacy. Curious about the dark windows, she hit the brakes and parked the bike.

Under the broken awnings, she peeked in the windows. The place was abandoned, with stools overturned on the floor and on the counter. The mirror behind the lunch counter was shattered, and the dark wood floors appeared water damaged. Sixteen years ago, if she remembered, the place didn't function as a pharmacy, but where everyone stopped in for lunch or a root beer float. Or so it seemed.

She reached for the door latch, stepping back when it gave way. "Hello? Anyone here?"

She made a slow turn, inspecting the dust and dings of the historic building. This room had to be well over a hundred and twenty years old. The fountain's scarred and chipped dark wood countertop looked like a dying piece of history.

"There's a story here," she said. Not just Alderman's but Sea Blue Beach. She sensed it.

A thump from the back startled her. "Hello?"

She peeked through the dim light to see a man rushing in, dropping a leather case on the far end of the counter. He seemed self-assured, dressed like a man who lived and worked in a beach town—jeans with a light blue button-down and brown suede shoes.

"I'm sorry I'm late," he said, pulling out a laptop. "My sister showed up and—" He shot her a fixed smile before looking down again. "You don't want to hear about her."

"Déjà vu," she whispered, recognizing him instantly. First with her heart, then with her eyes. Caleb Ransom.

His lean teen frame had filled out with a man's muscles, and the sun streaks were gone from his dark hair, but there was still a spark in his blue eyes.

"Give me a second . . ." He set his laptop in the middle of the counter and turned the screen toward her. "Here's Alderman's original drawing." He clicked to another image. "This is a rendering of what we can do with the refurbish. I also ran some numbers, keeping in mind you want to maintain all of this historical detail." He stepped forward and offered his hand. "Caleb Ransom. Nice to meet you, Jenny." He paused, then backed up. "You're not Jenny Finch."

"No, but I can be if you want."

Caleb laughed and pressed his fist to his lips. He walked toward the back of the room, then faced her, arms akimbo. "You're . . . I can't believe . . . What?" He pointed to her, then ran his hand through his hair, laughed again, and finally said, "Emery Quinn. *The* Emery Quinn."

"Live and in person, every night at seven. Tips appreciated." She joined his laugh. "So *the* Caleb Ransom. I thought you'd fly far away from Sea Blue Beach."

"I recently flew back." He remained on the far side of the pharmacy. "Emery Quinn. I'm-I'm . . . stunned."

"Thank you. I always thought I had a certain shock quality about me."

Another laugh, which felt deep and bassy in her chest, and Caleb moved closer, a bit of wonder in his gaze. "Still beautiful," he said. "But maybe you're married or engaged, and I shouldn't say such things."

"I'm not married or engaged. So please feel free to call me beautiful any time." She was flirting. Emery Quinn never flirted. "I'm the new editor-in-chief of the *Gazette*."

"What? Really? I think half the town is expecting the *Gazette* to push up daisies."

"Push up daisies? Hopefully not on my watch."

"Emery Quinn. In Sea Blue Beach." Suddenly he scooped her up and whirled her around.

Caught off-guard, she clung to his shoulders, inhaling the fragrance of body wash and fabric softener. When he set her down, she stumbled a little and fell against his chest, her cheek landing in a familiar place.

"Sorry. Dizzy." She jolted back to gather her bearings. "So, um, why are you back in town, and who is this Jenny person?"

"I came back six months ago. Mom had surgery for thyroid

can—" He stopped with a motion to the pharmacy walls. "This place, can you believe it? The old girl needs some love. I'm meeting the owner, Jenny, to go over renovation plans for this place. I'm an architect."

"It's okay to say *cancer*, Caleb. It doesn't upset me. Though I'm sorry to hear that about your mom. How is she?"

"Good. In remission."

"Good for her. Really. And you're an architect. Not surprised. As I recall, you preferred things in structured and neat lines."

"And you, a writer, our new *Gazette* editor. I'm surprised you came back to Sea Blue Beach."

"That makes two of us." She made a funny face, and he smiled. "But here I am." She started for the front door. "In fact, I'm late to meet Elliot Kirby. Hey, it was good to see you."

"Same here. Where are you staying? I'd love to—"

"Caleb, finally. Excellent. Did you get my text saying I was going across the street for a coffee?" A curvy woman with dark bouffant hair and a two-thousand-dollar Hermès Birkin bag swinging from her elbow charged into the pharmacy. She was serious and commanding, focused on Caleb, completely ignoring Emery. "Let's see what you got."

The brightness he exuded two minutes ago faded as he began dealing with this force of nature named Jenny.

Emery escaped outside and picking up the bike, she walked to the corner before glancing back at the old pharmacy.

So . . . she and Caleb Ransom were both in Sea Blue Beach. She'd not seen or talked to him in sixteen years, yet it felt as if she'd just talked to him yesterday.

4

EMERY

Then . . .

The beach! In Florida! And the place where they were staying, the Sands Motor Motel, was pretty cool. The seven cottages sat right on the sands of Sea Blue Beach in a horseshoe around the courtyard, with string lights between them. In the center was a courtyard with a low, smoldering firepit.

Dad was loaded up with motel trivia and randomly fired off facts during the fifteen-hour drive. "Did you know *hotel* first appeared in the English language in the 1600, but *motel* didn't come along until 1925? Probably a portmanteau from motor and hotel. Motel."

"He just likes to say *portmanteau*," Mom said.

"Maybe I do." Dad reached over to squeeze Mom's hand. "The Sands is what you'd call a motor court, where the cottages sit around a courtyard."

"Dad, please . . . One more fact and I'll die before we get there."

Did that stop him? Nope. Welcome to Douglas Quinn Land, where knowledge reigned supreme.

So, on a June afternoon, Emery arrived in Sea Blue Beach fully informed about motor motels but clueless about what to do with her endless summer days. When Dad and Mom had proposed the idea of a summer in Florida, she'd resisted.

"I have basketball camp in July. What about my friends? We were going to hang at the pool."

Then Emery's friend Brianna said two critical words that got her to see the beauty of a summer holiday in Florida. *"Rocking tan."* Plus, Emery loved hanging out with her parents, even at sixteen. She'd be off to college soon. This would be a summer to remember.

Dad rarely taught summer classes and had finally talked Mom into using her horde of vacation hours. Her job at the bank had been super intense after last year's housing collapse. She looked beat-up every night after work. More than once, Emery had found her asleep on the couch when she came home from school.

Mom never came home early. She never napped on the couch.

Dad packed sandals, socks, shorts, and T-shirts. And so many books that his suitcase weighed down one side of the Volvo. Mom brought all the "soft clothes" she loved but never wore to work, along with her crochet and a pile of novels. Emery brought half her wardrobe and shopped for two new bathing suits.

Day one, she went at it too hard. Burned herself bright pink from head to toe, front and back. Day two, she stayed inside, reading. The only electronics allowed on this vacation was the cottage's radio for playing oldies.

Day three, she overdid it again. After her shower, she lathered on half a bottle of lotion and dressed carefully. The rough edges of her jean shorts scraped the back of her legs as she gently pulled them on. She hoped it rained tomorrow.

After dinner and a game of Uno with Dad, she said, "I'm going to sit outside." The sun was still high but far enough west to leave a portion of the courtyard safely in the shade.

Getting this burnt was not the best start to the Quinn Family Summer of Fun, as Mom had coined the trip. She seemed fixated on making memories, but so far the only memories were of grocery shopping at a place called Biggs, Dad nearly burning off his eyebrows trying to light the gas grill, and Emery's you-must-be-a-tourist sunburn.

Delilah popped out of Cottage 1 in workout gear, waved, and started down the Beachwalk at a clipped pace. Emery settled down in the Adirondack, keeping as much of her legs as possible away from the sunbaked wood slats.

"Nice burn," a male voice said from the edge of the motor court.

Emery twisted around. "And you are?"

"Caleb." He leaned his bike against the side of the cottage and pointed to her legs. "You should get some aloe for that." He stepped closer. "Next time wear sunscreen."

"Where were you two days ago? And this morning?" She regarded him for a moment. He was cute, if not "gorg," as Brianna liked to say. Tan, of course, with lean muscles and a flop of dark hair that needed wrangling. But his eyes . . . so bright. Like a pure blue sky.

He peered through the cottage window. "Your parents?"

"Yes, and my father knows Krav Maga."

"Excuse me?"

"Krav Maga. It's dangerous and—" She jabbed the air with her finger. "Lethal."

"You have no idea what Krav Maga is, do you?"

"No." She motioned to the chair next to her. "Tell me your name again and why you're sneaking up on me."

"Caleb Ransom. I was following my sister—well, trying to anyway. She left with a guy in a Jeep."

"You were following a Jeep on your bike?"

"I know. Stupid."

"I'm surprised they got away. Did they jump to light speed?" He laughed easily. "Why were you following her?"

"Because . . ." Caleb leaned forward, elbows on his knees. "She's been fighting with my parents. I think she has a secret boyfriend—or had one. Something happened. She's changed. A lot. I thought if I followed her, I'd find out what she was up to, tell her to chill out, talk to me."

"A car would've been better. To follow, you know."

"No kidding, but if she spotted my truck . . ." He motioned toward the cottage door. "You got a brother or sister in there?"

"I'm an only."

"Lucky you." When he gazed down, he pointed to her swollen feet. "Take some aspirin. And seriously, wear sunscreen. Where are you from, Yankee?"

"Cleveland, Ohio."

"You know my name, Cleveland, but I don't know yours."

"Emery Quinn."

"Emery Quinn. I like it. Sounds like a character in a spy novel or something. How long are you here?"

"You're nosy."

"Fine. Don't tell me."

"Oh, don't pout. We're here for the summer. My dad's a professor at Case Western Reserve—"

"Where he teaches Krav Maga?"

She spit-laughed and decided she liked this sister-chasing-guy-on-a-bike. "Where he teaches molecular and microbiology. My mom is a bank exec. What about you?"

"Born and raised here. Dad's a logistics supervisor for a big

46

warehouse. Mom works for a lawyer. You already know my sister is crazy."

"Only that you think she's crazy."

After that, talking became easy. They were both sixteen, going into their junior year. He played football (what else?), and she played volleyball and basketball. He was into his drafting courses because he liked structure and neat lines. She worked on the school yearbook and wrote for the school newspaper.

"How many girlfriends?" she asked.

"None. How many boyfriends?"

"Liar. And none."

A lady came out of Cottage 3 and snapped a sandy towel in the air, glanced at the two of them, then went inside.

"You're the liar," he said. "*I'm* the one telling the truth."

"So, what's up with your sister?" she said, swiveling in the chair to face him.

"I don't know." Caleb slumped down in the Adirondack. "She started acting funny in the spring, bucking the house rules and curfew. Then, right after school let out, she found her inner Godzilla. Got all mean and snarky. Only comes home to sleep or do laundry."

"Maybe something's wrong."

"You think?" Sarcasm ruled the night. "Mom suggested seeing a doctor, but Cassidy refused." He reached for the stick lying by the firepit and snapped it in two. "We used to be close, but now she hardly talks to me."

When he looked over at Emery, she felt like she'd known him forever. Her skin tingled with a heat generated from inside, not her sunburn.

"Is it lonely being an only child?" he asked.

"Can't say. I don't know anything else." He wasn't looking at her so intently now, so she could watch him for a moment. "It's pretty cool at Christmas."

"I bet."

"Emery, who's our visitor?" Dad stepped out of the cottage looking like a nutty professor with his hair all wild, wearing his thick, ratty sweater, holey slippers, and black ankle socks.

"Caleb Ransom, sir." He stood to shake Dad's hand.

"Donald Quinn, Emery's dad. You're a local boy?"

"Yes, sir. We're off Pelican Way."

Dad pulled his phone out of his pocket. *Uh-oh, Dad, what are you doing?* "Enter your name and home number, Caleb Ransom. Do you have a cellular phone?"

"Um, yes."

"Enter that with your father's cellular number. He also has one, I assume."

"Y-yes, he does."

"Dad, good grief, what are you doing?"

"Watching out for my girl." When Caleb handed back the phone, Dad pressed the call button and held the phone to his ear.

Caleb glanced back at Emery. She shot him her best, "*Sorry!*" expression.

"Mr. Ransom? Douglas Quinn. Your son is over here at the Sands Motor Motel talking to my daughter by the firepit. Well, the pit doesn't have a fire, it's just dark, but he's here and I wanted to make sure he was an upstanding young man, as well as introduce myself to you." Pause. "Yes, we're down for the summer. From Ohio." He handed the phone to Caleb. "He wants to talk to you."

Caleb turned away as he pressed the Nokia to his ear. "I don't know . . . He just asked for your number. Okay, bye." Caleb handed over Dad's phone. "Emery tells me you know Krav Maga. I was wondering if you could show me a few moves, sir."

"Krav Maga? Do I look like a man who could take you out with my bare hands?" Dad turned back for the cottage. "Don't stay out late, Em."

She laughed when Caleb returned to his chair. "You are so gullible, Caleb Ransom."

"Better than being a pathological liar."

"Pathological. Wow, that's a big word." She sat up straight, deepening her voice as she said, "'I was wondering if you could show me a few moves . . . *sir*.'" She slapped his arm, laughing.

"I see how it is, Emery Quinn. I see how it is."

"Okay, maybe he doesn't know Krav Maga, but I promise you this, Caleb Ransom. Dad is the Boyfriendinator. The father who scares off any boy sniffing around his daughter. His words, not mine."

"The Boyfriendinator? Let me guess, he's a fan of Arnold Schwarzenegger." He had the cutest smirk on his full lips, and her heart plunked a little. "So, does it work? The Boyfriendinator?"

"I'm not sure. He's only tried it once." She glanced sideways at him, grinning. "And you're still here."

Now . . .

Gazette Editorial

Sunday, January 12th

By Emery Quinn
Editor-in-Chief

For the past three days, I've reacquainted myself with Sea Blue Beach and its lovely citizens, listening and trying to discover how this newspaper can best serve you.

With so much news available twenty-four seven, the *Gazette* seeks to be a microlocal newspaper—stories about you and the community, your neighbors and friends. Which seems in keeping with the vision and traditions set by Rachel Kirby when she took over the *Gazette* from her father and grandfather.

The *Gazette* is one of you. (Soon I'll feel comfortable saying "us.") This newspaper is a viable member of the community, telling the stories of your lives.

The staff—Rex Smithfield, Jane Upperton, Junie Hollis, Gayle Hamilton, and Tobias Elling—and I are committed to quality stories and quality production. We'd love to hear your thoughts at editorial@SBBGazette.com

5

CALEB

"Knock, knock." He peeked around the door of Emery's office where sunlight covered the southern window, the floor, and her desk, even catching the highlights in her hair. "Rex escorted me in, said you were staring at the wall." Caleb held up the One More Cup caddy he carried. "Lattes. Please tell me you're a coffee drinker."

She leaned toward the open door. "Rex, you're fired." Then she reached for the coffee. "Thank you, I drink this by gallon." When she smiled, he had that I-just-won-the-lottery feeling. "How'd your meeting go with that lady? Jenny something? She seemed like a force to be reckoned with."

"Jenny Finch knows her own mind, which makes my job easier." Caleb sat in the chair across from her desk. "Alderman's went on the block a few years ago when there was no one left in the family to take care of it. Jenny launched a website selling high-end clothing, and it's so successful her accountant told her to lose some money before the government took it all. She loves historic preservation, found Alderman's, and bought it with the intention to preserve its historic significance. It's hard for a pharmacy to compete with the chain stores on the West End, so she'll reopen it as a lunch counter. These days it seems the only thriving businesses on the East End involve food."

"And roller-skating. The Sands seems to be busy. I've only been here a week, but all the cottages are booked."

"Delilah has her regulars. The same with the Starlight. Sometimes I think the Starlight, the Sands, the Blue Plate Diner, and *Gazette* are the only things holding all of Sea Blue Beach together. They remind us of who we used to be, maybe who we're supposed to be." Caleb raised his coffee cup. "Look at me waxing sentimental."

Even more, pouring out his thoughts to Emery as if he'd seen her every day for the past decade and a half. He'd only known her seven short weeks, really six if he thought about it, when they were sixteen.

"So why are you staring at the wall?" he asked, reigning in his thoughts. "And are you really firing Rex?"

"Wouldn't dare. The dude runs this place. I don't know why Elliot didn't hire him. I think he didn't want it."

Caleb wanted to say *I'm glad he didn't* but thought it sounded too . . . something. Like not what a man says to a woman who walked back into his life after a long absence. "And the wall?"

"I was just remembering things." Emery lowered her gaze to her coffee cup. "I reread my Sunday editorial and it sounds like I was trying too hard."

"Not at all. It was a good piece. To the point. A nice introduction."

"The emails don't think so. People want to know why Elliot didn't hire a local, someone who knows the town. A few said we don't even need the *Gazette*, that it's a rag with occasionally large holes where ads were supposed to be. And one email, all caps, 'THE WRITING STINKS!'"

"People can be rude, Emery. Don't think those voices represent Sea Blue Beach."

"I reported hard news in Cleveland for the *Free Voice*. The founder, and my mentor, Lou Lennon, was a stir stick for controversy. I cut my teeth on people hating my stories—or rather, the *Free Voice* stories. But this, I don't know, feels personal. It shouldn't. It's just—" She stared out the window as if the rest of her thought might walk by. "I had this idea in my head about coming here. It's stupid—"

She glanced over at him, eyes glistening. That's when he realized coming here was more than a job. It was about her mom.

He sipped his coffee to give her a moment. After a second sip and more silence, he said, "Anyway, I came by to say hi, bring you the best coffee in town—but don't tell Paige at the Blue Plate I said that—and to say I'm glad you're here." He stood and took a step toward the door. "Also, I wondered if you'd like to go to lunch with a handsome, albeit at loose ends, architect. Of course, handsome is only an opinion. Feel free to fill in your own adjective."

He was trying to be funny. But he sounded a little pathetic.

Until Emery smiled. "Handsome will do. And it's good to see you. You're my only friend in Sea Blue Beach."

"You have Shift and Jumbo and—"

"They're still around?"

"Living and working in the West End, the traitors. But yeah, they're around. I know they'll never forget the Queen of Operation Revenge."

"Oh my gosh. I forgot about her."

"How could you forget? She was iconic. Made that whole summer special." Reminiscing about that summer wasn't easy for Caleb. It took him back to the pain of Cassidy. But seeing Emery reminded him he'd also fallen a little bit in love. "So lunch? One o'clock? Food truck or Blue Plate? One More Cup has great sandwiches . . ."

"I'd love to, but—" She looked at the stack of bound papers on her desk. "I have a lot of work to do. I don't have an advertising director, so I'm wearing that hat for now, and I loathe the schmoozing required for ad sales. I'm also head of human resources and a beat reporter."

"You need a hat rack," Caleb said. "I'm not a newspaperman, but I handled the finances for my Seattle firm when we started out. If you need any help—"

"Call someone else?"

"Exactly. You read my mind, Quinn."

"Hashtag don't call me," she said

"Hashtag I'll call you."

"Hashtag we sound so 2018." Emery laughed.

"Hashtag so about lunch . . ."

Caleb paused to check his ringing phone. The caller wasn't in his contacts, so he sent it to voicemail. Three seconds later, it rang again. Same number. When he answered, it was the principal's office at Valparaiso Middle School, asking him to come as soon as possible.

"Emery, sorry, I have to go. My nephew is in the principal's office."

"Is everything all right?"

"Don't know. Can I call you later?"

"Of course." She waved him out the door. "Go. Good luck."

Caleb had walked from his house to One More Cup, then to the *Gazette* office, so he didn't bother going home for his truck. The middle school was only a half mile, if that, from the middle of downtown. With a quick jog under scattered clouds, he'd be there in five minutes.

He was still catching his breath when he walked into the principal's office. "Caleb Ransom for—" The receptionist pointed to the closed door marked *Principal Tucker*.

Okay, guess he was going on in, see what he would see. Bentley sat across from the principal, head bowed, his thick towhead hair matted with sweat, his cheeks caked in mud, blood, and tears.

"Hey, buddy." Caleb knelt in front of him. "What's up?"

Bentley tumbled into his arms, clinging to him as Caleb dropped to the floor. Trembling and sobbing, he soaked Caleb's shirt with tears.

"Shhh, it's all right." Caleb held him tight.

"I'm sorry, I'm sorry."

"I know you are. Come on, take a breath. Everything will be all right."

When he'd calmed down, Caleb moved him back to the chair and accepted a box of tissues from Mr. Tucker.

Bentley wiped his nose and face, muttering. "Mom says boys don't cry."

"Really? Is your mom a boy?" Bentley's green eyes widened as he shook his head. "Listen to me, I'm a man, and you can cry anytime you want. Just don't let your emotions steer the ship."

Bentley's shoulders relaxed, and he finally looked Caleb in the eye. "I'm sorry, Uncle Caleb."

"Bentley," Tucker said. "Why don't you go clean up and get some water. Then come back."

When he'd gone, Caleb faced the principal. "What happened? He's only been in school a day and a half."

"Your nephew is having trouble adjusting."

"Define *trouble*."

"Did you know this was his fifth school in two years?" Tucker said.

"I knew it'd been more than two. But five? Wow. Okay. My sister is a bit of a nomad."

"I remember Cassidy. She was a bright student. I wasn't the

principal in her day, but I had her for math class. So, what's the story with Bentley? He said he's living with you."

"My sister has a new boyfriend who doesn't like kids. She asked me to take Bentley for the rest of the school year. We enrolled him last Friday."

That'd been a weird day. Coming down to the school with Cassidy, being listed as Bentley's guardian, the one to call in emergency. They had lunch at a food truck afterward, set up Bentley in the bedroom next to Caleb's, then Cassidy drove off, smiling. Not a care in the world. But Caleb felt every one of them. He wondered if Bentley did too.

"So, who started it? Bentley or the other guy?"

"Bentley, I'm afraid. He took offense at something. I'm still trying to figure out what exactly happened, but the other boys involved—"

"Boys?"

"Two. Seventh graders, good students, leaders for the most part. But they're also a bit of a clique with some other kids. Look, if Bentley apologizes and promises no more fighting, I'll let this one slide. I've talked to the boys' parents, and they are willing to let it go if this is a one-and-done."

"Yeah, sure, I'll talk to him. Mr. Tucker, he's a good kid."

"I can see that, Caleb, but he's also hurting and confused."

Caleb should've suspected something brewing beneath the surface. Bentley seemed fine with everything, even chipper, over the weekend. He talked nonstop as he moved into his room. He ran back and forth between his grandparents' place and home. Went to church with them Sunday while Caleb slept in. Not once did he speak of his mom.

Bentley returned to the office with a clean face, hair slicked into place, holding a bottle of water. Mr. Tucker informed him of his consequence. Bentley agreed to apologize and never fight again.

Caleb waited with him while the other boys were summoned. They were a good three inches taller and fifteen pounds heavier.

Bentley looked each boy in the eye, said he was in the wrong, and promised not to start anything again. The boys shook hands and accepted his apology, then the three of them headed back to class.

"I'll pick you up later," Caleb said as they parted ways in the hall. "I'm proud of you, okay?"

After school, they said nothing as they walked toward Avenue C, the beach, and the Sands Motor Motel.

"Want to tell me what happened?" Caleb leaned to see Bentley's face.

"They wouldn't let me sit at their table. Then someone said I was a crybaby."

"For no reason?"

Bentley shook his head. Caleb kept walking as Avenue C connected to the Beachwalk behind the motor motel.

"Are you hungry?" Caleb asked. "How about something to eat?"

"Can we get tacos?"

At Tito's Taco Truck, Caleb ordered two Taco-Taco-Taco meals, then carried the food to one of the Beachwalk benches.

"Good choice, Bent. These are my favorite." Caleb bit into his first taco with a side glance at Bentley, who sat there, staring toward the sea blue waves lapping against the sandy beige shore, his food untouched. A single tear splashed down on the taco wrapper.

"No one wants me," he said, lowering his head.

"Hey, buddy, that's not true. I want you. Grandpa and Grandma want you. Your mom—"

"Dumped me off with you because Pluto doesn't want me."

"Pluto? I thought his name was Arturo."

"I call him Pluto," Bentley said. "He looks like an alien."

Caleb grinned. Man, he liked this kid.

"I just wanted to sit with those guys at lunch," Bentley continued. "I liked them. They made me laugh in math class. Then someone told them I was crybaby. Crying in the bathroom after gym."

"And were you?"

"No."

His monotone reply said otherwise. "You know you can tell me anything."

"Yeah."

"It's okay to miss your mom." Caleb took a bite of his taco.

"I know."

"So, you said you were in the same math class as those seventh graders?"

Bentley opened one of the tacos but didn't take a bite. "I'm good at math."

"Not surprised. So was your mom. Be proud, Bent." Caleb slurped his soda, leaving space for Bentley to talk. When he didn't, Caleb went on. "Do you think the boys will be nice to you now? They seemed like good guys in the principal's office."

"No. Why would a bunch of guys at school like me when my mom doesn't?"

"Hey, look at me," Caleb said. "Your mom likes you, it's just she—" *Likes herself more.* "She's figuring out a few things right now."

"She's always figuring things out. She left me home alone a lot until she decided I should live with you."

"I bet she misses you. And I know she loves you. Tell you what, we'll FaceTime with her tonight, okay?"

"Okay. But she'll probably be busy with Pluto." Bentley grabbed the first taco for a large bite. "Hey," he said with a mouth full of food, "can we go roller-skating?"

"Don't see why not. But, Bentley, really, no more fights. Talk to me if something is bothering you. Or your grandparents. Or your teachers."

"I promise." He took another bite of taco, then glanced up at Caleb with a sly grin. "I took on two of them, and I was winning."

Caleb kept a straight face. "That's what every guy thinks until he starts losing. No more fights, dude. Come on, you promised."

"No more fights."

Their conversation found a rhythm with Bentley telling Caleb what he loved about the classes he managed to attend before the fisticuffs. His math teacher was cool, while his science teacher was boring, and his English teacher, Ms. Ware, was really pretty.

When they'd finished their tacos and downed the last of their sodas, Caleb walked him toward the Starlight, Sea Blue Way, and home. At the old, defunct splash pad, Caleb surveyed the East End. Just past the Starlight was the West End line, where the brick portion of Sea Blue Way converged with smooth, well-cared-for blacktop.

Everything east of the Starlight was old, run-down, and breaking. Sea Blue Way's bricks needed replacing, the Victorian lamps were rusty, and all the planters were either broken or empty. Several storefronts needed repair, and he saw what the mayor talked about last week.

About to step off the curb toward home, Caleb backed up when a semi crept slowly down the street, elaborately painted images on the side. *Fantastic Carnival.*

"A carnival!" Bentley exclaimed. "Can we go?"

The Fantastic Carnival? They were back town? Last he knew, they'd not come to the north Florida coast in years. Mom mentioned it now and then.

Last time he'd gone to the carnival was the summer of Emery Quinn. Caleb wasn't one to believe in signs or coincidences or fate, but what were the odds of the carnival coming to town a week after Emery Quinn returned?

"We should go." Bentley tugged on Caleb's sweater. "I promise no more fights."

"The Starlight, the carnival . . . you're getting a long list of wants, buddy." He hugged Bentley close. "We can do whatever you want as long as you don't make me ride the Ferris wheel."

At the house, he set Bentley to do his homework, then clean his room. Since Cassidy didn't believe in chores, Bentley had no grid for getting things done well or in a timely manner.

Meanwhile, Caleb answered emails and returned a few texts. Simon asked if Caleb would make some sort of presentation at the Tuesday night town council meeting about the Org. Homestead houses. Anything to spark interest.

Jenny Finch sent a long, bulleted document, outlining her plans and timeline for the Alderman's job. Her contractor would arrive a week from Monday and wanted to meet with Caleb at nine o'clock sharp.

"Please bring your completed plans so we can file for approval and permits."

In one sentence, she defined his work for the next week. Other than the job for Simon, he had nothing to do. He'd bid on a job in Panama City, but it would be weeks before he heard anything. And he had an email from Pierce Austin.

"There's still room in St. Louis for you."

Caleb clicked out of the email without responding. As much as he appreciated the offer, he was still betting on himself, Ransom Architecture, and Sea Blue Beach. Things around here just got a little more interesting with the arrival of Emery Quinn.

Reaching for his phone, thinking to text her about the carnival, he realized he didn't have her number. He'd forgotten to ask in the wake of heading to the principal's office.

"I'm done." Bentley bounded into the office. "Can we go skating now?"

Now? Caleb skipped through his to-dos. Alderman's plans. Town council presentation. Getting Emery's number.

"Let's go for inspection first."

Upstairs, Bentley's room and bathroom looked exactly how an eleven-year-old with no cleaning skills might "clean." He'd moved his clothes from the floor to his bed in one cohesive pile. He'd moved his bathroom towel from the floor to the back of the toilet. Caleb was about to instruct him on how to fold clothes and hang up a wet towel, but you know what? Good enough for beginners. One step at a time.

"So you want to go skating?" Caleb handed Bentley a twenty for skate rental and a snack from Spike's Concession. Spike had run the rink's concession for almost forty years before retiring and handing over the Starlight to Simon. But for posterity, and all that was good about the rink's concession for the past sixty years, Simon kept the name.

Bentley snapped the twenty-dollar bill, then tucked it into his jeans pocket. "Please."

"Sure. Why not. Might be fun."

Walking toward the rink, Caleb called the *Gazette* to get a hold of Emery, but voicemail picked up. He didn't leave a message.

At Sea Blue Way, he thought of the passing carnival semi and fell into a memory of *that* summer, Emery Quinn, and how the girl from Cleveland had stolen his heart.

6

CALEB

Then . .

Here goes nothing.

Caleb tapped lightly on Cassidy's door. "Hey, it's me."

It was Saturday morning, and he knew she was holed up in there because last night when Mom asked her to unload the dishwasher, she *unloaded* on Mom instead. Caleb volunteered to do it, but Mom refused. She went toe-to-toe with Cassidy until Dad called a truce and sent Cassidy to her room. She slammed the door and that was that.

"Cass?" He heard a thump on the other side just before the door swung open.

"What?"

"Just wondered if you were still alive." Caleb moved into her room as she fell back into bed, burying herself under the covers so all he could see was her long, dark hair spreading over the pillow. The morning sunlight warmed her room.

When they were kids, everyone thought they were twins. Guess they were sort of—Irish twins. Only eleven months and two weeks apart.

After a second, she sat up. "Would you care if I wasn't? Still alive?"

"What do you think? Come on, Cass. What's going on with you? Where'd you go the other night with the dude in the Jeep?"

"None of your business."

Caleb swiped his finger over the dust on her spelling bee trophies, then looked to her bookshelf, where she'd tacked first- and second-place math ribbons.

"I heard a girl transferred to Nickle High to play softball," he said, moving on to Cassidy's softball trophies. In the spring she was named Female Athlete of the Year. "Do you know her? Is she good?"

"Yeah, she's good."

Last year, Cassidy led the Nickle High Eagles softball team from the "circle" to regionals. And then colleges had come calling.

"When's softball camp?"

"I'm not playing." Her muffled voice came from under her blanket.

"What?" Caleb sat on the edge of the bed. "You've played your whole life. The team needs you. You're predicted to go to state. You could get a scholarship to play D1."

"I don't want to play, okay? Am I allowed to make my own choices? Why does everything in this house have to be about sports and school and good grades and church and stupid trophies?" She burrowed under her pillow. "Just go."

Caleb paused at the door. "By the way, Shift called. The West End Panthers trashed our beach. And by trashed, I mean stuff from like dumpsters or something. Shift said it smelled like a sewer."

Cassidy threw aside her pillow and scrambled out of bed. "When? How do you know it was the West End?" She peered out her window. "Who did it?"

"Who else? The football team. They've been pranking us every summer since we started winning the rivalry game. We've never retaliated, but this year, we want revenge. Want to come?"

"No." She turned from the window. "It's so dumb, trashing the beach over a football game." Cassidy picked up a brush from her dresser, then set it back down. "Wh-who all was with them?"

"How should I know? Those cowards work at night. All because they can't beat us on the field. And yes, it's dumb, but they started it." Caleb started to leave but stuck his head back in for a final word. "Give Mom and Dad—especially Mom—a break, will you?"

She said nothing as he closed her door, just stared at the floor, looking lost and sad.

He met the team on the beach with trash bags, a cooler of drinks, and a whole lot of grumbling about the smell.

"We have to get revenge this time," Jumbo said to Caleb as he passed out the trash grabbers he'd borrowed from his dad's refuse company.

Hollingsworth set up a speaker for some tunes, and the Eagles football team got to work. Shift drove his dad's ATV over the sand, collecting full bags.

A photographer from the *Gazette* snapped a few pictures while a reporter asked questions.

When the sun rose high and hot, a couple of the guys abandoned cleanup for a pickup game on the beach.

"My nose can't take it anymore," Kidwell hollered.

"Come on, Kidwell, Alvarez, get to work. Then we can get up a game." Caleb reached in the cooler for a Gatorade, and as he tossed one to Shift, *she* walked by. The girl from the Sands Motor Motel.

"Hey! You . . ." He moved around the cooler toward the Beach-walk.

Emery slowed, glanced over at him, lifted her chin, and kept going.

"Hey, Quinn, what's up?" Caleb started to follow. One of the guys let loose with the "Brick House" whistle, but Emery didn't even break stride.

"Okay, I see how it is. You too good for me, Emery Quinn?"

She slowed this time and looked at him through the loose hair blowing around her face. She wore shorts and a T-shirt, and her sunburn had faded to a soft tan.

"It's me, Caleb Ransom," he said. "How's the Boyfriendinator?"

"He's great, practicing Krav Maga." She pointed to the trash bag in his hand. "Punishment for some criminal activity?"

"No, this was done by the idiots at our rival school. Emery, come meet the guys!" She waved and started on down the Beach-walk. "Yo, Emery Quinn, you leaving me hanging?"

When she disappeared inside the Blue Plate, Caleb returned to picking up trash, checking every few minutes to see if she'd exited the diner. But what if she left out the front?

Yanking off his gloves, he handed his trash grabber to Clubber, who'd done nothing but drink Gatorade and toss the football for the last hour. "Here, put yourself to good use."

"Bro, where are you going?"

"To see a girl." He spotted her in the back booth, going over the menu, and slid in across from her. "Look, Quinn, I know you're *way* cooler than me, but really? Shooting me down in front of the bros?" He slapped his hand over his chest. "How could you do me that way?"

"I gave you a look." She proved it by recreating that coy glance. "Even smiled and waved. What do you want from me?"

"I want you to—"What did he want? To hold her hand. Work up the nerve to kiss her. The warm flush on his cheeks was em-barrassing, so he grabbed her menu and ducked behind it. "Did you order yet?"

"Hey, Caleb." He looked up to see Sarah, a girl in his class, setting down Emery's orange juice. "I thought you were picking up trash with the rest of the team." She gave him a flirty smile before dully asking Emery, "What'll it be?"

"I don't know, someone stole my menu." She made a face at Caleb, who promptly handed it over.

"The Big Breakfast Plate is good," he said.

"I don't know if I can trust you." Emery deliberated, ordered the Big Breakfast Plate, handed the menu to Sarah, then eyed Caleb. "If it's not good, you're buying."

"No problem." Caleb ordered the same, along with a Coke.

Sarah jotted on her order pad, asking Caleb about his summer and if the Eagles planned to retaliate against the Panthers for trashing their beach.

"Don't know," he said. "But if I told you, I'd have kill you."

"Such a cliché, Caleb." Sarah squeezed his arm. "Anyway, some of us are going to the Fish Hook later. It's bonfire night. You should come."

"We'll see," he said.

"She's into you big-time," Emery said, when she'd gone.

"She's a flirt. Dates my buddy Jumbo."

"You'd better warn him. And where did he get the name Jumbo?"

"You'll see when you meet him."

"You think I'm going to meet him?"

"Of course, when you start hanging out with me."

"What makes you think I'm going to hang out with you?"

"I have no idea. I'm shooting in the dark here, Emery."

"Speaking of the dark, did your sister come home the other night?"

"She did. About four a.m." He looked up when Sarah set down his soda. "I tried to talk to her this morning, but she's not giving up much." Talking about Cassidy made him sad. And he didn't want to be sad while sitting across from Emery.

"My mom was into punk in her teens," Emery said. "She wore combat boots and chains. If my grandparents hated something, she *loved* it. Next thing you know, she's in college, majoring in business, joining all these clubs and honor societies. Then she met my dad, got an MBA, engaged and married, had a baby while rising in the banking ranks, became a senior vice president, and drove a Mercedes. Punk Rosie would never believe Adult Rosie would do corporate America. So give your sister a break. She'll come around."

Caleb reached for her hand. "Thanks. That means a lot."

He thought she'd pull away, but she held on, gripping his right with her left. Caleb softly moved his thumb back and forth, only letting go when Sarah loudly arrived with their food. He sat back, grateful to pull himself together. Another minute and his heart would've thumped right out of his chest. He'd heard about a girl making a guy feel nutso, but he thought it was hooey. Until now.

Being an Irish twin with a sister, Caleb was comfortable around girls. Cassidy had a boatload of friends who were always running in and out of the house. Some of them "liked" him over the years, but none make him feel the way Emery Quinn did.

Across the table, she cut up her pancakes and took a small bite. Caleb did the same. Even though he was starving, he didn't want to look like a buffoon.

"What was Sarah talking about? With the other high school?" Emery said after a minute.

"We're rivals with West End High. The Panthers," he said. "The East End of Sea Blue Beach is the original settlement. The Nickle High Eagles are the original high school. The town was founded by a prince and—"

"Nuh-uh. A real prince?"

"Yeah, from Lauchtenland. He built the Starlight roller-skating rink and half the town. A man named Nickle, who was a freed slave, saved the prince after his yacht crashed during a storm or something. Nickle High was named after him. In the nineties, some developers came in and built up the town west of the rink. Everything new is on the West End. Everything old is east. West End High was built in 1994. Nickle High was built in, like, 1900. The football teams became rivals. They started pranking each other. Toilet-papering the courtyard, hauling beat-up old cars to block the field house. The last four years, we've owned the rivalry game. And every summer, they trash our beach."

"And then you trash theirs?" Emery said.

"We have not. But the seniors are saying it's time." He shoved in another bite of pancake, followed by scrambled eggs. "The guys talked about the retaliation all morning. It's going to be epic. Four-years-of-trashing-our-beach epic. You want trash, we'll give you trash."

"Don't they get into trouble? I mean, if the principals or parents know their team is trashing the beach . . . isn't that public property?"

"Oh, they know. All we hear is 'keep it civil.'"

"Ransom!" Jumbo stood at the front of the diner. "Sarah told me you were in here. Slacker. Let's go."

"Look who's talking." Caleb shoved in another mouthful of pancake. "Jumbo, Emery. Emery, Jumbo." He tilted his head toward Jumbo with an "I told ya" smirk. Jumbo was six-four, two hundred and thirty pounds of muscle.

"Now, Ransom." Jumbo and Kidwell yanked him out of the booth.

"See ya, Quinn," he said with his best flirty wink as his teammates dragged him toward the door.

"Wait, you can't go yet. Caleb, your breakfast . . . who's going to pay?"

EMERY

Now . . .

"I'll handle the town council meeting tonight," Emery said, checking off the items on her assignment board—which was a single document on her laptop screen. At the *Free Voice,* Lou had a large whiteboard on the wall outside his office. He assigned stories using color-coded magnets. Checking that board was imperative for every reporter in Lou's world.

Despite all the hats she wore as editor-in-chief, the small staff and simple production of the *Gazette* made it easy to feel like she was doing her job adequately. She didn't have much to do with her first edition on Sunday, but she had a hand in Wednesday's edition.

Elliot checked in Monday afternoon with a corporate-like pep talk, then confessed his sister Henrietta still made the case for selling. Dad called in the evening for a professor-like pep talk and update on the wedding planning.

"*The Glidden House became available on May tenth.*"

"*May tenth. They're getting married May tenth?*"

"*Mark your calendar. And, Em, rock Sea Blue Beach with your editor skills.*" Rock Sea Blue Beach? Dad was so cute when he tried to be hip.

"Jane, what are you working on?" Emery glanced at the woman across from her. A graduate of the University of Florida, she was bound for a major news outlet until she met a fisherman during spring break. Now she lived in one of the small cottages on Rein Boulevard, just north of the Original Homestead.

"My husband heard a developer is looking at the Org. Homestead. Since our neighborhood is adjacent, we could be impacted. I want to look into it. Besides, that's the oldest part of town," she said. "We'd lose a big chunk of history if those houses are destroyed."

Emery liked it. Jane's story had hard-news vibes. Lou always paced, clicking his pen, when a reporter dropped a hint of something nefarious going on in Cleveland. "See what you can dig up. Maybe I'll hear something at the town council meeting. Rex, anything more with the new sports facility at West End High?"

Rex Smithfield covered sports and hospitality for the *Gazette*—or any other beat not covered by their very lean staff. "Nothing, other than it looks like a small college campus."

"Where'd they get the money?"

"Town budget. It's all above board. I checked." Rex was a thirty-something surfer-looking dude with blond curls and an in-depth knowledge of the *Gazette's* inner workings and small-town Florida. Rachel Kirby hired him five years ago, right before she got sick. Emery loved that Rex, Junie, and Gayle were connected to Rachel, thus the paper's past, present, and future. "The West End rules the roost. Simon tries to fight them, but town council members who live on the East End are spineless."

"There's more to that story," Emery said. "So what are you working on now?"

"There's an amateur surfing competition in Melbourne Beach coming up. We've got a couple of surfers from Sea Blue Beach and Fort Walton entered. I think I'll write a piece on it."

Jane laughed. "You just want to surf with them."

"Never claimed otherwise, Jane."

Rex deserved a surfing break. He'd run this place until Emery was hired. He still ran the place as she was learning.

"Okay, we have some wire stories, a couple of fluff pieces banked from you two. I feel like I need another microlocal story to fill out the paper." So far, there wasn't much hard news in Sea

Blue Beach. The police blotter looked like Mayberry, save for a few West End break-ins.

"You should look through the digital morgue," Rex said. "Go over the old editions. Rachel kept everything." He leaned forward. "Let me see your laptop."

"Did he tell you he's part-time IT when Ambrose isn't available?" Jane said. Ambrose worked for the city and moonlighted for the *Gazette*. "Emery, if you don't need me, I've got some research to do."

"Yeah, go. Thanks Jane."

When Rex turned Emery's laptop around, he'd connected her to a server containing all of Rachel's archives. "There's a physical morgue in the back of this place." He pointed at the wall behind him. "But Rachel had the foresight to store it all digitally. You have sixty years' worth of *Gazettes* in the database as well as her own personal correspondence. There's some pretty cool stuff." Rex clicked on the drive, then on a folder labeled *Royals*. "In the late eighties, she became friendly with the future queen of Lauchtenland. You know the story of saving the Starlight rink from demolition, right?"

"I heard the story a long time ago."

"Weren't you here as a kid?"

"As a teen, yes." Since running into Caleb her first day in town, she started sifting through her old, stored memories. "They tried to bulldoze the rink to start all the western development."

"Right. But through a wild series of events, the town learned the land and the rink were owned by the Royal House of Blue in Lauchtenland. Prince Blue deeded the land to his home country. They couldn't knock the rink down without offending the royals, so it was saved. You can read the story and Rachel's correspondence with the royal family, mainly the queen, in the morgue." Rex headed for the door. "The paper's been put to bed, files zipped and ready to FTP to the press. Unless you want the town council story in tomorrow's edition, we're good to go."

"Nothing seems to be that important. We can wait until Sunday. If we need to, we can update the online edition." Which was even more anemic than the print version of the *Gazette*. Last month, they had thirty hits. Half of the stories were from last year.

"Then I'm out, heading to my folks' in Chipley. Got a date with a girl I used to know."

"Sounds promising," Emery said, clicking through the morgue files.

"I hope so. We've known each other since middle school. So what's up with you and Caleb Ransom?"

Emery laughed. "Where'd that come from? Nothing's up. We hung out the summer I was here as a *teen*."

"There's nothing romantic going on?"

"Rex, I've been here seven days."

"Is he the reason you took this job, moved to Sea Blue Beach?"

"Wow, this is really bringing out the reporter in you," Emery said. "I needed a job. I liked the potential of this one. As for Caleb, we've not talked in sixteen years. Then I ran into him at Alderman's."

Rex made a face. "What were you doing at Alderman's?"

"Same thing you're doing now—snooping."

He laughed. "Fair enough. I hear he's a good guy."

"He was when I knew him."

She shooed Rex out of the office so she could dig into the morgue before the town council meeting—by way of Sweet Conversations for a sandwich.

Emery clicked on a folder marked *Photos*, then on the first .jpeg. A gorgeous photo of Rachel Kirby with Queen Catherine of Lauchtenland displayed on her screen. They were dressed in ball gowns and bedecked with jewels. Simply stunning.

"Hey, Rex." Emery ducked into the newsroom, catching him

as he packed up. "Have any of the Royal Blues ever visited Sea Blue Beach?"

"Not in this century, no." He slipped his laptop and a battered notepad into a well-worn leather case. "Maybe not the last. The prince left in 1916 to fight in World War One."

"Not even to see the Starlight? To see the place founded by one of their ancestors? Do any of the Nickle descendants visit?"

"I believe most of them grew up here but have since moved away. One dude owns a ranch in New Mexico, the other is a lawyer turned judge. There's a sister who visits, but no details on when and why." Rex paused. "To be honest, I think the West End believes *they* founded Sea Blue Beach. The East End is like the old grandpa you lock in the back room when guests arrive."

"I never figured you to be hyperbolic. Is it really that bad?"

"Wait until the town council meeting. You'd think Alfred Gallagher, the big Realtor on the West End, and Bobby Brockton, who maintains every piece of government-owned land and then some, and Mac Diamond, a golf course developer, invented dirt."

7

CALEB

Long day. He was exhausted. Not from work, but from wrangling an eleven-year-old boy. Which started the moment the kid opened his eyes. What an ordeal. Caleb had to constantly move him from one thing to the next.

Wake up. Get out of bed.

"Bent, shut off the game. Let's go."

Get dressed. Then eat breakfast.

"What is the TV doing on? Go brush your teeth. Now."

Make his lunch. Grab his backpack. Then run back inside for the books that go in the backpack.

"Did you get your lunch? From the counter? Now why would I pick up your lunch for you when you have two eyes, two arms, two hands, two legs, and two feet?"

By the time he dropped him off at school, he was ready for a nap. But Caleb banked on Bentley getting used to the routine and executing things on his own.

Caleb cruised by One More Cup for a latte and egg frittata before heading home to wrap up the last of his work for Jenny Finch and then prep something for Simon and the town council meeting. He'd hacked together a rough budget last night while watching college basketball, but he needed to design a couple of examples.

In Seattle, Caleb worked on restoration projects whenever he could. He felt like he was saving history, saving the dreams of those who'd given blood, sweat, and tears to building the country.

In the afternoon, he picked up Bentley, ran to Biggs for a few groceries, then came home for an after-school snack and homework. Bentley talked nonstop from the moment he got in the truck—about his classes, roller-skating, Grandma's chili, his latest level on Minecraft—until Caleb said, "Buddy, I've got to get some work done. Remember you're going to Grandma and Grandpa's tonight. I've got a meeting."

By six o'clock, he was satisfied he had enough to pique town interest. Then he packed up his laptop for the presentation, walked with Bentley to the folks' for dinner, and headed to city hall. He'd tried to entice Mom or Dad into going, but they refused.

"The members from the West End control everything. It's heartbreaking."

"Then come with me. Fight for our side."

"They never listen," Dad said.

Simon met Caleb in the foyer. It was a beautiful space with Italian marble floors, a staircase constructed with ash wood, and a chandelier of handblown glass. Caleb had written a paper on the interior for his senior high drafting class.

"Are you ready?" Simon ran a handkerchief over his forehead. "It's like 1987 all over again. When I ran for mayor three years ago, I wanted to help the East End, unify us with the West, and end the competition, but the divide is wider than ever."

"It'll be all right. We're just getting started."

"I've roped you into my efforts. Now they'll label you as my ally and their enemy."

Someone called for Simon, so he excused himself. Caleb made his way into the meeting room, where a couple dozen citizens talked among themselves in groups of two and three. Emery sat alone in an aisle seat of the second row. Caleb slipped in next to her.

"Are you new here?" he said, extending his hand. "Caleb Ransom, architect, befuddled uncle, single."

Emery grinned and shook his hand. "Emery Quinn, editor, befuddled sister, single."

"Sister? Weren't you an only child?"

"I was . . . I am . . . sort of, but not anymore. It's complicated. Well, not complicated technically," she said in a low tone. "It only feels complicated. Is there a way to make me stop saying *complicated*?"

Up front, Simon called the meeting to order.

"Ah, saved by point of order." Emery tapped on her phone to record the meeting, then opened her Notes app.

"Did you see the carnival is in town?" Caleb whispered.

"Hard to miss with all the lights and sounds." A message pinged on Emery's phone. She swiped it away, but not before Caleb saw *QuinnFam* as the heading.

After the Pledge of Allegiance and Pastor Troy's opening prayer, Simon moved through old business before addressing new. Since all business these days seemed to revolve around the West End, there were no objections.

"Onto the matter of the old homes in the northwest corner of town," Simon said. "I've asked Caleb Ransom—"

"Who's Caleb Ransom?" Mac Diamond made a show of looking round the room.

"I'm Caleb Ransom." He rose up, waved, and sat back down. "Architect. Just moved back to town. We've met before, Mac."

"So what do you want him to do, Simon? Have we approved this?"

76

Simon already looked defeated. "I've hired him to work on a refurbishment budget for the Org. Homestead. Show a couple of designs that fit the era of the homes. They'd make great low-cost housing, which we need. I've also asked Caleb to work on a Main Street initiative."

"Main Street initiative?" This from Bobby Brockton, a contemporary of Caleb's, and part of the beach-trashing cabal. "Our main street is stellar. Recently paved, new lights and foliage. We need to talk about development and expansion of our infrastructure. The West End needs room to grow. We've been talking to a developer who—"

"Bobby, the West End is not separate from the East End," Simon said. "We're all Sea Blue Beach. We've got to stop thinking like we're two different entities with one budget."

"Maybe we'd like to change that too," Bobby said with a look toward Mac Diamond, who gave a slight head shake.

"Who is that guy?" Emery whispered.

"Mac Diamond," Caleb said. "A renowned golf course developer. Moved to Sea Blue Beach in the early 2010s."

Emery tapped notes on her phone.

"We've been talking with Thorndike Alliance about development on the East End." This observation came from Alfred Gallagher, real estate mogul.

"Excuse me?" Simon morphed from defeated to determined. "I've not talked to anyone from Thorndike."

"We're going to bring you in, Simon," Mac said. "So hold onto your horses."

"Hold onto my horses." Simon slammed down his gavel. "I'm the mayor of this town, and if anyone is driving the horses, it's me."

"Exactly." Mac's patronizing tone was grating. "Go on with what you and this architect want to do."

This architect?

Simon shot Mac a couple of visual daggers and returned to his agenda. "If we're to preserve our town, our culture and history, we need funds to fix up the streets, paint and beautify, reclaim and reuse. I've invested my own money into purchasing Doyle's Auto Shop and other properties. Caleb, do you want to bring your presentation for the Org. Homestead?"

He whispered to Emery as he stood. "Welcome to Sea Blue Beach, eh?"

While he set up his presentation, Simon reminded the citizens and the town council that those old homes were built by town founders Prince Blue and Malachi Nickle.

"If we do any refurbishing of those homes, or anything on the East End, we'll go with JIL Architects, Simon," Bobby said. "They're proven and—"

"Owned by your brother-in-law," Caleb added.

Bobby fancied himself the "mayor" of the West End. He owned the largest lawn and landscaping business in the region. His ads and billboard said, *If BB Lawns & Garden isn't caring for your yard, you're not caring for your yard.*

"All right, Caleb, show us what you got, but really, those old homes need to go. Sea Blue Beach is a modern town with modern amenities. People don't want to stay in a fixed-up Florida Cracker home when they could live in a brand-new build."

"Sorry, Alfred," Caleb said. "I couldn't hear you over your wallet talking."

"There's not a wallet in this town that doesn't talk, young man." Alfred looked around for approval. "Well? You just going to stand there or show us what you got?"

Was it okay to loathe that guy? Arrogant and rich, trying to rule the town with his greed. Caleb was all for capitalism but not at the expense of everything that made this town the gem of the north Florida coast.

Meanwhile, Emery sat in the meeting expressionless, like a good stoic, objective reporter.

His presentation was short and sweet, getting to the bottom line and the wow factor of how beautiful those old homes could be.

"We can use sustainable and reclaimed materials," he said, "which I've done before. It will cut cost and waste. Still, the cottages are old and will need to be updated for today's codes, including foundation work, new plumbing, and electric."

He also presented Main Street ideas for the East End—new Victorian lamps, fixing the brick portion of Sea Blue Way, buying new planters and plants, maybe a few banners, and painting the storefronts. "Like Simon suggested, a Main Street initiative will help bring in new business for the East End."

Caleb advanced to the last slide—the budget slide—and Alfred, Bobby, and Mac laughed.

"Where are you going to find that money?" Mac asked.

"We have some reserve," Simon said. "It will get us started."

"That money has been earmarked for easements on the West End for the new rec center." Alfred's voice boomed through the room. "You know we're becoming a destination for pro tennis players and golfers, which opens doors for service and support jobs. They can't afford country club fees, so we need the rec center."

"They'll need places to live too, Alfred. Not everyone will be able to afford a home in the West End. The Org. Homestead is a good place to start." Simon matched Alfred's tone.

"I think you're forgetting where most of our revenue comes from, Mayor."

"How could I forget when you remind me every council meeting?"

"I think the mayor has forgotten that all spending goes to a council vote." Mac sounded like the voice behind the curtain in Oz.

Besides Bobby and Mac, Millie Leaf was a West End council member. Adrianna Holmes and Lester Walsh were East End members — who sat there like bumps on a log.

"The mayor has authority for discretionary spending up to three hundred thousand dollars." Simon faced the citizens in the hall, not his council. "All I'm asking is for some funds to go to the East End."

"And we know you have a good many properties in the East End, don't we, Mayor?" Mac said.

"Yes, and I'm setting all my interests aside. Frankly, I'd like to see us do away with all this East End–West End business. We need to be one unified city. Those old Cracker homes tell our story. Just like the Starlight or the Sands Motor Motel or the *Gazette*." He nodded at Emery. "Or the Skylight on the west side. Or the Tidewater Tavern on the far corner of the west. It's all a beautiful story. Folks, you're here because you care. Let us know what you want."

Crickets.

Bobby rose slowly to his feet. "He has a point. I move we fund a Main Street initiative and release funds to fix up the old downtown, try to build up business on Sea Blue Way. The old splash pad is an eye sore." He glanced at the council members. "We all have memories of running to Alderman's for a float after skating at the Starlight, or going to the Blue Plate for all-you-can-eat pancake breakfasts."

Caleb closed his laptop and returned to his chair next to Emery.

After some discussion, Simon called for a vote, and it was passed to start the first Sea Blue Beach Main Street initiative and given a budget to restore parts of the old downtown. As for the Org. Homestead, it was tabled until further notice.

"They're throwing us a bone," Caleb whispered to Emery. "One yes for a hundred nos."

But he took this as a win. By the look on Simon's face, so did he. Then Emery stood.

"Emery Quinn, the *Gazette*," she said. "Mr. Gallagher, or Mr. Brockton, what are your views on preservation? Are you saying no money or effort should be made to restore and rebuild the town's Original Homestead?"

"Well, Ms. Quinn, since you asked," Mac Diamond said, "I think the whole East End should be bulldozed. It's in the way of progress."

EMERY

"How do you like that guy?" Caleb huffed.

Emery sat across from Caleb at the Blue Plate Diner. She had been in the middle of recording her notes at the meeting, stretching her journalistic muscles, when Caleb had whispered, "I need a drink," and steered her out of building and down Sea Blue Way.

Hurrying alongside him, she voiced the last of her thoughts into her phone. When they slid into a front booth, Caleb didn't bother with the menu but ordered two tall, tall chocolate shakes with extra ice cream and extra chocolate.

"Whoa, Caleb, slow your roll. Extra ice cream, extra chocolate?" Emery smiled. He did not. "What's going on?"

"I don't know . . . It's just . . . Mac saying the Org. Homestead Neighborhood should be bulldozed reveals way more than any of us want to admit. The East End is dying."

"Seemed a rather bold declaration," Emery said. "But after nine years of reporting in Cleveland, not much surprises me." She sorted through her notes from the meeting, squinting at a very weird autocorrect. "Alfred, Bobby, and who's the other guy? Mac? You could say they're in the way of preservation." She glanced up at Caleb, then made a note for Jane Upperton's West End story. "Talk to me about those West End council members."

Emery shifted as their server, Elsie, set down two ginormous milkshakes. She jammed her straw through the thick ice cream and drew a long, cold sip. She never imagined a town controversy was brewing when she accepted this job.

"West Enders. Born and raised. Except for Mac. He's a recent transplant. The prejudice between the two sides grows wider and deeper each year. I've not lived here for almost fourteen years, and while the tension was tangible when I was a kid, it was cordial. Now it's taken a seat at the table. Literally."

"Okay, but why such hate and loathing in Sea Blue Beach?"

"My guess? Rivalry, greed, envy, jealousy—all the seven deadlies." He stirred his shake with the straw, then took a sip. "You're the reporter. Go ask."

"Jane's working on a West End story. She and her husband own one of those houses bordering the Org. Homestead. If the West End wants to bulldoze one street, they'll want to bulldoze more. They've put a lot of work into their place. That reminds me . . ." She looked down at her notes. "Who is Thorndike Alliance?"

"Investors. They get behind small-town projects where the town votes in a small tax to pay them back."

Emery tapped a note on her phone before setting it aside. "This feels like more than east versus west for you, Caleb." And just like that, she stepped onto an old, familiar lane. One she'd forged with Caleb when they were teens. Bonded by friendship and laughter, by sorrow.

And love. Caleb was her first kiss. Her first love. She'd forgotten until now.

Her gaze must've lingered on him too long because he said, "Why are you looking at me like that?"

"Am I giving you a look? Sorry. Just thinking." She shook free from reminiscing and tried to make a dent in the massive milkshake.

She'd moved to Sea Blue Beach to work and build a career, not rekindle an old flame. Or the fantasy of a flame.

"When I lived in Seattle, I saw how the rise in housing costs affected hardworking people with good-paying jobs. If we take land to build another vacation condo complex or hotel, or develop another gated subdivision, where will the cashier from Biggs live? Or the support personnel at the golf and tennis clubs? The Org. Homestead is just a symbol of what Sea Blue Beach is meant to be—a place for everyone."

"You should run for town council."

"That'd be the day," he said with a soft laugh. "I'll do my part from the vantage point of Joe Citizen."

"Mr. Ransom Goes to Sea Blue Beach City Hall."

"It has a ring to it, doesn't it?" he said. "So, will you join Main Street with me? I could use an ally."

"I'll come as a reporter to let the town know what you're doing. In fact, give me some details and I'll write up something for Sunday's *Gazette*." Emery shoved her shake aside. She was going to need a to-go cup. "We need more local news for the paper, stories about the actual people and businesses that make up the town."

They discussed the Main Street project, and Emery took more notes in her phone. Caleb texted Simon, asking for an inquiries email on the town domain.

Caleb suggested Thursday night for meetings. Every other week. Seven o'clock. He asked Simon if they could use the Starlight Museum.

Emery summed up her notes. "The first Sea Blue Beach Main Street initiative meeting, Thursday, January 23, at the Starlight Museum. Email for more information." She glanced at Caleb. "Send me the email addy when you get it."

"No backing out now. The *Gazette* has the information."

Emery tucked her phone away. "Can I ask you something?"

"You can." Caleb said, his attention on her.

"Your sister had a son and he's living with you? Are you and Cassidy friends again? I know it's been sixteen years, but the last I heard she'd decided to drop out of school and move in with a friend."

"Friends? No. But we're cordial. She's a hippy-dippy wild child, marches to her own beat. She takes too many risks, in my opinion, especially with a kid. She thinks I'm an uptight corporate guy. Bentley's arrival *did* kind of heal things with the family, lowered the walls a bit. Now she has a new boyfriend who's not kid-friendly and wants to give the relationship a chance. She asked me to take him for the rest of the school year."

"At least she asked you and not strangers. What happened at the principal's office?"

"He got in a fight. Wanted to be friends with some older boys. He seemed excited to live with me, so I missed any signs of him hurting, missing his mom. He thinks no one wants him." Caleb finished his story with a long sip of his shake. "Can I ask you something?"

"Yes, but I'm not promising to answer."

"You have a sister?"

"I have three sisters—and a stepmother." Emery knew this would come up sooner or later.

Caleb knew Mom died of cancer. They'd messaged once on Facebook. Then she stayed off social media. Too many photos of Mom popping up on someone's Wall, along with sympathy notes and memories.

"I can't tell. Is this a good thing or bad thing?"

"For a long time, it was a hard thing. Then a good thing because Dad was so happy. They married a year after Mom died. The next year I was off to college. But I have to admit I always felt more the welcomed guest who came along with the new husband and new father."

"So your stepmother had three daughters?"

"Two. Ava and Elianna. Dad adopted them since their father was dead. A year later, Blakely was born." Emery pressed her finger against the tear resting in the corner of her eye, surprised by her surfaced feelings. "My allergies are getting to me."

"Must be an ice cream allergy." Caleb stretched across the table to take her hands. "Hey, you don't have to talk about this if you don't want."

"It's okay. It feels good to talk about Mom." She pulled free of his grasp. "Anyway, after we left Sea Blue Beach, I decided Mom wasn't going to die. I went around shouting, "Listen up, cancer, you can't have her!" to sun and moon, stars and sand, and anyone within earshot."

"Emery," he said, tipping his head to see her downturned face, "I'm sorry I wasn't there for you. Especially that night . . ."

"You had your own battles to fight, Caleb."

"But no one died. Emery, wow, I should've kept in touch."

"You sort of did until I deleted my social media accounts. And as I recall, you lost your phone in the Gulf."

He sat back with a soft laugh. "I was so mad."

"Look at us now. Mature, stable adults. We survived."

"You survived more than I did, Em."

"You two want anything else?" Elsie set the bill on the table. "We're about to close."

"No thanks." Caleb reached for the check. "I got this. If I remember right, I owe you one."

"You finally remembered. Wow, Ransom, I'm impressed. And FYI, you owe me more than one." She gave him a gentle punch as they walked toward the cashier. "You left me with a twenty-dollar breakfast bill. I had to run home to find money for a tip."

"What's your beef?" he said, waving the check at her. "I said I got this one."

"And the next one," Emery said. "And the one after that."

"Whoa now, this shake and maybe a couple of coffees and we're even. That's more than twenty bucks plus tip. We have to calculate inflation."

"Inflation? Dude, I'm adding interest, compounded daily."

"Compound interest? You're killing me, Quinn."

She loved when his laugh rumbled in his chest, and how easy it was to find their old friendship.

He seemed, in some way, unsure of what he was doing in Sea Blue Beach. Yet confident he'd figure it out.

But Emery saw a kind, intelligent, passionate man. One a girl could trust with her heart—if she wanted.

"Can I walk or drive you home?" he said as they exited the diner's back door and onto the deck.

"Is that your subtle way of asking where I live?"

"Is that your subtle way of telling me it's none of my business?"

"Goofball. Let's go. I'm at the Sands." Emery passed the couple lingering on the deck, talking softly and headed for the Beachwalk.

"Don't tell me you're in Cottage 7."

"I am. I know it seems crazy, but—"

"You want to feel close to your mom." Caleb moved around her to walk on the beach side.

"Yes. And I think *not* being there would be harder than being there."

They walked under the light of the Victorian lamps and past the dark and quiet food trucks in a comfortable silence.

"So, do you like your stepmom, if I can ask?"

In the peace of the beach, with its humming ocean and wide, glittering sky, Emery finished her story. "I do. We're friends. She loves Dad, so that's a win for me. Mom and Dad knew Joanna from their social circles. Four months after mom died, he sat next to Joanna at a dinner party. Dad never thought he'd fall in love again. Joanna was focused on her girls, wary of bringing another man in their lives. But at the dinner, it all changed."

"Love is a powerful force."

"Said like a man with experience. What's your romantic story, Caleb?"

"I believe," he said with a lilt, "we're still talking about your dad and Joanna."

"The rest of the story is they married a year after Mom died. In November, Blakely joined the family while I was at Ohio State. I like to joke she was the whole to meld the halves. But she's lucky. She never knew anything but Dad and Joanna as parents, and Ava and Elianna as her sisters. And me, I guess. For a while I was the mysterious one who only came home for holidays."

Caleb stepped behind her, one hand gently on her back, to let another couple pass on the Beachwalk.

"Ava and Elianna's father died when they were very young, so Dad was really all they knew. I, however, didn't want a mother or a mother figure—which I made known rather rudely, I'll admit. More than anything, Dad with another woman meant Mom was truly gone and we'd never, ever be a family again. When she died, our family died. My childhood died. It took me a long time to reckon with it."

They arrived at the motel's courtyard, where a couple of men sat by a winter fire, playing guitar. Delilah sat in one of the Adirondacks on the opposite side, head back, eyes closed, singing softly.

"Delilah," Caleb said. "She has a story to tell, doesn't she?"

"Maybe. I'm just not sure she wants to tell it."

Emery lingered, not wanting to disturb the moment in the courtyard. Caleb waited with her, and when he shifted from his stance, his hand brushed hers. Such a simple touch. Such a warm spark.

"I should go," Caleb said when the song ended. "Mom's with Bentley. Who knows what he'll talk her into. Grandma Ransom is nothing like Mom Ransom."

"See you at the Main Street meeting." She backed toward her cottage. "If not before."

He waved before disappearing down the dark Beachwalk toward the center of town.

At her door, she looked into the courtyard, hoping to see him there, feeling the slight sink in her middle of missing him.

8

EMERY

Then . . .

"Pssst. Emery." The jalousie window next to her bed rattled. "You awake?"

Pulling out of a dead sleep, she cranked open the window. Between the hum of the ceiling fan and the cha-chunk of the old A/C unit, Emery's room sounded like an old Cessna airplane. The digital clock on the nightstand blinked eleven thirty.

"Caleb? What are you doing?"

"The carnival is in town. Want to go?"

"Maybe. Who wants to know?"

"Me," he whispered, his lips pressing against the screen. "I'm off work tomorrow."

"Stop kissing the screen. If my dad sees a sloppy lip print . . ." Since their breakfast at the diner—where he'd stuck her with the bill—she'd seen Caleb every day. He'd stopped by a few times. Then she ran into him at the Starlight when Dad "rallied" the troops for an evening skate.

Caleb was becoming a good friend. He was cool. And cute— really, *really* cute. She'd filled her journal with descriptions of his

89

cuteness. This evening, she'd sent him a Facebook friend request. So far, he'd not accepted.

"So, the carnival?" Caleb wiped the screen with the hem of his T-shirt, showing off his taut, tanned belly. "You want to go?"

"Gee, I don't know if I can hang with a guy who disses me on Facebook."

"Disses you on Facebook? What are you talking about?"

"You haven't accepted my friend request." She tried to sound somewhat irritated, but sounded flirty instead.

"I hardly look at Facebook. Too much drama. Especially since you-know-who went all crazy on us." Over the last week, Emery learned that his sister continued to cause tension in the family. "But you, I'll Friend. As soon as I get home. So, are we going?"

"Em?" Dad knocked on her door. "Everything okay?"

Caleb dropped out of sight as she fell back on her pillow. "Huh, what?" Did she sound sleepy? She *needed* to sound sleepy.

Dad peeked in. "I thought I heard voices. I know it's hot, but don't leave your window open. Delilah called her A/C guy, he should be here tomorrow. And close your blind. You never know who's walking along the beach."

Yep, you never know who might walk down the beach, tap on your window, and set your bones on fire. No, siree.

When Dad had gone, Caleb popped up again. "Shew, I escaped the Boyfriendinator. What time should I pick you up tomorrow?"

"Talk to me after you've Friended me."

He grinned, pulled out his phone, tapped the screen a half dozen times, then turned it toward her. "Done."

"See you tomorrow, Caleb." She cranked the window closed and fell back down on her pillow, smiling.

In the morning, before Mom had even started breakfast, Caleb knocked on the cottage door. "Mr. Quinn, I'd like to escort your daughter to the carnival this afternoon."

He's asking Dad? The Boyfriendinator? Gutsy.

"Escort my daughter?" Dad tried not to laugh, and Emery swatted his arm. "I don't know, Caleb, what are your intentions?"

"Intentions?"

"Oh, good grief," Mom said. "His intention is to have fun. Honestly Doug, this is not the 1920s. Of course she can go, Caleb." Lately Mom answered a lot for Dad, and it always felt like she was trying to show or teach him something.

Caleb thanked Mom and said he'd be back in the afternoon. Dad, after giving him the evil eye, said, "That'll be fine. But I may be calling your father. Just in case."

"Yes, sir, he'd be glad to hear from you."

After breakfast, Emery cleaned the kitchen while Mom showered, and Dad stepped outside to take a call. When he came back in, he went straight to their bedroom. They'd had a lot of closed-door conversations since arriving at the Sands. They whispered a lot too. While sitting in the courtyard Adirondacks, while cooking or washing dishes.

Cottage 7 could fit in their Cleveland home's living and dining room, so maybe they wanted privacy, but still . . . it was weird.

"Emery." Dad returned to the kitchen. "Your mom and I are going to see a friend of mine in Jacksonville. You have fun at the carnival. Check in with Delilah when you get back."

"You have a friend in Jacksonville? How long will you be gone?"

"Just the day. We'll be home late. It's a five-hour drive over and back."

Emery made a face. "You're driving ten hours to see an old friend? For a day? Why aren't you staying over?"

"We want to get back, enjoy our time in Sea Blue Beach. And we don't want to leave you overnight. As for Todd, we've only recently been in touch. Don't feel the need to spend the night."

"But you want to drive ten hours to see him?"

"Yeah, your Mom and I thought it'd be fun. Besides, this summer is really about making family memories."

"Then why don't I go with? Meet your old friend."

"Well, sure, you can come if you want. Rosie, Em thinks she might like to ride along."

Mom came out of the bedroom dressed in jeans that bagged around her hips, no makeup, and her hair in a loose ponytail. She looked nothing like the bank exec heading out the door, ready to kick butt and take names. "Of course we'd love to have you come." She looked at her watch. "You'd better get ready. We need to get on the road."

Mom and Dad started gathering their things, but Emery didn't move.

"Em?" Mom said. "Better grab a book. Maybe a pillow. Once Dad starts talking shop with Todd, who knows when we'll get out of there."

Okay, fine. They called her bluff. She didn't want to sit in the car for ten hours, then at dinner while Dad reminisced with Todd.

Besides, Caleb braved the Boyfriendinator for her. "Well, I told Caleb I'd go to the carnival with him."

"And a woman must keep her word," Mom said, leaning to kiss Emery's cheek. "Doug, she'll need some money. And the spare cottage key."

Standing in the courtyard, with a twenty in her pocket and the cottage key in her hand, Emery waved good-bye to Dad and Mom. She startled when Delilah hooked her arm around her shoulders.

"There's no need to worry," she said.

"What do you mean? Worry about what?"

"Oh, nothing. Just when your parents drive off and leave you behind in a new place for the first time, it can be kind of scary." Delilah smiled down at Emery and squeezed her shoulders. "But

I've got a hundred bucks for the girl who can clean the two cottages vacated this morning. My regular cleaning service is running behind, and new guests are checking in at noon."

"Where do you keep the cleaning supplies?" Emery said.

By lunch, she was a hundred dollars richer and considering a career as a motel owner. Back in Cottage 7, she showered, ate a quick sandwich, then picked her outfit for the afternoon—the new jean shorts she bought before coming down, a pink tank top, new Converse, and her crossbody bag.

At three o'clock, Caleb came knocking.

"I don't think your dad likes me," he said as they walked past his truck, up Avenue C, toward the lights and music of the carnival.

"He likes you. He just likes me more."

He laughed. "My sister says our parents like me more. But it's not true."

"Is that why she's causing trouble?"

"Nah, I think it's whatever happened in the spring."

The carnival was set up in the lot by the abandoned Doyle's Auto Shop, and Caleb stepped up to the ticket window for two passes.

Emery walked with him toward the crowded thoroughfare. "So, what do you want to do first?" He paused by the Serendiporama machine. "Want to know your future?"

She glared at the mystical mechanical man at the top of the machine, with the wild, kaleidoscope eyes and lopsided turban. "No. That guy gives me the creeps. Do you really think this machine knows the future?" She tapped the name of the machine. "Serendiporama isn't even a word."

"Maybe not on earth, but—"

She chuckled and playfully nudged him. "Not even on Krypton."

"Okay, then just for fun."

"Or to throw away your hard-earned money."

Caleb slipped two quarters in for himself and handed Emery

two. She groaned as he closed his eyes and crossed his fingers. "Say I'll be a millionaire, a millionaire." Then *bleep, bloop, bloop*—the Serendiporama spit out a white card. Caleb pressed it against his abdomen. "Okay, you go. I won't look until yours comes out."

"Fine, but if I get a curse, I'll never forgive you."

"You won't. But if you get the millionaire one, it's mine."

"You wish."

"Hey, who gave you the quarters?"

"*Oookaaay*, I'll give back your quarters when I'm a millionaire."

"Even better, we split the million. Deal?"

"Geez, Ransom, I'm beginning to see why Cassidy hates you." Emery heard her words as she paid the machine the required fifty cents. But it was too late. She meant to be light and airy. Teasing. But her comment changed Caleb's expression, and a dark glint flickered through his blue eyes.

"Caleb, I'm sorry." Emery said as the machine spit out her card. "I didn't mean it."

"Forget it, whatever. Let's go." He walked off without waiting for her.

"Caleb, stop, I was trying to make a joke. I'm horrible at jokes." She tucked her card in her pocket and ran after him. "I'm an idiot. Big, fat idiot. Bad Emery. Bad."

He stopped short and turned to her. "I never said she hated me. But now, I don't know, maybe she does."

"I take it all back. What do I know? I've never even met her." Emery mimed eating her words, then locking her lips and tossing away the key. "The piehole is officially closed."

Caleb stared at her, then broke with one of his grins. "For the rest of the day?" He plopped his arm on her shoulders. "Who am I going to talk to, Em?"

"Me. Only if you forgive me." She wanted to hug him, but

that'd be weird. What if he pushed her away? "I'm an only child who talks to adults most of the time, which makes me a bit of a smarty-pants."

"You're forgiven," he said with a soft sigh, staring toward the carnival rides. She wasn't sure, but she thought he blinked away tears. "Cass was my first best friend. We were a close family, though she always tested the boundaries. Especially with Mom. But now—" He glanced down at her. "Want to find a ride? Get some food?"

"Again, I am so sorry."

"Forget it." He pulled her in, holding her so close she could hear his heartbeat beneath his Nickle High Eagles Football T-shirt. She hugged him back, breathing in his clean scent.

They moved on to the fun—hot dogs and sodas, a funnel cake and ice cream. Bellies full, they hopped on the carousel, knocked each other around in bumper cars—her side still hurt from laughing—and took a turn on the mechanical bull. She got tossed the moment the machine started. But Caleb hung on for the full eight seconds.

Onlookers cheered when the event staffer—also known as the ride jockey—rang a bell, blew an airhorn, and handed Caleb a cheap, aluminum belt buckle that said *Champion*.

"What next, Champ?" she said, leaning against him as she admired the buckle. "Ferris wheel?"

"How about the pony ride over there?"

"For a bull-riding champion? No way, it's the Ferris wheel or nothing." She grabbed his arm and tried to drag him toward the line, but he remained planted. "What gives?"

"If you must know, rusty bolts holding up big, circular wheel is not my idea of fun. Plus, I don't do heights."

"You just rode a bull."

"Yeah, a mechanical one."

"Come on, please." She grabbed his hand and leaned back, tugging. "It'll be fun, I promise."

"Emery, I'm serious. I can't." He freed himself and wiped his hand down his shorts. "Just thinking about it makes me—"

"You're really scared?" She pointed to the giant wheel. "They wouldn't run the thing if it wasn't safe. And it's not that high."

"How do you know it's safe? 'Cause a couple of dudes say so? No, no way. If that thing fell apart, we'd drop, what? Three hundred feet?"

"So are you worried about safety or heights?"

"Both."

"Nope. One or the other. Like when your mom took you to the store as a kid and said you could only get one treat, but the Skittles and the M&Ms both called to you."

"Quinn, this is not *even* the same."

"I'm making it the same, Ransom. Is it safety or heights?" She braced herself for his answer, ready to counter.

"Well, I guess . . . safety."

"Perfect. Let's go. The ride is safe or else the carnival would be buried in lawsuits." She shoved him from behind this time. "Fears are meant to be overcome."

"No fair, I don't know your fear."

"Guys who hate the Ferris wheel. Keep walking, Ransom."

Finally. She got him to the line, but he shifted from side to side, cracked his knuckles, ran over to talk to a passing friend.

"Caleb, let's go. We're up."

"I can't believe I let you talk me into this." He climbed into a bucket, shaking it, leaning over the side, over the front, inspecting the rig.

He turned to the event staffer. "Is this thing safe?"

"As far as I know." The tatted man squinted at Caleb through a twist of cigarette smoke. "Man up, bro, you got a pretty girl with you."

"Hey, Caleb," Emery said, "if you really don't want to go—"

"Forget it. I'm in. I'm in. Let's do this." Caleb jiggled the metal bar locking them in. "Want to make sure it doesn't come loose."

When the wheel moved to fill the next bucket, Caleb closed his eyes, breathed deep, and white-knuckled the safety bar.

"Open your eyes," she said. "Experience the thrill."

"What happened to closing your piehole?"

"Wow, okay, I guess we're—"

"Emery, please, I'm trying not to freak out and embarrass myself." He tensed as the wheel rotated higher.

She regarded him for a moment. He was really and truly scared. She regretted goading him onto it now. With a slight hesitation, she gently set her hand on his jiggling leg.

It seemed like forever, but the ride finally started going round and round, up and down. Caleb stopped shaking his leg but jumped at every creak or squeak, clinging so hard to the safety bar he might have to take it home with him.

"This thing was built during the Roman conquest," he muttered. "Listen, can you hear the bolts straining? Feel the swaying? Hey, we're stopping. Why are we stopping?"

"To see the view." Emery scooted closer and slipped her arm through his. "We can see the whole town from here. We're higher than the Starlight sign, and I can see fishing boats way out there. Oooh, and the lights of the Sands and the Beachwalk and Sea Blue Way. It's magical, Caleb."

Suddenly, she felt him relax. "Everything looks so small," he said.

"At home, in winter," she said, "we can see all the way down the street. I never see Mrs. Myrtle pushing her husband's wheelchair in the summer. Too many leaves. But in the winter, she takes him for a walk every morning. People don't like hard things, or winter, but Mom says that's when our perspective gets fine-tuned."

"What do you see when the old lady pushes her husband down the street in winter?"

"Love." Emery blushed and scooted away from Caleb. "I see true love."

"I've never met anyone like you before, Emery."

"I certainly hope not. How would I be unique if there were a dozen of me?"

"I'm glad there's only one of you." His eyes searched hers as if he wanted to say something else. "Emery, can I—"

"Hey." She flashed her white Serendiporama card. "We never looked at our fortunes." She scooted another inch away from him. He was going to kiss her! "What does yours say? That you're going to be a millionaire?"

Caleb read his card, making a face. "It says 'Immanuel, God with us.' That's not a prediction, that's the town motto." He leaned toward Emery. "Read yours. Remember, if you get 'Be a millionaire,' we go halfsies."

"Mine says . . ." She looked up at him. "'Immanuel, God with us.'"

"You were right." He reached for her card. "Serendiporama was rigged."

"You seriously didn't think a machine could predict your future, did you?"

Caleb ripped up the cards and tossed them into the wind, then shifted closer to Emery and clasped her hand in his as the wheel kicked into motion, slowly moving toward the ground.

After a moment, Emery exhaled and gently rested her head on his shoulder. She'd never been this close to a boy before. She'd only witnessed romance by watching her parents or friends at school—which was mostly drama and heartache.

Caleb felt like belonging. If this was love, it was the best feeling in the world.

Now . . .

Town Council Agrees to Fund Main Street Initiative

By Emery Quinn
Editor-in-Chief

The Sea Blue Beach town council recently approved measures to establish the first-ever Main Street initiative with architect Caleb Ransom heading up the project.

"While we've enjoyed the westward expansion of our town, we've neglected the original settlement east of the Starlight," said Mayor Simon Caster. "This section of Sea Blue Way, along with the business owners, needs some attention."

Main Street America, a nationally recognized organization, has helped small towns across the country to revitalize for more than forty years.

"We hope to learn from those who've gone before us," said Caleb Ransom. "But we also want to do what's right for Sea Blue Beach. We're a unique city. We want to capitalize on the things that make us special."

The first Main Street meeting will be held Thursday, January 23, at the Starlight Museum, 7 p.m.

"We're looking for volunteers," Ransom said. "Come on out, Sea Blue Beach. We need your creativity."

Developers Looking at Development in the East End

By Jane Upperton

Thorndike Alliance, one of the largest real estate investors on the Eastern Seaboard, is looking at Sea Blue Beach.

"We see so much potential in this town. Our goal is to bring revitalization and industry to the gem of the north Florida coast," said Terry Burton, CEO of Thorndike Alliance.

"We have a lot of confidence in Thorndike," said Alfred Gallagher, owner of Gallagher Realty, a multimillion-dollar company. "The shacks on the northwest corner of the East End, the Org. Homestead Neighborhood, are beyond repair. With or without Thorndike, we need to modernize the East End."

Mac Diamond, owner of Diamond Dog Golf Courses, thinks the location is perfect for a nine-hole course and clubhouse. "We live in the Sunshine State, home to golf and tennis pros and amateurs," Diamond said. "Think of the revenue a golf course could bring to the to the East End. Much more than fixing up a couple of Florida Cracker homes."

But not everyone agrees with the progressive view.

"I've never understood how we became East versus West," said Teddy Gardner, a long-time Sea Blue Beach resident and owner of a fishing charter in the West End. "I don't want to see the Org. Homestead destroyed."

Misty Harden, owner of Sweet Conversations, also wants more attention on the East End. "Our businesses are vital to tourism as well as the locals. We all want to succeed."

While the West End voices are loud, Mayor Simon Caster has no plans to work with Thorndike or any developer. "Right now, our focus is on strengthening business in the East End through the Main Street initiative," Caster said, "Which will strengthen all of Sea Blue Beach."

9

EMERY

The first edition of the *Gazette* with her fully at the helm hit the street on a blustery Florida winter Sunday. And she felt a little proud. It was only four pages—with one of them being the comics—but the local content was strong.

Junie was an experienced paginator who'd started with the *Gazette* when her last child went to kindergarten. Gayle in advertising makeup also had years of experience. Rex was not only a talented writer, but also a brutal editor. Emery hadn't seen so much red on one of her pieces since her first year at the *Free Voice*. Made her wonder if Lou cut her too much slack over the years.

On Saturday evening, after they put the paper to bed, she was restless with excitement. She'd produced the *Free Voice* many, many times, but always with Lou looking over her shoulder. If not in person, in spirit.

She slept in her clothes and set her alarm for five a.m., ready to hop out of bed, grab one of the motel's bikes, and pedal through the cold dark toward the *Gazette* office, where the "paperboys"— about two dozen teenagers and retired couples—prepared the paper for delivery. Almost every paper went into a rack or business. None to private doorsteps. Yet.

She'd met Owen, the head paperboy, earlier in the week. When she arrived at the office, he handed her a copy of the *Sunday Gazette* the moment she stepped onto the wide front porch.

"Congratulations," he said.

"I'll never tire of holding a freshly printed newspaper." She loved everything about it—the feel, the smell, the stories. And as of today, her name on the masthead.

She rode back to the motel, where she made a pot of coffee with Elianna's beans, and on the settee where Mom used to read her books and nap, Emery read the paper from front to back, top to bottom, writing ideas and small areas for improvement in the margins. Then she read it again and again.

Jane's story was short and to the point, objective, which was what Emery expected for the *Gazette*. Rex's piece on the surfing contest was fantastic—rich in detail, with an engaging human-interest angle. One of the surfers had a prosthetic leg. And the photos, taken with his iPhone, were crisp and clear, full of color.

At ten a.m., she started a Notes file for a growth plan, then emailed the staff. *Thank you all for making my first* Sunday Gazette *a success.*

Cut from old school journalism, Lou would grumble at her for that one. She could hear him saying, *Don't get giddy over people doing their job. Get giddy when they do more than their job. Like break a Watergate-level story. Even then, just give them a nod of "well done" and tell them to find another one of equal or greater magnitude.*

By the afternoon, she'd cranked open the jalousie windows to let in the brisk Gulf air, napped under a pile of blankets, taken a long, hot shower, and tucked the newspaper in her laptop bag for Tuesday's staff meeting.

Now what? The courtyard was quiet. The guests in Cottage 2, 3, and 5 checked out yesterday. Delilah had sent a text that she'd be gone all day Sunday.

Emery hadn't seen or heard from Caleb since the town council meeting, though he was never far from her mind. Stepping out of the cottage, she looked toward the center of town, wondering what he was doing. Something with his nephew? Maybe a family day. If memory served, his grandparents had a hobby farm northeast of town.

Back in the cottage, she sat on the settee and peered out the window toward the beach and the bluish-green Gulf. And missed her mom.

"Do you have any more advice for me, Mom?" She understood a person died once, then stood before God. But she wasn't sure if they stopped hearing words from the living.

Mom tried to stuff every ounce of wisdom she had into Emery before she died. Many of those moments were right here in this cottage. Only she couldn't remember what she said, only that death took her mom and her future as a daughter.

Okay, enough of this line of thinking. The day was too gorgeous to stay inside and feel sorry for herself, especially with such newspaper success. Heading out in her yoga pants and an oversized Buckeye's sweatshirt, Emery started for the Beachwalk, but the distant sounds of the carnival gave her another idea.

Back inside, she changed into jeans and pullover, wrangled her hair into a braid, tucked her phone, cottage key, and a couple of twenties in a crossbody bag, and headed up Avenue C against a stiff northern wind.

She purchased a ticket, then made her way through the crowd—between parents with strollers and kids on leashes, hand-holding teenagers, young couples, older couples, ladies in purple hats, men in ballcaps. She squeezed past people in Alabama, Florida State, Clemson, and Ohio State T-shirts.

She snapped a picture of one couple from the Buckeye State and sent it to Dad.

Emery:
We're everywhere.

Dad:
Never doubted it.

She made a note to research the Fantastic Carnival's relationship to Sea Blue Beach, see if she could find a story there, when she suddenly found herself in front of the Serendiporama.

"You"—she pointed to the crazy-eyed mechanical man in the crooked turban—"are evil." She kicked at the machine. "You cannot tell the future."

She didn't have her white card from sixteen years ago, but she remembered what it said.

Immanuel, God with us.

The town saying, according to Caleb. And what did it mean? God didn't feel near when Mom was dying.

Her phone pinged again. She expected to see an Ohio State meme from Dad, but it was Ava to the QuinnFam thread.

Ava:
I purchased my dress! AHHHHH! It's stunning.
I'm a bride!

Emery enlarged the photo for a better look. The dress and Ava were beautiful. She wore her long dark hair in an updo—to see how she'd look on her wedding day—a bright smile and otherworldly glow in her eyes. She was going to knock Jamie's socks off.

Elianna:
It's even more gorgeous in person, Aves.

Blakely:
I'm wearing it when I get married, so don't spill
anything on it.

Ava:
OMG, Blake, let me have my moment, will you? Emery, dear big sister Emery, this dress calls, yearns, for a set of gorgeous pearls. 😄

Really, Ava? Leave it. She was obsessed with Mom's pearls. The pearls that the Force women handed down for four generations.

Emery:
Check Walmart. Their prices are reasonable. Love the gown, Ava. Stunning.

Ava:
Walmart. Ha, ha, very funny. 🙁

Emery:
Thank you. I'm here every night at 7. Remember to tip your server.

Blakely:
Ugh! Em's turning into Dad.

Then a private message came from Joanna—who wrote every thought on its own line.

Joanna:
We miss you.

With the wedding coming up so fast, we have to host the shower in March.

I know you're focused on your job.

But it would mean so much to Ava if you could come.

We all want you there. It'd be incomplete without you.

Dad and I will pay for the flight.

I've checked the airlines, just in case.

You could leave late Friday afternoon.

And return early Sunday morning.

Also, I'm sorry Ava keeps bringing up the pearls. I'll talk to her.

But did you know you left them here? I was surprised to find them in your room.

I hid them in your father's wardrobe.

> **Emery:**
> Thank you. Re: pearls. I didn't know I'd left them. As for the shower, we only have two editions: Wednesday and Sunday. Friday and Saturday are production days for the Sunday edition, which is our biggest issue. So I'm not sure I can leave. I'm just getting started here.

She was finally getting a handle on all of her job duties. While the paper was small and Rex could produce a Sunday edition in his sleep, Emery still ran the staff, acted as ad director, planned future editions, and wrote stories. It was too soon to take a weekend off. What if the mysterious missing ads thing happened? What would she say to Elliot?

While he'd given her free rein, he also made it clear he and his sister expected a quality production with an eye on the future. She also sensed the threat to sell was always on the table—in a far corner, but on the table.

> **Joanna:**
> I understand, but keep it in mind, please.

"Everything all right?" Emery looked up to see Caleb, dressed in nice-fitting jeans, a long-sleeved polo, and his hair loose about his face. "Are you waiting for the bus to the future?" He nodded at the machine.

She grinned and tucked her phone into her bag. "Don't look now, but we're in the future of our past."

"'We're in the future of our past.'" Caleb leaned against the other side of the machine. "Nice, Quinn. Very poetic. Did you read that somewhere or make it up on the spot?"

"Just made it up." She snapped her fingers. "I'm that good."

"So," he said, giving her a Rhett Butler smirk, "you come here often?"

She laughed. "Never. Come on, buy me a hot dog."

Down the thoroughfare, he shielded her from the crowd, taking all of her hits, blocking her from folks who spent too much time at the beer truck.

"Beer and carnival rides do not go together," Caleb said, shoving a large teetering man aside.

"Write me a letter to the editor on it." Emery ducked behind Caleb to avoid a child wielding a large stick of cotton candy. "Letters to the editor are the voice of the community. Anyone can submit one. That's the hallmark of the *Gazette*."

"To be microlocal, right?"

"You remembered—and such a big word too."

"Keep talking smack, Quinn. Keep talking." Caleb put his arm around her, guiding her through an angry crowd arguing about cutting in line at the pony ride. "How about I write about how architecture and politics don't go together?"

"I'll expect it in my inbox this week." She curved into him to avoid a band of teens walking five abreast. "Are you here alone? Where's your nephew?"

"Wandering around with my folks. They wanted to bring him

after church. But I know for a fact Dad is useless without his Sunday afternoon nap."

"If you need to meet up with them—"

"Nope, I don't." She like the way he looked at her. Only today she didn't feel like melting. She felt beautiful.

"Any updates from the town council meeting?" she said.

"No, but I've been working on designs for the Org. Homestead among other things. Emery, if we can get the funds, not only will we preserve a piece of our founding but we'll have housing for seniors, singles, and young families. The councilmembers from the West End aren't thinking about everyday citizens."

"I love that, but there's only twelve houses, Caleb."

"True, but they are the very first houses in Sea Blue Beach. And it's a start for preservation. A nod toward affordable housing."

When they arrived at the hot dog stand, Caleb suggested she find a table while he ordered. She tried to hand him some money, but he refused.

She snagged a spot under a giant oak with swaying Spanish moss, near the Super Himalaya ride blasting Boston's "More Than a Feeling."

She was checking her phone for more texts from QuinnFam when he arrived with their baskets of food and a caddy of drinks.

"You looked pensive by the Serendiporama." He passed over a basket with a hot dog and fries.

"My family was texting. My sister found her wedding dress, and Joanna, her mom, wants me to come to her bridal shower in March. But it's too soon. I'm just getting settled here. And the weekend is all-hands-on-deck for the Sunday edition."

She was exaggerating a little bit. Gayle had all the ads designed by Thursday afternoon. Junie had the pagination done by Saturday morning. All Rex or Emery had to do was hit a couple of keys to flow the final stories. Jane only came into the office for the staff meeting. Rex was training Emery on the *Gazette's* production process and June was teaching her to paginate. Even Tobias, the janitor, gave her an overview of his chores.

"I get it," Caleb said. "I'd probably feel the same way." He hoisted his soda cup. "Here's to your success of today's *Sunday Gazette.*"

She tapped her cup with Caleb's. "I know it was only four pages, but they were *my* four pages as editor-in-chief." She wiped a bit of mustard from her hand. "I shouldn't be, but I'm proud of it."

"You have every right to be proud. My first design from college is in a frame on my office wall."

"From the University of Florida? That was your destination back in the day, if I remember right."

"I was headed to Gainesville until I got accepted into Cornell."

"Cornell? Ivy League. Wow. I never took you for the jaunty-sweater-tied-around-your-neck kind of guy."

"I would've been if I'd gone to school in the 1950s." Caleb's manner was so confident. "Cornell was great. I was a fish out of water for the first year, mostly because it was so darn cold. But I adapted. Loved it."

"I loved college for all the usual reasons but also for the distraction from Dad and his new family."

Caleb gave her a look. "Do you think if she was your biological sister you'd go? To her shower?"

Emery studied Caleb for a long moment, fielding the weight of his question. "Never looked at it that way before, but yeah, I guess I'd go. Feel more obligated, anyway." She shoved her hot dog basket aside. "Here's the truth, and it sounds childish and immature, but Ava, the engagement, all the wedding planning . . . Caleb, it only reminds me of what I don't have. Her mother is alive, and mine is dead. I know, I know, grow up, Emery, but every time I think of the wedding, I get sad and anxious, knotted up. Joanna gets to celebrate this momentous occasion with her daughter—who is now my dad's daughter. I'm working on being more gracious, but all this reminds me that death robbed some part of my life before I had a chance to live it. I feel like an orphan, which I'm not, but there's my gut truth. Joanna and the girls love me. I love them. I'm just not one of them."

"Emery, at least you're honest with yourself," Caleb said. "Most people can't express themselves like you did. I didn't have a parent die, but I've wrestled with Cassidy and the family dynamic she creates. I've come to realize love doesn't require perfection."

"Nor fairness. Is it fair I don't have a mother while Ava has her mother and my father? Joanna didn't kill Mom. Dad did a wonderful thing adopting Ava and Elianna. They love him. Yet here I am with one foot out the door."

"To me, you're more in the door than you realize. Otherwise, none of this would bother you."

"Maybe." Emery gave him a small smile. She'd spilled more than she'd intended. But somehow saying it out loud helped her make sense of her tangled emotions.

The conversation shifted to life updates since the summer of '09. Caleb asked more about Ohio State, and she wondered how he'd liked living in Seattle.

"I didn't know it rained so much," Caleb said with a laugh. "But five years in Ithaca trained me for weather. Besides, I was busy building a new firm. What about you? How'd you land at the *Free Voice*?"

"I kept sending Lou Lennon, the founder and editor, clips of my stories in the *Ohio State Lantern*. He ignored me for a while, then emailed me out of the blue before I graduated." Emery loved recalling that story. "I wanted to learn everything I could from him. He was tough, but he taught me the nuts and bolts of journalism."

"And there are honestly no boyfriends in your wake?" He peered at her over the rim of his soda cup.

"There was a guy my junior year. When the spring semester ended, he shook my hand and said, 'Have a nice summer.'"

"So a real classy guy." Caleb expression made her laugh.

"Oh, the best. Ending it was fine with me. I didn't take our relationship seriously. Love is a bit scary. You never know when the one you love could be ripped away from you. I never thought Mom would die so young. I don't want to ever want to be blindsided like that again." She pointed at Caleb. "How many broken hearts in *your* wake? Tell the truth."

"One. I think. Hard to tell with Lizzie. We were semi-serious for about a year. When I told her I didn't want to go to the next level, she stormed out of my apartment shouting, 'Seek help, Caleb,' and slammed the door."

"Did you?" Emery said with a glance skyward. During their short lunch conversation, clouds had gathered over the carnival, obscuring the sun's distant warmth. "Seek help?"

"Yeah, I called building maintenance. She broke the brass plate around the knob when she slammed the door." Caleb checked the darkening sky and started gathering their trash. "Should we catch some rides before it rains?"

"Let's do it." Emery took a final bite of her hot dog, then tossed the basket and the last of her drink in the trash. "Let's head for the Ferris wheel. It'll be one of the first to close down."

"Or . . ." Caleb headed for the thoroughfare. "We skip the Ferris wheel and ride the carousel."

"Skip the Ferris wheel?" Emery fell in step with him. "Are you still afraid of it?"

"No, only I prefer to ride the plastic ponies first." He grabbed her hand, tugging her toward the other rides. "The carousel is completely empty."

"So is the Ferris wheel."

"But remember, when we first came here that summer, we rode the merry-go-round first."

"You're just hoping we'll get rained out."

"Yes, absolutely. I'm not ashamed to admit it."

"Caleb Ransom, you have to ride the Ferris wheel. Fear can't win."

"It's not fear, more like wisdom." He pointed at the colorfully lit wheel. "I can hear the bolts buckling from here, Emery."

"No, you can't." She released his hand to push him from the back. "Here we go, overcoming all our fears."

Caleb dug in his heels. "Did you feel that? A sprinkle. They're shutting down the rides, Quinn. Aw, too bad."

"We have a chance. There's a few people getting on."

She pushed, and he resisted, yet somehow she managed to get him there in time for the last bucket. "You almost missed it," the ride jockey said. "We're shutting down after this one. Storm's coming."

"What luck, eh, Caleb?" Emery nudged him. "Last spin before the rain."

"I'm buying a lottery ticket if we get off this thing." He anchored himself against the seat, feet pressed against the footrest, hands gripping the safety bar, his gills a little green.

"You don't have to hold so tight." She tried to ease his grip. "We're still on the ground."

Still he held fast. "How is it, sixteen years later, you've got me on the dumb thing again?"

"Don't know," she said. "Must be love." She meant it as a

joke, yet the air between them sparked with a subtle truth. "Just kidding."

But when she looked over at him, nothing about this moment seemed funny.

"Hey, ride jockey." Emery pounded the side of their seat. "Get this bucket of bolts moving."

IO

CALEB

Love? She just said *love*, and the notion sank in deep. But come on, be serious. Emery Quinn did not love him. They hardly knew each other. Seven weeks one summer followed by sixteen years of silence was barely a recipe for friendship, never mind love.

Yet, man, he *loved* being around her. So much so he didn't care she witnessed his embarrassing phobia of Ferris wheels. Again.

He eased his grip a little when the ride started. The threat of rain had turned the afternoon sky an eerie, inky blue. Were he on the ground, Caleb would stand on the beach to watch the storm roll in. Instead, he was on a lightning-attracting metal wheel of creaking bolts and flexing steel.

As they neared the top, the bucket shimmied through a gust of wind. Caleb white-knuckled it while Emery scanned the horizon like she was the queen of the world.

"You're crazy, you know that?" he said.

"Being back in Sea Blue Beach, the resting place of my last carefree days, feels a little crazy. Might as well lean into it." When she looked back at him, the wind shoved a lock of hair over her eyes, and he flashed on the image of her walking down the Beachwalk the day he and the guys were picking up trash left by West End High. The twist around his heart felt the same as it did then. "Caleb, why'd you come back to Sea Blue Beach? Are you sure this is where you want to be?"

"You get me three hundred feet off the ground and ask me a loaded question?"

"At least you can't walk away. . . ."

Everything in her hazel eyes said she cared. She wasn't being a reporter or filling space with conversation.

"A few months before turning thirty-two, I looked in the mirror and thought, 'What are you doing in Seattle?' I'd always had this idea of who I wanted to be, what I wanted to do, and Seattle wasn't it. A month later, Franklin and I had a talk about our struggling business. Then Mom had surgery for thyroid cancer. The choice to leave Seattle became easy."

"Do you think we make choices for unknown reasons? Like, we think we're moving for family or a job but something bigger is going on? Would your sister have dropped Bentley off in Sea Blue Beach if you weren't here? Would she have driven him all the way to Seattle? I can tell you like having him around."

"She wouldn't have brought him home. Nor would she want him so far away in Seattle. She does love him, in her weird way. And yes, it's fun having him around. He dashes everywhere. Through the house, up the stairs, down the stairs, into the kitchen." Caleb laughed softly. "It's only been two weeks, but I'm already dreading when he leaves at the end of the school year."

"Look at the two of us. You left a big city with lots of job opportunities to live in a small, politically locked, albeit magical small town, to be with your family. Me? I left the big city because the only job opportunity was in a small town—which I partially accepted so I could get away from my family."

Emery subtly rested her head on his shoulder, and he felt

115

like she left part of her burden with him. In that second, Caleb knew he could fall all the way in love with Emery Quinn, and shoulder all of her burdens.

Maybe she'd help shoulder some of his.

Suddenly, the ride jerked to a stop. Their bucket swung back and forth.

"We're not moving." Caleb peered cautiously over the side to see what was going on.

"Caleb," Emery said, trying not to laugh. "Relax. It's so beautiful up here. You can see for miles. Wow, the West End really has expanded since I was here last. It's so bright, especially against the dark sky. And the East End, oh, it's so cozy and quaint, like a Rockwell painting. And the Starlight sign reflects on the waves. I never knew that old neon sign was so powerful."

"Yep." One word. Try as he might to be the brave man here, all the fuzzy feelings of sharing this bucket with Emery had just dropped out the bottom.

"I'll won't ask you ride the Ferris wheel again, Caleb." Emery wrapped her hand around his arm, and when he looked over, she was right there next to him, holding on to him. "But thanks for this time."

Two inches. That's all he had to move for his lips to be on hers. And he wanted to taste those lips, hold her close in this swinging bucket of bolts.

"Emery—" Her name came on a coarse whisper.

The ride jerked into motion and tossed her off his shoulder. Then they paused again.

He wanted to tell her he got on the dumb ride just to be with her. She was worth it. Wasn't that a metaphor for love? Doing what he didn't want to do just to be with her?

But he wasn't ready to say those words. He had a sense she wasn't ready to hear them.

Finally, they were at the bottom, being released from their seat.

"All done." Emery popped him on the arm. "Way to go, Ransom, I'm so proud."

"All right, enough of my Cowardly Lion routine. The wind is cold and it's going to rain. Let's head to One More Cup for a hot chocolate."

"Be still my heart," she said, falling in beside him as he headed down the all-but-empty thoroughfare toward Sea Blue Way, toward the café, the rain only stalling until they were safely inside.

On Thursday evening, when Caleb walked into the Starlight Museum for the first Main Street meeting, Simon met him with a grim expression.

"Two houses on the Original Homestead sold today, the ones right in the middle of Port Fressa. They were in foreclosure at the bank. A private buyer snapped them up, but I suspect it was Mac or Alfred. I was wrong about the bank owning ten of the twelve homes. Four of them were simply abandoned, and enough time has passed we can evoke adverse possession claim for anyone who wants to occupy one."

"You think Mac and Al will tear their houses down?"

"They'd need a permit." Simon smirked. "I have some sway in that department."

Caleb grinned. "Careful. If we fight fire with fire, we could get burned."

"True. They are a bigger flame. Mac will act like he's a team player, but as the rest of the homes continue to rot, he'll make some magnanimous move to rescue the East End with a nine-hole golf course. It's only a matter of time." Simon pulled a couple of chairs off a storage rack. "Though I heard today Thorndike ended their talks with Sea Blue Beach. This has always been about Mac and his golf course."

"When I decided to move home, Simon, it was to build a business." Caleb joined Simon in setting up chairs. "I'm glad to help, but I can't afford to tick those guys off."

Simon set down two more chairs. "I know it's not appealing for a young man building a business to get stuck trying to save twelve one-hundred-and-forty-year-old homes."

"Simon, I love Sea Blue Beach. I love preserving our history. Your generation saved the Starlight, it's our turn to save the Org. Homestead. But I'd like to do business on the West End too."

"I'm on your side, Caleb." Simon paused to count the chairs. "We've got twelve. Should be enough."

The Main Street email had a lot of inquiries, but neither Simon nor Caleb had a guess on how many actually planned to attend.

But by seven, only Adele Olsen and Mercy Kinney, two retirees, had arrived, toting one cake and one pie, paper plates, napkins and forks. Food was a requirement for every town gathering.

A minute later, Ivan Grissom, another retiree, came in with a pencil behind his ear and a folded sheet of lined notebook paper. Duke Pettrone, the owner of a startup company focused on uses for seaweed and sargassum, entered with his iPad tucked under his arm. By ten after, when no one else arrived, Caleb started the meeting with three retirees and one successful entrepreneur.

Simon's expression told him, *Work with what you got.*

Adele took a seat and pulled out her knitting. "I do my best thinking when the needles are clicking."

"You must be Caleb." Mercy sat next to Adele. "Thank you for helping our East End. Everyone, I've cut up the pie and cake and set out plates for whenever we're ready."

"We're going to be the slums of Sea Blue Beach if we're not careful," Ivan said. "Or worse. Bulldozed, like Mac Diamond wants. The Starlight will be all that's left of the Org. Homestead. My great-grandparents lived there when my grandpa was born. But mark my words, if we don't get on the ball, one day they'll get the whole downtown. The Blue Plate, the Fish Hook, the Sands Motor Motel."

"We don't technically own the Starlight, remember?" Simon said. "Prince Blue deeded the rink and the land it stands on to his home country. The Starlight is safe."

"We can't ignore the fact that the West End revenue makes up a majority of the town budget," Duke said. "We've let them steer the ship for too long. It won't be easy to pull them back."

"What Duke said." Caleb scrolled through the scattering of notes on his iPad. "This Main Street initiative should help balance the scales. I've talked with some Main Street cities and —"

Emery Quinn swept into the museum and without trying, Caleb suddenly relaxed.

"Sorry I'm late," she said. "I got lost."

"Lost? In Sea Blue Beach?"

Easy there, Ivan. Caleb motioned for her to sit next to him. "Everyone, this is Emery Quinn, the new editor-in-chief of the *Gazette*."

Ivan pursed his lips and sounded "Taps" out the side of his mouth.

"Hush, Ivan," Adele said. "The *Gazette* is well respected."

"Ever since Rachel passed, it's a rag. Some days there's no ads. Just tiny print of what the ad was supposed to be." Ivan leaned toward Emery. "Ain't y'all paying attention to what you send to the printing press?"

"Yes, we are," Emery said. "And hopefully, Mr.—"

"Ivan, just call me Ivan."

"—Ivan, no more missing ads."

"You hope," he said.

"Okay, let's give Emery a break," Caleb said, "and focus on why we're here."

Simon presented a budget to the group, and Caleb presented his initial list for revitalizations: replacing the rusting Victorian streetlamps, applying for historical markers, mending the broken bricks of Sea Blue Way, adding planters and banners, and getting the empty storefronts filled.

"Can we string those lights, you know, like folks have in their backyard, across Sea Blue Way?" Mercy said. "I saw it done on one of those home shows."

"Now you're talking," Ivan said with an exaggerated eye roll. "Good thinking. Lights will save the East End."

Double easy there, Ivan.

"I like the idea." Caleb added it to his list. "We can also ask shop owners to freshen up their front façades. Some of the money should go to those projects."

"Best make sure you distribute funds equally, or you'll have owners fighting like they did in '62, when Doyle's Auto Shop opened up and Garrett from the haberdashery thought it unfair Doyle got a bigger tax break."

"Noted," Caleb said with a glance at Simon. "In the meantime, we need incentives to increase business. One idea is to ask shops and restaurants to stay open late one night a week to draw in customers. Right now, the Blue Plate and the Fish Hook, along with the rink, are the only businesses open after seven o'clock."

"We used to do street parties," Mercy said. "Why not do that again?"

"I remember those from when I was a kid." Caleb added *street parties* to his list. "They were fun."

"What about a mural?" Adele said. "I saw that on a home show too."

"One that depicts our town history," Mercy added.

120

"I like it." Duke's deep, bassy confidence settled on all of them. "It's visual. People can *see* what we're about on this end of town. Maybe a bit of affection for the East End will spill over to the West Enders."

When Simon offered the east-facing side of Doyle's Auto Shop to be the canvas, the group started buzzing with ideas.

"It would be the first thing folks see when they drive into town," he said.

"What do we have to do to get a mural, Caleb?" Adele's knitting needles flashed and clicked. "Emery, when you write the story, can you say I came up with the mural idea and how I think best when I'm knitting?"

"There you go, tooting your own horn." Ivan's pencil was still behind his ear and his piece of paper remained folded on his leg. "Ever since we were kids on the school playground."

"Maybe, but I'm still nice. What happened to you?"

Duke leaned toward Emery and whispered, "You'd think they were married. Nope, just longtime friends." Then to Caleb, he said, "I know the boys in the West End pretty well. Let me see if I can convince them this Main Street initiative is good for us all. Also, I'll donate funds to help with the mural." He smiled and nodded at Adele. "It's a great idea."

"I have a friend who is a muralist," Caleb said. "I'll reach out to her. In the meantime, why don't you all email me your ideas for the mural. Simon, can you get a meeting with East End business owners? They need to know what we're planning."

"All this thinking is making me hungry." Ivan headed for the dessert table. "No use letting all this good food sit here, rotting."

Whether he wanted to or not, Ivan adjourned the first-ever Sea Blue Beach Main Street meeting. For a piece of pie.

10

CALEB

Then ...

On a deserted stretch off Highway 20, Caleb sat in his truck bed with Shift, Jumbo, Crammer, and Kidwell, drinking Dr. Pepper and planning revenge on West End High.

"What's our plan?" Jumbo crushed his empty soda can between his palms.

"Trash them back," Caleb said.

"I say we start collecting garbage." Crammer downed the last of his soda. "Put the trash in bags behind Jumbo's gramps' barn to rot in the sun."

Caleb laughed as they bumped fists.

"When should we execute Operation Revenge?" Shift said. "When they start two-a-days?"

The group disagreed, and Caleb was relieved. He wanted to get them back but not ruin their first day of practice. *That* would be going too far. He wanted no excuses when the Eagles trounced them in the final game of the season.

They tossed around a few more ideas before deciding to collect all the trash they could for the rest of the week, then execute.

"But let's not put it in the sun," Caleb said, "or we'll end up smelling worse than the field."

Agreed.

Jumbo crushed another empty soda can between his hands. "Ransom, you still hanging with the hot chick at the diner?"

"Yeah, Ransom. When do we meet her?" Kidwell was the Romeo of their group. All the girls loved him. He was stupid good-looking but also sincerely charming. In eighth grade, he stole Shift's date to the dance and Shift said, *"I can't even be mad, he's so nice."*

"Meet her whenever you want," Caleb said as nonchalantly as possible. "She's from Ohio. Down here with her family for the summer."

"Are you two going out?"

"No. Maybe. I don't know. We're friends."

"Move on, Kidwell," Crammer said. "Let Ransom have one. He's never even kissed a girl, as far as we know."

"Shut up, Crammer." Caleb lobbed a crushed soda can at his friend then hopped out of the truck bed. "Get out, boys, I have to go home."

"We know, it's Thursday night." Kidwell dropped to the ground. "Ransom family dinner night."

More than once Kidwell had offered Caleb his college fund, his weekly allowance, even his brand-new Nikes, for a year at the Ransom family Thursday night dinners. Because the wealthy Kidwell clan was a gong show. Which was probably why the dude was so nice and sincere, as a reaction against the chaos in his household. Caleb always thought he had a look of longing in his eyes.

He used to invite him home a lot during the school year, where Mom fussed over him and Cassidy flirted. But lately, the Ransom household wasn't much better than Kidwell's.

Slipping in behind the wheel, Caleb startled when Jumbo knocked on the passenger window. "Hey, just wanted to let you know my sister seen Cassidy out at a West End bar. Said she was pretty trashed. Could barely stand." He glanced back as Crammer left, skidding and fishtailing in the dust between the palms and palmettos. "Didn't want to say nothing in front of them."

"Thanks, dude. Appreciate it."

"Also, she was hanging on Coach Sanchez."

"Sanchez? No way." He was the offensive coordinator for West End High, their rival. "She's not that dumb. Isn't he, like, twenty-four? And engaged?"

"Just telling you what she saw."

Caleb fired up the truck but sat there for a moment, wondering what had gotten into his sister. Drunk? Hanging on Coach Sanchez? If she was home, he'd say something. It'd lead to a fight, but so what?

But when Caleb parked in the driveway, the house looked dark. He hung his keys on the hook by the kitchen door and flipped on the light.

"Mom?" He yanked open the fridge for a water. "Are you ordering takeout? I vote for Chinese." Mr. Po's had recently opened by the Starlight Museum. "Mom?"

Caleb bounded upstairs two at a time, his footsteps echoing in a cold and ominous house.

He texted his parents.

Where is everyone?

Then he texted Cassidy.

You coming home for dinner?

Her reply came quick.

124

Um, duh, noooo.

Mom:
Sorry, Caleb, I had to work late.

Dad:
One of our biggest jobs got scrambled. Still not all the way there. Eat without me.

In his room, Caleb fell face-first onto his bed. His family was imploding. Maybe that's what happened over time. Families changed. Traditions unraveled. He'd been naïve enough to think things would go on forever. That he'd bring his kids to Grandma and Grandpa's for the traditional Thursday night dinner, along with Cassidy's family.

He dug in his pocket for his phone and rolled onto his back. He started a text to Emery, then decided against it. Why dump on her?

He grabbed his iPod, plugged in his headset, and hit play on the Eagles *Their Greatest Hits* album. The music was smooth and melancholy, and the last thing he remembered was having a "peaceful, easy feeling."

An hour later, he woke up from a deep sleep, grumpy and hungry, with sounds coming from downstairs, along with the living room's light. Caleb grabbed his shoes, then headed to the bathroom to splash water on his face, an idea forming.

"There you are," Mom said in her cheery, fake voice. "Did you eat?"

"Not hungry." He took his keys from the hook.

"Caleb, look," Dad said. "Your mom and I realize things have been—"

"Weird? Yeah, really weird. And where's Cassidy?" He yanked open the door. "I texted her about coming to dinner and she said 'Um, duh, noooo.'"

"What?" Mom went to the stairs. "Cassidy? Honey, we're home. You hungry?"

"I'm telling you, she's not here. Didn't you see her car was missing?"

"She told me she'd be home." Caleb waited, listening, as Mom walked up the stairs, down the hall, opened Cassidy's bedroom door, then came back down. "Well, where is she?"

Maybe at some bar. Hanging with a West End coach. But Caleb didn't want to add fuel to the fire.

"Do you think something is wrong with her?" Mom said. "Maybe she's having a breakdown or something. In the spring she was doing so well in school and on the softball field. . . . Caleb, has she said anything to you?"

"Nope. I've asked."

Dad suggested again that they make an appointment with a doctor. "She may need serious help."

"I'll be back," Caleb said, his tone soft, sorry he snapped at his parents. "I'm going to see my friend Emery. Dad, her dad's the guy you talked to a few weeks ago."

"Fine, but don't be—" He regarded Caleb for a moment like he wanted to say something parental but instead ran out of steam.

"I won't be out late."

In his truck, he took a minute to process. *Could* something be wrong with Cassidy? He looked toward the lights of the kitchen. Maybe he'd just stay home and order pizza, see if Mom and Dad wanted to play a game. But it was almost eight. Mom took her nightly bath at eight thirty, and Dad sat in his chair with one of his many books.

Besides, Caleb wanted to see Emery. She made him feel like his world wouldn't always be messed up.

At the Sands, he'd hoped to find her sitting by the firepit. But when he arrived, the courtyard was dark, except for the string of lights and the golden windows of the occupied cottages. From one of them came a bit of music and laughter. He glanced toward Cottage 7, still feeling knotted up from the all the day's weirdness. Even Operation Revenge felt pointless and wrong.

He started to knock on Emery's door but lost his nerve and turned to go.

"Leaving so soon?" Emery appeared in cottage doorway, the light from inside embracing her.

"Hey, sorry," he said. "I didn't want to disturb y'all."

"Then why'd you come over?"

"It's okay. I should probably go."

Emery peered at him. "You need to talk, don't you?"

"I thought maybe Delilah would have one of her summer fires going." His weird way of saying yes.

"Dad," Emery called over her shoulder, "can we make a fire?"

The man came out in socks and sandals, T-shirt and plaid shorts, greeted Caleb, and grabbed a few logs from the pile. "I feel I should remind you," he said. "I know Krav Maga."

Caleb saluted. "Noted, Mr. Quinn. I'd still like a few lessons."

"Perhaps toward the end of our stay, when I'll no longer need to reserve my secrets."

While Caleb helped Mr. Quinn build the fire, Emery disappeared inside, returning a few minutes later with her hair in a braid and some gloss on her lips. "Let's walk on the beach first. Dad, we'll be right back."

They walked in silence through the courtyard toward the runner of moonlight on the sand. Finally, he confessed, "Thursday night is family dinner night. Only my parents worked late, and Cassidy was a no-show. A friend's sister saw her at a West End bar, drunk. She's not even eighteen. It feels like everything is changing around me, and I can't find a way to feel right about it."

"Maybe you're not supposed to feel right about it." Emery's

hand swung against his, so he hung on. That was all he needed for his world to get a little brighter.

"Maybe." He squeezed her hand. "I feel a little stupid. Always complaining about my family."

"Doesn't feel stupid to me. If I had a brother, I'd want him to care about me like you care about Cassidy."

"I like you, Emery Quinn. A lot." He caught the edge of her white smile in the angled glow of the Beachwalk lamps.

"I like you too." She held his hand a bit tighter.

"Are you going to break my heart, Quinn?"

"Not if you don't break mine, Ransom."

They arrived at food truck row and Caleb bought a couple of tacos from Tito's Tacos before they headed back to the motel. *What just happened? Did they confess they liked each other? Should he make it formal? She was leaving before the end of summer. So he should just let it be.*

Back at the courtyard, a soft fire flickered, and music drifted down from the speakers. Emery took one Adirondack. He took the other. They ate their tacos, and when she looked over at him, smiling, the fire's flame in her eyes, Caleb knew without a doubt that Emery Quinn would definitely break his heart.

11

~

Main Street Initiative Underway with Historical Mural

By Emery Quinn
Editor-in-Chief

January 26th—Sea Blue Beach's Main Street initiative is launching several projects. First up is a mural to be painted on the eastern wall of the defunct Doyle's Auto Shop, recently purchased by Mayor Simon Caster.

"The East End is the original site for Sea Blue Beach," said Mayor Caster. "The mural will depict our history from when Prince Blue landed on our stormy shore."

Lulu Chan had been commissioned for the work. Chan is internationally recognized as a premier muralist.

"She one of the best in the world," said Caster. "We're lucky to get her. But our window to get it done is small. Still, we're really proud to get rolling on improvements for the East End."

Members of the Main Street initiative will determine the mural's focus.

"We want a historical portrayal," said architect Caleb Ransom. "But also something that shows the heart of Sea Blue Beach, what our town is really all about."

Chan, born and raised in Seattle, has painted murals from California to Maine, and across the Atlantic in France and Italy.

Her pastoral scene of the French countryside won the Horizon Muralist Award.

"We'll be looking for volunteers to help Lulu get started," said Mayor Caster.

Sea Blue Beach was founded in 1882 by Prince Rein Titus Alexander Blue of Lauchtenland and freed slave Malachi Nickle. The two men developed a lifelong friendship, overseeing the town's growth and development into the gem of the north Florida coast.

Prince Rein, also known as Prince Blue, died on the Somme during World War One. He was sixty-two. Malachi Nickle died in 1950, just shy of his one hundredth birthday.

"My great-great-grandfather and Prince Blue wanted a town where men and woman of all nationalities lived in harmony," said attorney Bodie Nickle of New Orleans, a descendant of Nickle's. "A freed slave and a prince? Who'd have ever thought they'd meet, let alone be best friends. I'm happy to see measures being taken to preserve the history of the East End. Sea Blue Beach is a special town. Let's not forget."

From: sandyfayes@aol.com
To: editorial@SBBGazette.com
Subject: Main Street Thing

Love the idea of a mural. Why haven't we done it already? When is the next meeting? My grandmother was good friends with the Nickle family.

From: lukehall@hallindustries.com
To: editorial@SBBGazette.com
Subject: Move on!

You can spin it any way you want, but SBB needs to move into the twenty-first century. A mural isn't going to make a lot of difference. We can't afford to preserve the part of town that's falling apart. We've got the Starlight and the old Sands Motor Motel, what else do we need? Move on. I like the idea of a golf course.

From: hearmeroat@proton.com
To: editorial@SBBGazette.com
Subject: I missed it!

I missed the Main Street meeting but I'm all for preserving the East End. Why shouldn't we? Didn't we all grow up skating at the Starlight? Famous mobsters slept at the Sands. Even Frank Sinatra, if the rumors are true. (Which I believe. My great-grandmother saw him there.) The mural is a great start. Let's band together, SBB, to love our town. All of it. Not just the West End.

EMERY

Her third edition was in the can. So far, so good. She'd spent last Thursday and Friday courting advertisers. Her pitch went something like, "Do you want to advertise in the *Gazette*? We have amazing rates." Yet potential clients stared at her as if to say, "And?" So she blathered on about the value of a print paper, then ended with "Please, please, please buy an ad. I promise it won't go missing."

Okay, maybe she didn't say the last part, but that's how she sounded to herself.

When she returned to the office Friday afternoon, she emailed Elliot. *"Please hire an ad salesperson. Even part-time."*

Nevertheless, she'd landed a couple of accounts—small Mom-and-Pop businesses—and on Saturday morning, she sent over the contracts.

Now it was Sunday afternoon, and she was alone in the office, reading the paper. She reread her piece on the Main Street initiative. Every time she heard or read about the prince and Malachi, she was moved.

Sea Blue Beach, remember who you are.

Reaching for the banana left over from her Friday lunch, Emery made her way to Rachel Kirby's digital morgue. What if she created a "From the Archives" section and ran old stories about the town? It would add interest to the initiative. And it fit the brand she wanted to establish for the *Gazette*.

Taking a bite of banana, she began clicking on folders, looking for a place to start. The morgue had only a few issues from the first year the paper was in production, but she found with a photo of Malachi Nickle and Prince Blue roller-skating at the Starlight.

Emery downloaded the archive and emailed it to Junie. *"Do you think this will print well if we create an archives section in the paper?"*

She emailed back almost instantly. *"Yes."*

The afternoon sun sat in short blades across her office floor by the time she emerged from the world of the morgue. Fascinating. She'd found emails between Rachel Kirby and members of the House of Blue's Chamber Office, even the queen herself.

But more than anything, the stories and history made her fall in love with this special town. And she almost felt called to remind everyone.

Night was falling when she gathered her things. She was about to shut off her office light when an idea hit and started to sink in. *Nooooo.* It was crazy, right? Even if it wasn't crazy—which it was—she couldn't possibly . . .

She paced around the newsroom desks, once occupied by a half dozen reporters but now sat empty. She'd have to think about this. Pros and cons. Even the best idea had a few cons. Crazy ideas had even more. Think. And talk to Caleb. Even Simon. Or maybe she should just do it, then wait and see.

But first, think. Sleep on it, as Mom used to say.

She walked down Rachel Kirby Lane to Avenue C, considering her idea. What were the cons? They'd say no. What were the pros? They'd say yes. Then, of course, that would start a whole other list of pros and cons, but her idea was worth a try.

She arrived home—already the Sands Motor Motel felt like home—to find Delilah by the fire, wrapped in a blanket, head back, eyes closed. The guests from Cottage 4 sat across from her, playing guitars and singing.

"Michael, row your boat ashore . . ."

Emery took the chair next to Delilah.

"There's nothing like folk music," Delilah said. "It's got heart."

"You should know, since you were one of the queens of the genre." Emery sat forward to see Delilah's face.

"So they say, but I don't live in the past, Emery. Music is something I love, but it wasn't my calling. Not for my whole life, anyway."

"That's a gutsy declaration. Most people find their calling or passion and cling to it."

"It crushes some of them too. They have no sense of who they are outside of their so-called calling."

"Are you about to tell me why you walked away from an amazing career?"

Delilah reached over and patted Emery's arm. "No. Just enjoy the music."

Emery sank down in the Adirondack and closed her eyes, drifting away on the melodies intertwined with the crackling fire. Then Delilah was shaking her awake. The fire had died, and the guitar players were gone.

"It's too cold to sleep outside, darling." Delilah offered her a hand. "See you tomorrow."

"Yes, see you tomorrow." Emery stumbled to Cottage 7, feeling cold and out of sorts. She'd been sleeping so sweetly.

She'd was ready to tumble into bed when Joanna texted.

Emery, so sorry, I should've texted or called
early.

But we're so busy between the three cafés.

Elianna and I really need a home office, so we're
taking your old room.

I hope you don't mind.

We're installing a Murphy bed.

I slept on one at a hotel once and it was comfy!

So, when you come home, you'll have your
room and privacy. Just our desks along the wall.

They're built-ins. Very nice. You would still have
plenty of space in the room.

Guess that's all for now.

We love and miss you. XOXO

Any thoughts on coming to the shower?

Emery slipped into bed, wishing for the peace and warmth
of the music and fire.

CALEB

Monday afternoon, Caleb ducked out of his under-the-staircase
office into the living room, seeing it as if for the first time. The
clutter of moving boxes marked *Kitchen* or *Bathroom* remained

against the living room wall, waiting to be unpacked. Or maybe moved to another place altogether.

Also, there was evidence of Bentley—two pairs of sneakers plus socks on the floor and three before-bed cereal bowls growing fuzzy things on the coffee table.

Come on, Bent. You can do better.

Caleb could do better too. He'd not set much of an example with his unpacked boxes. He carried the dishes to the kitchen, gave them a good rinse, and set them in the dishwasher. He 409'd the counters and started a load of laundry, giving himself a bit of a pep talk.

"Come on, Ransom, you can do this. Build a business in your hometown and take care of your nephew. And unpack. What's your hesitation?"

However, the morning had been slow. He'd finished the plans for Alderman's refurbishment and met with Jenny's contractor. No word from Simon on the Org. Homestead project, and the client looking to build in Preserve on the Bay had ghosted him. The Swansons weren't ready to pull the plug on the Lake Lorraine home, and the Tallahassee project he'd bid on had emailed Friday afternoon. *"Budget cuts. On hold."*

But what did he think would happen when he returned to Sea Blue Beach? Doors would fling open? He knew what he was up against with JIL and the West End. Yet he'd thought things through, considered his options, even tossed a prayer to God for guidance.

Then last night, while he posted on his Instagram account about the possible marriage of restoration and green architecture, he saw a buddy from Cornell had been listed by *Architectural Digest* as an architect to follow on social media. Mitch Dawson? Really? The guy turned in every project late. Caleb pulled a couple of all-nighters just to help him out.

Comparison was the devil's playground—Grandma's mantra—but he still took a ride on the Why-Me Whirlybird and the Regret-o-Rama.

In the good news column, Lulu Chan, the muralist he'd contacted, happened to be free the first week of February. She quoted Caleb the friends-and-family rate, which Simon loved, especially since Duke's contribution covered two-thirds of it.

Back in his office, he realized he'd not texted Emery lately. Which was surprising since he thought about her often. She'd gotten under his skin the day they met at the carnival. Making him ride the Ferris wheel—again—and wrapping her hand around his arm, leaning so close he could kiss her.

Yet he had doubts about taking up where they'd left off sixteen years ago. The summer of "then" was about two teens falling in love—at least for him—their first kiss, and making his troubles at home fade away.

Caleb:
Hey, Em. Can you put something in the paper about the next Main Street meeting on the 30th? The mural project is moving fast. We are lucky we caught Lulu between commissions. How's your day?

Emery:
Can get the announcement in the Wed. edition. Visited more businesses about advertising. I'm not a salesperson. Blergh! That's how my day went. You?

Caleb:
I have faith in you. Go get 'em. Things are slow here except for cleaning up after an 11 yr. old.

Emery:
Ha! I bet.

He stared at his phone, wanting to invite her to dinner, then Lizzie's voice ran through his head. That he needed help. That he didn't *do* relationships.

Was Sea Blue Beach his final stop? Was it Emery's? Chances were the *Gazette* was a springboard for a larger paper.

Back in his office, he emailed the Main Street group about the next meeting. *"Lulu will want preliminary ideas from us. If you have, get them to me now."*

By the time Bentley dashed into the house, calling, "I'm home" and dropping his backpack on the hardwood with a thud, Caleb had a dozen emails from Adele, Mercy, and Ivan. One from Duke. Two from Simon. Most of them suggested images of the prince and Malachi Nickle, of the Starlight, the Sands Motor Motel, the Tidewater, and the Sunset Bowling Parlor.

Simon insisted on Immanuel being included. *"We're not Sea Blue Beach without Him. He is 'God with us.' He saved the prince from drowning by washing him onto our shores. Then sent Malachi Nickle to bring him home. I think that's the part of our heritage we're forgetting. So Immanuel must be included."*

Caleb wrote down all the suggestions, circling *Immanuel, God with us.*

Coming out of the office, he greeted Bentley, who had a fresh bowl of cereal sitting on the coffee table while he worked Minecraft magic.

"Take your bowl to the kitchen when you're done, buddy," Caleb said before he wandered into the crisp, cool air of the back porch.

Growing up in Sea Blue Beach, every kid and every adult knew about Immanuel, God with us. The mural at the Starlight depicted Immanuel as a woodsman of sorts, dressed in a long coat and a *Crocodile Dundee* kind of hat, his brown hair tucked around his collar. But it was his radiating eyes that captivated and perplexed Caleb.

Prince Blue had hired a renowned Italian artist to paint a picture of Him on the panels of the Starlight, with children of every nationality skating toward Him. The prince had experienced Immanuel with his own eyes, walking toward him through the storm, by the light of a single star, as the Gulf's tempest waves washed pieces of his wrecked yacht ashore alongside him.

Was He real or the result of a desperate man on a desperate night? Caleb hoped against hope He was real. Mom and Dad believed. But not Cassidy.

Leaning against the rail, Caleb watched a new set of dark clouds roll in, promising to make a ruckus later. The lawn's winter grass needed to be cut, which seemed like a good chore for Bentley. But since Caleb was restless, maybe he'd break out the old push mower tomorrow, clear his head with the scent of freshly cut grass, stretch out a few tense kinks.

Back inside, he was about to tell Bentley to do his homework when he paused by the first box along the living room wall. It was marked *Mementos*.

Mom sent him to Seattle with this box of football trophies, the medallion from winning the county-wide middle school spelling bee, his high school diploma, and the framed acceptance letter from Cornell. And the last family photo when Cassidy was Cassidy.

Ripping away the packing tape on the box, Caleb pressed the flaps back and laughed. Sitting on top of his letterman jacket was the cheap belt buckle he'd won for enduring the carnival's mechanical bull. He'd forgotten all about it until the carnival came to town. How had Mom known to pack it? He'd had it with him in Seattle that whole time?

Setting the buckle on the coffee table, he reached for his letterman's jacket. He was struggling with the snaps when Bentley peered over the back of the couch.

"Hey, what's in the box? Is that your jacket?" He wrinkled his nose. "It doesn't fit."

"Yes, it's my jacket. No, it doesn't fit since I'm all the way grown. Hey, finish your game and then homework."

"Can I try that on?"

Caleb regarded the dark blue and white jacket with the *N* letter and the cluster of pins he collected for the years he lettered in three sports. He shrugged it off and tossed it to Bentley.

"Hey, it fits." Bentley stood on the couch, arms wide. "Almost. Can I keep it? Until I earn my own?"

"Sure, but, buddy, I don't think Minecraft is a sport."

"I'm trying to talk Principal Tucker into making pickleball a school sport."

Caleb smiled. "Are you now? Good for you." In that moment, Bentley was his mother. She was always coming up with new ideas, challenging the norms. Asking, "Why not?"

Back to the Mementos box, he found a picture of Cassidy and baby Bentley. He carried it over to the bookshelf. That was a nice memory.

Around dinnertime, Mom called to see if they wanted to join them. Caleb declined since they'd eaten at his folks' five nights out of the last seven. But Bentley wanted to go, dashing out the door and across the yard before Caleb could stop him.

He heated up leftover lasagna, poured a glass of wine, cut off all the lights but the two framing the sofa, and lit a fire. Reaching for the remote, he turned on SportsCenter. But the house was still too quiet . . .

Which gave him too much head space to think of Emery. Why didn't he just call her? Ask her to coffee, or lunch, or dinner? Nearly all of their interactions had been random. The awkward yet surprising exchange at Alderman's Pharmacy. Running into her at the carnival. Then the town council and Main Street meetings, which she attended in an official capacity as editor of the *Gazette*.

Dude, just call her.

As he took a fortifying bite of lasagna, his phone rang. He smiled when he saw Emery's name.

"I was just going to text you," he said. "What are you doing? Torturing some man by making him ride the Ferris wheel?"

"No, no, I reserve that fun for you."

"I feel so special."

"I'm standing on your front porch, freezing."

When he opened the front door, Emery stood under the amber-colored porch light, wearing an Ohio State hoodie and socks for gloves.

"No one told me Florida winters were so cold." She held up her hands. "I left my gloves in Cleveland."

"It's the wet air. It sinks into your bones. Come on in."

As she crossed the threshold, Caleb exhaled a breath he didn't know he was holding. She felt right in this space. She looked good in this space.

"Caleb, wow, your place is gorgeous." She pointed to the boxes. "And I love what you've done with the corrugated cardboard. Very green-forward. Is that part of your sustainable design plan?"

He laughed. "No, but now that you mention it . . ." He started for the kitchen. "Have you eaten? How's leftover lasagna and a glass of wine sound?"

"Like heaven." She tugged off her sock gloves and tucked them into her hoodie pocket. "Hey, do you have any contacts at the amphitheater? I've called and called about press passes to an upcoming Beach Boys concert, but no one will return my call."

"Really? You're the editor of the *Gazette*. Don't they know about the power of the press? And no, I don't have any connections there." He moved into the kitchen. Emery followed.

"I'd reach out to Mac Diamond or Alfred Gallagher, but I know their kind. Favors always require payback."

"You'd do better trying to sneak in."

"Is Bentley here? I've not met him."

"He's at my folks'."

"Then another time." She crossed her arms and leaned against the counter. "So why haven't you unpacked those boxes?"

"She goes straight to the hard questions, ladies and gentlemen." Caleb set a square of lasagna on a plate and popped it in the microwave. "I don't know. Lazy? Or maybe because I'm not sure this is permanent."

"Why isn't this place permanent?" She leaned forward to see his face, her eyes bright and sincere.

"For one, business is not good."

"But you didn't know that when the boxes arrived."

"Then I don't have an answer. Maybe I should just throw all the stuff out. After Grandma died, I helped Grandpa clean out her things. And guess what, Emery? You can't take it with you. Other people won't want your stuff unless it's near priceless or really sentimental."

"Mom went through her things before she died. She hired someone to come in while Dad and I were at school and work. We didn't know what she was doing for a couple of weeks. Then I saw some photo albums and her high school yearbooks in a box marked *Garbage*. I rescued those. After she died, we realized how much she'd given or thrown away, but the house . . . the place where she cooked dinners and decorated for holidays and entertained was still there. For me, it felt like she was still with us. Then Dad met Joanna, got married, and we moved. That was hard because it was like a final good-bye to Mom."

"But you kept the things that really mattered." The microwaved beeped, and Caleb decided the lasagna needed another minute. "Look in that drawer by the sink for utensils."

"I have her pearls." Emery selected a fork from a rather nice collection. "I'll be the fifth generation to wear them on my wedding day. I like to think Mom will be with me."

"Do you want to get married?" He shot a glance her way but didn't linger.

"I love the idea of being in a committed relationship with someone I love. And who loves me. My parents were a good example. But I'm not sure I know how to find that guy. I'm starting to realize how much Mom's death affected me. Like I don't cling to things. I reserve my heart. I get scared the other shoe will drop, like something happening to Dad. I want to move past that way of thinking, though, because Mom always chose to love."

"She'd be proud of you, Emery."

"I'd hope so. What about you? Is marriage on the drafting table?" Emery followed him to the living room with her plate and glass of wine.

Caleb wished her *bon appétit* and considered his answer. With the fire and lamplight low, the living room was cozy and romantic, perfect for being vulnerable for half a second. And it was Emery Quinn. The one who made things right. *The* girl against whom he'd measured all others.

He washed down a bite with a sip of wine. "I want to get married." He glanced over at her. "To the right girl."

When she smiled, heaven help him, he wanted to set aside their plates and pull her onto his lap and hold her. Kiss her. But the slamming kitchen door ended that idea.

Bentley dashed into the room. "I'm home. Early." He skidded to a stop, his eyes on Emery. "Hello."

"You must be Bentley."

"And who are you?" He glanced at Caleb with sly grin. "Is this why you didn't want to eat at Grandma's?"

"No. Emery stopped by just as I was getting ready to eat."

Bentley's sly grin widened. "How convenient."

"Bent, politely introduce yourself, then get to the shower," Caleb said. The boy was too clever for his own britches.

"I'm Bentley, the nephew," he said, shaking her hand, then rocking the house as he bounded up the stairs and down the hall.

"Make sure to pick up your wet towel when you're done!" Caleb called after him.

"I can see why you like having him around," Emery said. "My little sister Blakely was always asking those poignant or embarrassing questions at his age."

"So, what would you tell him if he asked why you came by tonight?" Caleb stabbed at his lasagna, waiting for her answer.

"I'd say to see his Uncle Caleb, my only friend in town."

12

EMERY

Then . . .

When she came in from the beach, Dad was pulling burgers off the grill.

"I hope you're hungry." He held up the plate of meat. "Or did you eat your fill at the food trucks?"

"I didn't take any money, so I'm starved." Her first-day sunburn had faded enough for her to tan golden brown. She sort of liked becoming a beach baby.

Inside, Emery set down her bag, taking out her towel, water bottle, and book. Mom was on the settee under the window, dozing with her head cradled against her arm.

Let her sleep. Dad would be loud enough when he came in. But as Emery passed by, Mom looked up.

"Are you having a fun summer?" She held out her arm, inviting Emery to join her. "You look beautiful."

"I'm having fun. Are you?" Emery sat on the ottoman next to the settee.

"I am." She'd been spending more time by the window, pretending to read but falling asleep. "Did you see your friend Caleb today?"

"No, he was working at the Starlight. Mom, are you okay? I mean, you seem kind of tired. You and Dad disappeared for another day again. Where'd you go?"

"We told you. To see friends of Dad's. And anytime I'm near you, I'm having fun."

"He has friends in Jacksonville *and* Gainesville?" For that trip, they left before dawn and arrived home well after dinner. "Why don't you take me with you?"

Mom gave her a weak smile. "You want to be in the car with your Dad and me when you could be on the beach with that boy?"

Mom had trumped with that line before. "He's really nice, Mom."

"I can tell."

"Burgers are up." Dad set the plate on the island. Delilah came in behind him with a cake. "Delilah offered me cake in exchange for a burger."

"You're playing his tune, Delilah," Mom said, shoving off the settee. "Emery, put on some music. Oldies, like Samson Delilah."

"Rosie, please, you don't have to play my music."

"I would, but you told me no electronics," Emery said, clicking on the old radio. "Sorry, Delilah."

"I like the oldies station on that radio just fine. Now, what do we have for the burgers?"

Emery helped set out the burger fixings and dumped a bag of chips into a bowl but kept one eye on Mom.

"Hey, Dad, is Mom okay?"

"Of course." But he didn't look at her. "Why do you ask?"

"She seems really tired. And I think she's lost weight."

"Her stomach has been bothering her. She'll be all right. You know her job is stressful. You focus on having fun."

145

"We're supposed to make memories together. You keep driving away, leaving me here."

"Well, no more driving away. How about we go roller-skating tomorrow night? Delilah has some friends visiting this weekend. She wants to have something called a guitar circle. We'll sit around the fire and listen to music."

Okay, that sounded a bit more normal.

While they ate, Delilah told them stories of her music heydays and how she and Samson toured with the Beach Boys. "We made a lot of music and a lot of money."

"So why'd you leave the business?" Emery reached for another handful of chips.

"I met Jesus in '72. He changed my life."

"Did your life need changing?" Mom said.

"More than I knew."

Emery crunched softly on a chip, waiting for more, but all Delilah said was, "Doug, that was a delicious burger."

"Caleb's dad gave me a few pointers." He glanced at Mom, who smiled and suggested a game of cards after dinner.

Emery volunteered to clean up, then partnered with Dad for a game of euchre, winning over Mom and Delilah. She was about to curl up in bed after her shower when Dad peeked in her room.

"Caleb Ransom is here to see you."

When she entered the living room, he jumped up from the lumpy cushion where he chatted with Mom and Delilah. "Hey, I was wondering if you wanted to go for some ice cream."

"Now?" She looked at Dad, who nodded. "Um, sure. I'll be right back." She dashed into her room, tripping over her own jitters. What should she wear? Yanking her wet hair out of a tie, she shook out her waves with an eye on her favorite shorts and T-shirt.

"Be home by midnight," Dad said as she walked out with

Caleb. "And Ransom?" He swung two fingers from his eyes toward Caleb's.

"Yes, sir. You know Krav Maga."

Emery didn't laugh until they left the cottage. "I'm sorry. He's a nut."

"I don't mind, but, um, this way." Caleb led her to his truck instead of the Beachwalk. "I hope you don't mind if we don't go for ice cream."

"No ice cream?" She'd been reaching for the door handle but stopped. "Then I'm out."

"Instead," he said with some urgency, "we're executing Operation Revenge on West End High. Do you want to come?"

Well, this was interesting. She'd never been one of the guys before. And she wanted to go. To be with him.

"What sort of payback? Will I get arrested?" She opened the door and climbed in. "If I get arrested, I'll never speak to you again, and when you die, you'll be cursed to ride a Ferris wheel for all eternity."

"You will most definitely *not* get arrested." When he clapped his hand on her leg, it felt hotter than the noon sun. "So? You in?"

"I'm in." All in. Too far in.

She'd only know him a little over a month, but he'd become a huge part of her heart. She barely thought of her friends in Cleveland. Yet in a few weeks—it was already July—she'd be gone for the rest of the year. Maybe the rest of her life.

Caleb cranked the radio as Kenny Chesney sang "Everybody Wants To Go To Heaven," slowing as they stopped for the East End's one traffic light. When it flashed green, Caleb headed out, swerving down the first side street and straight into a driveway.

"I'll be back," he said. "Got to get Shift." Caleb pressed his finger to his lips with a gentle "Shhh."

"Shift? Who names their kid Shift?"

"His name is Harvey, but everyone calls him Shift."

A broad, stocky boy ran from the side of the house with two huge garbage bags. He tossed them in the bed, then ran back through the shadows, returning with three more huge bags.

He popped open the passenger door and climbed in next to Emery, crunching her against Caleb.

"Shift, this is Emery." Caleb backed out of the driveway. "Emery, Shift."

"So you're the great Emery Quinn?" Shift leaned back and whispered behind her, "Dude! She's hot."

Caleb laughed. "Duuudde, she can hear you."

One by one, Caleb acquired more teammates. They hopped into the truck bed along with their stuffed garbage bags.

One of the guys peered into Caleb's window. "Jumbo and the rest will meet us in the West End." Then he nodded at Emery. "Hey, Emery, Abe Hollingsworth, but everyone calls me Hollingsworth. Thanks for coming. You're our good luck charm."

"Am I?" She looked at Caleb. "You've been talking about me?"

"Only a little."

Emery glanced at Hollingsworth. "Please don't get me arrested."

"We won't get you arrested." Chorused by Caleb, Hollingsworth, and Shift, almost in three-part harmony, so she had to believe them.

Back onto Sea Blue Way, they drove from the older, more narrow Way onto the newer, wider, multilane Sea Blue Way, with its bright lights, hotels, restaurants, and tourist attractions.

"It's like going from the farm to Oz," Emery said.

After a couple of left turns, then a right, West End High came into view. But Caleb went off-road, heading through thick clumps of palmettos, palm trees, and pine, where guys named Alvarez and Jennings waited, their F-150s overflowing with bags of trash.

"Jumbo parked down a ways," Alvarez said. "He's got his dad's work truck and so much trash."

They fist-bumped and praised themselves as Shift passed around a box of latex gloves.

"You learn a lot about germs living with a mother who's a nurse. Who's got the ski masks?"

Clubber passed out black ski masks, then everyone, including Emery, grabbed trash bags and crept through trees, shrubs, and shadows toward the stadium.

"Aren't they going to know it was you guys?" Emery whispered.

"Shhh." This from a voice in the back. "You'll jinx us."

At the locked stadium gate, they hoisted bags after bag of trash over the chain-link gate. One of the guys exhaled a string of curses when his bag leaked on his leg.

"Who didn't tie this up tight? Carter? Was it you?"

"Hush," Caleb said. "Just leave it. Check your bags before you toss them over. We don't want to smell like trash when we get home."

Home? If they even made it home because they were getting arrested. Definitely. Yet she was in. All in.

Once the bags cleared, Jumbo, the center most likely bound for a top college football program and eventually the NFL, started launching guys over the gate.

"All right, Emery, you're up." Jumbo waved her over. But when she put her foot in his hand, he fired her so high she cleared the gate and then some. Caleb scrambled to catch her.

"Sorry, Emery," Jumbo said. "But you don't weigh nothing compared to these guys."

"Hush up. Want someone to hear us?" Caleb asked, still holding her while Jumbo tossed another guy to the top of the gate.

When the last man was over, Jumbo cleared the top with his own brute strength. Then, and only then, did Caleb set her down.

"Careful, everyone." Shift ripped open the first bag. "We don't know what all's in these things, but—" He gagged. "Keep it low to the ground. Don't fling it and hit one of us. Let's get 'er done."

Operation Revenge dumped trash in the end zones, on the panther mascot in the center of the field, then dragged open bags on every yard line. They worked quickly, efficiently, and quietly. Emery tried to keep upwind of the smell. They'd just emptied the last bag when headlights bounced through the bleachers. Car doors opened and slammed closed. One after another. Then voices.

"I saw Jumbo's dad's truck." The deep, loud voice was angry.

"Scatter!" Caleb whisper-shouted, and every Nickle High boy took off, leaving Emery standing under the goalpost alone. Which way? Which way?!

"Wait, wait—" Panicked, she yanked off her mask to breathe. She tried to run, but her legs wouldn't move.

"Em, this way. Let's go. Hurry." A masked Caleb hooked his arm around her, but she twisted free.

"I'm going to get arrested. I'm sixteen. I can be tried as an adult." She turned left, then right, then left again, running smack-dab into a mountain of a boy. When she looked up, he snarled down at her.

With a scream, she raised her knee like Dad taught her, connected, then ran. Like *Forrest Gump*. Through the woods, not caring that palmetto shrubs scraped her arms and legs. Or the thick roots bit at her toes. Somewhere along the way, she lost her mask, but who cared? Emery Quinn was not getting arrested tonight.

Caleb caught her when she finally arrived at his truck, swooping her up and spinning her around. "That was crazy. Emery, you're awesome. Did y'all see her? She ran into Bobby Brockton, kneed him where the sun don't shine, and outran us all. Even you, Alvarez."

"Emery Quinn." Shift raised her arm. "The queen of Operation Revenge." They gave one shout to the queen, then Shift passed around a plastic grocery sack. "For your gloves. Leave no evidence behind."

One by one, Operation Revenge peeled off their gloves then dashed to their trucks. One of the guys tossed Emery's mask inside the cab.

They drove with their lights off until they cleared West End High and headed east, toward home. Caleb and Shift rolled down the windows and blasted "Summertime Blues." Clubber, Hollingsworth, and Kidwell hung over the truck bed, banging out the beat.

By the time Caleb dropped off the guys, celebrating with each one, midnight neared. Later, he would tell her that every one of the boys fell a little bit in love with her that night.

He slowed for the red light, and she considered moving toward the door since Shift got out, but she liked sitting in the middle. Sitting next to him.

"You didn't get arrested," he said.

"Not yet anyway."

When they arrived at the Sands, Caleb cut the engine but the radio continued to play.

"Do I smell like garbage?" She leaned toward him. "I took a shower before you came."

"No, you smell like flowers."

"Well, I'm going to have to leave my sneakers outside but—" When she looked up, he was inches from her face. "Guess I'm babbling."

"I like your babbling."

"Tonight was awesome, Caleb. Very wrong. But awesome." She laughed. "I never do anything I'm not supposed to do. So what's next? Nothing criminal."

"I've got an idea," he said as the Eagles' "Take It Easy" played softly. He cupped his hand around her neck. "I'm running down the road . . ." He pressed his forehead to hers. "I've got Emery Quinn on my mind."

"Caleb—"

She wasn't ready. But there was no going back. His arm slipped around her waist, and she fit against him. Then he kissed her—so soft and warm—and it was everything she might have imagined. She shivered, eager to kiss him back. Was she doing it right? Was she any good? The kiss ended slowly, like their lips didn't want to leave each other.

"I could do this all night." His words were thick and husky. "But it's midnight."

"Caleb?" she said. "I never kissed anyone before."

"Me neither." He grinned and laced his fingers with hers. "Best first kiss ever."

13

EMERY

Now...

Doyle's Auto Shop sat at the eastern entrance of Sea Blue Beach. Used to be everyone in town trusted Doyle to fix their cars until more modern shops opened in the West End.

Doyle hung up his oil rag and retired to the Bahamas, eventually selling the large cinder block structure with a dusty concrete floor to Simon Caster.

The wall facing the town entrance was the perfect canvas for Lulu Chan's mural.

On the first Friday in February, she projected a full-color drawing onto the freshly painted white wall to check her design. She lined up the paints and brushes. A couple of city workers constructed the scaffolding.

Emery stood with Caleb, studying the images that would depict Sea Blue Beach's history.

Dark edges framed the town and got lighter and brighter as they moved toward the center. From midnight blue to cerulean to cobalt—finally exploding in the middle with a brilliant royal blue haloed in a holy white gold.

Lulu created motion with foaming Gulf waves washing ashore. The sand seemed so soft and real, and reflected the blueish tinge of the Starlight's neon sign.

In the center of the blue and holy gold was Immanuel, God with us, the man on the Starlight's wall, legend of the town's founding.

"He seems so lifelike," Emery said, more to herself than Caleb.

"Immanuel? He always does."

Somehow Lulu captured more than His face and arms, hair and hat; she captured His essence. Immanuel seemed to walk out of the painting into the town. Into Emery.

She took a step back, bumping into Caleb. "You okay?" His arm loosely rested around her waist.

"Y-yeah, just for a moment I felt like—" How did she put it into words? That the painting of a God she'd never seen or heard suddenly felt more real than her own heartbeat.

"This thing is going to be amazing," Caleb said. "Adele's idea may have jump-started an East End revival."

"This will be a tourist attraction for sure." For the *Gazette*, Emery was covering the story herself. And she'd hired a renowned professional photographer, Kadasha Collier, to cover the progress. It cost more than a month's salary, but beautiful pictures in the paper would boost the *Gazette's* reputation.

Lulu set the Starlight and Prince Blue, the old sawmill and Malachi Nickle on either side of Immanuel, and somehow with her art, showed the town growing around them. The Sands Motor Motel, the Beachwalk, and the food trucks, with a hint of a carnival Ferris wheel anchored the left side of the wall. On the right, a large, glowing West End hotel, shopping centers, the Skylight, the Sunset Bowling Parlor, and the Tidewater Inn.

Lulu included milestones like the 1952 Nickle High state football champions and the 2006 West End girls' volleyball champs.

"I don't know how she did it, but I feel like I'm part of the mural," Emery said. "Wanting to preserve the past while embracing the present." She looked at Caleb. "We can do both, right? We don't have to give up history for progress. Or progress for history."

"I think that's what Main Street is about." The light in his eyes seemed to tie up all her feelings about the mural, Caleb, and returning to Sea Blue Beach. As if she was supposed to be here by some divine ordinance. Not because it was her only option.

Caleb Ransom, what are you doing to me? One thing she knew for sure. She didn't come here to fall in love.

"Kids, I think we're ready." Lulu had finished setting up painting stations. She was tall and thin, with a mane of dark hair gathered underneath a scarf. In her mid-fifties, she had an air of *get out of my way, I'm not done yet.* "I've divided the wall into sections . . . and what an amazing space. I feel rather blessed."

About a dozen folks stood around the scaffolding—kids from Nickle and West End High art classes, several local artists, and a couple of commercial painters. Caleb's parents joined the party with Bentley. Bobby, Alfred, and Mac from the town council stood around, watching. Simon was dressed to paint, along with the Main Street crew.

The February day was perfect for the rejuvenation of a town. The sun blazed through a blue sky. The air had the right amount of chill. Paige from the Blue Plate set out breakfast sandwiches, coffee, and tea. Misty from Sweet Conversations donated donuts, scones, and sweet breads.

Someone sounded an air horn, and Caleb introduced Lulu Chan. "She's painted murals all over the world, and we're very lucky to have her. So, listen up. She's going to tell us what to do."

Lulu explained how the day would go, assigning groups to cover the wall with various colors. The kids were assigned sections on the ground, while experienced painters and adults were on the scaffolding.

"Above all, have fun," Lulu said. "Don't worry about being too exact. I can fix what I don't like. Consider this a giant paint-by-color. Next week, I'll start painting the details."

"When do you have to file your story?" Caleb asked.

"I told Rex I'd have it to him by four. He'll break my heart by slicing it to pieces with his red pen, then I'll rewrite. The photographer promised to send pictures by five. We've set aside a two-page spread for this. I even managed a few premier advertisers for it." She nodded to the aloof town council members. "Are they supporting or plotting?"

"Who knows. If possible, both. Elections are coming up next year."

Emery was about to pick a section of wall to paint when Lulu tapped her on the shoulder. "You and Caleb . . . up on the scaffold with me."

"Me?" Caleb stepped back, and Emery reached for his hand.

"It's the best place." Lulu angled toward them, grinning. "No one drops paint on your head."

Emery nudged Caleb as he inspected the structure, giving it a good shake, muttering, "It is high. Very high."

"You don't have to go up there," she whispered. "Paint with Bentley."

He glanced around, then at her. "Don't make it easy for me to wimp out."

After another shake and quick inspection of the nuts and bolts, he climbed up, muttering to himself. Emery followed, not laughing. No. Not laughing at all.

"The prince would be proud, Ransom. And Immanuel. Tell yourself you're doing it for the town."

Lulu positioned Emery in the middle with the gold paint and Caleb next to her with the rich dark blue.

Moment by moment, the wall began to tell the story of Sea Blue Beach in vivid color, inspiring those who came to reminisce, recalling tales from their parents and grandparents. Simon and others talked about Tuesday Knight, who used to run the Starlight. And eighty-five-year-old Dr. Marvin Crane's grandfather smoked cigars with Prince Blue before he went to the Great War.

Emery continued piecing together her story, thoughts on how sharing this moment brought people together, reminding them of their place in the town history. "History feels like it began the day one was born. But it began long before," she said into her phone.

Caleb stoutly and bravely did his part, working alongside her, looking like a natural, talking to Simon most of the time, occasionally glancing over at her with a childlike grin. *"Look at me, no hands."*

Emery had just finished painting the top middle section an amazing, brilliant gold when someone called her name.

"Emery Quinn, hey, someone's here to see you."

"Who? Me?" Everyone she knew was painting the wall. But when she looked down, Ava stood next to Bobby Brockton. "Ava? W-what are you doing . . . Oh no, what's wrong?" She shoved her brush at Caleb, missing his hand and smearing his shirt with gold. "I knew it. I knew coming here would lead to disaster."

Caleb glanced at his painted chest, then Emery. "What's going on? What are you talking about?"

She felt cold and weak as she climbed down the scaffold. "Is it Dad? Tell me. Tell me now. Why didn't someone call?"

"Can we talk somewhere?" Ava tried to pull Emery aside. "Please."

"About what? Ava, is Dad okay?" She could not be in Sea Blue Beach *again*, hearing her only parent was sick and dying.

"Yes, yes, he's fine, I'm sorry. I should've called first, but I—" She looked horrible. Circles under her eyes, hair in a messy topknot—not the sexy kind. Her blouse was wrinkled, and her baggy jeans had a mustard stain. This was not Ava.

"Hey, are *you* all right?" Emery gently touched her arm.

"Yes. No. Well, of course it must look strange for me to be here, and well, no, Emery, to be honest, I'm a mess." When she looked up, there was a looming sadness in her eyes. "Otherwise why would I be here looking like I rolled out of bed, bought an airplane ticket, ate a hot dog with too much mustard and"—she pointed to the mural—"interrupted my sister while she paints . . . what *are* you all doing?"

"Painting a mural of the town history."

Ava moved for a better look. "Is that Lulu Chan? I love her work. Wow, how'd you get her?"

"She's a friend of Caleb's." Emery waved at him, staring down at them, kneeling and gripping onto the side of the scaffold with both hands.

"That's Caleb? Your summer love?" Ava's wide eyes exposed her thoughts. "From, like, sixteen years ago?"

"How do you know about him?"

Ava made a face. "How do you think? Dad."

Emery sighed. "Yes, that's him, and we're just friends."

"He's gorgeous."

"I know, but we're not here to talk about him." Emery removed her gloves. "Have you eaten anything more than a hot dog today? Why don't we grab some lunch?"

"Yes, please."

She texted Caleb she was taking Ava to the Blue Plate. Up Sea Blue Way, they walked in silence. There was no use for small talk at this point, though Ava had reassured her everyone at home was healthy and thriving.

At the diner, the hostess sat them on the deck, near the firepit. They each ordered a hot chocolate and the eggs benedict.

"Mom and Elianna have taken over your old room," she said. "Joanna texted."

"That doesn't mean you can't come home and make it your room again."

"I know." But it sure felt that way. "But you didn't fly down here to talk about my old room."

Ava sat quietly for a moment, gripping her mug. "I don't think I can do it."

"Do what, Aves?"

"Marriage. The house, the bills, adulting."

"Ava, you were adulting at ten."

"I was a smarty-pants. Living securely with my parents. But, Em, this is for real. I don't know if I can marry Jamie. Is he *the* love of my life? Or am I in love with love? One of my friends seems to think I am. And on top of everything else, you're not coming to the shower. Why aren't you coming?"

"Because of my job. I'll send a present. And the rest sounds like a dumb *Cosmo* article or one of those relationship podcasts hosted by no one who's actually ever made a relationship work. Who's this friend? Dump her."

"Kaitlyn Bernard." Ava made a face. "And you're right, I've been reading online articles about marriage, and, Emery, no one seems to think it's a lasting gig. I woke up three days ago, panicked. I thought I'd shake it, work myself out of it, but it sank deeper. We had an appointment to look at a house, and oh my gosh, it was a stunner. Like a dream home for someone who's worked ten or twenty years. Or fifty. It's bigger than our house. You should see the back deck with an outdoor fireplace and dining, all facing three beautiful acres, trees and landscaping everywhere. A pool. I can't do landscaping, Emery. Plants die in my care." Ava's hand trembled as she held up her phone, showing Emery a picture of the home in Gates Mills. "And the price. Did you see the price?"

"Jamie's a successful lawyer, Ava. He made partner. Don't you know how much he makes?"

"I do now." She tucked her phone away. "I wanted a starter home for a young, newly married couple with eclectic furniture, some old, some new, a creaking staircase. This place is for *House Beautiful*. Just move in and live. It's a frozen dinner. Heat and eat."

Emery grinned. "Then tell him. And don't read articles about marriage. Talk to real people. Marriage works. Look at Dad and Joanna. Dad and my mom. Caleb's parents have been married for forty years."

Ava looked pensive. "There's the couple across the way who are always hosting their friends and family. They went jogging in matching outfits a few days ago when the temps hit forty-five."

"Do you love Jamie, Ava?"

"I do." Ava dropped her forehead to the table. "For now. But what if I can't do this? Be his wife forever. What if he goes into politics, and I have to wear pantsuits and one of those coiffed hairstyles?" She bolted upright. "We happened too fast, didn't we? Be honest. We did, right? You never liked how fast Dad and Mom got together."

"That's because my mom had recently died. Ava, are you running away?"

"Yeah, I think I am." She looked Emery in the eye. "I've watched you do it enough times."

CALEB

On Saturday evening, Caleb turned on the patio lights, built a fire in the outdoor fireplace, and roasted bratwurst with Bentley.

His neck and arms were sore from a day of holding a paintbrush over his head, but the side of Doyle's was starting to look like something beautiful. The mural already had the desired effect—stirring excitement in the East End.

Folks came by all day, and at least forty or fifty people wanted to grab a brush, lay on some strokes, become a part of something happening on their side of town. Mac Diamond used the occasion to do a bit of soft campaigning for mayor until the current mayor told him to knock it off. Gutsy man, Simon Caster.

Being divided was killing Sea Blue Beach. The two sides had become like siblings, fighting all the time. They couldn't separate because they were family, but the tension always existed.

In the chair next to him, Bentley hovered over a book while roasting his bratwurst, only occasionally checking his progress. Cassidy was missing this season of his life. He was discovering things, making his own observations and conclusions. He was smart and funny, lovable. If he still believed no one wanted him, he hid it well.

He'd tried to FaceTime his mom three times this week. She never answered or called back.

Yet, he had a blast working on the mural. Came home covered in paint.

"Geez, Bent, did you get any on the wall?"

"Hey, I was on the bottom. Y'all on top splattered us."

When Bentley's brat caught on fire, Caleb suggested it was done. They sat at the table with coleslaw, chips, and iced teas, Caleb lost in thoughts of the day. Bentley, his book.

Emery never returned to the mural. Between her sister's sudden appearance, writing her story, and getting the paper to bed, he didn't expect to see her. He thought to text her, but even something like *"The mural looks great"* felt like an attempt to find out her business.

While on the scaffold, he'd painted part of the golden light where Lulu outlined Immanuel. His sixth-grade civics teacher taught Immanuel as *"Sea Blue Beach's own rich lore. A fairytale-like legend."* Legend or Lord? Which was true?

As a kid, Caleb found comfort in the idea of God appearing to a lost and shipwrecked prince on a dark and deserted beach. Then sending a freed slaves to rescue him. Maybe it meant He was with the townspeople. With Caleb. With Emery. With Bentley.

He'd just taken a bite of bratwurst in a bun of mustard, cheese, and onions when Bentley said, "You should marry her."

Caleb choked. "What?"

Bentley glanced up, his cheek chipmunked with food. "You should marry her. I mean, you are a full-grown man, you said so the other day. And you're making money, right?"

"Marry who?"

"Emery. She's good-looking."

Caleb laughed. "Good-looking? I didn't know boys your age said *good-looking.*"

"I'm well-traveled. You hear things out there on the road." The wise, philosophizing Bentley slurped his tea. "Emery's not what you'd call pretty. Maybe beautiful, but eh, that's overused. Good-looking is like—" He pumped his fist. "You know, good. And looking. Like no one else." He shrugged and sighed, done with his ruminations.

"Nice to know. Eat your coleslaw, Aristotle."

Good-looking? Emery had been pretty as a teen, with light freckles and wavy blond hair, curves in the right places. When Caleb first saw her at Alderman's a month ago, he was a little bowled over. Like, wow. She was beautiful. Or to go with Bentley's definition, good-looking. With a couple of exclamation marks.

"Hey, Bentley." One of the Feinberg boys from three houses down rode his bike through the yard. "Want to hang out? My mom made brownies."

Bentley closed his book while shoving the last of his brat in his mouth. He started to dash away until Caleb called, "No, you may not."

"Why not?"

"First, you ask. Second, did you pick up your clothes and towel after your shower?" Caleb heard echoes of his own dad in that question. And Bentley wasn't even his kid.

"Be right back."

The Feinberg kid munched on chips while Bentley thundered through the house—Caleb could hear him all the way to the patio. When he burst out of the kitchen door, he grabbed Caleb's old bike from the porch and said, "Can I go?"

"Home by eight."

"I picked up my stuff," he said, riding off. "You should unpack your boxes."

"Hey, I'm the adult around here."

But the boy wasn't wrong.

After cleaning up dinner, Caleb left the porch light on for Bentley, then headed into the living room with a glance at his boxes—when did Bentley use them for a fort?

He found a good game of college basketball—Ohio State was up on Purdue by ten in the second half. Was Emery watching? He glanced at the time. Seven thirty. She was probably at the paper. He started a text, then deleted it. He had more confidence with girls at sixteen than at thirty-two. Maybe he should heed Lizzie's advice. Seek help.

But deep down, he already knew the answer. Emery. She'd been in the back of his mind since the summer they met. When she left, she took a piece of his heart. He was soaking in this revelation when someone knocked on his door and the Ohio State point guard knocked down a three-point buzzer beater at the half.

Emery stood on the porch in a pair of jeans and hoodie, her hair in a braid.

"Can we go for a walk or something? I mean, if you're not busy." She buried her hands in her pocket, shivering. "I'm sorry to barge in on you like this, but I didn't know where else to go. I knocked on Delilah's cottage, but she was out."

"You can bother me anytime, Em." He pulled her in for a hug. "What's wrong?"

"My sister is getting cold feet about marriage. She's panicking. We went round and round. . . . Then I had to get to the paper. I wrote my story, worked through Kadasha's photos. She's amazing. Put the paper to bed and went to the cottage to check on Ava. She's sleeping. So I took a shower and came here." She leaned away from him to see inside. "Who's playing?"

"Your Buckeyes." Caleb stepped aside to let her in. "Let me get my jacket. Unless you want to watch the game? It's halftime."

"I can't sit. I need to move, walk, talk. How did the rest of mural painting go?"

"We accomplished everything Lulu wanted. People came by all day to check it out. A lot wanted to help. There's buzz about improvements for the East End. And your boy here stayed on the scaffold the whole time."

She laughed softly through her tired expression. "I'm impressed."

"Come on, let's go out the back."

"Where's Bentley?" Emery said, exiting the kitchen onto the porch.

"With a neighborhood kid. He's finally making friends."

They walked up Pelican Way and through the cold night warmly lit with the glow of houses and streetlamps.

He stopped by the Feinbergs to tell Bentley where he was going. "But at eight, head to your grandparents. Got it?"

"Got it." He looked up at Emery. "Going walking? That's old-fashioned. You kids have fun."

"What was that about?" Emery said as they started off again.

"Bentley being eleven. By the way, he thinks you're good-looking. Not pretty or beautiful, but good-looking."

"Oh, how nice of him to notice. Tell him thanks. I think. Is good-looking cool to an eleven-year-old?"

"Extremely cool." He should add his thoughts, but . . .

They went up the slight hill of Pelican Way to Port Fressa Avenue. "Have you ever been here? This is the Original Homestead," Caleb said. "These houses are the ones Mac and his crew want to bulldoze."

"No, I haven't, but I should have. These are adorably shabby." Emery started up one of the broken, uneven walkways to a Florida Cracker porch. "Yet there's something romantic about them."

"It's hard to imagine families living in them, kids running up and down the street. But other than Sea Blue Way, this was the heart of our town." He pointed to the house on the corner. "I've seen black-and-whites of that one. Proverbial picket fence, family with a dog gathered on the porch."

"Now it looks sad. Even haunted. Do you really think they're worth restoring?"

"I think everything is worth restoring." Caleb glanced back at her, then continued down the lane, pausing by a couple of the houses, making mental notes. He'd have to walk the street in the light of day, choose one to refurbish first, then see what Simon could do for backing and money. "Mac will have to buy the houses on either side of this neighborhood to build his golf course. I'm not sure he can do it, but I bet he's playing a long game."

"Why hasn't anyone done anything with them before now? How long have they been abandoned?"

"Lots of reasons. Red tape. Owners died, left it to family who live somewhere else. Unpaid taxes, foreclosure, if there's a loan. The city has to prove the property is abandoned, which requires a lot of due diligence. Some of the houses may have the taxes up to date, but no one pays for upkeep. Frankly, we've been so busy building up the West End, I don't think anyone noticed the Org. Homestead."

"Well, they care now, don't they?" Emery said as they'd stopped in front of the last house on the street. Beyond was a dark wood. "She told me I run away."

"Who told you—ah, Ava said you run away?"

"Yeah, after she confessed her panic over marrying Jamie, which sounds to me like nothing but freezing cold feet and varying expectations. I asked if she was running away, and she said she'd seen me do it enough times."

Caleb started up the walkway to the porch. The sidewalk, the front walks, all of it would have to be redone to restore the Org. Homestead. "Is she right? Do you run away?"

"This morning I would have said no, but now I don't know. Maybe."

"I'm going to need evidence, Quinn. How'd you run away? If it wasn't from a fiancé, Ava may not have a case." He liked that she laughed.

"She may have reset the bar. No fiancé for me."

"Then how'd you run away?"

"According to her? Sports, friends, college, my career. Living a block from the *Free Voice* instead of near them. Missing family events. When I moved home out of necessity, I didn't really join in, according to her. She's probably right. But the *pièce de résistance* was accepting a job nine hundred miles away the night she got engaged."

"Isn't that life? You were seventeen, right? When your dad married her mom. A senior in high school. I was so busy my senior year I was hardly ever home. Then I went to a college twelve hundred miles away before moving to the West Coast."

"She admitted her reasoning wasn't sound before clarifying I was more emotionally absent than present. She claims I never put my heart into the family. I *emotionally* ran away, she said."

"What do you say?" Caleb sat on the bottom step of the dilapidated porch and patted the space next to him.

"I never intended to stay on the outside, Caleb. But I didn't want another mom. I didn't want sisters. I didn't want to share my dad." Emery picked up a broken twig next to the step and started peeling away the dried bark. "Yet I wanted Dad happy. I understood he couldn't build his life around me. Still, after Mom passed, I thought he'd drink craft beer with his fellow professors and have a weekly poker night, visiting me when I was living in Costa Rica for a year. Not create another family."

"Did you live in Costa Rica?"

"It's a metaphor, Ransom."

"As for the family, you are part of it. Like it or not."

"I know, I know, but I never felt like I was. Not deep down. And Ava felt it too."

"I did a bit of pushing away with Cassidy. I wished she'd just go away and never come back. Stop making things hard and uncomfortable. I feel bad about that now. But she scared me. When love hurts, we disconnect. Find other things to occupy our hearts."

"Is that why you didn't want to commit to your ex? Is that why she told you to seek help?"

"Pretty astute observation, Quinn." He could chuckle about it now, but that night . . . "We never officially verbalized it, but yeah, she probably picked up on a few things."

"From where I sit, you're not afraid to love. Maybe she just wasn't right for you."

"Maybe." Most definitely. "Now I get scared for Bentley. That

Cassidy is going to hurt him. She chose a man who doesn't want kids, Emery. She dropped him at his uncle's for the rest of the school year. What does that say to him? He tried to FaceTime her again this week. She never answered."

"He's got you, Caleb, one of the good guys. You can help him understand her."

"But he'll always carry that wound," he said more to himself than Emery. "Hey, do you ever think about our summer?"

"Lately, quite a bit. No offense, but I tried to forget everything about the year my mother died, except for her."

"I wanted to forget Cassidy and remember you."

"Was she *really* so bad?"

"Probably not, but I was angry at her for so long. Did I tell you she dropped out of high school? Her senior year. Our parents were devastated."

"You did. Caleb, she's not the first kid to rebel and choose a different path. If we ever have kids, we'd have to—" She angled back, laughing. "Hold up, I didn't mean 'we' as in you and me. Just the general 'we.' People who might one day have kids. *And* moving on . . ."

She was pretty when she was flustered—so very pretty. Bentley hadn't seen this side of her—the slightly lost and unsure girl, forgetting what she possessed. Caleb liked how their sixteen years apart melted the moment they found each other again. At least it seemed that way to him.

"So, your sister," he said. "What are you going to tell her?"

"I don't know. Maybe 'I'm sorry' since she believes I was emotionally absent. Then encourage her to have an honest conversation with Jamie about how she's feeling and what she wants. I've known him a long time, and he's definitely in love with my sister. He'd give her the moon if possible." Emery looked over at him. "That's the right answer, isn't it?"

"Come on, Quinn. You don't need me to tell you what's already in your heart. You just said it out loud."

She leaned against him. "Thank you," she said softly. After another minute or two, she stood. "I'm cold and should probably get my emotionally unavailable self back to my sister."

Down the street toward Caleb's, she paused and turned back to the Org. Homestead. "I wish I had the money to save each one."

"Me too. But saving it needs to mean something to the town. If it doesn't, we'll end up back here in another, what, fifty years? Maybe that's why we're so divided. Do we invest in our past history or our future history? Most people just want to have a nice place to live and a steady job and hope for their kids. A chance to dream a little."

"Isn't that what this neighborhood stands for, Caleb? If you can restore one of the houses, I think people will see the Org. Neighborhood as a really beautiful part of the city. I'd live here."

"I just don't know if the East End has enough clout to sway the West. They have more control than we like to admit."

"Then we need to find a way to bring everyone together."

"All ideas are welcome." He liked that she said "we," as if Sea Blue Beach was already her home. Even more, he liked walking with her through the quiet night. "I'm glad you came over."

"I interrupted your basketball watching."

"Let's see . . . watching sweaty guys toss around a ball or have a deep conversation with the lovely, sweet, perfumed Emery Quinn? Not a hard choice."

At the end of Port Fressa Avenue, they cut across Pelican Way to pick up Bentley at his parents. Mom fussed over Emery, welcoming her back to Sea Blue Beach. Dad asked about her dad, which made them all laugh.

When they left, Bentley ran ahead for his nightly bowl of cereal, though Caleb was pretty sure he'd just finished one at his folks'.

"Can I give you a lift to the Sands?" he said in the light of his kitchen windows.

"Nah, you have Bentley," she said with a shiver. "If I keep moving, the cold isn't so bad." She tugged on Caleb's hoodie sleeve. "Thanks again. For the tour and the talk, Ransom."

"Anytime, Quinn. On your walk home, remember one thing: Ava may claim you were emotionally unavailable, but you were the one she ran to when she needed help."

14

EMERY

Ava sat outside Cottage 7 under a blanket in an Adirondack next to Delilah. A fire roared in the stone firepit, and soft music drifted from hidden speakers. Guests from one of the other cottages sat on the other side, talking quietly.

"Hey, you're back." Ava rose from the chair. "Delilah was telling me she used to be a big-time folk singer. Em, she even toured with the Beach Boys. Isn't that wild?"

"You're talking about your past?" Emery leaned around her sister, her eyes wide.

"Your sister is very clever. Wrangled a bit out of me. But all of that was a long, long time ago." Delilah pushed up from her chair. "Em, sit here. Enjoy the fire." Delilah tucked her blanket around Emery, then brought out a glass of wine. "Are you covering the Beach Boys concert on the twenty-first?"

"I couldn't get tickets or press passes. The amphitheater never returned my calls." Emery glanced up at the beautiful folk singer. "The *Gazette* has lost so much clout. What we need is a couple of big stories. Prove our worth. I don't suppose you could get me tickets?"

"Honey, those days are long over for me. Most of the boys I toured with are gone. Mike Love might not even remember me," Delilah said, her attention stuck on something over Emery's head. A picture from the past, perhaps. "Well, good night. Ava, it was lovely to meet you. Emery, you never told me you had a sister."

And . . . thank you for that, Delilah. Emery sipped her wine with a side glance at Ava. "It wasn't intentional. Just never came up."

Ava curled up in the chair, facing Emery. "I think it's hard for me because I was so happy to have a big sister. You'd think I would resent it being the oldest myself, but I thought I'd have someone to confide in, talk girl talk with, tell people, 'My big sister is taking us shopping this weekend.' So some of this is on me. I'm disappointed in you because of my own imagination."

"Ava, I'm sorry I was none of those things. I am. Maybe they were your imagination, but they're also very real things sisters do."

"Probably, but none of my friends with sisters had that kind of relationship. I watched too much TV. Read too many books."

"First off, you can never read too many books. Second, how about if I'm a big sister right now? The kind I know I can be." Ava sat forward, listening, waiting. "Maybe you've done the same thing with Jamie. You've built up an idea of marriage in your head, then when you have to deal with real life—deal with a real man with real ideas of his own—you think it's not right. You think he's going to be like me. Emotionally unavailable. But he's not. He loves you, Ava. Trust me, I've known him a long time, and he's never been with anyone like he is with you. You're the one for him. He's the one for you."

"I called him tonight," she said softly. "He was scared I'd call off the wedding. Then he was upset I didn't tell him how I felt about our first house. He thought the one he wanted proved he could provide for our family. He wanted to give me something grand and nice, something beautiful. But he understands my point of view, wanting to start out small and messy, grow into each other, work out our likes and dislikes."

"How do you feel about getting married in May?"

Her smile was so like Joanna's. Wide and winning with a dash of tenderness. "Excited. I do love him, Emery. Very much. I feel stupid for panicking and running away. Jamie's going to ask our realtor to look for something smaller and less grand."

"Good." Emery raised her glass in toast. "I went for a walk with Caleb tonight, and he pointed out that despite our issues and how *emotionally unavailable* I am—"

"You're never going to let me live that down, are you?"

"—you *did* come to me for help. And no, I'm not."

"To be honest, I thought your lack of emotional interest in me would point me in the right direction."

"Then you're welcome." Emery took a sip of the wine, which was smooth and slightly sweet. "Little sister."

Ava grinned and leaned toward Emery. "So, do tell. What's up with Caleb? Delilah told me a little more about your summer of love. Dad left out the juicy details."

"Juicy details? Then Delilah is making stuff up." Emery looked toward Cottage 1 with its framed windows watching over the courtyard. Two hundred yards away, the Gulf hummed a night song against the shore. The moon, the great pearl in the sky, hovered over them. "He's just a friend."

"What happened the summer you were here with Dad and your mom?"

"Our third night here, I was sitting where you are when he walked into the courtyard and commented on my sunburn." Emery smiled at the memory. "I saw him a few days later, picking up trash on the beach with his football team, and he followed me into the Blue Plate Diner. After that, we started hanging out as much as we could. I thought Mom, Dad, and I had come down to build memories as a family, but Mom was sick, which I didn't know, so she was happy to let me run around town with a nice kid, making happy memories, knowing she'd be gone in a few months."

"Why didn't you ever tell us about him? Then again, you never told us much of anything." Despite her last comment, a tenderness remained in her tone.

"You were ten when I met you. What'd you want me to say? 'Hi, I'm Emery. I met a boy in Florida last summer. He's really cute.'"

"I'm not ten now."

"It's not a big deal."

"Em, is anything a big deal to you?" Ava finished her final swirl of wine. "Except your mom's pearls." Emery looked over sharply, and she immediately apologized. "I'm sorry. That was out of line."

"Okay, little sister, since we're confessing things, what is with you and Mom's pearls? You didn't even know her."

Ava set her glass on the pavers and leaned toward Emery. "Mom asked me the same thing. And when I found myself at the airport with a small carry-on and an eight-hundred-dollar airline ticket, I asked myself, 'Why are you going to see Emery? She hates you.'"

"Stop, Ava, I do not hate you."

"You certainly don't like me, or Elianna, very much—at least you didn't. Though we all love Blakely. We can't help it. Anyway, at the airport, it hit me. I want to know why you don't like me. Why you don't want to be my sister. Why you don't like being a part of our family. *Your* family. I've never understood it. Flying here meant you'd have to face me, deal with me, counsel me in your cool, emotionally unavailable way. I was going to force you into being my big sister." She laughed softly at her confession. "It's the same feeling I get when I ask about the pearls. They're like a visual of our relationship. 'The pearls are unavailable to you, Ava Quinn.' Yet if you *actually* loaned them to me, it would mean you liked me. Approved of me. It would mean we are sisters."

Emery listened with her glass cupped against her chest, waiting for Ava's honesty to sink in before answering.

"First of all, I do like you and Elianna. And you're right about Blake. We can't help but love her." She glanced at Ava. "I just never looked at the situation from your point of view. I was still grieving Mom when Dad and Joanna married. Then, in some ways, I was grieving the loss of Dad, our relationship, the family we had for sixteen years. The months after Mom died, we got really close. Even after he connected with your mom, Dad and I were always there for each other. Then he married, adopted two little girls, and for first time ever, Ava—*ever*—I had to share him. And I didn't want to share."

"So we're both guilty of not seeing each other's side. For Ellie and me, Mom would tell us every day about how lucky we were to get a new dad *and* a sister. How we'd all love one another, and yes, disagree, but in the end, we'd have each other's backs. Elianna and I were young when our dad died. We have so few memories of him. We loved Doug Quinn the moment we met him. And you know why? Because of you, Emery. He had one great daughter and believed he could have two more." She looked toward the sound of the ocean. "But Mom didn't prepare us for a sister who didn't want to be a sister."

"Well," Emery said, swirling her wine, "thank goodness we're sorting this out now. Do you realize we've spent more time talking about me and you than you and Jamie?"

Ava laughed softly. "This convo has been a long time coming," she said. "Also, I recognize that Elianna and I were pretty annoying. I'm not sure I'd have appreciated us either in those early days."

"You weren't *that* annoying. But at the time, I felt left out. Like Dad replaced Mom with Joanna, and me with you two."

"Before Dad, Mom was sad all the time," Ava said. "I used to hear her crying in her room. Then one morning, she came out for breakfast, smiling, and made us French toast, made us laugh. She'd connected with your dad the night before. Our whole lives changed from dark to light."

"He is pretty great, isn't he?"

"We have more in common than you think, Em. We both lost a parent. We love Dad. We're professional businesswomen. We both run when we're panicked."

"Do you really think I run when I'm panicked? I went to college. I worked summers in Columbus. I came here for a job. How's that panicked running?" Emery reached for the stick to stir the fire, but the last log was well on its way to embers. Without the heat, the courtyard grew cold.

"You were stuck. Nothing was happening for you."

"I was not stuck."

"Em, come on. The job you loved abruptly ended. You could no longer afford your beautiful apartment."

"My lease ended."

"You were writing freelance, which you hated. The only guy I remember you going out with made you pay for your meal. More than anything, you had to move into your parents' house, into the bedroom you lived in for a hot second."

"Wow, this is the beginning of a Shakespearean tragedy." Emery laughed. "I was stuck, wasn't I? Still, I deny that I ran away. I *moved* away. To college. To a new town."

"Okay, okay, maybe I'm the one who runs. I've learned my lesson. Though when I woke up wanting to get away, you were the person I wanted to see."

"I'm glad. And I mean it. So, what are your plans now?"

"My ticket is for Monday. There's a hotel about five miles from here that has some rooms. I can take an Uber—"

"You're staying with me." With the fire dying, Emery motioned for them to head inside. "Little sister."

"You do like me, don't you? I knew it."

"Okay, okay, don't push it." Emery wrapped her arm around Ava as they walked to the cottage. After all, she *was* a big sister.

While she showered, Ava made Joanna's Sophisticated Sips hot chocolate. They drank their mugs on the settee under the window.

"Mom was sitting here when she told me she was dying," Emery said softly. "She gave me the pearls that night."

"What was she like? Your mom?"

"Like yours, to be honest. Loving, but didn't take a lot of guff. Being a bank VP, she could be very direct and business-like. She was the prettiest mom at my school, at least to me. Adored the snow. She used to brush my hair all the time, which I loved." She stretched her foot to Ava's leg. "I'm glad you're here."

"Me too." Ava set down her hot chocolate, and said she'd be right back. Ten seconds later, she returned with a boar bristle brush. "May I?"

Emery's eyes filled. "Yes" was all she could manage.

On the settee where Mom used to sit, Emery's sister brushed her hair until she drifted to the space between awake and asleep, to the place in her memories where Mom still lived.

EMERY

Then . . .

A float of orange and red clouds reflected off the water as Caleb walked Emery from the beach volleyball game toward the motel.

His arm brushed hers when the sand gave way under his step. "Sorry," he said with a light laugh. Then she slipped and fell against him. "Sorry," she whispered.

That's when his hand clasped hers. It was warm and strong and magically filled her with the colors in the clouds.

"You're still going home in two weeks?" he said without looking at her.

"I asked Dad if we could stay another week." Dad's answer was noncommittal, almost distracted, but he seemed more anxious to get home than she liked. Apparently he had an additional class this fall, and Mom had things to "tie up" at the bank, whatever that meant. Still, she was hopeful for an extended stay.

Emery was not ready to leave Sea Blue Beach. Funny to say since she didn't want to come in the first place. Since the trashing of the West End High football field, she'd spent every day with Caleb. If he was working at the Starlight, she'd skate the late session, then hang out with him afterward.

Today, while playing volleyball, Jumbo said West End High was pretty ticked about the trashing and demanding those responsible to come forward.

"But we're not talking, right?" Jumbo leaned into the huddle of Caleb, Emery, Alvarez, Kidwell, Crammer, Shift, and Hollingsworth, and zipped his lips. They all followed. "Loose lips sink ships."

Emery loved being a part of their crowd. She loved sharing a secret with Caleb.

"I never thought I'd say this 'cause school means football, but I don't want this summer to end." He slowed as they neared the motel and pulled Emery into the shadows of the palms along the Beachwalk. "This is the best summer. Because of you."

"Even though I made you ride the Ferris wheel?"

"I made you trash our rival's football field." His laugh resonated in his chest.

"And I didn't get arrested."

"Nope. I trust those guys with my life. Hey, my mom asked if you'd come to dinner one night. Your folks too."

"You mean Mr. Ransom and Mr. Quinn will meet face-to-face? Not sure the world is ready for it."

"I'm not worried about our dads. It's my nutcase sister that scares me." Still holding her hand, Caleb's tanned arm rested against hers, which was finally a lovely burnished brown.

"Still trouble in River City?"

"That starts with *C* and rhymes with pass? Yeah. She was blaring her music the other night, and when Mom asked her to turn it down, she cranked it louder. I grabbed my keys and left."

She squeezed his hand. "Wish I had some advice for you, but being an only—"

"Talking to you is enough." He drew her into a hug, and she inhaled his scent—suntan lotion, salt water, and sand. He embodied everything she imagined about true love—trust, affection, friendship.

"Better get you home," he said, releasing her too soon. "I don't want to get in trouble with the Boyfriendinator."

But she didn't want this moment to end. She wanted to stay with him. Listen to his heartbeat.

"I love you, Caleb." The words came with a soft sigh.

"What?" He snapped back, taking his warmth and affection with him.

"Nothing." She spun around and made tracks for the Sands. What did she just say? Why, why, why? So dumb. He'd asked, "What?" but he heard. She knew by the way he released her. By the look on his face. Way to ruin everything, Emery Quinn.

"Emery, wait." Caleb ran in front of her to cut off her escape. "I love you too. Can't believe it, but I do."

"Stop, stop." She pressed her hands over her flushed cheeks. "It's okay, you don't have to say you love me. I don't know how those words came out of my mouth without my permission, but you don't have to say it back. Just forget—"

He was kissing her, covering her moving lips with his. There was no going back now. His arm cinched around her waist as she raised her arms to his shoulders. His mouth was hot and salty, the kiss more perfect than the one in the truck. Because love came first.

The moment ended slowly, then he touched his forehead to hers and gazed into her eyes. "I swore I wasn't going to fall in love until I was twenty-five. You're making a liar out of me." He kissed her again. "You got some sort of power, Emery Quinn."

His final kiss goodnight was sweet, drawing a second "I love you" from her. Then he whispered the same in her ear, igniting chills down her sunkissed arms and legs. She watched him go, her fingers resting on her tingling lips.

When she turned for the courtyard, Mom sat by the fire, wrapped in a blanket. She called Emery to sit with her.

"Why the blanket?" Emery sat on the ground beside her. "It's hot and humid out here."

"I had a bit of a chill. Delilah wonders if it might be a summer cold. I'll be fine." Her soft palm stroked Emery's wild hair. "Why don't you get your brush?"

Mom brushing her hair was Emery's favorite pastime. In the cottage, Dad was hovered over his computer with a serious expression.

"Hey," she said, "whatever happened to our unplugged summer? No work. No TV or videos." She ruffled his curly hair. "No computer."

"Just researching." He looked up, bleary-eyed. "Did you see your mother? How was she?"

"Good, I guess." Emery ducked into her bathroom. "She wants to brush my hair."

Dad reached for her as she headed back out. "Did Caleb behave himself?"

"Always. Oh yeah, his parents invited us to dinner at their house." Emery glanced down, blushing, wondering if Dad could see through her. That she was in love. "Can we stay longer? Please?"

"We'll see." Okay, that was progress. Closer to a yes than a no.

Back at the firepit, Emery rested against Mom's blanketed legs. With each pass of the brush, she drifted away with the sound of the night.

"You're so tan," Mom said. "I thought your Irish blood would never allow it."

"How do you know if you're in love, Mom?"

"Goodness, that's a big question in this small moment."

Emery twisted around to see her face. "I'm serious."

"Are we talking about Caleb Ransom?" Mom said.

"Are there any other boys I hang around with?"

"Well, you're young, but not so young to know love means you don't count the cost. You don't hold grudges or offenses. You forgive. You sacrifice. You can imagine a life with them. Be with someone you can live *with*, not live without." Mom ran the brush through her hair from the nape of her neck and then over the crown of her head. "You might be a bit young to decide on a life partner, but if he makes your heart go pitter-patter, and if you want good for him over yourself, you might be in love."

"He kissed me, and I thought I'd fly away and melt all at once."

"Goodness, that was some kiss," Mom said. "The first boy who kissed me, Randy Needleman . . . hmm, it was like kissing a toad." Mom's pretty laugh fluttered in the wind, along with a few embers from the smoldering fire. "I've not thought of him in eons. Anyway, I told him if he ever kissed me again, I'd knock him down."

"Way to go, Mom." Emery raised her hand for a backward high five. "How old were you?"

"About your age. He'd asked me to dance at a friend's party." There was a moment of silence, and Emery began to drift away when Mom said, "Emery, about being in love . . . be careful, hear me? I want to take home the same girl I brought down here."

"What?" Emery popped awake. "Why wouldn't you?"

"Meaning I don't want my girl *losing* anything on the beach or in the back of a Chevy S-10." She made a face—brow arched, eyes wide.

"Oh." Emery shrank down. Mom gave her part of the "the talk" when she was ten, then again when she was thirteen. But since Emery never had a boyfriend, the nitty-gritty details seemed more like theory than reality. A one-day-in-the-future-moment.

With Caleb's kisses, the future had arrived. While their declarations of love seemed innocent enough, she wondered if he'd expect more than a kiss before she went home. Naw, not Caleb. He wouldn't . . . would he?

"You know I want you to wait. You're too young for sex, Em. There's more to it than physical affection."

"I know," she muttered, shrinking down further so Mom could only brush the top of her head.

"But if you feel things are getting out of hand, talk to me. Do you hear? I'll have your father kill the boy."

"Mom!"

She laughed. "Okay, just kidnapped until we leave." She reached down to raise Emery's chin. "Listen to me, you have command of yourself. No one can make you do anything you don't want. I joke about Caleb, but we shouldn't have to kidnap him because we know and trust you. Understand?"

"I understand."

Mom's honesty blew away some of Emery's romantic clouds. Nothing was ever as it seemed, was it? She continued to brush her hair, humming softly, as the fire burned lower and lower. Delilah popped out of Cottage 1 to see if they needed more wood. But Mom said they were going in soon.

"What do you and Delilah talk about all the time, Mom?" Emery said.

"Life. Death. Jesus."

"Jesus?" Emery said. "Why? We have love. We have each other. We don't need religion."

"Delilah's not talking about religion." Mom leaned on Emery as she tried to stand but lost her balance and fell back into the chair. "Goodness, I'm a bit weak tonight."

"Mom, what's going on?" Emery took the brush, then helped her to her feet. "Do you really just have a cold, or is there something else? You sleep a lot. You've lost weight. I don't believe you and Dad visited old friends when you disappeared."

Mom started for the cottage ahead of Emery. "How about we go in and read? What happened in the chapter we finished, Miss I've-Just-Been-Kissed?"

"Mom, don't tell Dad about the kiss, okay? Just you and me." Emery folded Mom's blanket and hurried after her.

"It's our secret." But Emery suspected she'd tell him the moment they were in bed and the lights were out.

"Mom, can I ask you one more thing?"

"Anything."

"You said kissing Randy Needleman was like kissing a toad?" Emery cocked her head to one side, resting her hand on the cottage latch. "When did you ever kiss a real toad?"

The Sunday
GAZETTE

February 9
Happenings Around Town

West End
The Beach Boys!
Sunday Night
February 16
7 p.m.
Blue Shell Amphitheater
Tickets available online.

East End
Starlight Roller-Skating Rink
18 sessions a week.
Tickets at the door.

Fish Hook Bonfire
Open Mic Night
Monday, February 24
First come, first serve.

Mural Painting
By Lulu Chan
Call city hall for more
information.

15

CALEB

Now . . .

The mural had the desired effect. At the next town council meeting, more citizens than usual filled city hall, chatting about "their
town," wondering what else could be done to energize the East
End.

Just before Simon brought the meeting to order, Emery took
the chair next to Caleb. He'd not seen much of her since their
Org. Homestead stroll, though they were able to grab a dinner
last night, where she'd updated him on Ava—she and Jamie had
a good long talk and found a smaller home in Gate Mills that
suited them both.

"Though they're planning a few updates."

"While planning a wedding?" Caleb said.

*"You haven't met Ava. She'll have it all researched, organized, and
contractors hired by the end of the week."*

"Maybe I'll meet her one day." That sounded more hopeful than
he'd intended. But he was curious about Emery's family. Wouldn't
mind seeing the Boyfriendinator again either.

Up front, Simon reviewed old business, beginning with the

success of the mural. Then Mac Diamond interrupted the proceedings when he rose to his full six-foot-five.

"Before you go on and on about piddly stuff like murals and banners and mending bricks on Old Sea Blue Way"—his tone was bold yet even, like one of his commercials advertisings his golf courses—"those of us council members representing the West End want to declare an intent to separate from the East End and become our own municipality."

At his podium, Simon visibly froze. The air seemed to stop moving. Next to Caleb, Emery tapped furiously on her phone. Mac gazed steadily around the room, from Simon to the council members, to Caleb and Emery, and to the citizens surrounding them.

"As I hear no objection, please let the record show—"

"I object." Simon was a volcano about to erupt. More objections fired around the room from the East End council members, Caleb, and the citizens in attendance.

"Mac Diamond," Adrianna Holmes said with dubious surprise, "you actually want to tear the town apart?"

"Wake up, Adrianna, the town is torn apart. We're just tugging on the last thread."

"Point of order," Simon said, his voice reflecting his fiery demeanor. "Nothing is decided just because Mac declares it. We have to have a discussion to even start the research of such a move."

"This makes no sense," Emery whispered to Caleb. "A month ago, they suggested bulldozing the Org. Homestead. Now they want to leave the town and go on their merry way?" She raised her hand. "Mr. Diamond, Emery Quinn, the *Gazette*." He looked like he was trying to suppress a laugh. "Don't you need the East End for your development plans? Wasn't your plan last month to bulldoze the Original Homestead neighborhood?"

"Ms. Quinn, you're new here—"

"Answer the question, Mr. Diamond. How do you plan to keep developing your hotels and golf courses without the East End?"

Alfred Gallagher launched to his feet. "There's plenty of land on the other side of—"

"What Al means," Mac said, "is we have other opportunities. We just thought the East End would like to cash in with us."

"What if everything isn't about money, Mr. Diamond?" Emery was on fire tonight. "What if it's about community, history, and planning for future generations to know who they are and where they came from? What if restoration is more valuable than dollars?"

"I can see you're not a businesswoman."

"Come on, Mac, save your insults," Simon said.

"But I'll agree not everything is about money. But there's not a man or woman in this room who doesn't want a little bit more money." A soft amen came from the gallery. "We're just trying to leverage our options."

"By destroying Sea Blue Beach?" Simon came from around the podium to confront Mac face-to-face. "What game are you playing?"

With that, the whole room was off to the races. People shouting and accusing, pointing fingers and blaming.

Finally, Simon returned to the podium, grabbed his gavel, and hammered the room to order. One of the sheriff's deputies stepped up beside him, which really calmed things down.

"Now look, everyone." By *everyone*, Simon meant Mac because that's where he focused. "There's a lot that goes into breaking off and incorporating into a new municipality. There's feasibility studies, budget, and infrastructure to consider. Last, but not least, you need approval from the Florida legislature."

"Certainly, certainly, all those things," Mac said in a sweepingit-under-the-rug tone. "I've already spoken to Congresswoman Abbott. She is more than willing to help us investigate this process."

Caleb leaned to Emery. "Camille Abbott is an avid golfer. You can put the rest together."

She made notes in her phone while letting the recording app play.

"Listen, folks, we don't mean to cause dissention." Mac again. "We love Sea Blue Beach, but if y'all are determined to maintain the old ways and the old town . . . Listen, I just got word on an environmental study that we can build—"

"What environmental study?" Simon again, with a lead tone and steely glare.

"My company always does a study on potential property. I can't pursue an investment only to find there are issues." Mac walked toward the gallery. "People, we could have a luxury nine-hole golf course and sweet little clubhouse with a pool up and running by Christmas. I can give you numbers on then increased revenue to the East End." A couple of business owners nodded, buying what he was selling. "The clubhouse, by the way, would be open to the public for a very small fee. Small enough for our lower-income folks." He pointed at Caleb. "Ransom, we saw your sustainable design ideas on social media. That's the kind of stuff we're envisioning. You could be our architect."

"Mac Diamond." Simon slapped down the gavel. "Sit down. I'll see you in my office first thing in the morning."

Mac made a motion toward the mayor. "See, this is what I'm talking about, folks. If you can't join 'em, you have to leave 'em."

Simon never gained control of the meeting after that comment. Some citizens protested. Others asked questions. The council members argued. Caleb slipped out with Emery.

"That was *Gazette* gold," she said, tapping more thoughts on her phone.

"You think? It's coal for the town, Em."

"You're right, but do you think Mac, Alfred, and Bobby can actually pull off the West End becoming their own municipality??" She made another note in her phone. "That's a huge ordeal." She tapped out a message to someone. "Man, I can't even shout, 'Stop the presses!' We're already put to bed. Note to self: Change the freaking Wednesday deadline. And start an online edition." She stopped for a breath. "Sorry, I don't mean to be excited about the town's troubles. I'm just excited to get into some hard news. I texted Jane to see what's she's heard from the West End."

They walked down Salty Sea Street, away from the city hall lights, toward Sea Blue Way and the Starlight. Caleb churned with the sound of Mac's voice, declaring his sustainable designs were right for this new course and clubhouse. No one had ever said that to him. Except Pierce, but Caleb never thought he was a hundred percent sure of the idea.

A contract to build a Diamond Dog golf course clubhouse would rocket-launch his career. Way more than refurbishing an old pharmacy-slash-soda fountain or a 1902 Florida Cracker home. Mac's golf courses were legendary in the south.

When he looked around, Emery wasn't with him. She stood a few paces back, looking all agog.

"What? Does Jane have more to the story?" he asked.

"No, you. Your face. Oh my gosh, you're thinking about Mac Diamond gushing over your designs."

"No—"

"You are. Caleb. He just Mr. Pottered you in front of everyone. You're his George Bailey." She puffed out her chest and strutted around. "'How's twenty-thousand dollars a year sound? You could have a nice house, go to Europe once a year.'" She grabbed his shoulders for a good shake. "Snap out of it. Tell him he's a scurvy little spider."

"You tell him. You're writing the article." He walked off, toward the skating rink, his skin hot with the truth. He got Mr. Pottered. But in the end, he'd have woken up, realized he was being played. Probably. Hopefully. Oh man . . .

"I can think it, but I can't write it. Well, unless you say it. Can I quote you? 'Mac Diamond is a scurvy little spider, said Caleb Ransom, owner of Ransom Architects.' Otherwise, I'm an objective observer. Just the facts, ma'am."

"No, you can't quote me." He grabbed her hand. "Come on. Let's roller-skate."

"Skate? Don't you have to get home to Bentley?"

"Mom's with him and his bowls of cereal. I need to move."

Inside the wide lobby with images of past skaters on the wall, Caleb bought two tickets and passed one to Emery as she studied the rink's memorial wall.

"Who are all of these people? This wasn't here in '09."

"Stars of the Starlight. In one of the rooms at the museum, they have even more." Caleb pointed to a black-and-white of a lovely older woman. "That's Tuesday Knight. She ran the place for years. In my parents' day, not mine."

"Right. Her grandson is Hollywood A-lister Matt Knight who's married to Harlow Hayes."

"I met her once," Caleb said. "Long time ago. I was a kid and remember thinking she was really nice." He pointed to a photo of Simon. "He's standing with Spike, who ran the rink after Tuesday. Then he retired and handed it over to Simon, who managed the expansion of the Hayes Cookie franchise across north Florida."

"Do you think Matt Knight and Harlow Hayes might be helpful in this town strife?"

"Simon's the one to ask. But I saw a headline on the cover of *People* saying they were filming a movie in Europe."

Caleb greeted a few folks he knew in high school who now had children, a couple even in Bentley's class. He selected a pair of brown rentals with Emery and laced them on at the benches.

"Don't laugh if I fall. I've not done this in eons," she said.

"Don't get mad if I trip over you when you fall. I've not done this in a long time either." Yet he was ready to go, ready to *move*, cleanse his soul of even considering Mac's idea.

Kool and the Gang's "Good Times" came on as they hit the floor. The shufflers whizzed past. Caleb was tempted to join them, but he wasn't ready to make a complete fool of himself in front of Emery just yet. The Ferris wheel incident was enough for now.

When the two of them had gone around for few songs, some fast, some slow, Emery said, "Caleb, what did you mean Tuesday handed the rink over to Spike and Spike to Simon? Sounds more like management than ownership."

"You should look up the story in the *Gazette* archives. I can't remember all the details, but when they tried to knock down the Starlight to start development to the west, Tuesday, Matt, and Harlow stood in the way. Turns out one of the descendants of Malachi Nickle—Bodie or Booker, one of them—knew the rink and the land belonged to the Royal House of Blue."

"And that ended the demolition plan?"

"That ended the demolition. Of course, they found other ways to expand, which has been good for the town. Until now—"

"When they want to come east," Emery said. "Any chance the Original Homestead is deeded to another country?"

"It was only the Starlight. The West End has a lot of power, and if Mac, Alfred, and Bobby are determined to consume the East End, not even the House of Blue can help us. Maybe breaking away, becoming their own municipality, would be best for all."

"You don't mean that, Caleb."

"No, I don't." He wobbled a bit going around the turn as he glanced over at her. "To be honest, I don't think they do either."

EMERY

On Thursday morning, she rode one of the motel's beach bikes down the Beachwalk for a breakfast burrito from the taco truck. Next she grabbed a latte from One More Cup, then sat on a bench to watch the sunrise.

The air was crisp and cool, slipping around her legs and through her hair. The calm Gulf reflected the colors of the dawn, and being by the sands of Sea Blue Beach was heaven.

She washed down a bite of burrito with a sip of her latte and wrestled with an idea, one she'd had for a while now. But was it a good idea? Since she'd never had one like this before, nor did she know anyone who did, her reference points were nonexistent.

Just do it. No guts, no glory. With those clichés rattling around in her head, she finished her breakfast and let her thoughts drift to Caleb—which was happening more often than not these days. Skating with him had been fun. When he held her hand for the couple's skate, she felt sixteen again.

Snippets of their long-ago summer would come to mind while she worked on the *Gazette's* budget or while cooking dinner. In so many ways, he was the same Caleb Ransom who made her laugh, who made her do crazy things like trash a football field and fall in love. Yet so far he'd not made any kind of romantic move.

Her phone pinged with an incoming text.

Ava:
Just thinking of you. Thanks again for putting
up with my crazy.

        Emery:
        Any time.

Ava:
What's happening with you and the hunky
architect?

        Emery:
        That's what you want to know on a Thursday at
        eight a.m.?

Ava:
I'm working on invitations. Is he your plus-one?

        Emery:
        Probably not. BTW, I've not approved the pink
        color for the bridesmaids' dresses.

Ava:
You're joking, right?

        Emery:
        Not joking. No human can see me in
        unapproved pink.

Ava:
Especially a hunky architect.

        Emery:
        ☺ We're just friends, even partners in some
        civic happenings, not so much potential lovers.

Ava:
Put yourself out there, girl. Dad said Caleb was
hot for you back in the day. I'll send you a fabric
swatch in the mail.

Emery:
You talked to Dad about this again? SMH.

Ava:
He blabbed when I mentioned Caleb lived in Sea
Blue Beach.

Emery:
Please inform him there's nothing between
us. He's not my date for the wedding. Emery
Quinn, plus-zero.

Ava:
Bummer. We're going to have a live band at the
reception. Who will you dance with?

Emery:
I don't need Caleb to kick up my heels. Look,
we liked each other as teens. Can't assume we'd
work romantically as adults. People change.

Ava:
Are you telling me or yourself?

Emery:
Have a good day, Ava.

And with that, the sun had fully risen. She biked back to the
Sands for a shower before the morning staff meeting.

"What's everyone working on?" Emery sat on one of the empty
desks in the bullpen and faced her small staff.

"Dr. Wheeler is retiring," Rex said. "I'm working on a long
piece about his years of medical practice and philanthropy in
town. Junie, could you pull some stuff off the digital morgue for
me? Like when he started his foundation? And I think his first
office was above Alderman's Pharmacy."

Jane was digging into the West End notion of becoming their own municipality. "All my contacts have gone dark, Emery. The best I can do is write up a piece on what's involved in a town splitting. I've called Congresswoman Abbot's office. We'll see if she responds."

"Good, and how about a story on Diamond Dog Golf Courses? Where are they all located? How did Mac acquire the land? Cost of each course? Did the cities contribute at all? Anyone want this one?"

"I'll take it," Rex said. "I do most of the sports reporting. Emery, I just filed my piece on the Tanagers Country Club joining the national pickleball circuit."

Gayle heard a rumor that a small contingency of health advocates were starting a petition to remove all food trucks from the beach.

"That's sacrilege," Junie said. "Sea Blue Beach is known for their amazing food trucks."

Jane wanted that story since her West End investigation stalled.

"Are you thinking what I'm thinking?" Emery said. "That the West End might be stirring up trouble?"

"Nothing will surprise me," Jane said.

The meeting adjourned, and Emery donned her ad director hat to visit businesses on the West End. It seemed the East End was tapped out. Either they already advertised or couldn't afford to advertise, even with the *Gazette*'s cut rates.

By the time she returned to the *Gazette* that evening, she'd made fifteen sales calls, each one more exhausting than the last, and secured one small account. A maid service called Maid For You. The owner agreed to a quarter-page ad for the Sunday-only edition. Which Emery won by throwing in an eighth of a page in the Wednesday edition for free.

Setting her things on her desk, she retrieved a bottle of water from the kitchen fridge and headed through the solemn, quiet newsroom to her office. The *Free Voice* had been nothing like this. It was loud and busy, phones ringing, keyboards clacking, reporters hollering to one another.

"One day, *Gazette*. One day."

She entered the ad details for Maid For You for Gayle to make up tomorrow. Then she closed her office door and returned to her brewing idea.

Was she going to do this . . . *thing*? It had sat with her all day. Was it dumb? Yes. Would it produce anything good? Probably not. Yet she had to try. Logging into the email server, she searched Rachel Kirby's archives for *House of Blue*.

Finding a private email address for the royal family, she read a couple dozen exchanges between Rachel, members of the Chamber Office, and the queen herself. If this idea had any chance of succeeding, Emery needed to use proper names and protocol.

The winter sun had tucked in for the night when she finally started an email from her editor-in-chief account. She had to be honest about her identity. Fingers crossed their royal system with their spam filters would recognize the domain. And not think Rachel Kirby emailed from the grave.

To: PrivateRK@chamberoffice.gov.LL
From: EQuinn@SBBGazette.com
Subject: Greetings from Sea Blue Beach!
To the Lord Chamberlain, House of Blue

Dear Sir,
My name is Emery Quinn, editor-in-chief of the *Sea Blue Beach Gazette*. I discovered this email address while going through the archives of Rachel Kirby, the *Gazette*'s former owner and editor.

Sea Blue Beach has grown into a lovely town, if not a divided one.

Something of a rivalry has developed between old and new, east and west.

The East End, founded by the House of Blue ancestor Prince Rein Titus Alexander, needs historic preservation as well as business revitalization. While some members of the town council are eager to allocate funds for projects, others are not. There has even been talk of razing the homes on the Original Homestead for a nine-hole golf course.

We love progress in Sea Blue Beach, but we also love history, especially one as rich as ours. Sea Blue Beach is still "the gem of the North Florida coast."

As far as we know, no royal Blue has visited the town since Prince Rein's departure for World War One. As there was a great affection between the royal family and the Starlight's former mangers, Tuesday Knight and Spike Chambers, as well as with the *Gazette's* owner, Rachel Kirby, my simple request is for a member of the House of Blue to visit our humble town. Perhaps his or her presence will remind us all what we're about: Unity. We need more restoration for more than just buildings. We need one for our hearts.

I believe the founders—a prince and freed slave—would agree. Thank you for your consideration.

Respectfully yours,
Emery Quinn

She pushed away from her desk, knocking into the credenza. When she did, a white envelope fell to the floor. Picking it up, she set it on the desk, then hovered over her laptop, rereading the email. She edited a couple of lines, then cursor to the send button.

"Do it," she whispered. "It's now or never." With an inhale, Emery closed her eyes and clicked send, with the whoosh of her request launching into cyberspace.

197

A spear of anxiety was defeated by true, genuine excitement. What if they said yes?

Closing her laptop, she grabbed her bag. She'd sent it, now forget it. What will be, will be. She was about to shut off the office lights when she spotted the envelope.

Inside she found two press passes for the Beach Boys concert Sunday night at the Blue Shell Amphitheater—which allotted her backstage access and a ten-minute interview with Mike Love and Bruce Johnston.

Two. Backstage. Passes. But from who? Delilah's "no" was adamant the other night. Besides, how would she have access to official press passes?

Emery tapped the envelope against her palm. The tickets felt like a message. *"Come to the West End."*

"I see you, Mac Diamond. You can't buy me, but I see you."

16

CALEB

"Cassidy, stop. You can't just barge in here and—"

"Who says?" She scooped Bentley's socks and underwear from one of the dresser drawers and dumped them into his little suitcase. "Bentley, get your shoes."

"I don't want to go," he said.

"Then you shouldn't have cried to your uncle how I never call you."

"But you don't."

Caleb stepped between Cassidy and her son, placing his hand on Bentley's head. "Hey, buddy, go see if Grandpa needs help with dinner. It's his turn to cook tonight, and you know how he likes to burn things."

He didn't have to tell the boy twice. Bentley shot out of his room, dashed down the stairs and out of the house.

"Bentley," Cassidy called after him. "Get back here. Pack your stuff." She gave Caleb a steely gaze. "Way to undermine me, *Uncle* Caleb."

"Cassidy, I told you if I took him, it was for the rest of the school year. And you agreed."

"If he wants to talk to me, he can talk to me at my house." She tossed Bentley's sneakers from the closet to the center of the room.

Caleb returned them to the closet. "Will you stop throwing stuff? What's going on? All I said in my text was he misses you and to please call him."

"I'm busy, okay?" She left the room and came back with Bentley's toothbrush. "We're not staying for dinner. I can't believe Dad is still burning good food hoping Mom will let him get out of his night to cook. Why doesn't he just grill out?"

"It's his version of blackened." That actually got a laugh from Cassidy. "Mom made your favorite, chicken and noodles, the other night. There's leftovers."

"I don't eat that southern comfort food anymore." Cassidy wadded Bentley's T-shirts into the suitcase. "Too many carbs."

While Cassidy had always been a bit of a loose cannon, her behavior today reminded him of the summer she fought their parents at every turn. When she seemed to be at war with the whole world.

"What's happened? Something with Pluto? Did you two—"

"His name is Arturo, you jackwagon, and yes, we broke up. There, you happy?" Cassidy shot down the stairs and through the kitchen, the back door slamming behind her.

Caleb chased her out to the patio, where she paced, weeping and swearing like a ticked-off football coach. He flipped on the string lights, then retrieved a long lighter from his outdoor storage container.

"This always happens to me, you know? I find a good guy and then BAM! He takes off with another woman."

As he listened, Caleb stacked wood in the brick fireplace, glancing at his phone to see that Emery had texted.

Emery:
Beach Boys concert the 16th. Wanna go?

Caleb:
I'm in.

"We were engaged," Cassidy said, scowling as Caleb tucked his phone back in his pocket. "I was planning a wedding."

With a couple of twigs for kindling, the dried logs caught quickly. Caleb set the lighter aside and perched on the table.

"I'm never good enough. Not for anyone—not for Mom or Dad. You. Perfect Caleb."

"Woah, where'd that come from? No one ever said I was perfect, Cassidy."

"The good son who did as he was told. And now the perfect uncle, knight in shining armor. Taking in his crazy sister's kid cause she's a relationship disaster."

"No one is saying that, Cass."

"They're all thinking it."

"Are you sure it's over with Arturo?"

"Yes. Over. Finito. How many times does the love of my life have to walk out for me to learn my lesson? Once, twice? Three times? Four? No, no, I'm done. From now on, it's Bent and me. Deuce."

"Fine, but where are you going to live?"

"I don't know, but not in Sea Blue Beach. Under Mom and Dad's condemning eye. Or yours. And all of their friends. My former friends. Forget it. I can hear all the whispers. 'There goes Cassidy Ransom, Hayden and Billie's messed-up daughter. She had *so* much potential.'" She made her way over to the fire, stretching her hands to the warmth. "You want the truth? Here it is: I'm a nobody. No. Body. Not worth the time and effort."

"How do you make that out?" Caleb took his sister by the shoulders and turned her to him. "Cassidy Ransom, you're a somebody. Listen to me! You are your father's daughter. Hayden Ransom has given you a name—*his name*—and maybe people today don't think that means anything, but it does. You are not alone. *You are your father's daughter.* Start acting like it."

"I'm not anyone's anything." She shook her head and pulled away. "I have a job in Mobile. I'll find a place to live there."

Caleb wanted another stab at convincing her of the power of being Hayden Ransom's daughter. Of having a family that loved her. But he'd pressed enough

"Do you need any money?"

"No, and even if I did, I'd not ask you." She looked toward their parent's place, then started inside Caleb's. "I'm leaving. Bentley can stay here. I'll send you my new address and try to call him more." She stopped on the steps to look back at Caleb. "By the way, little brother, what's with all the boxes? Unpack, you moron."

"I just haven't gotten around to it," he said. "Stay overnight, please. Talk to me."

She shook her head, tears in her eyes. "There are some things I can't tell even you."

CALEB

Then . . .

In one hour, one *very* long hour, he was picking Emery up for dinner. With his parents. He'd never brought a girl home for dinner before.

He went to the eighth-grade dance with Sally Peterson, but he met her at the school, and her dad sat in the bleachers the whole time. Caleb barely touched her during their one slow dance.

Inviting Emery had really been Dad's idea. *"Might cheer up your mother,"* he'd said.

Cassidy had been home most of this week with a brutal attitude, which made Mom cry a lot. Then she started disappearing again, staying out late, ignoring everyone when she came around for food.

Mom insisted Caleb invite Emery and her parents for dinner. He took a risk and invited them for Friday night. No way Cassidy would be home before dawn.

Her parents declined since her mom had a cold. But Emery was coming.

He worked an extra shift at the Starlight, then ran by Biggs for a bouquet of flowers. At home, he showered, gelled his hair, and snuck a splash of Dad's Hugo Boss. In the kitchen, he asked Mom what he could do to help with dinner.

"You can set the table." Still in her work clothes and covered with a big apron, signature slippers on her feet, Mom checked the lasagna. The whole house smelled of meat, cheese, and sauce. "Was Cassidy with you at the rink?" she said. "I called her and left messages, but she never called back. What's the point of paying for cell service if she's not going to use it."

Oh, she used it. Just not to talk to Mom. "She wasn't at the rink." He hoped Mom would leave it at that because he knew where Cassidy had been all afternoon: at the beach, wearing a bikini that made him blush, while some muscled airman from Eglin wrapped his tattooed arm around her naked waist.

"Are you excited?" Mom said. "About this girl? What's her name?"

"Emery. She's just a friend."

"You've been spending a lot of time with her."

"She's cool. The guys like her."

"The guys? Like Shift, Jumbo, Hollingsworth?" Mom said, properly impressed. "Well, personally I like how her father called your dad. He's looking out for her." She stepped to the back porch facing their neighbor on the right. "Caleb, I'm going to see if Cassidy is with Allison. Her phone must've died."

Allison was Cassidy's best friend and co-conspirator. Mom was knocking on the wrong door there.

Ten minutes later, she arrived home from Denial Town. "Alli said she's at the Starlight." Mom looked pleased with that answer. "You must've missed her." At the fridge, she collected the salad fixings. "Apparently Riley Stebbins is in town visiting her grandparents, and she dragged Cass to the rink. Although . . ." Mom paused, talking to herself more than Caleb. "Jennifer and I played cards last week, and she never mentioned Riley coming to town."

"I'm off to pick up Emery, Mom." It was a bit early, but another minute of Mom's reasonings and he'd break, rat on his sister—who absolutely deserved it—but tonight was about Emery coming to dinner.

When he pulled up to the Sands, Mr. Quinn waited outside Cottage 7. "Come on in," he said, offering his hand. "Want a Coke or Dr. Pepper? Em, Caleb's here."

She came out of her room in a pair of white shorts and a pink top, flowers in her braided hair. Her tawny complexion had even more freckles—which made her hazel eyes look super cool. She was the prettiest girl he'd ever seen.

"How do you like her hair?" Mrs. Quinn said. "We picked the flowers from Delilah's garden."

"Nice" was all he could manage, since his heart was banging against his chest. But she was so much more.

"Bye, 'rents." Emery kissed her mother, who'd retreated to the small couch under the window, pulling a blanket over her legs. "Bye, Dad, and yes I have my phone, and yes I'll be home by ten."

"Please thank your parents for inviting us," Mr. Quinn said, with a look over at his wife. "Hopefully we can make it another time."

Caleb held the passenger door for Emery as she climbed in, filling him and the truck cab with her soft, clean scent. Every part of him was intensely aware of her. Could he just stare at her all night and not be a weirdo?

Dinner was just the four of them—Dad, Mom, Caleb, and Emery. Thank goodness Cassidy was a no-show. The knot in his gut eased away when Dad said grace and Mom offered Emery a glass of sweet tea.

The table conversation was peaceful and fun. His folks peppered Emery with the usual questions: Where she was from? What did her parents do for a living? How did she like school? They were impressed she was an honor student who lettered in two sports. Even better, she made Dad laugh with a story about snowboarding into a tree.

"Our daughter is a talented athlete," Mom said. "Have you met Cassidy?"

"No, not yet." She glanced at Caleb. "So you're going to be the starting quarterback?"

"Yes, yes, of course," Dad said. "He's got quite an arm and a good football IQ."

"Cassidy can launch that softball from center field to home plate." Mom dished more salad onto her plate. "Emery, more lasagna? You must take home a couple of pieces for your parents."

"Thank you. Dad is crazy for Italian food. Can I help wash up, Mrs. Ransom?"

"No, no, I'll let them soak while I mix up the brownies. You and Caleb can set up the game he wanted to—" The kitchen door banged against the wall as a very drunk Cassidy stumbled inside.

"I'm home." She flung her arms wide, wearing a stupid grin. Her hair stuck out like she'd been in a wind tunnel. "And I'm *drunk*." She dropped into the chair next to Emery's, laughing. "Hey, you . . . you're Emery. My brother is in *looove* with you."

"Cassidy, shut up."

"Why? I know you are, little bro." She slurred every word and almost slid out of the chair. Twice. "So you ..." Cassidy tapped Emery's chest. "Don't go breaking his heart. Or I'll have to kick your a—"

"Caleb," Dad said. "Why don't you take Emery to the Beachwalk for dessert?" He took a couple of tens from his money clip. "Emery, it was nice to have you here."

Mom said good-bye, standing at the sink with her back to the kitchen. "Nice to meet you, Emery."

Caleb tried to swallow it, but he seethed with every bitter and foul name. Emery walked quietly beside him past the Starlight to the Beachwalk. Seeing the Gulf, Caleb kicked off his flip-flops and raced for the water.

"Caleb, wait." Emery ran after him. "What are you doing?"

"Cooling off." He dove into a low curling wave, staying under as long as he could before bouncing to the surface, smacking into Emery, who'd lunged for him, knocking them both back under the water.

"You idiot. You scared me," she said when they surfaced, the flower from her hair floating in the sea foam.

"It's only a teeny, tiny Gulf of Mexico wave, Em." He caught her with one arm and held her steady as the surf dragged along the ocean floor, tugging their feet, trying to pull them under.

Emery grabbed his shoulders to stay upright. "Is that how she always is?"

"That was a new low," he said, walking against the tide, gripping Emery by the waist.

On the beach, they plopped next to where Emery had flung her purse. Water drained from their skin and clothes, making a pool around them. At eight o'clock, the sun was too far west to dry Emery by the time he took her home.

"What will your dad say when you come home with wet clothes?"

"Nothing, when I tell him I had to save you from drowning."

"Oh, okay, I see how it is." He laughed low. "I swim like a fish, for your information." He gently swept aside a lock of her hair curling over her eye. The tip of his finger barely grazed her skin, and now he wanted to kiss her. "She wasn't always like this. Mad at the world. I think something happened right before school let out, but she won't talk to me, or anyone. Dad wanted to take her to a doctor, and she flipped. Refused to go. If Mom says it's a nice day, Cass goes off about melting polar ice caps. I used to love being home. Now I get a knot in my stomach when I walk through the door."

Caleb flopped down on the beach and listened to the waves, cooling the last of his angst. When Emery stretched out next to him, the world almost felt right again.

"I'm working at the Starlight this weekend," he said, searching for her hand and hooking his little finger with hers, wondering if she could *feel* the power of his heartbeat. "You should come."

"Do I get the employee discount?"

Caleb grinned. "You're so special, Emery Quinn."

"So are you, Caleb Ransom." She looked over and brushed something from his hair—the twisted, limp stem of a flower.

He tried to weave what remained into her braid, but the damage had been done. He dropped the flower to the sand. "Want to get dessert?"

They decided on cinnamon buns and a Diet Coke from Mr. Callier's truck, Delicious Dave. When Caleb handed him a soggy ten, he didn't ask. Just pressed it between two napkins and counted out the change.

Sitting on the nearest Beachwalk bench, they ate and slurped, not saying much. When he glanced at her, she smiled. Once, he looked up to see she was watching him. The warmth in her eyes inspired a brand-new set of sweat beads.

At nine forty-five, he walked her toward the Sands. "I had fun."

"Me too." Her hand brushed his.

"Maybe I'll see you tomorrow?" Because he couldn't imagine tomorrow otherwise.

"Maybe," she said, slowing as they approached the motel's beachside courtyard. When she turned to him, her eyes were on his lips. He pulled her close and rested her hands on his chest.

"Emery, I was wondering if I could—"

"You're home early, Em. By five minutes." Mr. Quinn stood in the doorway of Cottage 1. "Delilah was playing some of her records for Mom and me. Did you have fun? Emery, why are you wet?"

"I had to rescue a drowning kid." She tiptoed up to whisper in Caleb's ear, "See you tomorrow, Ransom."

"I told you lifeguard training would come in handy," her dad said.

Emery ducked under his arm into the warm, peaceful-looking atmosphere of Cottage 1. Peace. That's all Caleb wanted. Peace again. "Good night, Mr. Quinn."

"Night, Caleb."

Heading down the Beachwalk toward home, passing under the old lamps and palm trees, he realized that when Emery left for Cleveland, she'd be taking his heart with her.

17

EMERY

Now . . .

It didn't seem right that she had tickets to the Beach Boys when the Sunday *Gazette* was a disaster.

Their beautiful Sunday edition with an extended mural story, along with more of Kadasha's stunning photographs, Rex's piece on Diamond Dog Golf Courses, and Jane's discovery of an advocate group wanting to shut down the food trucks, was a disaster.

Thousands of dollars' worth of missing ads. Big holes on every page where a display ad was supposed to be.

She spent the better part of two hours fielding calls from angry advertisers—the ones she convinced to trust her—promising them recompense, talking to Elliot, trying to make him understand what she didn't, then digging in with Rex to figure out what happened. They found nothing. Ambrose even came in after church to help, suggesting that maybe the old Atex system simply needed to be replaced.

As a test, they resent the zipped files to the press and all the ads were there.

What now? Even Tobias, who came in to finish cleaning the floors and carry out the weekend trash, peeked over their shoulders for a look-see. However, the man could barely use his smart phone, so he was more moral support than anything else.

By the time Caleb picked her up at the *Gazette* office for the Beach Boys concert, she was exhausted and frustrated. As temporary ad director, she finally knew what it felt like to labor in sales only to have production go belly-up.

"We don't have to go to the concert," Caleb said as they drove from the East End into the West.

Emery glanced over at him. "Yes, we do." The iconic sound of the Beach Boys filled the truck cab from the playlist on Caleb's phone. "It's just . . . how? I can't stop thinking about how every ad was missing, yet when we re-sent the file this morning, they were all there."

"Glitch? Something happened while sending the file?"

"We don't think so, but it's on a schedule, so who knows."

"Wish I could say it'll be okay, but I have no idea. In the meantime, how do you like my ensemble?" He tugged on the collar of his Hawaiian shirt.

She laughed. "Very beachy. And how do I look?" That morning, she'd slept in. Taken a long, hot shower. Was about to enjoy the *Sunday Gazette* while dining on a Sweet Conversations pastry with a cup of Sophisticated Sips coffee beans when Rex called.

"Have you seen the paper?"

She jumped into a pair of yoga pants and an oversized Ohio State T-shirt, wrapped her wet hair in a topknot, and ran out the door.

Caleb gazed at her for a long moment, and she felt suddenly shy and tugged the tie from her hair.

"Maybe you shouldn't answer that question," she said.

"You look pretty. Or should I say good-looking."

"Bentley would be proud, but I'll take pretty, even if I don't believe you."

"I'm serious. Your hair is all wavy. And it smells good."

Emery rested against the back of the seat. "Okay, Quinn, get in the right mindset. You're about to interview the Beach Boys. Oh—" She sat forward. "Delilah said, 'If the boys remember me, tell them hi.'"

"Delilah Mead, the woman who still holds sales records, thinks they won't remember her?" Caleb slowed for one of many West End traffic lights. "You think she'll ever tell you why she walked away from music?"

"I think her story is very special to her. Like deeply personal. She's not going to share it until she's ready."

"You think she played a part in you getting last-minute back-stage passes?" Caleb eased off the light when it turned green. The narrow two-lane Sea Blue Way in the East became six in the West.

"I think Mac Diamond gave me these tickets."

"Really?" Caleb cut her a side glance as "Wouldn't It Be Nice" played in the truck. "And FYI, he's not reached out to me, in case you're wondering."

"I'm not."

"He didn't Mr. Potter me."

"Sure looked like it that night."

"Well, he didn't. By the way, we have a Main Street meeting this Thursday."

"I'll be there."

"Good. Maybe we can grab a bite to eat before or after."

"Caleb Ransom, did you just ask me out on a date?"

His side grin was so cute. "You asked me first."

"Since when?"

"Um, now. I'm going to a Beach Boys concert with you. You don't need me."

"I had two passes."

"Could've taken Rex or Jane, even Delilah."

Emery stared out her window. "I'd be okay with dinner."

His laugh resonated through her and once again took her back to riding around in his Chevy S-10, blasting music and Caleb reaching across the bench seat to pull her closer to him.

"What's Bentley doing tonight?" Emery spotted the amphitheater up ahead as Caleb navigated the concert traffic.

"Skating with the Feinberg boys." He made a left into VIP parking. "That kid . . . I told him if he got tired of the rink to call Dad and Mom. He says, 'I don't have a phone.' So, this afternoon I bought him a prepaid dumb phone, programmed in emergency numbers, and handed it to him, thinking 'Not bad, Uncle Caleb.'" He shook his head. "Bentley curled his lips and said something about a *real* phone, a smart phone, and I said, 'If you think you're getting a thousand-dollar phone at age eleven, you've got another thing coming.'" Caleb powered down the window to show their press passes to security. "Know what he said? 'Okay, what's the other thing coming? I need to check my options.'"

So, with a bit of laughter, they parked, then followed the signs to the press room, Emery shoving aside the missing ads debacle to focus on the opportunity ahead.

She'd solve the *Gazette's* problems tomorrow. She would. There's no reason an intelligent, educated woman couldn't figure out what had happened. For now, head in the game. She was about to interview two of the legendary Beach Boys: founding member Mike Love and longtime vocalist and contributor Bruce Johnston.

"You have ten minutes. Not a second more, so don't ask." A bearded man with Rocky Mountain muscles gave Caleb the once-over. "Who's he?"

"My photographer," she said. Caleb popped a wide grin and flashed his phone.

"No photos in there." The man shoved Caleb against a wall and ushered Emery to her seat across from Mike and Bruce. Suddenly she was nervous. While she'd interviewed a few celebs in her time, and a great number of political figures at the *Free Voice*, this was for the *Gazette*. Her paper. And a little bit for Delilah.

"Delilah Mead says hello," she said right off the bat, and immediately the atmosphere changed. Mike and Bruce perked up and peppered her with questions.

"Delilah Mead, of course we remember her. Man, how is she?"

"She's great," Emery said.

"When we toured with her, every show was a blowout. What a voice." This from Mike Love.

"Where is she these days?" Bruce said.

"Yeah, what's she been doing the last forty years?"

Emery hit record on her phone and answered their questions as best she could. No, she didn't know what happened to her or why she walked away from a stellar career. Yes, she'd love to know the rest of the story too.

"As far as I know," Emery said, "she's been running a motor motel in Sea Blue Beach for the last four decades."

"Tell her to get in touch." Mike handed over his card, then Bruce's. "I wish she was here tonight. We'd pull her on stage."

"My mom said there was no voice like Delilah in the late sixties, early seventies." Emery tucked away their cards, treating them like gold.

"All true. Her last album had a sound that lives on," Mike said. "Samson thought he was the brains and talent, but when they split, he never produced anything worth listening to again. Delilah was the genius behind their success."

The mention of Delilah had turned the green room into a living room, and for thirty minutes, Mike and Bruce told stories. About their early days. About Bruce filling in for Brian Wilson in 1965. About how the two of them toured longer than any other Beach Boy.

When their muscled man finally said, "Boys, you have to move on" for the third time, Mike and Bruce hugged Emery as if she was a long-lost friend and shook Caleb's hand, looking at him like, *Were you here the whole time?*

Emery braved a request for a picture, which Mike granted, handing her phone to a hovering assistant. The four of them squeezed together, smiling. She exited the green room into a sour-faced huddle of print and TV reporters. She'd stolen their time. Sorry, but bazinga, she had a stellar story for the *Gazette*. And for Delilah.

"You were magic in there." Caleb grabbed her hand.

"Mentioning Delilah did it."

"Maybe Delilah got you in the door, but the rest was all you. They were comfortable. You have that effect on people."

"Do I?" Being tutored by a man with hard-news sensibilities, she'd viewed herself more of a gentle bulldog. Get the story. Convey the facts. Ask questions. Challenge the answers. Think through problems and situations. She'd never considered herself comforting. After losing Mom, she considered comfort a luxury.

Heading down the ramp to their seats, they passed a group of men in polos and pressed khakis. Bobby Brockton stood among them, with a lovely woman and another couple.

"Caleb?" Bobby said. "What'd you do, sneak backstage?"

"No sneak to it." Caleb raised his press pass. "Emery was interviewing Mike and Bruce. Great guys. You remember Emery Quinn, editor-in-chief of the *Gazette*?" He introduced her to Bobby's wife, Wren, and her brother, Tommy Lake, and his wife, Dani. "Tommy owns JIL Architects. He's good, gets all the West End jobs."

"Nice to see you all." Emery shoved Caleb toward their seats in the center of the second row, bumping him with her hip. "Don't antagonize those guys. He'll tell Mac Diamond not to give you the golf course clubhouse."

"Very funny. I'm not interested in his clubhouse. Nevertheless, it's true. JIL wins just about every West End job."

"Forget them. Caleb, we just spent thirty minutes with two men from one of the most iconic groups of the twentieth century. I'm buzzing. I don't even care anymore about the paper's missing ads." Emery started typing in her Notes app. She'd just thought of a great opening line for her story.

Caleb announced his need for concessions and headed off, returning with hot dogs, chips, and two large souvenir tumblers of Diet Coke. She took a bite of her dog and a sip of her drink before going back to her notes.

"I can't think with all this noise. I should listen to the recording, but I didn't bring my AirPods."

"Want me to tell everyone to pipe down?" Caleb said.

"Would you?" She patted his arm without looking up. "That'd be great."

"Em, you're in an outdoor amphitheater with ten thousand people waiting to hear the Beach Boys. Stop working. Have fun. Soak up the atmosphere."

She looked up, smiling. "I've not had a story this fun since my crime and corruption piece on Ohio's Speaker of the House." She started typing, then looked up at him. "I don't want to forget anything, hearing how it was in the early days of rock-n-roll, how they developed their sound, how it feels to have such an enduring legacy. I'm going to weave in a bit about Delilah Samson."

An older couple took the seats on the other side of her. The man leaned in to say, "We fell in love dancing to the Beach Boys. Fifty-eight years later, asking her to dance was the best decision of my life."

She shook his hand. "Emery Quinn, editor of the *Sea Blue Beach Gazette.* Can I ask you a few questions?"

She interviewed two more couples before the opening act, Dave Mason, brought the crowd together. The noise amplified, so Emery tucked her phone away and tried to escape into the music, but the story—*the story*—beckoned her.

When the Beach Boys took the stage, she tried for photos from her seat—she should've hired Kadesha again—but the angle was weird. She nudged Caleb to get some shots of the crowd.

"Can't we just enjoy the concert?" he said.

"Darn it, I wish we had a Monday edition," she said, snapping a picture of Mike Love, then tapping a note on her phone. "The crowd went wild when they sang 'wish they all could be Florida girls' instead of 'California girls.'"

When the opening chords to "Good Vibrations" hit the air, even Emery couldn't resist the energy of the crowd, and the way the Beach Boys transported so many of them back in time when the post-war world was changing.

The couple next to her danced a slow dance in the aisle to "Surfer Girl," and Emery snapped a couple more photos and jotted in her notes. She lost herself in "Fun, Fun, Fun" and danced the swim in front of the stage with a couple of well-dressed, gray-haired women who were probably former prom queens.

Somewhere in the back of her mind, she heard her mother's subtle advice. *"Be present, Emery. Everything comes in good time. If it doesn't, it was never yours."*

Too soon it was all over, and she walked with the energized crowd to the parking lot, singing "wish they all could be Florida girls." Heading home, Caleb stopped at 7-11 for a couple of waters.

"I needed tonight," she said after a long drink. "Wasn't it fun? Meeting Mike and Bruce, talking to couples who grew up in that generation, feeling the vibe of the crowd, and hearing the music. I really have to get Delilah to talk to me."

"You've got a great story for the *Gazette*," Caleb said, not matching her enthusiasm. Somewhere toward the end of the concert, he'd gone quiet on her.

At the Sands Motor Motel, the courtyard was lit by the fire and the lights strung from cottage to cottage, the Beach Boy's music playing from mounted speakers.

"All right, Ransom, what's up?" she said as he walked her to her door. Delilah's cottage was shut tight, but Emery sensed the ambiance of the courtyard was her doing.

"All right, since you asked. First, I had a blast. Thank you for inviting me." He walked toward the firepit, then turned back to her. "You know how the couple next to us danced to 'Surfer Girl'? I, um, wow, now it sounds silly, but I wanted to dance with you to that song." He laughed. "Ever since you invited me, I had it in my head, some romantic notion of—" He waved off his comment.

The bass chords and the harmonic "oooohs" of "Surfer Girl" dropped into the atmosphere. He glanced at her and laughed softly. "I think Delilah is spying on us." He held out his arms. "Can I have this dance?"

"All you had to do was ask," she said, resting her cheek in the strong spot of his chest, listening to his heartbeat as she followed him through the rhythm of the music. "At the concert, I mean."

"Let's always do this," he whispered close to her ear.

When she looked up at him, he bent toward her until his lips found hers. It was the first, next kiss, in a sixteen-year gap. New and exciting, yet familiar and known. Everything she remembered about *that* summer.

When the song ended, they continued in a slow sway, stealing kisses and forgetting a world beyond the Sands and Sea Blue Beach existed.

"Maybe you'll knock on my window tonight like you did that summer?" She laughed as if she were teasing but she felt the eagerness in her voice.

"Maybe I will. Your dad's not here to put some Krav Maga move on me." Caleb kissed her one last time as she leaned against the doorframe. "But I still fear the Boyfriendinator."

EMERY

Then...

When she came in from the beach holding Caleb's hand, Dad was once again pulling burgers off the grill, and Emery Quinn made a decision. Actually, two.

One, she loved Caleb Ransom. At sixteen, almost seventeen, she'd found her forever man. Wow! She'd never, ever, ever imagined she'd like a boy so much to think he was The One. Not until after college. But why not?

Grandma and Grandpa Force, Mom's parents, met at sixteen, married at eighteen. Caleb told her his Ransom grandparents fell in love at fourteen and married after his grandpa came home from Korea.

As Dad would say, *"There's precedent for it."*

Two, she was never leaving Sea Blue Beach. That's as far as she'd gotten with that one. The logistics were complicated. What about Dad's professorship at Case Western? Or Mom's power job at the bank? Or Emery starting as point guard for Hawken School? Details, details. Florida had universities. And banks. Nickle High had an exceptional girls' basketball team. Emery had meet several of the players this summer. They were super cool.

In six-and-a-half short weeks, she'd become a bona fide member of Sea Blue Beach. Even a queen, according to Caleb's friends. Queen of Operation Revenge. Two nights ago, when Caleb worked the Starlight, Emery went skating with Shift's sister and her bestie. Had a blast.

"Young Mr. Ransom," Dad said, trying to sound stern but fooling no one. Last night he told Mom how much he was going to miss "that boy." He hoped Emery would find a nice kid like him back home. But there was only *one* Caleb Ransom.

"Tell your father thanks for the grilling tips," Dad said. "I've become the grill master I've always wanted to be."

"Hayden Ransom is your guy, Mr. Quinn." He released Emery to help Dad with a platter of meat.

"After dinner, can I go to the Starlight with Caleb? He's not working, and it's eighties night." Emery tossed her beach towel over one of the Adirondacks. She'd become more tan and more lean over the last month from all the beach volleyball and bike riding.

"We thought we'd have a family dinner tonight." Dad motioned her inside. "Just us three."

"Okay, but can't Caleb stay?" He was family to her. She reached for his hand after he handed the platter to Dad. "There are six burgers here. We can't eat all of them."

"Another time," Dad said, smiling. But there was something sad in his eyes. "Caleb, we'll see you tomorrow."

Emery walked him out to his truck. "I'm sorry, I don't know why he's being so weird."

"I get it," Caleb said, popping open his truck door. "He wants a family dinner. I'd want that too if Cass wasn't a freakazoid." He kissed her quickly on the cheek. "See you tomorrow."

She waited as he drove off, waving one last time.

Back in the cottage, Dad set out the mustard and ketchup and a plate of sliced onions and tomatoes. Mom set the seventies-style dishes on the table. They were eating at the table? Guess they were serious about this family dinner.

Dad put Emery in charge of the potato salad, coleslaw, and baked beans. He filled glasses with ice, and Mom poured the sweet tea.

Oldies played softly on the kitchen radio, but dinner wasn't their usual lively affair with Dad telling corny jokes and Mom trying not to laugh, Emery sharing anything and everything about her day.

Dad was preoccupied. Mom looked more tired than usual. Emery couldn't stop thinking about Caleb and their inevitable good-bye as she choked down her hamburger, which sat in her stomach like a rock.

At the end of the meal, Dad wadded up his napkin and said, "Let's sit in the living room."

"Here, Em." Mom patted the settee, a rectangular velvet box resting in her lap. The Force family pearls. "I want to give you these."

"The pearls? Why?" Emery wasn't partial to pearls. No one her age wore them. But these were special. A family heirloom, given to a Force woman for her wedding. Tradition dictated that the bride's mother hooked the choker necklace on the inheriting daughter the moment before her father walked her down the aisle. "I like Caleb a lot, Mom, but I'm not ready to get married just yet." Her laugh sounded hollow. What was going on here?

"I want to give these to you now since I won't—" Mom smiled faltered, and her eyes filled her tears. "I won't be here to give them to you for your wedding."

"What are you talking about?" Emery looked at Dad, then Mom. "Why won't you be here?"

Mom gathered Emery's hands in hers. "When you were born

. . . I was so happy. Finally, I had my baby. We'd tried for so long." Mom's tears spilled over and slipped down her cheeks.

Emery pulled away, standing. "I don't know what you're going to say but—"

"Will you please sit down? I have this whole speech prepared, and I'm going to say it." Mom patted the cushion again, and Emery sat with a huff. "Your dad and I always planned to give you the Force name. It's your heritage and your character." She opened the pearl box for Emery to see the white strand resting against the black velvet. "You come from a line of loving, kind women who understood the power of family and motherhood. They stood up for things even when it wasn't popular. Shelby Force Canton was the first to wear the pearls. Her parents went all the way to Tiffany's to buy them. She gave them to Elizabeth Force Jones, who gave them to Grace Force Wilder, who gave them to me, Rosie Force Quinn." Mom set the pearls in Emery's hand again. "Now I'm giving them to you, Emery Force Quinn. Be strong, Em. Be a force for good. Don't look back, don't give up. Yet lean on those who love you and care for you. L-let God into your life."

"All right, that's enough." Emery was on her feet again. "Tell me right now. Why won't you be here when I get married?"

Mom wiped her wet cheeks with a wad of tissues. "Don't wear them until your wedding. Have some woman you love hook them on for you. I don't have a sister, nor does your father, but—"

"Mom! Stop talking about my freaking wedding and tell me right now. What's wrong?" But she knew. She felt it in every part of her trembling being. *I won't be here to give them to you.*

"—whatever you do, don't let your friends try them on or borrow them. They're not for a prom. They're for your wedding. But be generous whenever and wherever you can. As I don't know what the future holds for you and your dad, you can share with—"

"Me and Dad? Me and Dad?" Emery paced through the small living space, into the kitchen, back to the living room, gripping the side of her head, fingers twined with her hair, shaking so much she feared she'd lose it. Flat-out lose it. "Are you . . . dying? You're only forty-nine."

"Em," Dad began, sad and low, "your mom has stage-four brain cancer. The days we disappeared? We were checking with specialists in Jacksonville and at the University of Florida."

"I knew you weren't visiting old friends," she whispered. She waited for him to say more. "And . . . ?"

"And there's nothing they can do. She could go through surgery and chemo, but it will be hard on her physically and mentally. At best, she'd live three or four months longer, sick more than not the entire time. Mom has chosen to forgo treatment and be present with us for her final days."

Emery snapped the pearl box closed and tossed it on the settee. "So let me get this straight. You and Dad have been on a journey discovering you're going to die without saying a word to me? Letting me run all over Sea Blue Beach with a cute boy as if life was all sunshine and lollipops? I feel like I've been living a lie. Why didn't you tell me any of this? I'm sixteen, not six. When did you find out you had cancer?"

"May," Mom said softly.

"May? And you're just now telling me? It's mid-July." She faced her father. "So this whole summer was a fraud. We're not here to make family memories. We're here to say good-bye to Mom. For you to give me the Force pearls. Well, I'm not wearing them. Ever." She ran out of Cottage 7, Dad's voice calling after her.

"Emery, please come back inside."

She crossed the courtyard and kicked a fallen pine cone. When her bare feet hit the beach, she ran toward the water, stopping on the edge of the low tide, where the sands of Sea Blue Beach washed out from under her feet with each receding wave.

Tipping back her head, she screamed against the wind and toward the last bit of gold, red, and orange resting on the horizon, then raised her fist at the first peek of the full, luminous moon, the *pearl* of the night sky.

"You can't have her. You can't."

18

CALEB

Now...

Work had finally started on Alderman's Pharmacy. Liking hands-on experience, and to keep an eye on the historical elements, Caleb joined the construction crew removing rotting beams and floors and the odd wall someone added in the seventies to the upstairs apartment.

Thursday afternoon, Jenny Finch arrived in her high-heeled, high-fashion manner to check on the progress. Caleb rolled out the printed plans across the long, dark mahogany counter where Alderman's used to serve milkshakes, floats, and fizzes.

"Excellent, Caleb. I love it." Jenny compared the plans to the pictures she'd acquired when she bought the place. "I want to walk into 1902 when I pass through that door. Let all the modern stuff be behind walls, under the floor, and in the attic."

"Sourcing some of these items, like the pulls for the old soda fountain, will be pricy. We may have to order custom made."

"Do what you have to do. I want the detail, Caleb. I picked you because I knew you'd make sure the pharmacy was restored to its original beauty."

He regarded her for a moment before rolling up the plans. "What brought you to that conclusion?"

"I do my homework." Jenny slid her arm through the arched handles of her Hermès handbag. His ex, Lizzie, had educated him on Hermès Birkin, Prada, and Louis Vuitton. "Listen, I got a call from a Mac Diamond. He offered to buy me out. Says he has plans for the East End and doesn't want me to lose my investment. But I don't roll that way."

If Caleb didn't respect Ms. Finch before now . . . "Mac wants the entire East End as his money-making playground."

"So I gathered. Listen, if you need anything from me, let me know. And what's this about something called the Org. Homestead?"

"He told you about that too? It's more of a street, really, with twelve Florida Cracker homes. Mac wants that area to be a nine-hole golf course with a clubhouse. It's prime real estate, for sure. Higher ground, lots of trees."

"But you want to restore the homes?" Jenny leaned in for his reply.

"Yes, get people living in them again. Progress is good until it rolls over history. They tried to demolish the Starlight skating rink in the eighties, but the town and a secret deed saved it."

"Fascinating." She headed to inspect the second floor, her high heels thunking against the old floorboards. "If you need money, let me know."

Duly noted.

For the rest of the afternoon, his conversation with Jenny clung to him, offering hope and relief. There were good people in the world. Okay, maybe Mac Diamond wasn't a bad dude so much as driven, ambitious, and callous toward the wants of others.

Swinging a hammer helped him process, along with hauling out large pieces of lumber to the dumpster. Lost in the demolition of the old kitchen, Caleb finally noticed the bright afternoon hues had faded to gray. What time was it, anyway? Six fifty-five. He hollered good night to the foreman, then scrambled for his truck. The Main Street meeting started at seven. He called Dad once he hit Sea Blue Way.

"Can you feed Bentley?"

"Already done. You got to get the rhythm of this parenting thing, son," Dad said.

"I'm trying, but being a single parent is no joke." Which made him think he should cut Cassidy some slack in that department.

At the Starlight Museum, he walked into the warm conversation of Adele, Mercy, Ivan, and Duke, along with the heady aroma of a chicken casserole. Dust fell from his jeans and shirt as he set his iPad on his chair.

"Sorry I'm late." You could hear his stomach rumbling all the way to Tucson.

"Help yourself to a plate, Caleb," Adele said. "It's one of my signature recipes."

"Adele, you don't have to bring food to the meeting." Which seemed hypocritical to say as he scooped out a large pile of steaming chicken in a creamy sauce, darn near weak with hunger. "But thank you."

"She can't help it, Caleb," Ivan said. "It's a disease with her. Got to feed and clothe everyone."

"Just doing what the good Lord told me to do. You do know the good Lord, don't you, Ivan? Immanuel, God with us? He's part of our town." She pointed to the replica image Immanuel. Same as on the wall of the Starlight. "He wrote a whole big book for us to learn about Him and His love. But you got to read it if—"

"Adele, will you hush up?" Ivan squinted at her. "Pastor does all the preaching I need."

"Okay, let's call this meeting to order." Caleb shoved in a few bites, then washed it down with cold, sweet tea. Man, he'd died and gone to heaven. "Simon couldn't make it tonight, so it's just us."

"Where's that pretty reporter?" Ivan said. "She's not really pretty, though. She's more good-looking."

Caleb choked down a swallow and glanced up from his iPad. "Have you been talking to my nephew?"

"What nephew?"

Right, Ivan didn't know Bentley. Never mind.

"Y'all, the mural is amazing," Mercy said with a satisfied sigh. "Well done, us. Lulu is a genius. What a talent. Her portrayal of Malachi Nickle pulling Prince Blue off the beach?" She pressed her hand to her chest. "I'm moved every time I go by there. And the image of Immanuel brings me to tears. I feel like He really *is* with us."

"Fine and dandy," Ivan said with a bit of a huff. "But is it going to bring tourism to our end of town? If'n folks have a mind to drive over here from the West End, all they got to do is head down Sea Blue Way, oooh and ahhh at the mural, then circle up Rachel Kirby Lane and head right back to Sodom."

"Sodom. Come on, Ivan," Duke said. "The West End is still *our* town, still Sea Blue Beach. Still part of Immanuel, God with us. If they're Sodom, we're Gomorrah."

"Quite right, Duke," Adele said, knitting needles clinking. "Such talk will further divide us. I'm one for all and all for one."

"Folks, meet Nickle High's head cheerleader, class of '72. Rah, rah, rah, sis-boom-bah." Ivan swung his arms about and kicked the air, which caused him to do something to his knee, making him jump up, moaning and groaning as he walked it off.

"Serves you right. Rah, rah, rah," Adele said as she soberly continued knitting. "Sis-boom-bah."

Caleb tried not to laugh, but he grinned wide enough. He didn't want to encourage the Laurel and Hardy of the Main Street set too much.

"The new Victorian lamps are going in this week," he said, "thanks to Mayor Caster and discretionary funds. I also found a company to make historical markers for Sea Blue Way, the prince's home, and Alderman's Pharmacy. These are unofficial with regard to the state, just ones we want for our town. Simon is working on the funds. He's also done some research and is working on plans to make Doyle's a craft beer brewery."

"That'll get the younger set coming our way," Ivan said, still tending his knee.

The door opened, and a gust of wind pushed Emery inside.

"Sorry I'm late, you guys."

"We know, you got lost." Ivan again.

"Actually, I didn't, thank you." She sat next to Caleb and stared at his near-empty plate. "What'd I miss?"

"Just Ivan hurting his knee," Adele said. "Sis-boom-bah."

"Never mind me." Ivan huffed and crossed his arms. "How about that paper of yours? Missing more ads?"

"Ivan, come on . . ." Duke didn't hide his frustration. "That's not fair. The paper had missing ads before she got here."

Ivan started pacing again and moaning over his knee. "Next agenda item. What are we going to do about fixing the street?"

"We may not have the budget for the bricks," Caleb said. "But we can move forward with planters and banners."

"We really need town money to work on some of the store-fronts," Duke said. "I took a walk past the old haberdashery and Lloyd's Hardware. They both need major renovations. The bait-and-tackle shop turned yarn shop has been empty for years. Marconi Jewelers, same thing, even though the vintage clothing shop tried to make a go of it."

"Are you still talking to West End leaders?" Caleb said.

"Simon and I played golf with Alfred Gallagher, Bobby Brockton, and Denise Fletcher last Saturday. Denise wants to build a big pier, like in Santa Monica, with a Ferris wheel and everything. She thinks the perfect location is the Sands Motor Motel lot."

"A Ferris wheel?" Emery tapped a note on her phone. "Caleb would love—" She turned to Duke. "Wait, what? Where the Sands is located? Why? It's a lovely historical motor motel."

Teach her to make fun of his Ferris wheel phobia. But she was right. The Sands must remain. What was wrong with those West Enders? He'd never even heard of Denise Fletcher. Duke said she owned a lucrative, boutique software company.

"I met my dear departed wife at the Sands Motor Motel," Ivan said. "She was working as a maid one summer, down from Dothan. Besides, we got the Starlight. We don't need no honking, ugly Ferris wheel like Santa Monica. The Starlight is the gem of this whole shoreline."

"True, but how do we get people over here? How do we fix what's falling apart?" Mercy said. "I was looking into how we can advertise online and in larger metropolitan newspapers for small businesses to come to our side of town. Independent bookstores are starting to take hold. Even specialty shops, like Christmas decor, do well all year round. Pet daycares are popular now. Which would be lovely for those on vacation with a pet but want to take a day out to Crab Island or go out deep-sea fishing."

"Adele, see what Mercy just done?" Ivan leaned over her shoulder. "She's bringing good ideas. You're just knitting and clicking."

"Insults come from the small and insecure. Keep it up, Ivan, and I'll carry you home in my pocket."

Caleb laughed. He couldn't help it. Adele had Ivan's number. "Mercy," he said, "you should be leading this project. Let's talk later. Emery, a story in the *Gazette* about setting a business here might spark some ideas."

"Done," she said. "Mercy, can you stop by the paper tomorrow? I'll help write up ads for the *Tallahassee Democrat* and the *Pensacola News Journal.* What about the *Montgomery Advertiser?*"

"Go for it," Caleb said. "Simon will pay."

"It'd still be nice to have something really big to draw attention to the East End," Duke said. "No offense, Mercy, and all of us to what we're doing, but I feel like we're trying to put out a roaring fire with a garden hose. What we're battling is the energy and momentum of the West End leaders."

Duke dropped a weight of truth into the proceedings. Caleb thought to balance it with some levity, but he had nothing.

Then Adele spoke up. "You know our town lore," she said, setting her knitting in her lap. "If you look *really* close, you might see Immanuel walking among the streetlamps, between the shops and houses, among us. Now I ask you, ladies and gentlemen, *what* is bigger than God? Let the West End bring their roaring fire. We'll see what God can do."

"You want to invite God to our town," Ivan said with a sneer. "That's your plan?"

"No, goofball, He's already here. Caleb, does Ivan have to be on this committee?"

"Now, now, Adele, what would Immanuel say?" Ivan said.

"Oh, great day in the morning, now he's turning all religious on me. Have you no shame?" Adele had taken up her knitting again. "What about a street party to start things off?"

"We'd need the shops to cooperate," Emery said. "But I think they will. Should we meet with them? Set a date?"

Duke promised to keep working on his West End colleagues. Caleb gave an update on Alderman's and offered hope from Jenny Finch.

"She's interested in the Org. Homestead. Maybe if she invests, we could finish one or two of the houses to show everyone the possibilities."

"Sis-boom-bah, let's eat some cake." Ivan limped toward the desserts. "Mercy, did you bring your double chocolate delight?"

Caleb had just taken a bite of cake when the museum door opened. Mac Diamond walked in, bold as you please. "Sorry I'm late." He tossed his smarmy smile about the room, shook hands with Duke, and praised the food table.

"We don't need your kind here," Ivan said around a mouthful of double chocolate.

"My kind? I'm a loyal Sea Bluean, here to join this Main Street initiative."

"I thought you wanted this side of town bulldozed," Caleb said. "Or do you prefer to break away, make the West End its own municipality?"

"I've had a change of heart. Miss Adele, is this your chicken casserole?"

"Help yourself. It's one of my best recipes."

Mac helped himself all right—to the food, to the people in the room. He sat next to Mercy and started talking about revenue sources for the East End.

"I've had everyday folks like yourselves invest in my golf courses and let me tell you, the return is quite generous. Within two years of completion."

Adele and Mercy leaned toward him with wide eyes. Even Ivan stopped pacing, and chewing, to listen.

"Mac don't bring your propaganda in here," Caleb said. "We're talking about revitalization of the East End. You got any ideas?"

"A nine-hole golf course would do wonders." The man was a broken record. "Caleb, I got my eye on you for the clubhouse."

Caleb steeled himself from being Mr. Pottered. But what a sweet gig for his résumé.

"We're restoring those houses," Caleb blurted, in defense of the Org. Homestead. In defense of himself. "So find another place for your golf course and clubhouse."

For the next forty minutes, he tried to adjourn the meeting, but Mac charmed the room with his stories and supersized laughter. When Caleb finally shut off the lights and locked the museum door, even Emery spent a few minutes talking with Mac, saying good night.

When she joined him on the corner, Caleb huffed. "He's trying to buy the Main Street initiative. What was it he said? 'The return is quite generous.' Define *generous*. A dime on the dollar?" He started toward Sea Blue Way as a soft, misty rain swirled around them.

"He's a man used to getting his way, Caleb. He's wooing you," Emery said softly as she hurried alongside him.

"I resisted him this time. But, uh, from what I could tell, Em, he Mr. Pottered you. 'How's the *Gazette* going, Emery? Did you enjoy the Beach Boys concert? My golf course could be your largest advertiser.' You were his Mary Bailey."

"Excuse me, I was not wooed by him. I've interviewed hundreds of Mac Diamonds in my day. The trick is to let them think they are wooing you, then you put the truth in print. Trust me, eventually they get their due. Mary Bailey, my eye. Ha."

"Okay, fine. I just wish he could be a stand-up guy and help us restore the East End."

"Why can't you understand Mac Diamond's agenda is Mac Diamond? However, I do recall someone asking me to dinner before or *after* the Main Street meeting, but since he consumed a large pile of chicken casserole—"

Caleb stopped short. "Em, whoa, I forgot." He reached for

her hand. "I was demoing the pharmacy and lost track of time. Why didn't you text me?"

"Don't apologize." She dusted his work shirt. "I like this look. Rugged construction guy. Very blue-collar sexy."

Caleb slipped his arms around her waist. "Are you trying to make me fall in love with you, Quinn?"

"Now why would I want to do that, Ransom?"

The dampness of the cool rain that doused his ire over Diamond, along with the soft, hazy glow of the Victorian lampstands refracting through the mist and surrounding Emery that roused his feelings for her.

"If I say I've missed you, will you call me a liar?"

"Have you? Missed me?"

"I didn't know until just now. But yes, very much."

She lowered her gaze. "Are you trying to make me fall in love with you?"

"Maybe." He didn't know what he was saying, really, or doing, only that every instinct shouted *don't let her go.*

"We're not sixteen, Caleb."

"I know," he said, holding her closer, tipping up her chin to see her eyes. "But I'd like to find out who we are now."

The elements of the night were in her eyes. "I'm scared," she said so softly he barely heard.

"Of what? Me?" he said, sensing an unseen boundary.

"Of losing someone I love." She stepped out of his arms. "I-I can't do it, Caleb. I can't. It seems to me all good things end. Dad and me, the dynamic duo. My job at the *Free Voice.* I've never said this out loud, but I feel so . . ." She glanced toward the dark shore. "Fragile."

"Shhh, it's all right." He brought her close again, and she rested her head against his chest. In the same place she fit sixteen years ago. In the place she fit now.

The winter air chilled the mist as it continued to swirl around them, and Emery shivered.

"Come on." Caleb gently steered her across the street. "I'll buy you dinner."

The atmosphere of the Blue Plate Diner was welcoming, warm, and cozy, like walking into your grandma's living room. At nine o'clock, the place was quiet, with a few late-nighters eating the last of the day's special or claiming the final slice from one of Paige's pies. Standards from the forties and fifties played from the speakers.

Stars shining bright above you . . . Dream a little dream of me . . .

They sat in the booth in the back, the same one where Caleb stuck Emery with the bill. Life had a way of coming around in big and little circles. They ordered hot chocolates, and Emery, the grilled chicken plate. Small talk ensued, probably because it was safe, recapping the Main Street meeting and speculating about Mac Diamond's motivations.

When the server set down Emery's dinner, Caleb said, "Em, what you said tonight . . . about things ending. I never told you about the night I was supposed to meet you. The night your family left Sea Blue Beach."

She glanced at him over the rim of her mug. "Caleb, it was a long time ago. Things happen."

"I was on my way, I promise. When you texted you needed me, I was already on my way to—"

"Find Cassidy?"

"Yeah, the story of *that* summer. Besides you." He shoved his empty mug aside and leaned over the table. "I wanted to be there, believe me, especially if I'd known . . ."

234

19

CALEB

Then . . .

"Caleb, can you work the evening session?" Mr. Caster caught him on break in the concession area. "Brandon called in sick again. I'm going to have to let him go."

"Yeah, sure."

Mr. Caster patted his shoulder. "One day maybe you'll run this place."

Caleb doubted it. College couldn't come soon enough for him. Last night, Cassidy had announced she was *not* going to college and, in fact, was dropping out of high school.

"Not finish your senior year? Not graduate?" Mom looked like a cartoon character whose eyes and teeth bugged out of its head.

"You heard me." Cassidy slammed out of house. Never came back.

Caleb hid in his room, blasting Dave Matthews Band, wishing he'd stayed with guitar lessons, but football was more fun.

As the lights of the rink came up, indicating the end of the early evening session, Caleb wolfed down the last of his sandwich and drained a bottle of whole milk.

In the boot room, he organized and disinfected the used skates, checking the wheels and trucks for safety.

He volunteered for the ticket booth at the start of the next session, half hoping to see Emery. Since the night her father sent him home, he'd not seen or heard from her. He'd texted and called, but no response. Until tonight.

Emery:
Meet me at the palm tree stand?

Caleb:
Working until 10.

Emery:
See you then.

Caleb:
You okay? Where you been? Come by the rink.

Emery:
Can't. Stuff going on.

Caleb:
Like?

But she never answered.

The late session crowd was light. Thursdays usually were, so Caleb eased around the rink as floor guard, ignoring the flirtations of the girls stumbling past him. What did Emery mean about stuff going on? Was it her parents? Mr. Quinn seemed serious when he asked for a family-only dinner.

A little after nine, he looked up to see Dad by the boot room, waving him over. He looked drawn and sad, like he'd not slept in weeks. As Caleb skated over, Mom walked in, looking even more ragged than Dad.

"Do you know where your sister could possibly be?"

"Nope. I'm not covering for her, if that's your next question."

"Aren't you?" Mom said in a whisper.

"No, why would I?"

"Because she's your sister."

"Got news for you, Mom, the girl living in our house is not my sister." A kid stumbled next to him, and Caleb reached out to help him up. "Look, she's announced her plans to quit school, so let her go. Good riddance."

"Caleb Ransom." Mom snatched his arm. "We have to talk to her. This is serious. We can't just let her go. Wander off to God knows where, get into God knows what kind of trouble? All kinds of horrible things are happening to young women these days." Mom sobbed into her hand. "If anything happens to her . . ."

"Caleb," Dad said, patting him on the shoulder, "if you see her, tell her we just want to talk." His phone rang from his pocket. "Ransom," he answered. "Chief Kelly, yes, thanks for calling."

Mom waved good-bye and blew him a kiss as she followed Dad out of the Starlight.

So now they've involved the police. Cass had been gone a day and a half. Caleb guessed that'd be enough to worry a parent.

In the sound booth, he hopped on the internet and checked her Facebook wall. But she'd not posted anything since prom. Which he found interesting. He snooped her best friend Allison's account. She had plenty of pictures from the summer—Allison smiling at the camera, tucked between her friends, having a blast. In the background of one picture was the Driftwood Door, a Shalimar dive for airmen and local fishermen.

Caleb scoured the images for a glimpse of Cassidy, but she wasn't in any of them. Weird. Very weird.

Next, he called Jumbo, asked if his sister had spotted Cass in the wild. No luck there.

Back on the floor, Caleb tried to imagine where his sister

might hide out. As crazy as she was right now, he knew her. She was a bit of a chicken at heart. Hated being alone. Didn't like the dark. She might run, but no farther than Fort Walton to the west or Panama City to the east.

Thirty minutes before the end of the session, Caleb asked Mr. Caster if he could leave early. "There's only a dozen skaters left," he said. "I need to run an errand for my parents."

"Go on, I'll close up. Thanks for staying."

Out in his truck, he considered his plan. Mostly that he didn't have one. His gut told him if Allison had been frequenting the Driftwood Door, so had Cassidy.

In the fifteen-minute drive, he rehearsed some sort of "You got to stop this, Cass" speech in case he found her. If not, he'd deliver it to Allison if she was there. Neither one was old enough to be out drinking. Did they have fake IDs?

His phone chimed from the passenger seat with a couple of texts. At the next traffic light, he reached for his phone. He had one from Shift about upcoming football two-a-days and one from Emery.

Emery:
Could you come early, please? I need you.

> **Caleb:**
> Em, you're scaring me. What's wrong?

Emery:
Everything.

> **Caleb:**
> Had to run an errand. Meet you at the stand of
> palms ASAP.

The light turned green, and he hit the gas, the Driftwood Door on his mind, but his heart pounded with the words, *Turn around. Go see her. She needs you.*

He was only two minutes from the bar. He could see the lights of the sign. Two minutes there, five minutes to talk to Cassidy, and fifteen minutes home, calling Mom and Dad on the way to let them know she was alive and well—if he found her —then off to see Emery.

In the parking lot, he squeezed his little S-10 between two monster trucks and headed inside. At the door, an oversized tattooed bouncer grabbed him by the collar.

"ID."

"I need to see if my sister is here." Caleb held up his license to the man's flashlight.

"Who's your sister?"

"Cassidy Ransom. Blond. Blue eyes. Probably wearing too few clothes."

The man grinned. "Cassidy is your sister? She's hot. And spunky."

"Dude, she's my sister."

"What do you want with her?"

"Dude, she's my sister."

Bouncer stared at him a second, then pointed inside. "You've got five minutes, then I'm tossing you out."

Perfect. He found Cassidy dressed in a black tank and cut-off jean shorts, with an apron around her middle, carrying a tray of beer to a table of flyboys. She worked here?

As she set down their longnecks, she flirted with each one, leaning into the tallest of them until he went for kiss. Then she backed away, flirt-laughing.

When she headed to the bar, Caleb stepped into her view. Startled, she dropped her tray and hissed, "What are you doing here?"

"I think the question is, what are you doing here? You're not old enough to serve drinks."

"Will you be quiet?" She jerked on his arm, and the bartender came to see if everything was all right. "Dante, this is . . . my cousin. Fred."

Dante gave Caleb the once-over, grunted, and walked off.

"Fred? Your cousin?"

"You're embarrassing me." Something in the bar caught her attention. Caleb turned to see a couple of West End football coaches sauntering in—Sanchez and Martindale.

"Figures West End coaches would hang out at a dive like this," Caleb scoffed. "Spill drinks on them. They're the enemy."

"They're not my enemy, and they're good tippers."

"Even though they know you're a Nickle High girl?"

"Oh grow up. They're men, not boys. By the way, everyone knows it was a bunch of Nickle Eagles who trashed the Panthers' field."

Caleb caught her arm. "Don't say a word."

"Why shouldn't I? Were you there? Oh my gosh, you were. Ha! Wait until I—"

"Cass, come on."

"Fine. I'll keep your secret if you keep mine. Don't tell Mom and Dad I'm here."

"Why shouldn't I?"

She turned back to the bar. "Dante, let me take five." Cassidy leaned toward another curvy server with a sleeve of tattoos. "Posey? I'll be right back. Save the coaches' table for me." She shoved Caleb through the kitchen's double doors, then out the back, down a rickety ramp, and across the road to the marina. "Who told you I was here? Allison? She's such a—"

"I figured it out on my own. Mom and Dad are worried. They called the police. I just wanted to know you're all right."

"Well?" She held her arms out to her side, standing stiff as a board in the amber streetlight. "What do you think? I'm fine. More than fine. And could you please tell Mom and Dad to stop asking people about me? Allison said they've stopped by her house three times, and Dad called Dave twice." Dave was Shift's older brother. Cassidy went to prom with him.

"You don't get it, do you? They're *worried* about you. What is going on with you?"

"Tell them I'm fine, but don't tell them where I am. Say I texted you or something. And you keep your mouth shut about this place and I'll keep mine shut about the Panther field." They were locked in a Ransom steely stare until Cassidy broke it with a softening exhale. "Look, I know it's been weird, and I honestly don't mean to pop off like I do, but, Caleb, I have my reasons for what I'm doing. I'm ready to be on my own. I don't need high school. I don't need curfew. Can't I just discover the world—my world—on my own? I'll be eighteen in four months, a bona fide adult."

"I don't think one birthday makes you a bona fide adult." He wanted to hug her, tell her he loved her, to come home and be her old self. He wanted her to finish school, then decide her life.

She folded her arms and stared toward the water. "Please, don't tell them I work here, Caleb. If they find out, they'll get this whole place in trouble. I can't do that to them. I have a fake ID." She made a face. "Which Dante helped me get."

"They couldn't find a qualified person over twenty-one to work here?"

"They wanted to hire me, okay? I work hard. I'm good at my job."

"The West End coaches know you're not old enough to be here."

"Only Sanchez, and he's keeping my secret."

"Where are you staying when you're not home?"

"Posey has a cute apartment by the water."

Caleb's phone pinged with a text. Probably Emery. He pulled

it out to check, but Cassidy snatched his phone before he could see the screen, and without hesitation, hurled it toward the water. "Just when I was starting to trust you."

"Cassidy, you dimwit!" Caleb ran to the water's edge, but his phone was fish food. "Why'd you do that?"

"You were going to take my picture."

"I had a text. Probably Emery." He stood on the edge of the dock, looking into the dark water. "Guess our deal is off then. I'm telling Mom and Dad where to find you."

"Caleb, you promised."

"You threw my phone in the water."

The back door creaked open, and a couple of airmen emerged. "Cass, is he bothering you?"

"Um, no." Cassidy glanced at them, then at Caleb, her sly smile evident in the dim light. "But hey, fellas, why don't you take him for a joyride?"

Joyride? What is a—

Next thing Caleb knew, he was upside down and thrown into the back of a truck, held down by two airmen and driven to who knows where.

After what seemed like an eternity, the driver pulled over. The two brutes in the back dumped Caleb outside the entrance of Eglin Air Force Base and wished him a good night.

EMERY

Now . . .

"They just dropped you off in the middle of nowhere?" She'd leaned into Caleb's story from the moment he started talking.

Around them, the Blue Plate staff wiped tables and swept the floor. Paige brought out two pieces of cherry pie à la mode. "I don't want to throw them out."

Caleb dug in, forgetting he'd already had chocolate cake. This story made him hungry.

"I was disoriented. I'd never driven out there before. I started jogging down the road, away from the base. Didn't know which way was home. Then it started raining. I got lost. All I kept repeating in my mind was *Emery thinks I'm blowing her off.*' At the first convenience store, the guy behind the counter pointed me in the right direction. I didn't even think to ask to borrow his phone—not that I remembered your number anyway. It was six miles back to the Driftwood. Once I got to my truck, I beelined to the Sands and knocked on your window. When you didn't answer, I went around front, saw the windows were dark and your car was gone. I was exhausted, mad, sad . . . I sank down into one of the chairs by the firepit and apparently fell asleep, because the next thing I knew, Delilah was shaking me awake, telling me you'd gone, and I should get home. Why'd you leave so early? In the dead of night?"

"The night you helped Dad carry in a platter of burgers was the night they told me Mom was dying. She gave me the Force family pearls because she'd not be there on my wedding day."

"So that's why you never answered my texts or calls? I thought you were mad at me."

"I was mad at the world. Mom, Dad, and I had a million conversations in the following days. I cried so much I was probably dehydrated. I hated Cottage 7. I hated the Sands. I hated Sea Blue Beach. And for a moment, I hated you, because I'd spent most of my summer with you and not Mom. Then I realized I had to talk to you."

Emery picked at last of her pie. "I couldn't sleep, so I'd be up all night, refusing to believe Mom was dying. When Dad showed me the scans and data, it all sunk in, and I didn't want to leave her side. I curled on the settee with her for twenty-four hours straight. She told me stories of her childhood, of her college and early career days, what she learned along the way, what she thought were the important things in life. I wish I'd recorded those conversations. Dad, sweet Dad, brought us food and drinks, even read to us. Looking back, I can see that's when Mom let go of the facade and started to deteriorate. Two nights later, she said she wanted to go home. Dad responded with, 'Pack up, we're leaving.' Mom went for a walk with Delilah, and I texted you."

"Emery, I'm so sorry."

"It's okay, Caleb. I didn't know how to text, 'We're leaving and Mom's dying.' I sat in the palm tree stand crying, waiting . . . scared. The entire summer felt like a fraud. We didn't have this extended family vacation to make memories, to find *our* vacation place to come back to every few years. No, it was to say good-bye to Mom."

"When I got your text, the Driftwood Door was right in front of me. I figured I'd run in, find Cass, then head to you."

"I cried the first hour we were on the road, texting you over and over. I didn't understand why you didn't answer. I finally fell asleep, waking up when Dad pulled into a Marriott about dawn. At first I thought, *'What a horrible dream,'* then I saw Dad helping Mom out of the car." Emery shoved her plate aside and took a long drink of water. "I saw how frail she was, and there was no going back. While Mom slept, I wandered around some Tennessee town, crying off and on, trying to call you. I don't think Dad slept much at all, just drank gallons of coffee to get us home."

"I'm sorry, Emery. Sorry I wasn't there." He reached for her hands, his sincerity reflecting in his eyes.

"It's okay. I look back at the order of events and wonder if it just wasn't meant for us to have that final night, for me to cry on your shoulder." She laughed softly. "I had this idea we'd run away together." She dabbed the tears under her eyes. "I just wanted to be anywhere but in my life."

"I'd have been tempted, Em. But after confronting Cass at the bar, I swore to myself I'd never hurt my parents."

"So there is a silver lining to our clouds," Emery said. "Once we got back to Cleveland, I put Sea Blue Beach out of my mind. I was going to quit basketball, but Mom refused to hear it. If I wasn't in class or on the court, I was with her. By the end, she had a hospice bed in the living room facing the front window. She loved the fall leaves."

He reached again for her hand. "You loved her well, Emery"

"I tried. She liked you, by the way," Emery said. "So, what's the rest of your story? What happened when you got home? Did you tell your parents about the Driftwood?"

"When I got home, two police cruisers were in the street. Mom had tried to call me, but the fish weren't answering and she freaked. I didn't tell them where Cassidy was, only that she was okay and wanted to be left alone. The next few days were rough, but we found a new normal. Through other sources, probably the West End coaches, my parents found out she was at the Driftwood Door. By the time they went to see her, she was gone."

"Gone, gone?"

"Gone, gone. For about a year. But to give her credit, she occasionally texted. She showed up six months before I graduated, then left again. The next time she came home, I was a sophomore at Cornell, and she was very pregnant with Bentley." Caleb reached for the check, then left two twenties on the table. "It's been a roller coaster ride ever since."

"Roller coaster? Sure you don't you mean a Ferris wheel?"

Emery leaned against him as they walked out the deck door, into the mist settling on the beach.

He laughed. "I'm never living that down, am I?"

"I'm bringing it up at your funeral. 'Caleb is now riding the big Ferris wheel in the sky . . .'"

"You'll be at my funeral?"

"Sure, but many, many years from now."

Arms linked, they headed down the Beachwalk, through hazy amber light cloaked in mist. She loved the feel of Caleb's strong arm under her hand. She loved the sound of their even foot crunch on the sandy concrete.

Maybe being here meant the past did not have to shade her forever. Maybe the mist of time would wash away the sadness and leave behind the good.

Caleb gazed down at Emery, and the look in his eyes was more than friendship. "What do you think your mom would say about you living in Sea Blue Beach sixteen years later?"

Emery raised her face to the misty rain. "She'd be happy, I think."

"And what about me?"

"You? She'd be glad you were in Sea Blue Beach too." Emery wiped the dew dripping from the ends of his floppy hair.

She'd deflected his question with her answer, but it felt too soon, too intimate, to confess Mom would be thrilled that Emery was falling in love with Caleb Ransom once again.

20

CALEB

On Friday afternoon, Caleb attended a Valparaiso Middle School assembly, where Bentley won a prize for math.

After posing for pictures, Caleb shot off a text to Cassidy, while Bentley celebrated with his growing crowd of friends. In the last six weeks, his confidence had skyrocketed. He laughed more easily. He'd also gained another five pounds.

> **Caleb:**
> Bentley won a math award.
>
> Cassidy: . . .

After school, Caleb asked Bent if he wanted to FaceTime his mom.

"Nope," he said as he set the award on his desk. "Can I go skating?"

"Sure, but come straight home after. Maybe we can watch a movie." Caleb handed him a twenty for skate rentals and a trip to concession. "Hey, I'm proud of you. So are Grandma and Grandpa."

"I know." Bentley dashed down the stairs and out of the house.

Caleb, Mom, and Dad weren't the ones who mattered most. His mom mattered most.

You're losing him, Cass.

Downstairs, past his unpacked boxes, he browsed the pantry, then the fridge for dinner options. He should make a grocery list and head to Biggs, stock up for next week.

Kicking out the kitchen table chair to sit, he texted Emery a picture of a beaming Bentley accepting his award. She answered immediately.

Emery:
Way to go Bentley!!!!!!! I'm taking him
for ice cream.

Caleb:
Can his uncle tag along?

Emery:
Maybe. ;P

Last night, listening to each other's stories, sharing heart-to-heart at the Blue Plate, then walking home on a cold, misty night through the muted light . . . he knew he was falling for her. Flat-out. Even a nob like him could see the romance of it all.

In the meantime, he had some work to do. The Swansons called, wanted to move forward with their Lake Lorraine house. Again. Those Yankees from Minnesota, the Østers, who ghosted him about a home at Preserve on the Bay, also called, apologizing, saying they were ready to get started on their design. The husband deposited a large retainer in Caleb's account.

Caleb thought he'd drive over to the Preserve on Monday for inspiration, talk to a few contractors.

Simon had also paid for the Doyle transformation—from

mechanic's garage to hip craft beer brewery. Caleb had worked on a similar project in Seattle, so he felt confident knocking out the initial design by the end of the week.

What about the Org. Homestead? Simon continued to work things from his mayoral office. Caleb had half a mind to email Jenny Finch, see if she was serious about investing.

Finished with his bowl of cereal, Caleb headed to his office and caught up on email. He had several from Mercy about the street party idea and how to bring in new business.

> Current businesses are up for a street party. We'll put high-top spool tables down the center of Sea Blue Way for folks to use after they've gone into a place for food and drink. The Vine & Barrel will do a wine and cheese tasting. The band that plays weekends at the Fish Hook (can't remember their name) will play in front of Doyle's. Let's think of ways to keep the crowd circulating. More details at our next meeting.

Nicely done, Mercy. She'd put her experience as a former high school principal to work.

He also had a surprising email from Bobby Brockton, inviting him to speak at the Chamber of Commerce luncheon Sunday. *"I know it's last minute, but our speaker dropped out. We'd love to hear your experience in Seattle."*

The speaker dropped out? Sure he did. This was more of Mac Diamond Mr. Pottering people. But Caleb liked a challenge and accepted the invitation. He'd use the opportunity to address East End issues and maybe touch on Sea Blue Beach politics. The luncheon was at the West End's fine dining restaurant, the Skylight, a beautiful structure with part of the dining room extending over the water.

Caleb returned to the kitchen for more cereal, dumping in

a handful of blueberries to negate the bad carbs and bad sugar, then headed back to his desk to see Mac Diamond had slid into his inbox.

Caleb,
Diamond Dogs Inc. is in talks with a developer in West Palm. We'd love to bring you on board as our in-house architect. Your reclaimed and sustainable materials design is striking a chord with people.
Having you on board will enhance our projects and productivity. You'd be free, of course, to pursue Ransom Architecture jobs as well. Diamond Dogs is open to salary negotiations to suit your skill and experience.

Best,
Mac

Caleb shoved away from his desk. Really? *Really?* What a manipulative, brazen move.

Even worse, Caleb *wanted* to consider it. It was an amazing offer. It'd set him up for the next ten-plus years of his career. Ransom Architecture would become a name.

But it was from Mac Diamond, who had an agenda to destroy the part of the town Caleb loved.

EMERY

The Sunday *Gazette* printed with every ad in place. Such a relief. She'd barely slept last night, waking up every hour, ready to run to the office alongside the paperboys.

She hugged Owen when she saw today's beautiful, perfect edition. Too wired to go back to her cottage at the Sands, she popped into One More Cup for a latte and a hot cinnamon scone, then pored over the paper.

The headline was still the Main Street initiatives. Jane wrote a piece on tourism numbers if the East End added businesses. Rex's new piece on young golfers naming Sea Blue Beach's West End as their training home would probably add fuel to Mac Diamond's case against the Org. Homestead. But there was nothing to do about it. The *Gazette* belonged to the town and the truth.

For this edition, Emery published an article from the archives. In 1939, Earl and Inez Van Horn and Heddy Stenuf, famous roller skaters, put on a show at the Starlight. That same year, members of the Dixie Mafia vacationed at the Sands Motor Motel for a week.

"I think you're doing a good thing." Lupe, One More Cup's owner, set another latte in front of her. "On the house."

"Do you really think this little paper is making a difference?"

"I do. Even with missing ads." She sat across from Emery. "My grandparents came to Sea Blue Beach from Mexico in the late fifties. They started a trucking business and never looked back. They're gone now, and my parents moved to New Orleans for my dad's career. I came back as soon as I could. Met my husband here."

"Sea Blue Beach is a romantic town, isn't it?"

Lupe sighed with contentment. "How could it not be? Immanuel lives here."

"Immanuel," Emery repeated softly. "God with us, right?" She'd never experienced any sort of God or supernatural moment, but as a journalist, she'd learned to listen as much as to question. What were people saying between the words?

Lupe went back to work, and Emery made a note to get her family's story for the paper, then headed back to the *Gazette* office before Lupe offered her another latte. It was very generous, but after two rounds, Emery was wired.

At her desk, she made a list of things for the coming week. *Ramp up online presence. Talk to Elliot (again) about an ad director. Create a student section (???) from high school/middle school. Story on Org. Homestead. Pics of Alderman's refurbishments and reinvention of Doyle's.*

She glanced at her phone when it pinged. Ava had texted the QuinnFam.

Ava:
Wish you were here for the shower, Em. But I
understand.

Elianna:
I'll send pictures of everything, especially when
she opens your present.

Emery:
I know it will be a lovely day, Ava. Thanks, Ellie.

She'd barely remembered to send a gift. Dad reminded her late last week, sending a link to Ava's registry. She bought three since she didn't have the expense of an airline ticket.

Blakely:
Em, can I come for spring break?

Joanna:
Blake, by yourself? What happened to Mad
River Mountain with Sadie's family?

Blakely:
The usual drama. Sadie and Lucy had a fight,
and Lucy said she wasn't going, which means
Joely won't go. I'd rather go to the beach!

Emery:
Sure, Blake. If skiing doesn't work out.

She read the text thread again, kind of wishing she'd made time to go to the shower. Rex could've handled things at the *Gazette*. After Ava's visit, being a part of the Quinn sisterhood was beginning to matter.

She felt lighter and brighter about things after telling Caleb the rest of the story and closing the gap on their shared past.

Joanna:
Miss you, Em. Xo.

Emery:
Miss you all too.

Dad:
I like this spring break idea. Maybe we'll all go.

The flurry of texts following proved that the Quinn family was much too busy for a spontaneous vacation. Sophisticated Sips had a full calendar through the spring, never mind all the wedding planning.

Dad:
Okay, I give. Maybe in the fall.

Setting down her phone, Emery gazed out the window, full of thought and sentiment. Maybe this Quinn family venture was more beautiful than she'd allowed.

The rest of the day was too beautiful to stay inside. She texted Caleb to see if he wanted to ride bikes, then headed out, running into Tobias as he came in to clean. In his mid-fifties, he was stout and jolly, with a fisherman's tan.

"You're here on a Sunday?" she said.

"The fish were running yesterday. Had to take the boat out. I'm going to give the floors a good buffing." He was always buffing that floor. "You have to take care of terrazzo. But, Miss Emery, I got to tell you, if I run the sweeper over the newsroom carpet much more, the thing will shred completely."

"Be gentle with her." Emery patted his arm. "And next time, bring me some fish."

"Will do, Miss Em. Rats, I wish I'd known you liked seafood."

She'd just arrived at the Sands when her phone rang. Expecting to see Caleb's number, she stopped in the shade of Cottage 7 to see *Unknown* on the screen.

To answer or not to answer . . . that was always the question. She answered.

"Emery Quinn?" The masculine voice was elegant, bent with an aristocratic accent.

"Speaking." She shivered as if something grand was happening.

"This is Sted from the House of Blue Chamber Office. The royal family is delighted to accept your invitation to visit Sea Blue Beach. His Royal Highness Crown Prince John and Her Royal Highness Princess Gemma are available Friday evening, April twenty-fifth, and Saturday, the twenty-sixth, until four p.m. Will that work for you?"

Okay, this was a grand prank. "Rex, come on, is this you?" Emery made a face at her reflection in the dark window of her cottage.

"Pardon me? Hello? Miss Emery Quinn?"

"Speaking."

"Did you hear what I said?"

"I did. His Royal Highness Crown Prince John and Her Royal Highness Princess Gemma were available to visit Sea Blue Beach." She gazed around to ensure she was alone and not being punked. Never mind that she'd told no one about her royal request.

"Indeed I did. Were you serious about a royal visit to Sea Blue Beach? If not, I'll—"

"Yes, yes, I'm serious. You received my email? You're really calling from the House of Blue Chamber Office?"

"Yes, ma'am. April twenty-fifth and twenty-sixth are open on their royal highnesses' diary. If you confirm, we'll commence with the details. For security reasons, I'm texting you a code with instructions for a private email server."

Her email. It worked. "Thank you, thank you so much. Please thank the royal family."

"Excellent. Look for more information this afternoon. I'd like a call this Wednesday at ten a.m. Eastern Standard Time to begin preparations. We don't have much time to get it all organized. Does that work for you?"

"Yes, yes, of course." She was shaking, listening, memorizing everything the man said. "Wednesday at ten." When she hung up, she stood there, stunned and . . . more stunned.

The royal family was coming to Sea Blue Beach. This would change everything.

21

CALEB

His speech to the Chamber of Commerce was short and sweet. He'd gone to the dais with the never-ending ocean view behind him. The moment he began to speak, his phone, which he'd left in his jacket's breast pocket, began to vibrate.

He ignored the first set of buzzes, but the second, third, and fourth were distracting. What was going on? He stumbled over a couple of words. Lost his place. Then glanced at Dad and Mom in the front row to see if they were checking their phones.

Bentley was skating with the Feinbergs. So the vibrating probably wasn't about him. It probably wasn't Cassidy. She'd ring their folks in a true emergency. She'd done so once before. Was it Emery?

Across the room, every eye was on him, waiting, appearing impatient by the hesitations of their speaker. The few dozen on their phone did not look alarmed.

His phone went off again, but he ignored it and powered through, delivering his speech without conviction.

"What I learned in Seattle is simple: Trust and respect are paramount to every relationship, to business, to government.

This Chamber has supported business growth and recovery for years. It's time we focus on the East End. Opportunities abound for those who want to open a retail space. Take a chance. There are tax breaks and grants for start-ups. Attracting tourism to the East End is attracting tourism for us all. Which leads me to the biggest chore before us: unifying the East and West Ends. Sea Blue Beach deserves better. How did a simple rivalry between football teams grow into a—"

"We know it was you Nickle High boys who trashed our football field." The voice came from the back of the room. Caleb kept his head down and continued talking.

"You trashed our beach first." That was Shift, who'd come to support Caleb.

"With a few plastic bottles and ice cream wrappers. You dumped garbage on our field."

"I never forgot that smell." Another voice from the crowd.

From the corner of his eye, Caleb saw Mac move as if he were about to stand, take charge, be the man.

"You're right," Caleb said. "Simple high school pranks got out of hand, and somehow between now and then, the growth of the West End and a football rivalry divided us. We're us and them. The haves and have-nots. The old and the new. Our history is a royal prince and a freed slave working together to build our town. Who are we to tear it apart? Do we really want the West End to break off into their own municipality?" Low, rumbling voices rose from every table. "What will your history be then? That you used to be a town with royal and freedom roots, but now you're just about hotels, restaurants, tourist spots, and—" He glanced at Mac. "Golf courses?"

"The East End is dead weight," a voice called out.

"Stop shouting from behind one another." Caleb stepped to the side of the podium. Healing might as well start now. "Stand up if you have something to say." From his chair, Simon nodded, approving. Dad sat up a bit taller. "Look, I don't mean to preach here, but we need something, *someone* to bring us together. Sea Blue Beach deserves better."

"Caleb! Caleb." Emery burst through the doors, breathless and flushed, hair wild about her shoulders. "The hostess said you were—" She stopped. Froze, really, and glanced around the room. "Um, Emery Quinn," she said with a deep resonance. "From the *Sea Blue Beach Gazette*. Am I late?"

Nice save, Quinn.

"You're just in time," Caleb said.

He closed out his speech with a couple of platitudes he found on the internet and handed the room over to the Commerce president, Yolanda Vargas, and beelined for Emery.

"I'm so sorry," she whispered as they walked out of the Skylight toward the large dock over the water. "The hostess said the meeting was over. To go on in."

He pulled out his phone. All the calls and texts were from Emery. "What's going on? Why were you blowing up my phone?"

EMERY

Now that she was here, looking at Caleb face-to-face, she couldn't just blurt out the news. Not with Chamber members and Skylight patrons milling around, wine glasses in hand, walking on the deck as if walking on water.

She'd drawn attention to herself by barging into the banquet room, yelling for Caleb like she had no sense, awakening curiosities. She caught a few glances, smiled at his parents, their interest undisguised.

No, this news was too big to drop as casually as if she'd discovered a new muffin flavor at Sweet Conversations.

"Let's meet at your place. Wait, now that I think about it, I should tell Simon too." Emery paced along the dock's railing. "But just Simon."

"You drove all the way here and burst into the room just to say you want to tell me *later*?"

"I lost my head for a bit. However, I've found it now. It's best if we talk in private." She squinted through the shadowed glass wall of the banquet room. A handful of people were watching them, talking together. "Text Simon. Tell him we'll be at his place after dark."

"After dark. Got it. Should we dress in black? Wear ski masks?"

"Hey, that's not a bad idea, Ransom." She patted his chest. "I'm starved. Is the food any good here?"

"At fifty bucks a plate, it better be. Come on, let's go grab something from a food truck and pretend you don't have this big secret to tell. Am I going to like it?"

"You're going to like it. I think. Yes, you will. Oh man, I hope so. If not, I'm in trouble."

Thirty minutes later, they sat on a Beachwalk bench with sandwiches and soda, *not* talking about Emery's big news. The sun was high, warming the afternoon, and several spring breakers tossed a Frisbee on the beach.

Two bites in, Emery couldn't eat any more. She was full of excitement. The Royal Blues were coming to town.

After lunch, they passed the afternoon playing a game with Bentley until he went out to ride bikes with friends. Then the conversation turned to Caleb's unpacked boxes.

"Are they holding up the walls or something?" Emery peeked into the box marked *Mementos*.

"Bentley used them to make a fort. I can't mess that up, can I?"

Finally, the late winter sun set enough for them to knock on Simon's door. A dog barked. The porch light came on. An eager-looking Simon invited them in.

"Emery, this is my wife, Nadine. So, what's this all about?" Simon sat on the edge of the couch next to his wife.

The living room was beautiful and comfy, with rich hardwood floors, beams on the ceiling, and a western window framing the winter skyline.

"Well—" She glanced at Caleb, then Simon and Nadine. "I'm not sure how to say it now that the moment is here." She wanted to hold onto this special news a moment longer. It'd become a part of her. What if they didn't think it was a big deal? What if they rejected the idea?

"Em?" Caleb said.

"Here goes." She adjusted her position on the loveseat so she could see her audience better. "About a month ago, I wrote to the House of Blue in Lauchtenland, using Rachel Kirby's private email address to the Chamber Office." She paused for any questions. There were none. "The idea came to me after one of the Main Street meetings where someone, I think Duke, maybe Adele, said we needed a big event to bring attention to the town, especially the East End. And hopefully bring us all together. So I took a shot and requested a visit from the royal family. This morning Sted from the Chamber Office called. Their Royal Highnesses Prince John and Princess Gemma want to visit Sea Blue Beach at the end of April. He asked if that worked for us and—" The moment needed a drum roll or trumpet blast. "I said yes." Ta-da.

Her audience gaped at her, wide-eyed. What was her interpretation of their expression? Unbelief? Maybe, *"That's it? Your big news?"*

"Why are you looking at me like that? Did you hear what I said? The royal family, descendants of Prince Blue, want to visit Sea Blue Beach. I hope it's okay I said yes." This wasn't going *at all* like she imagined.

"Well," Nadine began, a bit breathless, glancing at Simon, "that is usually prom weekend."

"True." Simon nodded. "Emery, do you think they could come the weekend before or after?"

"What? Ask them to . . . You're not serious, are you?"

"Of course we're not serious." Nadine launched to her feet, shouting. "This is *incredible*. Emery, you brilliant, brave soul! How come we never thought to ask before?"

"Emery, you're going to get a Citizen's Star Award for this." Simon pumped the air with his fist so hard he strained his arm.

"You have those?" She waved off the compliment. "So do you think we can pull this off?"

"Absolutely." Simon started pacing. "I'll make *sure* we pull this off."

When she looked at Caleb, he was smiling so wide, so bright, so proud, she felt it in her veins. Without a word, he scooped her into his arms and whirled her around. "While I was making a speech about coming together, you were doing something about it."

"Not true, Caleb," Simon said. "You did something powerful today. You confronted the division. I was so proud."

"Not sure I did any good." He glanced at the small group. "How do we handle this?"

"Right now, the four of us will be the initial committee." Simon made a face. "Why does everything in this town begin with a committee? Anyway, since you're the contact, Emery, we'll follow your lead."

"I'd like to hand it over to you, Simon. You're the mayor. There's a call with Sted on Wednesday at ten. How about we meet in your office just before?"

"Emery, you've breathed life into me. I was beginning to lose hope. If the West End broke away on my watch, I'd have failed this town, the mayorship, and broken my own heart."

"Darling, I keep telling you . . ." Nadine said. "You're a wonderful mayor. Those West Enders are blowing smoke to get us to bend to their will. Forget them for now. The royals are coming. Let's celebrate. Who wants ice cream?"

They gathered in the kitchen for ice cream, strategizing on how to pull off a royal visit with order and dignity. When to let people know. How much they could beautify the East End between the first of March and the end of April.

"We'll know more on Wednesday," Emery said. "But I say we find the money to do what we can for the East End. Should I write something up, ask for donations without mentioning the visit?"

"Let's not risk sparking any suspicion." Simon tapped on his iPad. "We have eight weeks. We have the discretionary funds already in play for some of the improvements. I can release more."

"The owner of Alderman's might throw in with us. I think we can trust her. I'll tell her something big is coming. As reward for her donation, we can invite her."

"Fine, but play it very close to the vest, Caleb," Simon said.

Then Emery asked the elephant-in-the-room-question. "What about the West End? Do the royals tour over there, or stay on the East End? I mean, we can't preach unity and leave them out, can we?"

"I say we ask the royals what they want." Caleb took a big bite of chocolate ice cream. "Did your email to them indicate anything specific?"

"Hardly. I just invited them to visit."

Simon donned his mayor hat and said leaders from both sides would be invited. If the royals wanted to see how the town had grown, then they'd tour the West End too.

"But for now, this is our news alone. No royal stories from the archives, Emery. If I'm allowed to tell you what to do, Madam Editor."

"I can work with that request, Mr. Mayor."

"It's not the West End I'm worried about, but the rest of the world. Royal watchers, the media . . ."

Emery began to see the gravity of her brilliant idea. "I hope this visit isn't more trouble than it's worth. I never counted the cost."

"We're counting the cost now," Simon said with a big smile. "It will be worth it."

As she left the Casters with Caleb, all the excitement from before became a sober reality. A royal visit meant secrecy and security, a curated guest list, some sort of program, hospitality and food, on top of beautifying the East End. Where would the royals stay? Where would they eat? Who among the citizens should they invite?

They returned to Caleb's for her car. "Care to sit for a bit?" he said, sinking into one of the patio chairs. The lights from the neighbor's windows fell across the lawn in golden squares. "I'm too wound up to go inside."

"Should you check on Bentley?" Emery said, taking the chair next to Caleb.

"Mom's with him." He reached over to tap her arm. "Sorry we didn't get to go bike riding this afternoon."

"What? Oh, right, I'd completely forgotten." She loosely laced her fingers with his. "That would've been fun."

"Maybe later this week." He pulled her chair closer. "I have to tell you something. I had an email from Mac Diamond. He offered me a job as an in-house architect for Diamond Dogs."

"Caleb, wow. What did you say? Mr. Potter jokes aside, is it a serious opportunity?"

"It's a serious opportunity. I'd have my name on clubhouses and luxury venues across the south. He claims to like my sustainable design ideas, but . . ."

"Let me ask you this. Do you respect him?"

"No, I don't."

For a long time, they said nothing else, simply listened to the shifting sounds of the night. When the breeze brushed them with a wet chill, Emery crawled into Caleb's lap and rested her head on his shoulder.

"You know I don't want you to ever leave," he whispered, his lips close to her ear.

"Tonight, or in general?"

He laughed. "Both. But for now, let's say in general. I know you're not ready for more, but—"

Emery raised up, cupped her hand around his face, and pressed her lips against his. Tentative at first, then breaking when Caleb shifted so the side of her hip rested against his. When his warm arms came around her, she kissed him again, sinking into the heart and soul of Caleb Ransom.

"Are you trying to make me fall in love with you?" he said.

"No more than you're trying to make me fall for you."

His eyes locked with hers. "I think you stole my heart the first night I saw you at the Sands Motor Motel. You never gave it back."

"You never asked." She kissed him again. "You probably have mine in here somewhere." She tapped her hand over his thudding heart. "Once again, you were the last thing I expected to find when I returned to Sea Blue Beach."

"Even more than a royal visit?" He pressed his lips to her forehead.

"Okay, maybe not more than a royal visit, but, Caleb, ten million times better."

Mayor Simon Caster
cordially invites you
to meet

their Royal Highnesses of Lauchtenland
CROWN PRINCE JOHN & PRINCESS GEMMA

Friday, the 25th of April
5 p.m.
Reception on Sea Blue Way
&
Saturday, the 26th of April
10 a.m.
Brunch on the Beach
Noon
Tour of the East End
3 p.m
Skating at the Starlight

★ ★ ★

RSVP to the SBBRV@SBBcityhall.gov

Mr. & Mrs. Douglas Quinn
cordially invite you to share
in the wedding of their daughter

Ava Verbeke Quinn
to
Mr. James Allen Gelovani
at
the Glidden House

Saturday, the 10th of May
Ceremony to begin at 3 p.m.
with reception to follow.
Carriages at Midnight

22

CALEB

On the eve of the royal visit, he was exhilarated and exhausted. Sitting around the crackling firepit of the Sands Motor Motel courtyard, Emery curled in his lap, glass of wine in his hand, he finally, finally exhaled.

The jumble of voices and to-dos in his head went silent. After eight hectic weeks, Sea Blue Beach was ready. Once Simon hired Caleb to head up logistics for the royal visit, he zeroed in on all he had to do, found his stride, and got more done in the last two months than the previous six.

The Swansons' design was complete, and ground had been broken. The Østers' plan was still on the drafting table because Mrs. Øster kept changing her mind.

Alderman's Pharmacy reached the halfway mark this week—restoring history took time. Jenny Finch graciously donated to the East End restoration fund before knowing about the royal visit. She was bowled over to receive one of the few gold-embossed invitations for the Friday night reception.

On Saturday, one hundred and twenty town and business leaders, educators and students, city workers, first responders, doctors, lawyers, and senior residents of Sea Blue Beach would gather under a forty-by-sixty tent on the beach for a brunch reception.

Chief Kelly, along with the royal protection detail and a crew from the US State Department, was handling security. Simon and the town council were hosting, overseeing the reception line, and Misty from Sweet Conversations and Paige from the Blue Plate Diner were tapped to supply all the food.

Mac Diamond asserted that the Skylight—the finest restaurant in Sea Blue Beach (he stopped saying "in the West End" the moment he heard the news)—should cater the brunch, but Simon put a lock on the East End businesses.

Servers from about every café and restaurant in town volunteered to keep the champagne flowing and food platters filled. A team of twenty were selected. They'd wear blue Tommy Bahama shirts and khaki shorts.

The high school string quartet had been retained to serenade both events. Caleb was impressed when he visited their rehearsal this morning. The historical markers arrived, and a crew from the city cemented them in place last night.

The whole town buzzed. Every hotel and rental was booked, and as of yesterday, the East End crawled with tourists and security.

Hometown Hollywood legends Matt Knight and Harlow Hayes offered their lovely home at 321 Sea Blue Way for the royal couple's one-night stay. After all, Prince Blue was its builder and first resident. Descendants of the Nickle family had a private meeting with Prince John and Princess Gemma before the Friday night reception.

Royal watchers and photographers lurked against the barricade and roped-off areas. And Chief Kelly had assured Simon everything was under control.

Bentley continued to thrive, becoming more grounded every

day. When Emery ran her story on the royal visit, Bent read up on everything about the House of Blue and Lauchtenland, then generously shared his knowledge with Caleb at the dinner table.

He was grateful for this quiet moment with Emery.

"What's that pinched expression?" she said. "You did a fabulous job, Caleb. The program is beautiful."

"Dad gave me lots of logistical help. I was just running through everything in my head. What did I forget? Do you think the West End is really okay with the prince and princess only touring the East End? I have this feeling Mac will pull something."

"He'd be a fool to try. The itinerary was suggested and approved by the Chamber Office. It's what the Royal Blues wanted. As for getting everything done, babe, you had lists of your lists. You marked off everything."

Babe. A new term for them. One that came into play somewhere between "the royals are coming" and tonight, *they* had happened—Caleb and Emery.

During the last eight weeks, if Emery wasn't at the paper, she was at his house, helping source items for the East End's beautification, making calls, approving colors for the banners, making dinner, and enduring Bentley's fount of royal knowledge.

While plenty of kisses had been shared, there'd been no declarations of love. Yet he felt it with every ounce of his being.

"I can't believe we got it done in time." Caleb twisted his fingers through the ends of her hair.

"Delilah believes it's because of Immanuel, God with us."

"With the number of volunteers we had, I believe it."

The banners, the lights, the flower planters, the repaired and painted benches, along with the storefront renewals, were all done by volunteers. Bobby Brockton sent over a crew to fix the broken bricks of Sea Blue Way. On his own dime.

"I'm a fourth generation Sea Bluean," he said. *"How could I not contribute to this once-in-a-century visit?"*

Even Mac puffed out his chest and hired a team to trim the trees and cut back the ground cover in the Org. Homestead.

Caleb nodded toward Delilah, who watered the flowers she'd recently planted in the courtyard. The Sands Motor Motel was the royal couple's first stop after the brunch.

"I heard the princess is a fan of her music."

"Really? You must've read that somewhere." Emery pressed her laughing lips to his.

"I think I did. In a great little newspaper called the *Sea Blue Beach Gazette*." Caleb never spent a lot of time imagining his future—he knew how precarious relationships could be—but sharing all of this with Emery felt like the beginning of many, many lovely moments. Millions, billions of them.

"I was talking to Bentley last night after dinner," she said. "He really misses his mom. She's not called in a while."

"She's ticked that I wouldn't invite her to the royal brunch," Caleb said.

"There was a flurry of QuinnFam texts when the news broke. They all wanted to come, then pretended to be mad when I said no. But they really do understand. Are you sure that's not the case with Cassidy?"

"If I go by her word choice, she's mad. She has it in her head she's a nobody. The lack of an invitation is further proof. It's worse because her son is invited."

"Then I guess Bentley didn't tell you she texted him. Told him to invite her if he loved her."

Caleb glanced up at Emery. "He said that?"

"Yes. I thought you should be aware he feels guilty."

"I'll talk to him tonight."

Emery ran her fingers through his hair. He'd gone to the

barber earlier today, ready for the weekend, but Em could mess up his hair anytime. "Is anything else bothering you?" she said.

"Why do you ask?"

"You seemed distracted."

"You're not supposed to turn your trained journalistic eye on me, Quinn."

"You don't have to tell me but—"

"Mac emailed me this week. Wants to know my answer."

"And?"

"Usually I know exactly what to do. I assess a situation and decide. But this one . . . Am I turning down an opportunity because of my own prejudice?" With that, he kissed her and said he needed to go. "Bentley's home alone."

"Caleb, take the job if you want, but only if you honestly and truly want to work with Mac Diamond."

"Sound advice." He hooked her to him with one arm for one last kiss. "See you tomorrow."

"Are your clothes ready?"

He laughed. "Yes, all pressed. Bentley's too."

Last month, they'd searched online, at very expensive sites, for the appropriate upscale but casual wear, and learned they had very different taste.

"Light green button-down with a *subtle* pattern," he said, describing the outfit on which they compromised. "A pair of cream-colored slacks and mocha-colored canvas oxfords. Did I get all the words right? What about you?"

"Still deciding among my fifteen options. Joanna sent me a dress this week. It's at the top of the list. Which means my expensive purchases were for nothing."

"Shopping for a grand occasion? Four thousand dollars. Shaking the hand of a royal prince and princess—"

"Priceless."

Caleb kissed her forehead. "Get some sleep."

"I'll meet you at the reception. I've got to be at the paper early to prep for our special edition. The *Sunday Royal Gazette*. I'm meeting Kadasha Collier at noon, then off to Murph at Yes Hair Do for some sort of updo."

Backing away slowly, Caleb held onto her hand until their fingers slipped apart. On his way home, he stopped at Biggs for a roasted chicken, bag of salad, and a carton of mac and cheese.

At the house, he walked through the back door, bags swinging from his hands, picturing Emery that night after her first town council meeting. *"He just Mr. Pottered you."*

Was Mac still Mr. Pottering him? Was he a George Bailey—a restless soul wanting to change the world, but blind to the good in front of him?

"Bent?" He set the groceries on the counter and headed to his office, glancing twice at the fort of unpacked boxes. "I brought dinner."

The house was too quiet. He jogged upstairs to Bentley's room. The desk lamp was on, but his computer was gone. "Bent?"

He checked the bathroom, picked up the towel on the floor, then went back to Bentley's room. The space felt . . . abandoned. Caleb shoved open the closet. Empty. As were the dresser drawers. He checked the desk. Bentley's math award was gone. In its place, he found a note.

Came for Bentley. We're going on an adventure. Xx, Cass.

23

~

EMERY

"Hey." Rex peeked in her office, pointing at his watch. "You'd better go get ready. The reception is in three hours."

"How much primping do you think I need?" After meeting with Kadasha and sitting in Murph's chair for an updo, Emery returned to the paper, checking and double-checking the layout and banked stories, even running a test to the press to ensure the ads appeared.

"You're starting to get worry lines." Rex held up his hand, fingers crossed. "Everything's going to be all right."

"Elliot will have my job otherwise." She'd charged premium prices for ad space in the collector's royal edition. "The press run has to be perfect."

"Tomorrow we'll pick the best of Kadasha's pictures, flow them onto the page, zip it all up, and send it to the press." Rex gently shoved her toward the door. "Floyd will run the *Sunday Royal Gazette* ahead of the other jobs in case of a problem."

"And if there is, how do we fix it?"

"Prayer. Bye, go meet royal people."

Note to self—give Rex a raise.

At Cottage 7, she tried on several dresses before going with the obvious choice: the royal-blue-and-white print Tommy Bahama tasseled maxi dress, with the white and brown leather sandals Joanna sent.

I saw this while shopping and thought of you immediately. The dress said, "Casual day with a royal couple." No worry if you choose not to wear it. I also found these cool shoes. Love, Jo

Emery was a little more than moved that Joanna thought of her amid all the wedding preparation. Dad texted a few weeks ago saying she was starting to wear thin.

Joanna brought a sense of style to the Quinn closets. Dad's style improved from dotty professor to sophisticated academic. Joanna sent Emery off to Ohio State with a suitcase full of "college girl" clothes—which Emery never really acknowledged. *Thank you, thank you, Joanna.*

Of all her mom's amazing qualities, a fashion sense was not one of them. She was a banker who wore banker's clothes—dark suits and white blouses, heels. For a wedding or dinner party, she borrowed outfits from friends. But Mom had the pearls, which added class to everything.

At four forty-five, Delilah knocked on Emery's door. "I thought we could walk up together. I'm a bit nervous."

She wore a lovely pair of white slacks with a pink blouse, and white sandals. Her short silver hair was always neat, but Murph had insisted on running a curling iron through the top. At eighty-seven, she still had the leanness of her younger years, with high cheeks supporting her dark, all-seeing eyes.

"You've met royals before, haven't you?" Emery said. "Didn't you have an audience with Prince John's grandfather?"

"Many, many years ago. I'm out of practice."

"Princess Gemma is eager to meet you."

"Stay with me when I curtsy so I don't fall."

"We don't have to curtsy," Emery said, setting her phone, cottage key, and lip gloss in a small clutch.

"You say that now, but when you meet them, you will."

Walking up Avenue C under a fiery red, gold, and orange sunset, Delilah gripped Emery's hand as they rounded the old haberdashery and entered Sea Blue Way.

"Goodness." Delilah slowed. "It's a wonderland. Everything looks born again."

The banners flapped softly in the breeze, almost in rhythm with the murmuring voices. The glow of the shop windows spread a golden carpet over the red bricks. Even the vacant shops had light in the windows.

The high school quartet played Pachelbel, and the security teams, dressed in black, faded into the background.

"It seems like the East End has woken up from a long sleep," Emery said. "The whole place is glowing."

As they made their way under the string of crisscrossing lights, Emery began her article in her head, trying to find another word besides *magical. Glorious?*

The street was like a scene from a swoony movie where the hero finally scoops the girl into his arms and dances with her under the stars to her favorite song.

Somewhere in the gathering crowd, Emery hoped Kadasha captured the feel with her camera as much as the sights.

Down the center of the street, round high-top spool tables were decorated with lights and small bouquets of flowers. In short order, East End food vendors would bring out their specialties.

"Emery, over here." Simon beckoned from the small huddle of town council members. "I want you front and center. Delilah, you're next to Emery. The princess is a fan."

"Seems impossible, but all right." Delilah was so delightfully humble. "I haven't been on the music scene for over forty years."

Emery had just taken her place when she noticed Caleb in a deep conversation with Duke. Suddenly he turned, as if she'd called his name. His attention landed on her. And when he smiled, he challenged the brightness of every twinkling light. His presence wrapped around her, head to toe. *Caleb Ransom, you are making me love you.*

After a moment, he broke away from Duke and came over to her. "You know you're not supposed to upstage the princess."

"Very funny." Yet the glint in his eye said he meant it. "I couldn't show her up if I tried."

"Caleb, here, you tuck in next to your girl," Delilah said, pulling him into the line.

"No, no, I'll go on the other side of Simon," he said.

"Nonsense, you two need to stand together. You're the future of this town."

"Are we?" Emery said. What did Delilah know, or see, that she didn't?

"Does everyone remember the protocol?" Simon strode up and down the line of guests. "They'll walk the line, greet each of you. Shake their hand but do not crowd them, ask for a selfie, or tell them your life story." Simon turned to Ivan. "Hear me?"

"Of course I hear you, I'm not deaf. And I read the protocol. How dumb do I look to you?"

Emery smiled at him and gave a thumbs-up. He didn't look dumb at all. Dressed in a white shirt, bolo tie, and slightly too-tight suit, he was down-home handsome. Standing next to him was Adele in a soft pink dress with a matching knitted scarf. Mercy looked pretty in pale blue.

Across the way, Caleb's parents stood with the other guests, many of them the volunteers who worked tirelessly on the beautification of the East End.

For this first reception, they kept it small and intimate, inviting first responders, Dr. Crane and Dr. Wheeler, who started a general practice in the sixties and seventies, and a half dozen students from the high school and middle school.

"Caleb, where's Bentley?" Emery whispered, not seeing him among the students.

"With his mom."

"What? Really?"

"She picked him up last night when I was with you."

"Caleb." She turned to him. "Are you all right? Is he all right?"

"I think so. I called this morning, and she finally answered. For about sixty seconds. Bentley yelled something about having fun. They're on one of her adventures."

Without a thought, she slipped her hand into his. For a moment, it was almost too much—the fragrance of his skin, the gaze of his blue eyes from under his dark hair, the strong pressure of his fingers against hers, and this moment, sharing it together.

"Look at us sixteen years later, Caleb Ransom."

He bent to her ear. "Is it better than trashing West End High's field?"

She laughed low. "Yeah, almost, definitely better."

"Go time, everyone," Simon said. "They're coming out of the house with Bodie and Booker Nickle."

To her right, Simon greeted the prince and princess, along with the two Nickle family members—Bodie, a lawyer, and Booker, a rancher.

"I'm nervous," she whispered. "What if I suddenly freak out and scream?"

"Do you feel like you might freak out and scream?"

"No, but what if?"

"Thanks a lot. Now I'm thinking about it."

Simon walked the royals toward their side of the street. Mac Diamond stood tall and puffed-up, gripping the prince's hand like he was making a business deal, then bowing to the princess.

"Did he just *wink* at her?" Emery said.

"Yep, he just winked at her."

Simon moved quickly down the line until he was in front of Emery. "May I present Emery Quinn, the editor-in-chief of the *Gazette*. She's the one who sent the request for your visit."

"Thank you so much for inviting us." Prince John shook her hand. She'd seen plenty of pictures of him, but he was even more impressive in person, moving with ease and confidence, seeing the world through vibrant eyes. "We felt rather silly upon reflection. Why didn't we think of visiting?"

"We were thrilled you said yes," Emery said.

The princess greeted her next. Delilah was right, Emery couldn't help but curtsy. Princess Gemma was tall and beautiful, with the classic look of the girl next door. She wore a maxi dress with a pair of white sneakers, and her dark hair in a long French braid.

Emery *totally* felt like they could be friends.

The prince asked about Rachel Kirby and the *Gazette*, and how Emery got into journalism. She answered with clarity and swiftness, her nerves firing the whole time. Then Simon moved on to Caleb.

"Our hometown boy, Caleb Ransom, a talented architect who headed up the logistics for your visit."

"I hope we didn't cause too much work for you all. Everything you've done is lovely." Prince John shook Caleb's hand and went on to say how much he loved architecture and took courses while at uni. "Are any of the buildings in town yours?"

Caleb shook his head. "Not yet. But I'm overseeing the reconstruction of Alderman's Pharmacy, which you'll tour later in your visit."

"Well done then. I look forward to seeing it."

Princess Gemma greeted him, also mentioning her love for architecture. "You have to come to Lauchtenland, see our buildings. The Blue family is grateful to you, Mayor Caster, and the whole town, really, for preserving the Blue ancestry in Sea Blue Beach. It means a lot to Her Majesty, the Queen. She's anxious for a report from our visit." The princess started to move on, then stepped back, taking in Caleb and Emery together. She leaned in. "Are you two a couple?"

"They're a couple," Delilah interjected, not appearing nervous at all. "They just don't know it yet. Princess Gemma, a pleasure to meet you, I'm Delilah Mead." She held onto Caleb as she dipped into a perfect curtsy.

The princess threw her arms around the older woman, hugging her, swaying from side to side. In that moment, she wasn't a royal princess, but a small-town girl from Tennessee.

"My grandparents played your records constantly when I was growing up. Your songs are the soundtrack of my childhood." Then she leaned in again, whispering to Delilah, whose eyes glassed with tears, "Thank you for the music."

"Thank you, Your Royal Highness."

Down the line and back up, the prince and princess greeted everyone. Then Simon released the guests to mill about, enjoy fellowship, and partake in the food and wine.

"So," Caleb said, reaching out for Emery's hand, "seems we have royal approval to be a couple."

"Yes, it seems we do."

24

EMERY

"Darling, wake up." Delilah's voice was followed by a pounding on the cottage door, then the click of a key in the lock. "Emery, come quick. Hurry."

"I'm coming." She fell out of bed, thus ending the lovely dream of dancing at a royal ball with Caleb.

Last night, the two of them spent close to forty minutes with the prince and princess, tasting wine and cheese, talking about sports, education, art, and the state of modern media, like they were besties. Honestly, it was insane.

When the royal couple headed to 321 Sea Blue Way for the night, Emery was all agog, running to the paper to see Kadasha's initial photographs. They were stunning. The woman was worth every penny.

Caleb surprised her, waiting for her outside of Cottage 7, a fire in the firepit. She automatically curled into his lap—her favorite place to be—and they talked over each other while recalling the evening and dreaming about tomorrow's event.

"Never, ever did I foresee this when I accepted the Gazette *job. Me, guffaw-laughing with a princess."*

"She felt like a southern American girl and a royal all at the same time," Caleb said.

"Emery?" Delilah called from the front room. "You must come."

"What? What is it?" Half awake, she tripped into the living room, tugging on her yoga pants. "I was having such a good dream."

"Well, it's about to be a nightmare. Grab your shoes and sweat-shirt and follow me."

A nightmare? What sort of nightmare? Emery dashed to the window over the settee. Was it raining? Were dark clouds threatening the beach brunch? That *would* be a nightmare.

Emery slipped on her hoodie and sneakers, then hurried with Delilah toward the Beachwalk. Up ahead, the tent for the brunch stood tall against the breaking dawn—which seemed to be cooperating with their plan for a beautiful day with low humidity and gentle breezes. The Gulf lapped quietly against the shore.

"I see beauty, Delilah," Emery said, arms wide, drawing in a cleansing breath of salty air. "Where's this nightmare you speak of?"

"Brace yourself." Delilah left the Beachwalk to plow through the sand toward the tent.

"The princess seemed so moved when she thanked you for your music."

"Music is a powerful force."

"Delilah, will you please tell me your story one day?"

"Maybe, but right now—" They arrived at the tent. "You've got a whale of a story here."

Through the translucent sunrise, Emery surveyed the tent from one end to the other. "Wha—what happened?" She was accosted by a most vile odor. Trash everywhere. Piles and piles. She started to wade in, but Delilah snatched her arm.

"You don't know what's in there." She scanned the scene. "This is going to change today's plans, trust me. I'll call Simon. You go wake Caleb."

Emery ran all the way, stopping only to let a delivery truck ramble down Sea Blue Way. The street was dark and lonely with none of the beauty and charm of last night.

Cutting through the yards that butted up against Pelican Way, she landed on Caleb's front porch and banged on his door.

"Wake up, wake up!" She rang the bell, then pounded with her fist. "Caleb!"

When she heard footsteps, she stepped back, finally taking a deep breath. When the door swung open, she went breathless again. Standing there with a rumpled, rolled-out-of-bed vibe, she completely forgot her mission.

He was shirtless, wearing baggy shorts, his hair shooting in every direction, and a night's growth on his angular jaw. She wanted to smash into him, knock him back for a kiss or two.

"Em, what's wrong?" Concern filled his blue eyes as he looked her up and down.

"The tent—" She pointed toward the beach. "Trashed, Caleb. Someone dumped truckloads of garbage under the tent."

"They trashed the royal brunch?" He stepped onto the porch, gazing in that direction. "Are you kidding me? After my brilliant Chamber speech?"

"Maybe it stirred some old feelings, but there's vile-smelling junk all over the beach, under the tents, covering that expensive floor we put down."

"Trashing the brunch for the Crown Prince of Lauchtenland? Now that's going too far. It's political and social suicide. The State Department might even get involved."

"You have to see it. Shoot, I'm surprised you can't smell it. It's like dead fish, rotten food, I don't know what all, but we *cannot* let the prince and princess go there. Delilah's calling Simon."

"Where was security?" Caleb jammed on a pair of sneakers sitting by the door and yanked on the hoodie hanging on a nearby hook. One step out of the house and his phone rang from inside. He hesitated, then dashed up the stairs. "I bet it's Simon."

The mayor woke up every town council member and even the city manager, demanding crews come and clean up the mess. Emery stood in the living room just inside the door, waiting, listening to Caleb's half of the conversation.

"Simon's fired up," he said, dropping his phone in his pocket, then heading toward the beach. "He wants to know who did this."

"We can figure that out tomorrow, but what are we going to do about today?" Emery jogged alongside him. "They haven't even walked through the town, seen the rink, the mural, or Malachi Nickle's sawmill."

"We could move the brunch to the Skylight."

"Which is exactly what Mac Diamond would like."

"You think he did this?" Caleb stopped short. "Or Bobby? Some sort of delayed revenge?"

"All these years later?" she said. "Why? This ruins the whole visit. The town's reputation. There are national journalists all over the place. Every person with a phone and a social media account is a reporter. If those men want a thriving, progressing Sea Blue Beach, trashing a royal visit would not be the way to go."

When they arrived on scene, Simon was walking the tent parimeter, urgency in his movements. Kadasha was also on-site, taking pictures. That's when it hit Emery.

The *Royal Sunday Gazette* was not going to be at all what she'd planned.

"Mac denies any knowledge of this. So does Brockton," Simon said as he approached. "I've failed as mayor, allowing this level of animosity to fester."

"What happened to security?" Emery said.

"Chief Kelly's working on that now, checking the few cameras we have. This much garbage had to come from a large vehicle or a lot of small ones. Any tracks in the sand were covered. We didn't have security overnight."

"What are we going to do for the brunch?" Emery said. "Go to the Skylight?"

"We're not having a brunch." Simon motioned to someone arriving in an ATV. "The prince and princess left. Their protection detail saw the trash as a threat and made the call. Worried something more might happen throughout the day. Nothing says, 'Go away, we don't want you here' like a mountain of a stinking sewage."

"They left?" Emery said. She had six pages waiting for a special royal edition. She'd sold ads.

"Wouldn't you?" Caleb said.

"I'm the one who sent the invite." Emery pressed her hand to her middle. "They're going to think I'm behind this. That I wanted to go viral with a scandalous *Gazette* story. If it stinks, it leads."

"No, Em." Caleb stepped forward to survey the mess. "This is how they'll remember all of us."

"How can we apologize?" Emery tried to cast off her fear with the truth—this wasn't her fault—but she kept circling back to guilt by association. "We can't let them think we approve of this."

"I communicated that to their security team," Simon said. "But Caleb's right. This will certainly leave a bad mark on Sea Blue Beach."

"I'm going to the paper," Emery said. "I have to email them. Hopefully, I'm not already blocked on the royal server. After that, I have to figure out how to fill six pages." She saw Kadasha crossing the beach, camera raised.

Emery would have plenty of pictures. Just none of the ones she wanted.

CALEB

By late afternoon, city crews and volunteers had hauled off the trash, taken down the tent, and disassembled the portable floor and carted it away.

Standing where the reception should have been, he couldn't get free from the stench, despite the stiff Gulf breeze and the warm April sun.

What was happening to his town?

To his right, the town council members were locked in conversation with Chief Kelly and Simon. The State Department was now involved, making sure there were no other threats toward the visiting dignitaries.

Reporters appeared, stringers for major news outlets, and started filing stories. "Live from Sea Blue Beach, Florida . . ." Which put Simon and the town further under the spotlight.

But Emery was right. The real threat to their reputation came from all the royal watchers milling around with their phones raised, recording the cleanup and posting on every social media app.

Directly in front of him, his parents chatted with Ivan and Adele, and behind them, kids from Nickle High's football and basketball teams tossed Frisbees on the beach like today had been nothing more than a standard community-service project.

Caleb wanted to run in between each group, shouting, *"This happened on our watch. What are we going to do about it?"*

Yet he knew they wouldn't share his passion. Except for Simon, who now had to play the politician.

He pulled out his phone to text Emery. Even though he'd worn gloves during cleanup, his hands felt dirty.

Caleb:
How're you doing?

286

He waited for a response, but when she didn't reply, he slipped his phone into his pocket. She was busy. Maybe he'd pick up Tony's Pizza for the *Gazette* staff later.

With nothing else to do, he thought to head home, but being inside felt claustrophobic. Even worse, being inside alone. The house was stupidly quiet without Bentley dashing everywhere. Caleb had grown fond of Bent's footsteps thundering down the hall, then down the stairs. Almost like he was making sure he was heard.

"Caleb?" Bobby Brockton walked through the sand toward him. "Got a sec?" He held up his palms. "It wasn't me."

Caleb glanced over at him. "Didn't say it was."

"No, but you're thinking it. 'Cause I would if I were you."

"Do you have any idea who would do this? That was a lot of trash, Bobby."

"Let's not assume it was someone from the West End. Do *you* have any idea who could've done this?"

"If I did, I'd not be standing here."

Bobby gestured toward Mac Diamond and Alfred Gallagher, who were talking to a couple of city workers. "They're ambitious and calculating, but I don't think they'd stoop to insulting European royals. Mac's a networker. He'd want some royal connection to build a golf course in Lauchtenland."

"Know what's really behind this?" Caleb turned to Bobby. "The conversations we have in this town. East End versus West End. Us and them. Even tossing out the idea of becoming two separate cities." He motioned to where the trash site had been. "We've trash-talked each other for decades."

Bobby sighed. "A small football rivalry grew into a big mess, didn't it?"

"It's not football. It's the rivalry between old and new. Progress and history. Ever since those for progress lost the bid to tear down the Starlight, the festering started."

"There's some merit to that, I guess." Bobby kicked at the sand with his sneakered foot. "But Mac isn't going to stop. He wants a nine-hole golf course and clubhouse in the Org. Homestead neighborhood. It's adjacent to the new road coming in, which will bring tourists in from western Alabama and Louisiana. Come on, those houses aren't worth fixing up and selling, Caleb. You know it, and I know it. A hundred years ago, they might have been something, but now? Florida Cracker homes? Not on the list of classic architecture."

"Maybe I'll make it a classic style." Caleb's defenses were up.

"Okay, fine. Who's going to pay for them to be gutted and brought up to code? Who can afford to buy one when they're done? They're not big enough for anyone to buy at current prices. But over on the West End, we have new affordable housing developments. Let's be realistic for a second and—"

"What? Admit the East End needs to be bulldozed? That the town Prince Blue and Malachi Nickle built together should become a playground for tourists, with an amusement park and pro golf and tennis clubs? That's not the heart of Sea Blue Beach at all, Bobby."

"In the beginning, no. But Caleb, y'all are not going to win this one. I'm not trying to stir up trouble or side with Mac for my own gain, but look around. It's not 1900 anymore. Or 1950. Or 1987. Who has an old-fashioned pharmacy and soda fountain these days? Jenny Finch is going to eventually lose her investment in Alderman's. Sea Blue Beach is more than the gem of the North Florida coast. It's a gold mine." He started to walk off, then turned back around. "You should pay attention to what Mac is whispering to you, Caleb."

"He's not whispering anymore. He's shouting."

288

Three hours later, he sat around the Sands Motor Motel firepit, watching the sunset, Emery in the chair next to him, his arm resting on her shoulder, his fingers lost in the soft ends of her hair.

She'd called when the staff put the paper to bed, looking for some comfort and dinner. He grabbed a couple of steaks at Biggs and tossed them on the Sands gas grill while Emery put together a salad. But neither one ate very much.

Sitting with her now, the world almost felt right again. If he could just shake the heaviness of the royal disaster and Bentley's leaving.

"We did our best but—" Emery sighed this mantra all through dinner.

She'd ended up with three pages of *"gorgeous"* photos from the Friday-night reception with her story wrapped in between. Then three troubling pages of the brunch tent before and after the trashing and *"about fifty quotes of people wondering, 'How did this happen?'"*

"This is a pivotal edition for me. I mean, can you imagine a more diverse news day? This is one for the *Gazette* archives."

"You're doing your job. Reporting the news."

"I feel awful about everything." She sat forward, so his hand slipped away from her. "Prince John said he really wanted to skate at the rink his ancestor built."

"Now he probably never will."

"I'm not giving up on apologizing," she said, getting out of her chair and slipping into his lap.

"I don't think Simon will either." Caleb settled his hand on her waist, and with a soft sigh, held her close.

"So, is this our thing?" she whispered. "Sitting curled in Adirondack chairs by an outdoor fire?"

"Fine by me." He kissed her cheek. "One day I should take you on a proper date."

"To where? The Skylight?" She sat up to see his face. "Do you realize the West End is just a copycat? The East End has the Starlight and the Blue Plate Diner. The West has the Skylight and the Red Room. We're at the Sands Motor Motel, but six miles away, you can stay at the Shore Motel. The carnival came to the East End and now someone from the West End wants to put up a permanent Ferris wheel."

"Imitation is a form of flattery," Caleb said.

"Or stealing," Emery countered.

"Bobby Brockton made a point of telling me he wasn't behind the prank."

"Really? He avoided me when I interviewed the cleanup crews," Emery said. "You think it's deflection?"

Caleb thought for a second. "I don't think so. He was honest about their plans for the town. They want the East End for their business goals. He called it a gold mine. The true deflection is the bold announcement of breaking away, becoming their own municipality. That does not fit their plans at all."

"Scaring everyone into agreement."

"Right, and he, um, told me to pay attention to what Mac was *whispering* to me."

"Whispering? He's been shouting lately."

"My thoughts exactly. He's *shouting* how I can get in on the ground floor of all new development in the East End."

"More Mr. Pottering. George Bailey doesn't want any ground floors, remember?"

"Did you recently watch that movie? How do you remember all the lines?"

"We watched it every Christmas and Christmas-in-July when I was growing up. It was Mom's favorite."

"Do you have to go back to the paper tonight?"

"No, the files transfer to the press on a schedule. Floyd will let me know if anything goes wrong. And frankly, what can top today?"

"Let's go to the Starlight, roll away our troubles. End this day on a happy note."

Emery caught his face between her hands and gently kissed him. "Are you asking me on a date, Caleb Ransom?"

"Yes I am, Emery Quinn."

Just as they laced on their skates, the DJ called for a couples' skate. The lights dimmed, and the disco ball shot rainbow colors across the floor as Colbie Caillat sang "Fallin' For You." Instantly, Caleb was back to the moment he knew he was falling for a girl who would leave at the end of summer.

Only tonight, he determined to never let her go.

25

CALEB

Then ...

Getting comfortable wasn't easy after the bashing he endured from West End's defensive line tonight. And the interception he threw in the final two minutes of the game on fourth and goal played over and over in his mind.

He'd let the team down. Let himself down. And on enemy turf. But the Eagles' defense held the Panthers, and by the grace of God, Nickle High walked away with the W.

But more than a rough game powered by his mistakes, he missed his sister. In the past, she'd stretch out on the bed with him for a little post-game breakdown. Then they talked about life—school, homecoming, what they wanted to eat for Thanksgiving, what they'd get Mom and Dad for Christmas.

The absence of her voice rang in his ears. Her eighteenth birthday passed without any fanfare, though Mom sent her some money. She'd texted her thanks a day later.

Along with his almost-game-losing interception, he couldn't stop picturing the girl on the West End High sideline who looked like Cassidy. Only skinnier and with shorter hair. When he tried to get a better look, she was gone.

His parents had resigned themselves to the new way of life, which bothered him a little. Last summer he wanted them to kick her out; now he wanted them to go after her.

Mom kept all the family routines and traditions—like making a victory cake for Caleb after the game. He devoured it with Shift, Jumbo, and Kidwell.

In the middle of washing down a large bite of cake with a glass of milk, Shift asked, *"Whatever happen to Emery, Queen of Operation Revenge?"*

"Back in Cleveland." Short and sweet, leaving no room for questions.

Caleb gave up on sleeping, flipped on the small lamp by his bed, and reached for his laptop.

On Facebook, he searched for Emery Quinn, his heart ka-chunking when her pretty face popped on the screen.

He typed *Hi* on her Wall, then deleted it. *Hi? Don't be dumb, Ransom. Just send her a message.*

The only way to contact Emery was through Facebook. Dad was making him save up to buy his own phone, since he "lost it." Caleb couldn't bring himself to tell him Cass tossed it in the Gulf. He'd messaged Emery "Happy Birthday" in October, but she never responded. She'd missed his September birthday, but he didn't mind.

Then she posted her mom had died. He'd stared at the post for a long time, trying to understand. Mrs. Quinn was dead? It didn't feel real.

> Em, your mom died? Was she sick? Are you okay? I don't know what to say, but I wish I was there with you. I don't have a phone right now. Cass threw mine in the Gulf. Can you send me your number? I'll call you on the landline.

She'd never messaged back. But he understood. Now, scrolling Emery's wall, there were hundreds of condolences. As far as he could tell, she'd not responded to any of them.

He looked up when someone knocked on his door. "Yeah?"

Dad peeked in. "You okay? I saw the light on."

"I'm sore." He turned the laptop to his dad. "Just looking on Emery's Facebook wall."

Dad sat on the edge of the bed. "Losing her mom has to be hard. Especially when they were such a close family."

"Do you still have her dad's number? Could I call him?"

"Tell you what, why don't we run out and get you a replacement phone? Then you can call him, get Emery's number."

"What happened to saving up for my own phone?"

"Cassidy told Mom she threw yours in the drink."

"What? When?"

"She was asking if you had a new phone. Or a new number. I think she misses you. And you should've told me the truth."

"You think she'll come home soon?" Caleb said.

"I don't know. In a way, we're getting along with her better now that she's out of the house." Dad patted Caleb's foot. "Great game tonight. You took some hard hits."

"We beat the West End. That's all that matters."

"It's always nice to defeat the rival." Dad stood in the doorway, shadowed by the low, hallway lights. "Are you working at the Starlight tomorrow?"

"All day."

"See if you can get someone to cover a shift. We'll get you a phone, maybe grab a bite to eat."

When Dad had gone, Caleb glanced at Emery's Facebook wall one last time and decided on one simple message.

I miss you.

Sunday's Royal
GAZETTE
April 27

Sea Blue Beach Welcomes House of Blue Royals at Friday Night Reception

Site of Royal Brunch Trashed. State Department Investigating

EMERY

Now...

It was becoming her thing. She wanted to be the first to see the paper besides the paperboys. She woke early, showered, and rode her favorite motel bike to the *Gazette* office.

Riding down Avenue C toward Rachel Kirby Lane, the morning twilight fought the lingering ink of night and promised a clear spring day.

She was nervous. This paper had to be spectacular. Why? Because it was another chapter in Sea Blue Beach's story.

Social media was already propagated with its version of what happened, the royal watchers posting photos of the destroyed brunch site and others sharing it. Some posted photos of the royal couple from some other event and claimed it was Sea Blue Beach.

But the *Gazette* was telling the truth.

Last night, she'd kept checking her phone while skating with Caleb in case she missed a call from Floyd. Then while sipping a post-skate chai tea with him at One More Cup, she glanced at it every thirty seconds.

At one point, he settled his hand on hers. "It's going to be fine."

Now, pedaling toward the paper, she spotted the paperboys on the porch, folding and sorting. Owen met her on the sidewalk before she could stop the bike.

"You're not going to like this." He handed her a copy, then aimed his flashlight on the front page. "You might want to get off the bike first."

"Owen, please don't tell me." Her bike clattered against the pavement.

"The ads are missing."

~~~~~

Then . . .

During the school day, she'd almost forget. Caught up with her friends, classes, and sports, life seemed perfectly normal.

Then she'd walk through the parking lot under stark, bare trees toward her pre-owned yellow Jeep and remember.

Mom was gone.

Entering the quiet, dark kitchen after practice, she remembered.

Mom was gone.

No matter how many lights she turned on, or how loud she blasted the music, the house felt empty and cold.

Mom was gone.

When she sat with Dad at the grief counselor's, Emery definitely remembered.

Mom was gone.

Tonight, as she walked through the kitchen door, her phone blared from her backpack. She didn't recognize the number, but every now and then, one of Mom's old friends called her. To check in. But it only brought it all up again . . .

She answered with slow "Hello?" as she walked toward the large pane window, where a month ago Mom lay in a hospice bed, watching the summer green surrender to fall colors.

Now the trees were bare, and the colors faded to gray and brown.

"Hey, Em, it's me."

Caleb Ransom. Emery dropped to the swivel chair by the window and watched a passing car through watery eyes.

"I thought your sister tossed your phone in the Gulf."

"So you read my message?"

"Yeah, but—" She'd discarded all her Sea Blue Beach memories— and Caleb Ransom. She still had a message on her phone from Delilah, waiting to be answered.

"It's okay. I just wanted you to know I'm really sorry about your mom. She was always so nice to me."

"She was nice to me too." She laughed through soft tears. Caleb didn't say anything, just waited. "H-how's school?" she said. "How's football?"

She knew a little bit—Mr. Star Quarterback—from sneaking over to his Facebook Wall after his "I miss you" message.

"School's good. We beat West End, so we're going to district."

"Did you find any trash on their field?" The sound of his laugh made her smile.

"Yeah, the interception I threw on fourth and goal. Pure trash."

"But you won?"

"We won."

"That's good." She lowered the phone to cover a deep inhale, the one intended to guard against Caleb's warm, comforting voice. She felt fragile, like she'd break if she spoke one more word.

"Em, you okay?"

She cleared her throat. "Y-yes." But then she started to tremble with heavier tears.

"Hey," he said. "I was on my way to meet you that night. I wasn't blowing you off or anything."

"It's fine. Probably worked out for the best."

"Yeah, probably." She waited for him to say good-bye. "How was your birthday?"

"Fine." Emery pressed her fingers under her eyes to stave off the tears. "Mom threw me a party. At least she tried. Dad and her friends ended up taking over. Then she died three days later."

"Man, that's rough. Sorry, Em."

"I know." She caught a solo tear slipping down her cheek.

"I bet the party made her happy."

"It did, and we had fun." Emery focused out the window where clusters of dried leaves skipped over the lawn. "I should go."

"Yeah, of course. Hey, Em, I was thinking . . . maybe I can road-trip to see you. With Shift riding shotgun. He asked about you."

"No, Caleb, don't . . . I-I can't. I just can't."

"Oh, okay, sure, but if you ever—"

"Have a nice life, Caleb. I mean it." She hit end before he blurted out something irrational like *"I love you."* Because she'd felt love the moment she heard his voice. But being with him was impossible. Besides living a thousand miles away, she associated him with the saddest time of her life. But he also made her happy, and she didn't want to be happy. Not for a long time to come.

⌒

Now . . .

"Rough day?"

Emery twisted around to see Delilah joining her on the beach, where she sat on a copy of the *Sunday Royal Gazette*.

"I'm not good company right now, Delilah."

"Sometimes it all comes crashing down, doesn't it?" She kicked off her flip-flops and buried her feet in the sand.

"I don't know what you mean," Emery said, irritated Delilah had settled next to her.

"The images of Friday night, along with your story, were beautiful. I hardly noticed the ad holes." To this, Emery scoffed. "You did more than most, Emery. You tried to help Sea Blue Beach by inviting the royals."

She glanced at Delilah. "I'm a square peg trying to fit a round hole."

"I wanted a baby," Delilah said without any segue, and Emery was suddenly rescued from her downward spiral. "I'd just turned thirty, and after twelve years of singing in smoke-filled clubs, meeting Samson, hitting it big, touring the world, I ached to be a different Delilah Mead. A wife. A mother. Samson and I had created so much together that a child felt like a natural extension of us."

April's breeze was gentle and laced with an evening warmth as Emery listened to Delilah's story, picturing the wide-eyed beauty with full lips and a pixie haircut wearing a bright pink dress and white go-go boots on the cover of Mom's favorite record album.

"To my surprise, I was pregnant the next year. I was going to be a *mom*. No awards or success or cheering concert crowd, no amount of money, compared. Even Samson marveled, got swept up in marriage talk, looked into buying a house. We'd finally settled on a wedding day when I miscarried. Samson decided then and there that children were not our future. He slammed the door on anything outside of music."

Emery exhaled, waiting for the rest, sensing small sparks of hope popping on her insides.

"We recorded another album as the world changed around us. JFK and his brother were shot, as were Martin Luther King Jr. and Malcolm X. Our generation was protesting the Vietnam War. We did drugs to find the meaning of life, but there's not a drug in the world with the true answers. I know because I tried them all."

"Should I be writing this down?"

Delilah's soft laugh harmonized with the breeze in the palm fronds. "This story is just for you. Listen, Emery, *listen*. Sometimes the meaning of a person's story lies beneath the words." She tapped her chest. "You feel it here." She paused a moment, then said, "Samson became even more driven, and I began to wonder, 'Who am I living with?' I tried to stay in it, make Samson Delilah work, but I hungered for change. I was tired of the road, tired of being about nothing but music. Tired of the parties, tired of living with a man who refused to marry me."

"If you didn't find meaning in your music, then what?"

"One night I ended up at a Hollywood coffee shop with a bunch of long-haired hippy types who weren't stoned. They were full of light and life. Happy . . . no, joyful. Little did I know I'd walked into a room of Jesus Freaks."

"Jesus Freaks?" Emery made a face. "Never heard of them."

"They were as much a part of the counterculture revolution as the Summer of Love or Woodstock, impacting their corner of the world. A few months later, I met Jesus for myself, and my life changed, literally, from the inside out."

"And Samson? Your music career?"

"We broke up. Personally and musically. I recorded on my

own for a while, but when you step into a whole new identity, the old one doesn't fit. You see yourself and others differently. I didn't need music to feel worthy because I'd found the One who made me worthy." Delilah turned at the sound behind her, then patted Emery's arm. "That's how I ended up here. In a town with Immanuel, God with us."

She stood, dusting sand from her yoga pants. "Caleb is here."

CALEB

"Evening, Delilah," he said as she passed, gently squeezing his arm.

"Evening, Caleb. Take care of our girl."

"Will do." He sat in Delilah's place as the last of the sunset streaked gold and orange across a darkening ocean.

Emery scooped grains of sand to dribble on the exposed portions of the *Sunday Gazette*—while sitting on the rest. "Delilah was telling me her story."

"Really?" He glanced back at her cottage. "How'd that come about?"

"She just started talking. Said she left music because she found something greater." Emery stared toward the water as the seagulls swung low, searching for food, gliding on the current. "Ever wonder if life is against you?" she asked. "Even God?"

"Sometimes." He tucked a lock of her loose hair behind her ear. "Talk to me, Quinn."

"If I were Elliot and Henrietta, I'd fire me and sell the paper."

"Ever think you came down for more than a job?" Caleb rested his arms on his raised knees.

"Like what?" She shifted slightly toward him. "You?"

He glanced at her, surprised. "Maybe. Or to have some closure with your mom."

"I already had closure. I just didn't know it. She's always with me in my heart, in my memories."

"There you have it," he said.

Emery tugged on an exposed corner of the paper. "I really wanted the paper to succeed, Caleb. Wanted to prove I could do the job. Once I arrived, I was surprised by how much I loved this place, how every corner felt like a place I want to be, even with the memories of Mom. Then, surprise, you were here." She looked toward the stand of palm trees. "I didn't feel alone here."

"Sounds like Sea Blue Beach. None of us are ever alone."

"Because of Immanuel?"

"More than we probably realize."

"Immanuel aside," she said, raising up, pulling the paper out from underneath. "You've seen this?" Emery flipped through the pages. "The much-ballyhooed collector's edition has big blank spaces with teeny-weeny text in the middle saying 'Gallagher Real Estate' or 'Leman Pre-owned.'"

Caleb scooted toward her. "You could argue they still got their advertising. I can read these names. I get who's advertising."

Her laugh sounded sincere. Free. "Where were you when I was getting blasted by angry customers?"

"Call me next time. I'll be there."

"Next time?" She groaned. "Please tell me this won't happen again. There's no rhyme or reason to it, Caleb. Elliot hasn't called yet, but when he does, he'll want answers. By this time tomorrow, I might be out of a job, leaving Sea Blue Beach. Does Immanuel, God with us, come with us when we leave?"

He wrapped his hand around hers, and with a sigh, as if she couldn't keep her chin up any longer, fell against his shoulder.

"When Cassidy ran off, I remember my grandfather saying, 'Let's see what God will do.'"

After a moment, Caleb stretched out on the sand, taking Emery back with him so she rested her head on his chest. From the night sky, the first stars winked at them.

"Em?"

"Hmm?"

"I love you."

She stiffened. "W-what?"

"I love you," he said, gently rolling over to see her face, the light from the courtyard casting a soft glow against her hair. "I want to marry you."

"M-marry me?" Emery jumped to her feet, slipping on the sandy *Sunday Royal Gazette*.

He slapped his hand to his chest. "You stole my heart the summer we met, and I've been searching for it ever since."

His phone rang, but he ignored it.

"You're serious?" Emery said. "A minute ago, we were talking about my failure as the editor of a small-town newspaper, possibly moving on, and now—" His phone went off again, bouncing between rings and pinging texts. "Answer your phone, Caleb."

"I'd rather you answered me." He glanced at the screen. "It's Cassidy. She can wait."

"See what she wants. It seems urgent." Emery took a few steps, giving them space. "And I need a moment."

When he answered, Bentley's voice was loud and wild. "Uncle Caleb! Mom's crying. Like all the time. I'm scared."

"Okay, okay, buddy. Calm down. Are you all right? Is she all right?"

"I don't know. . . . She's in the bathroom and won't come out. I got to pee."

"Where are you?"

"Somewhere in Mobile. Did you see the text? I sent the address. Can you come, please?"

"I'm on my way. And go down to the lobby if you need a bathroom." Hanging up, he turned to Emery. "It's Bentley. He said—"

"I heard," Emery said, lightly brushing her fingers over his hair. "You need to go. He sounds scared."

"Feels like we've been here before." He gathered Emery in his arms. "My family having a crisis when I want—need—to be with you."

"I'd go with you if I didn't have my own crisis to confront. Plus I don't think Cassidy wants an audience."

"I'll call you," he promised.

"Unless she throws your phone in the ocean. Or a pool." She grinned. "Maybe the shower."

Caleb clamped her close for a kiss. Not one but two. "She won't. I'll call you."

She walked with him to his truck, and at the driver's side door, Caleb had one last thing to say.

"Em, I'm not trying to recapture some teen fantasy from our summer together. We both have bittersweet memories from that year."

"We do."

"But is it possible we met *then* for *now*? Sixteen years later, we're back to where we started. Only now we can say yes to love." At his truck, he raised her face to his. "You stole my heart a long time ago. Either give it back or love it. Love me."

"If I keep your heart, then I'll give you mine." She peered up at him. "But for this moment, can my kisses be enough?"

26

~~

EMERY

The light of her phone lit the dark room, and Emery slapped her hand against the night table, fumbling for it, yanking it off the charger. "Hello?"

From the corner, the old digital clock read 5:05.

It was too early to be Caleb. He'd arrived in Mobile late last night and booked a room for himself and Bentley. Cassidy remained locked away.

"It's a dive, but clean. Bent has an unoccupied bathroom."

"Hello?" Head still planted on her pillow, she waited for an answer, holding onto the depths of sleep where she was free, no longer the center of a royal scandal.

"Em, you got to come." It was Ava, her voice soft and frantic.

Emery sat up, snapping awake. "Why? What happened? Is it Jamie? If he broke up with you—"

"No, no, we're good. It's, um, Mom. Joanna. Dad's beside himself."

"Mom?" She pictured her mom, small and pale, wheezing the death rattle in her hospice bed. "I mean, Joanna? Is she all right?"

Emery threw off the covers and stumbled against the antique chest of drawers.

"She was standing in the café office and—" She began to weep, and a voice sounded in the background.

"Em, it's me, Jamie. Can you come? Doug and the girls are struggling. I know family is not your thing—"

"I'm on my way."

"Are you sure?"

"I said I'm on my way."

~~~~~

She'd never been in a hospital. Once she and Dad returned from Sea Blue Beach with a weakened Mom, hospice came to their house to care for her. Walking the white hall with brown doors toward Joanna's room—after fifteen hours on the road with a gallon of coffee and a gallon of Diet Coke—she was spacey and jittery, not braced for what awaited on the other side of the door.

Nevertheless, she peered into the room through the dim lights to see Dad perched by the bed, his hand locked with Joanna's, his expression drawn—a look she knew well. A look that defined her anxiety every minute on the road, no matter how loud she played the radio. No matter how loud she sang along. Nothing conquered her real and surprising fear of losing Joanna.

Ava rose first, her brown eyes tired but bright. She gripped Emery close. "Thank goodness you're here. We need you."

"You do?" she whispered. Really? Even with Dad and the sisters here? And Jamie?

"You're our rock." Elianna moved Ava aside to hug Emery. Blakely piled on, stretching her long arms around them.

"We're all here now," Ava said. "Though I'd rather stage this family reunion at my wedding, not in Mom's hospital room."

Emery bent over Dad, hugging his shoulders, resting her

cheek on his gray hair. "Everything's going to be all right." She tried to sound confident, though she knew nothing more than Joanna had collapsed. "What's the final diagnosis?"

"They ran tests," Elianna said. "She's dehydrated, and her blood pressure is whack. Between the cafés and the wedding, she's been going nonstop. This past weekend she worked in our warehouse without air conditioning or any fans. Never stopped to drink or eat."

"The temperature was ninety-five in that windowless building," Ava said.

"Em, can I get you something to eat?" Blakely rubbed her hand down Emery's back. "Cafeteria is closed, but the vending machine has Clif bars."

"I'm good." She pressed her hand on Blakely's. "I ate my weight in road-trip junk."

"I'll bring *good* coffee and pastries from the café tomorrow." Elianna stood on the other side of Dad, one hand on his shoulder, her attention on the silent machines checking Joanna's oxygen, blood pressure, and heart rate. "No offense to the hospital cafeteria."

Of all the scenarios Emery imagined she'd walk into—formed from Ava or Jamie's distracted, spotty updates—a cocoon of family was not one of them.

"They gave her something to sleep," Dad said. "But someone should stay with her. I don't want her waking up alone."

No, he wouldn't. He feared Mom dying between hospice shifts while he was teaching at the university. Or while Emery was at school. Or if someone stepped into the kitchen for lunch.

"Let's figure out who's staying," Ava said. "Dad, you need some rest. Elianna, you've got the cafés in the morning, and, Blake, you have school. I'll stay if someone can bring my laptop. I can get work done in the quiet."

"I'll stay," Emery said, glancing at Joanna, who looked so help-less and frail under the hospital blanket.

"Are you sure?" Dad said. "You've had a long drive."

"Positive." She patted the back of his chair. "I can sleep here. I did lots of chair sleeping with Mom."

Dad squeezed her hand as if to say, *We've been here before, haven't we?*

There was some debate over the next morning's schedule—who would relieve Emery—but in short order, she found herself alone in a dark room with Joanna.

Sitting in Dad's chair, she fixed a wrinkle in the blanket, then finger-combed Joanna's platinum hair, which was rarely out of place. Then cupped their hands together and waited, listening.

"Hey, you," she whispered. "You've been in my life as long as my mom. Maybe going forward, I could try a little harder? Because this is making me realize how well you've loved me. But I'm so tired. Why don't we just rest?"

She fell asleep on her folded arms, waking with a start when something touched her head.

"Emery?" Joanna said in a hoarse whisper. "What are you doing here?"

"Hey, Jo." She shoved a lock of hair from her eyes and scootched the chair closer. "I was going to ask *you* the same thing."

"Oh, you know, a girl likes a little drama once in a while," she said. "This is some pickle, isn't it?"

"A very sour one."

Joanna smiled. "Your dad likes to remind us how much you loved pickles as a girl. Is that why you're here? A big pickle moment?"

"I'm here because you scared the wits out of me, Joanna."

"Ah, just a bit of overwork. I knew I wasn't drinking or eating enough. That warehouse was so hot, but I wanted to get it organized before the wedding. Why, I couldn't tell you. I can't remember the last time I slept more than five hours."

"Listen, you can't do this to Dad and me." She pressed Joanna's hand to her cheek, washing it with a tear. "He's lost one wife. He can't lose another."

"I'm not going anywhere. Too stubborn."

"And I've already lost a mom, Joanna. I *cannot* lose another." Her gaze locked with Joanna's glistening one.

"You're not going to lose me. Not anytime soon. And it's good to know you want me around."

"I deserve that, don't I?"

"Emery, I love you like my own." Her grip on Emery's hand was soft and weak, but her message was strong and clear. "I never expected to replace Rosie."

"I know, I know. I just . . . convinced myself you all were a family without me, and it was up to me to remember Mom."

"How about we make a pact, you and me: to never forget Rosie. She's the unseen guest at the dinner table, the one we add to conversations. 'Didn't Rosie love tacos?' Or 'This is Rosie's recipe, one of our favorites.'"

"Or 'Put on a Delilah Mead record. Rosie loved her music.'"

"Perfect. Do we have a deal?"

"Yes, we have a deal."

The nurse entered on her rounds, so Emery escaped for a cup of coffee. It was hot and black, gut-rot, and after a few gulps, she poured it out.

"I'm sure she shot something into this tube to knock me out," Joanna said when Emery returned to the room. "Until I drift off, I want to hear the updates while I have you all to myself. I feel rather lucky. How was the royal visit? I saw the news about trash on the beach. What happened?"

Emery released every detail in one seamless breath—how excited the town was, how down-to-earth but unmistakably regal and impressive the royal couple were, and how the ensemble Joanna sent was perfect for the first night.

"I have to see pictures," she said, her words slightly slurred. "But when my eyes are open. Go on, what else?"

"The trashing? Still under investigation by government and local authorities. My royal collector's edition of the *Sunday Royal Gazette* printed without ads."

Joanna sighed. "Tell me about the boy. Ava called him a 'hunk-o-rama.'"

Well, that was one word for him. "Caleb Ransom. We met the summer Dad, Mom, and I were there. He was my first kiss, my first love. The moment I met him, I felt like I'd known him my whole life."

"You love him now," Joanna said. "I hear it in your voice."

"Do I? He says he loves me. Said I'd stole his heart when we were sixteen, and if I wasn't going to love it to give it back." Repeating it out loud painted a reality of life without him—again. After four short months in Sea Blue Beach, she could not imagine a future without Caleb Ransom. "I'm scared, Jo. I could love him too much. Maybe I already do. What if I lose him? I'm not sure I could bear it. I know, I know, I can't go through life fearing the people I love will die."

"Then don't, Em. Let the fear go. When I lost Eric, I lost my compass, my reason for being." Joanna's voice rebounded as she told her story. "We were so intertwined with each other as high school and college sweethearts. He was the only man I'd ever loved. But I had to grow up. I had to find faith and hope in God. I was a thirty-eight-year-old widow with two little girls. I resigned myself to being a dedicated mother and running our first café. Then I sat next to your dad at dinner."

"He says there's room in his heart for you and Mom. There's room in yours for Dad and Eric."

"The heart is a marvelous thing, Emery. Rosie gave him you. And now I have you. Eric gave me Ava and Elianna, and now Doug has two more loving daughters."

"And Blakely?" Emery laughed softly.

"Oh that girl . . . she owns all of us." Joanna's voice began to fade. "But what would the world be like without Blakely Quinn?"

"Yes, what would the world be like . . ." Emery rose up kiss Joanna's cheek. "Night, Mom. I'll be here when you wake up again." She bent to her ear. "I love you."

CALEB

"Cass?" He entered her Star Motel room Monday morning, hoping to see his sister out of the bathroom, composed, and sitting on the bed. But the room was dark. The bathroom door was shut. "I brought breakfast."

He set the carry-out tray from Fat Boys Diner on the desk under the mounted TV. Bentley was in the room Caleb rented, working on some school assignments. Principal Tucker called Caleb this morning, wondering about Bentley since he was absent from the Friday night reception and now, school.

"His mom wanted to go on an adventure."

"Is he coming back?"

"I hope so."

"I'll ask his teacher to email his assignments. He can keep up with learning no matter what."

God bless that man. And Bentley was thrilled.

"Cassidy, come on, please. Bentley is scared. He says you've been in there for two days." Caleb backed up to sit on the edge of the bed, phone in hand.

Emery had called during breakfast to say she was in north Alabama, on her way to Cleveland. She sounded tired and sad, yet resolved.

His news was nothing exciting. He'd slept horribly, but this morning he was hoping to lure Cassidy out.

"You know you said there were some things you couldn't tell me?" Caleb waited, hoping for a response. "Remember?" He paused again. Nothing. "But you can tell me anything. The truth is probably better than anything I could imagine."

Suddenly, the door jerked open and Cassidy emerged, dressed in a stained T-shirt and baggy shorts, her blond hair stringy around her face, in need of a wash. Caleb stood, pointing to breakfast.

"The food is on the—" She launched into him, knocking him back. Arms locked around his waist, her head buried in his chest, Cassidy's tense frame shook with deep, rolling sobs. Caleb wrapped her up.

"Hey, hey, I'm here, I'm here. Everything's going to be all right."

"I want to come home, Caleb. I want to come home."

"Then come home, Cass. Come home."

27

EMERY

On Tuesday evening, she walked into the Quinn household, which was fragrant with Blakely's taco efforts.

She'd spent the afternoon with Lou Lennon, who gave her a shot of encouragement as only he could do. In his gruff, put-on-your-big-girl-pants way. *"Do the job you were hired to do, Emery. Don't shrink back and hide."*

As she left Lou, she called Elliot and explained what happened with the paper and why she was in Ohio, assuring him Rex was at the helm until she got back.

He was kind, saying they'd talk when she returned to Sea Blue Beach. His steady, almost monotone, voice gave her no clue about the paper's future, nor her own.

A text from Rex brought her up to date with the Wednesday edition. After multiple tests to the printer—all of Sunday's missing ads included— he was confident the edition would print just fine. Nevertheless, he planned to stay on guard.

"Yay, Emery's here." Blakely greeted her from the kitchen, where she was browning fish in a cast-iron skillet. How many times had Blakely declared, "Yay, Emery's here," and Emery hadn't responded? Dozens. Pain and fear made her blind and dull.

"Look who's home." Blake pointed the spatula toward the family room, where Joanna reclined in her BarcaLounger, wearing a robe and fuzzy slippers. Dad sat next to her, reading a book. Elianna was ragdolled in the oversized ottoman, half awake. A game show was muted on the TV. "Just in time for Taco Tuesday, her favorite. Em, please, please, please make your guacamole."

"Yes, please," Joanna said with a nod at Emery. "It's one of Rosie's recipes."

"Who's going to help me cut up the avocados? Dad? Elianna?" Emery said, with a small smile at Joanna, and then feigned a stink when no one's hand raised. "Oh, I see how it is. Big sister and little sister are left on their own. Ha, shows you. We'll leave the cleaning up to you guys."

She'd just mashed the avocados when Ava and Jamie walked in, waving their marriage license.

"It's real now. No going back." Ava glanced at Emery, and everything in her expression said, *Thank you.*

"She's stuck with me," Jamie said. "Well, almost." He glanced at Emery with his own look of gratitude. Who knew the guy who hit her in the head with a Frisbee as she crossed the Oval would become her friend and, one day, her family?

Dinner was lively, with everyone talking at once, then among themselves, then across the table. Dad and Joanna presided from their prospective ends, Joanna's weak physical presence nothing against her inner strength.

By the time Emery crawled into her old room's very comfortable Murphy bed, she had confirmed she'd walk down the aisle in front of two hundred guests wearing pink. She'd also agreed that hunk-o-rama Caleb Ransom would be her plus-one.

She hoped, anyway. She'd not asked him yet. But he did love

her. And love was a powerful force. She'd done some research on the power of love and forgiveness, considering a series for the *Gazette*. Sea Blue Beach itself could use a bit of both.

Along the way, she read quite a few articles about the disastrous royal visit. *"What were the royals doing in Sea Blue Beach, Florida, in the first place? Princess Gemma does come from a shady, redneck background. Has she infected the royal family?"*

Funny how narrow-minded people can be so . . . narrow-minded.

But for now, she was tired and full of yummy fish tacos and the love of her family. She'd taken too long to accept what Dad and Joanna built.

"Em?" Blakely knocked on the door, then peeked in. "Your phone was pinging and ringing downstairs." She extended it toward her.

"I was about to miss that thing." She reached for the phone, seeing a missed call from Simon.

"Do you think I could come down for the summer since I didn't come for spring break? I could get a job and—"

"Do you really want to, Blake?"

"I promise not to get in your way or anything." She leaned against the wall, head down, voice unsure. Her demeanor was so unlike the vivacious, loud Blakely Quinn.

"Absolutely you can come. You could work at the paper or the Starlight skating rink or one of the coffee shops. Delilah might want help at the Sands."

"Honest?" She brightened and stood tall. "I'll help out, won't get in your way."

"Hey, come here." She patted the bed beside her, and when Blakely crawled in next to her, Emery wrapped her in her arms. "I love you, and I'm sorry if I ever made it seem like you were a nuisance or a bother. Or that I wasn't interested. That's on me and my fears, okay? You're amazing, Blakeley Quinn. I'm so very happy you're my sister."

And so Emery had her first sisterly laugh-cry with Blakely, then determined June would be the best month for her to come down. When she ran off yelling, announcing her plans to Dad and Joanna, Emery listened to Simon's message.

"Emery? Simon here. You won't believe it, but our special guests are returning. Small private gathering. But *they are*"—he put a lot of emphasis on *they are*—"coming back. Rex said you're out of town. Let's talk when you get back. Hurry home."

The Royal Blues were returning? What? How? Why? Ah, who cares, the royals were coming.

Emery jumped off the bed for a quick jig around her room. Thank God!

"Emery?" Joanna's soft voice sounded through the door. "I've been thinking about your missing ads and—"

Emery opened the door. "You've been thinking about the *Gazette's* missing ads?"

"Convalescing gives one time to think. Look, this is probably not on the same scale, but we had an issue with the café network going offline." Joanna laughed at the memory. "Drove us nuts. As it turned out, someone on our cleaning crew was unplugging the modem. . . ."

CALEB

Because Cassidy promised Bentley an adventure, and because she spent two days in the bathroom crying, and because Principal Tucker gave Bentley another day of excused absences, Caleb, Cassidy, and Bentley went exploring.

In between the Africatown Heritage House, Richards-DAR House Museum, the Colonial Fort Condé, and USS ALABAMA Battleship Memorial Park, Cassidy whispered her story to Caleb.

"Maybe it's too late for me to come home. Too late to turn this *Titanic* around." She motioned to herself. "Iceberg ahead."

"There are millions of people across the globe who turn their lives around. Who avoid the iceberg."

"Yet I keep running into mine. I try to change, and I end up right back where I started. Ripped apart. He was right . . . I'm nothing. No one wants me."

"Okay, enough of that, Cass. Who is this jackwagon who said you were nothing?"

"Look at Bent. He's having a blast." She smiled toward her son, who was snapping a million photos of the USS *Alabama*'s torpedo room with Cassidy's phone. "It all hit me this weekend. I'm trash. Then I imploded with all the stuff I've been holding in. The tears wouldn't stop. I locked myself in the bathroom so I *wouldn't* scare Bentley."

"You scared him anyway." He bent to see her face. "How are you trash? In all the years Dad told me to take out the garbage, never once did he say, 'Don't forget your sister.'"

She smiled for a second, then sobered. "Coach Sanchez."

"Sanchez? *Sanchez* said you were trash? When? Why?"

"Wow, it's tight in here." She bent to walk through the ship's watertight door, following Bentley for the rest of the tour. "The spring of my junior year, I met him at a party on the West End. At Ty Carson's house." Ty had been a star tailback for the Panthers. Ended up washing-out at the college level. "The moment I saw him . . . I can't explain it, something happened to me. He drew me in with some sort of pheromone-producing magnet. I couldn't look at anyone else. Thanks to Dad, I knew who he was—a former Florida State defensive end who'd gone pro until an injury ended his career. I never expected to see him in Sea Blue Beach. Never expected him at Ty Carson's place. Never expected to be so bowled over by him."

"He grew up in Pensacola," Caleb said. "But we were all surprised when he took the West End coaching job."

"Yeah . . . anyway, he winked at me, smiled, nodded in that sexy dude way for me to come talk to him. I *floated* over, literally, I'm not sure my feet hit the floor. Of all the girls in the room—and there were plenty—he picked me. I told him I was eighteen, on a gap year playing travel softball before going to Florida State. He pouted like he didn't want me to go away. Said something like, 'And just when I'd just met the most beautiful girl I've ever seen.' I was putty under his charm. He started telling me about FSU, the best places to live on or off campus, where to hang out, and named people he'd introduce me to once I got there, talking about how he'd come visit me whenever he could. Visit me? He made me feel so special. So wanted. And it's not like I didn't have that with Dad or you or Grandpa. But you're family. This guy, who could have any girl he wanted, picked *me*. Right then and there, I decided I'd met the love of my life."

"Didn't he have a fiancée?"

"Mom, look at this." Bentley pointed to the mannequin dressed as a World War Two sailor standing in the radio room.

"Cool, Bent. Think you want to join the navy some day?"

"Maybe." He aimed her phone all over the place with a snap, snap, snap.

"Have fun deleting most of those once you get home."

"I don't mind. We're making good memories after this rotten weekend."

"So, you and Sanchez." They continued from the radio room to the kitchen.

"I didn't know he was engaged. He asked me out and—" She

cut Caleb a sharp side glance. "Two weeks later, I was sleeping with him. My choice. He didn't force me. I honestly believed he was my one true love."

"Why didn't you tell anyone?"

"Because they'd tell him the truth, wouldn't they? That I was seventeen and still in high school. He was twenty-four and a high school coach. Didn't matter it was with the rival school. He'd have gotten in trouble, which means he'd break up with me and that could not, would not happen. So I skipped school and snuck around, which I liked. Allison covered for me when I stayed with him." She caught a tear in the corner of her eye.

"Was he the reason you dropped out of school?" Caleb said. "Did you really live with Posey when you left? Or with him?"

"Posey. The summer *plan* was to get him back in my life. We'd broken up because—Hey, Bentley, I don't think you're supposed to touch that, okay? Be careful." Cassidy paused as they walked through a makeshift operating room. "Must've been something to be at sea in one of these. Anyway, I was such an idiot." She moved forward. "And I hate myself for it, I really do."

"Why'd he break up with you?"

"His fiancée moved in. Which was a huge surprise to me. We were supposed to go to Disney World at the beginning of June, right after school let out, but he never called. Never texted. In my insane naïveté, I went over to his house, thinking he must be sick or something. He wasn't there, so I waited. Two hours later he came home with Tavia and about a hundred suitcases. She was drop-dead gorgeous with intelligent eyes, and I hated her instantly. He was shocked to see me but played it off, introducing me as the daughter of some West End boosters. I cried the whole way home. He said I was the most beautiful woman he'd ever seen, and I was going to hold him to it." Cassidy pounded her fist against her palm. "He was mine, so move over Tavia."

"Thus the job at the Driftwood Door." They took the stairs to the top deck and walked into the sunshine.

"I started stalking him. Online. In person. I sat in the bleachers when their preseason football practices started. I figured out when Tavia traveled for work and broke into his house. I thought if I got him alone, I could make him realize I was the love of his life. That's when he lost it. Called me a freak. A nobody. A loser. Trash. Told me to get out, and if he saw me again, he'd pelt me with rotten eggs."

She hurried forward, arm outstretched, as Bentley leaned over the edge of the ship.

"Rotten eggs? Who keeps rotten eggs in their house?" Caleb watched Bentley cross the ship under the massive guns. "Why didn't you talk to me? Or Mom and Dad?"

She shook her head, face turned away as she wiped her cheeks. "I was too ashamed. When he said all that stuff, I felt out of control. The heartache felt like knives. I went all *Fatal Attraction* on him. Can't even remember half the stuff I did. Then the *crème de la crème*: He broke up with Tavia that summer and started dating a West End teacher. That's when I had to get out of Sea Blue Beach. Everything reminded me of him and how dumb, ugly, and insignificant I was."

She turned to Caleb. "I know I owe you, Mom, Dad, and my friends a huge apology, but I'm not sure I can repeat this story again. And to be real honest, some days I think I'm not over him." She lowered her head, then looked up, eyes tracking Bentley as he explored. "Sanchez is not Bentley's father, by the way."

"Cass, you're living in the past—in the lies of someone who didn't love you. Come home, let your family tell you who you are. Look at your son. Is he the product of a loser? Of trash?"

Across the way, the eleven-year-old was talking to a Korean War veteran, listening and asking questions. "He's a star."

"Mom will freak when I walk in the door. She'll really love you now."

"Ha, she won't when I find Sanchez, wherever he is, and pelt him with rotten eggs."

Cassidy's laugh broke any remaining tension between them. "Caleb, I'm sorry . . . for everything." She didn't look at him, but Caleb embraced the sincerity in every word.

"Know what, me too. I'm sorry for my part. I wasn't always a good brother."

They drifted through a peaceful silence. Then Cassidy hooked her arm through Caleb's. "So tell me all about Emery Quinn. Bentley says you should marry her."

"Bentley!"

EMERY

She'd just carried her last bag into Cottage 7—she packed up more things from home—when strong arms gripped her from behind. "I missed you."

"You missed me?" She twisted around to see a tired but happy-looking Caleb. "It's only been three days."

"Forever to a guy in love." He searched her face with a bit of wonder.

She'd imagined this scene the moment she crossed the Florida line. Not before. Because she wanted it to be honest, and about the true Caleb Ransom, not her idea of him.

She'd spent far too many years believing the lie that she belonged on the outside looking in as the only way to preserve

Mom's memories. But if Delilah was right and there was a "God with us," then why waste time living in the past?

As for Caleb, every confession, every kiss, drew her closer to the truth. She loved him.

His kiss was firm, then soft, tasting of something sweet. His arms flexed tight around her, and with one exhale, she let love have its way.

"Have you talked to Simon? Did he tell you?"

"He told me. In fact, let's go see him." Caleb kissed her again, then pulled away, smiling. "What are you thinking, Emery Quinn? That your royal invitation has staying power?"

"No, but I'm glad they're coming back. I was thinking that I like it when you hold me." She pulled his face to hers for a kiss, then jerked away with an wild exclamation. "Oh my word, I've figured it out."

"Figured what out?" Caleb's brow furrowed.

"Wait. Let me think." Emery exited the cottage for the court-yard. "It was something Joanna said. About the missing ads. Caleb, I know why they're missing. It's Tobias and his darn terrazzo floors!"

28

EMERY

On the first Saturday in May, Emery walked with Caleb from his place to Port Fressa Avenue, claiming it was nothing more than a pre-dinner walk.

Cassidy noted, more than once, that Caleb was overdressed in his blue pullover, khakis, and brown suede oxfords. "And Emery too." She gave her navy blue print dress the once-over while she cut tomatoes for a salad. "Are y'all coming back for dinner?"

Emery gave her grace, though. Since Cassidy came back to Sea Blue Beach, she was desperate to make up for lost time. She cooked, cleaned, shopped, took her mom to lunch. Still, the road home was far from smooth.

"We're grabbing dinner out. Main Street business." Which was true. Only it was the main street of the Org. Homestead and dinner with a couple of royals. No big deal.

"Are you nervous?" Caleb grabbed Emery's hand as they started up the hill. "Is Delilah on her way?"

"She's coming in the Sands' golf cart. And yes, I'm nervous. And excited."

"Ever wonder if Prince John and Princess Gemma were a couple of Floridians living across town we'd be friends?"

"Except *they* are royal, and they live across the Atlantic." She grinned. "But yeah, I do."

Walking out from under the evening sunlight soaking Pelican Way onto Port Fressa, where the old oaks and pine trees cast deep shadows over the old brick lane, Caleb and Emery joined Simon and Nadine, Bobby and Wren, and Adrianna from the town council. Duke, Ivan, Mercy, and Adele joined from Main Street since the Org. Homestead was part of their focus.

Emery suggested Paige from the Blue Plate and Misty from Sweet Conversations join the visit since their hard work to cater the royal brunch got destroyed by the trashing.

Caleb had secured the second floor of Alderman's for supper after the Port Fressa tour. The front windows were boarded up for construction, so there was no concern about raising suspicions about lights shining from atop the old pharmacy.

Chief Kelly was along in plain clothes for, well, all the obvious reasons.

"Do you know how they are arriving?" Emery asked Simon. He and Chief Kelly handled most of the communication with the royal team. Emery would not be writing about this for the *Gazette*.

This week, she confirmed her suspicion about the missing ads. Tobias had indeed been unplugging the ads server to run his terrazzo buffing machine. Since he kept an erratic schedule, the missing ads were also erratic. After a brief discussion with Tobias about this, Emery mandated no maintenance on Tuesday and Saturday nights. Ever.

To be fair, the man felt awful about his faux pas and apologized profusely. Even brought Emery three pounds of fileted sea bass. But the coming months would be about repairing the paper's reputation and rebuilding advertiser trust.

"They didn't give details," Simon said. "We gave them the location; it's up to them."

"We don't even know where they're staying." Chief Kelly wore an earpiece to communicate with royal security.

"I'd forgotten the romance of this place." Wren walked toward the uneven, cracked sidewalk, stubbing her toe on a raised brick. "Are we going to allow Mac to bulldoze this for a golf course? I mean, really."

"Are we all here?" The group turned to see Prince John and Princess Gemma strolling up the avenue, hand in hand, dressed in jeans and sneakers, the princess in a puff-sleeved red top and the prince in a Tennessee Titans T-shirt. "Do we look local?" he said in a very fine American accent, adding, "Gemma's been teaching me."

And just like that, they were all friends, shaking hands and reintroducing themselves, then Caleb took the lead on the requested tour, talking about Florida Cracker architecture, when the Org. Homestead was founded, and what needed to be done to restore the area.

"Most of these homes are a hundred and forty years old, with plumbing and electric from the thirties and forties. The Cracker-style—low-slung, wood-frame with a large porch—are constructed from pine and cypress, maybe oak, milled at Malachi Nickle's sawmill."

"These remind me of homes in Hearts Bend," Princess Gemma said. "Only our Tennessee ancestors had stone to add." She walked toward the first house, stepping over all the cracks and staring toward the slanted roof over the broad yet tilting porch.

"We were going to do this at the brunch," she said. "And as much as we hated leaving the way we did—"The prince held up his hands as if to protest the broiling apologies. "We understand that day was a one-off for Sea Blue Beach."

"We're still investigating," Chief Kelly said, his tone defensive.

"Yes, very good, and we hope you find the culprits, but here . . ." Prince John handed Simon an envelope. "We've set up a fund in Prince Blue's name as well as Malachi Nickle's for restoring the Org. Homestead or whatever you need for the East End. The queen feels strongly that everything her great-great-great-uncle—" He turned to his wife. "Do I have enough greats, darling?"

"One more."

"Great-great-great-great-uncle built here in Sea Blue Beach be preserved. It's part of our family, thus our country. We are inextricably tied, you and I. Brothers and sisters of different mothers, if you will."

Emery slipped her hand into Caleb's. This was what it meant to be royal. Not a title, but the ability to be generous with an eye to restoration and forgiveness.

As the sun slipped away, taking the gold from the tree leaves, the Org. Homestead on Port Fressa Avenue had a second chance at life.

And so did Emery Quinn.

29

CALEB

"I always seem to have incredible experiences when you're around," Caleb leaned into Emery as they carried their skates to the benches.

"What do you mean *always?*" Emery tugged on one of her skates. "If we're going to keep skating, I need my own skates."

"Maybe *always* is a bit of a stretch, but I'm about to skate with a royal prince and princess, so let me be a bit hyperbolic."

After a smorgasbord of southern food at Alderman's, the royals toured the East End with Simon and Chief Kelly and visited the mural while the rest of them headed to the Starlight. The royal protection detail wanted to keep a low profile.

"Don't act like this is your first brush with royalty." She tugged on the laces. "Remember I was *queen* of Operation Revenge."

She wasn't prepared for the way he snatched her to him, his skates clattering off the bench to the floor, his warm lips landing on hers without reservation. Emery's fingers slid away from her laces to cup her hands over his shoulders and hang on.

She pressed her forehead to his chest when the kiss slowly faded. "I think you love me."

"I know I do." He reached for a skate, then looked over at her. "Will you ever say it back?"

"Can't my kisses be enough for now?" Her cheeks pinked as she returned to tying on her brownies.

The lights flickered to the beat of "Flashlight," a '70s skating rink classic. Ivan skated at his own pace with Adele. They were pretty good. But then again, they'd grown up at the Starlight. Bobby and Wren shuffled to the beat with ease, until Bobby kicked Wren's skate and sent her tumbling. From the lobby, more of the special guests arrived.

Emery tugged on her second skate. "It's not that I don't want to say it, Caleb."

He turned to her. "Then what?"

She worked the laces in silence. "I just don't want to be afraid when I tell you. It seems insincere."

"I can live with that, Quinn."

By the time the prince and princess arrived, Caleb and Emery were on the floor, going around to the Beach Boys' "Good Vibrations," which seemed fitting. A protection officer rolled smoothly behind the prince and princess, while another watched from the benches, sans skates.

The hum of "keep loving those good vibrations" hovered in the rink when Bobby Brockton skated next to Caleb. "Got a sec to talk?" He tipped his head toward the lobby. "Outside?"

"Business or pleasure?"

"Both."

Switching back to his shoes, Caleb shrugged at Emery as they headed outside.

"Think we'll ever find out who dumped the trash?" Bobby said, starting down the Beachwalk.

"Chief Kelly thinks so."

"I'm sorry it happened." Bobby said. "Honestly."

"So why are we out here?"

"Something Wren said the other night." Bobby slowed his

pace as they passed the first Victorian lamp. "She said you and I are the ones to change the culture of our town. All this East versus West stuff, the division we all feel has to end. We didn't start the rivalry, but our little pranks escalated it. Your speech to the Chamber of Commerce was dead-on. You ruffled some feathers, and maybe that's why the brunch got trashed, I don't know. But I'm going to start ruffling feathers with you. Let's challenge the things that divide Sea Blue Beach."

"What about Mac Diamond and Alfred Gallagher?"

"Wren had a few things to say about them too." Bobby laughed to himself. "She said I was blinded by their success and to wake up and smell the coffee."

"I still haven't replied to Mac's job offer."

"Are you going to take it? It'd be a great opportunity, but he'd own you, Caleb. I guess you know that already."

"I'm happy to work on the Org. Homestead. I have a few other clients. Simon wants to turn Doyle's into a brewery. That'll keep me busy."

"Wren wants to buy and refurbish the Sunset Bowling Parlor on our side of town. You interested in the job?"

Caleb grinned. "You and me working together?"

"Might just be the thing to start healing the divide."

Caleb offered his hand. "Friends?"

"Friends." Bobby shake was solid. "Now, when you going to marry Emery?"

"Ah, okay, I see, I see." Caleb laughed. "The real reason Wren sent you to talk to me."

"Come on, man, you've loved her since you first met her."

"Beg pardon, Bobby, but how do you know?"

"Wren dated Shift one semester. They went to prom. Don't tell me you don't remember. She was too beautiful for him."

"And you."

Bobby's laugh seemed to echo over the water. "By the way, I know it was Emery who ran into me that night you trashed our field. Kneed me where the sun don't shine. Took me out of the action."

"You think so?" Caleb grinned and turned back for the Starlight. "You're going to have to take that up with her."

30

EMERY

"The limo is here." Four little words never incited such panic and rushing about, but it was time to go. True to Ava Quinn's character, everything about this wedding was timed to the last second.

She *must* arrive at the church at three o'clock as the tower bells rang, emerging from the limo with Dad, walking up the stone steps, into the foyer, and down the aisle as the organist played "Jesu, Joy of Man's Desiring." In a twist of tradition, the bridesmaids would follow.

The ride from the house to the church was forty-five minutes with ten minutes to spare for unexpected delays. Yesterday Caleb and Emery drove the route four times with Ava while she made notes.

"If the limo driver goes too quickly, I'll have him slow down. If we arrive early, we'll go around the block. If nothing else, I'll be the first bride in history to walk down the aisle a minute early."

Dad and the wedding planner were equipped with walkie-talkies to ensure everything was in sync.

Yet now the limo had arrived, and no one moved for the door.

"Come on, we're going to be late." Emery peeked in the family room to find Dad facing the giant paned window overlooking the upper deck. Dressed in a black tux with a white tie, his silver hair trimmed and styled, he rocked back and forth with his hands clasped behind his back.

Emery locked her arm with his. "The limo is here. You okay?"

"I was just thinking about your mom."

"Mom? Why?"

"I don't know. Feeling sentimental. When you were born, we'd tuck you in bed between us, marvel at how beautiful you were, and dream of your future. Where you'd go to school—"

"—as if any place but Ohio State was an option."

"What career you'd choose. We imagined the man you'd marry. Your mom had mother-of-the-bride dreams while I held your little hand, tearing up because in twenty or thirty years I'd be giving you away. Yet we'd just brought you home." He peered at her. "I didn't get a chance to do that with Ava and Elianna."

She set her head on his shoulder. "Mom would love the family we made with Joanna and the girls. It took moving away and a few prods from Ava for me to realize it."

"And Caleb?" Dad said.

"Yeah, him too."

"Is he the one? You know the Boyfriendinator would be thrilled to have him as a son."

Emery laughed. "Then you should let him know."

"Doug, honey, Ava's about to come down." Joanna pressed her hand on Dad's back. She wore a silvery pink sheath gown with crystal-studded heels, her hair in a French twist with tendrils looped around diamond drop earrings.

Joanna glanced toward Emery. "Thank you for all your help. That dry run to the church—"

"It's what sisters do. We really should be going." Emery headed upstairs for the clutch Ava gifted the bridesmaids. Passing her old room, she met Ava in the hall. "Va-va-voom, Ava. Jamie's going to faint dead away."

She'd chosen a mikado and tulle gown with a basque waist, square neckline, and cap sleeves. The chapel-length train followed her like a snowy river. She wore the same French twist as Joanna with pearl drop earrings. There was nothing around her neck.

"I'm excited. I'm nervous." She grabbed Emery's hand. "Do you think it's okay to be nervous?"

"I'd worried if you weren't. But when you see Jamie . . ." Her eyes brimmed, finishing her sentiment.

Ava smiled, her eyes sparkling. "He's wonderful, isn't he? By the way, va-va-voom to you. Pink is your color."

"Whatever," Emery said. But Ava wasn't wrong. The pink was lovely. Why'd she make such a fuss?

"Girls, we're one minute off our timetable," Joanna called up the stairs.

"Go," Emery said. "I'm right behind you."

As Ava descended, Emery ducked into Dad and Joanna's room, retrieving the flat, black velvet box from Dad's wardrobe. The Force women pearls. She'd thought a lot about this and—

"Mom," she whispered, "I believe this is right, don't you? Force women are more than a string of pearls. We're generous and loving, and I was neither with this family for many years."

Emery sensed nothing except her heart's confirmation. She was the Force daughter in possession of the pearls. This was her choice.

She caught Dad and Ava in the middle of the sunshine-flooded walkway.

"Ava, please, wear the pearls for your wedding." Emery handed the box to Joanna. "Mom, you clasp them on. That's the tradition."

Joanna stared at the black velvet. Dad gruffly cleared his throat.

"What?" Ava peered at Emery from behind her veil. "No, no,

I can't. They're your mother's and grandmother's. I understand. I do."

"We don't have time to debate, Ava. We're two minutes off our schedule." She glanced at Joanna. "You see, Joanna and I have a deal: to keep my mom's memory alive whenever and wherever we can. So you have to wear them—for me, for Rosie Quinn. You're not stealing anything from me by wearing them. Well, I mean, you have to give them back, but—"

Ava brushed aside a rolling tear. "You're an evil sister for ruining my makeup."

"Payback for ruining my prom shoes," Emery grinned with a nod toward the limo. "Hurry, Mom. We're almost three minutes off the schedule."

This was the power of love. Conquering those little fears. Healing the hurts. Opening eyes. More than anything, being a family.

31

CALEB

New Year's Eve

Coming back to Sea Blue Beach, as it turned out, changed his life. Ransom Architecture was well on its way, having finished the Alderman's Pharmacy refurbishment and two of the Org. Homestead houses. Jenny Finch managed to get both the pharmacy and the Florida Cracker homes featured in *Historic* magazine, which opened the door to a half dozen consulting jobs.

The Øster home at Preserve on the Bay, still under construction, was going to be a showpiece. However, between the design and high-end materials, Mrs. Øster claimed she'd rather just look at it than live in it. Until Caleb gave her a bit of advice. *"A home needs love, or it's not a home. This place can handle your noise, your dirt, and your mess."* He received a thank-you text from Mr. Øster that night with ten exclamation points.

Mac Diamond audaciously came around with another offer. Caleb turned it down. Golf course clubhouses were not his brand. Instead, he partnered with Bobby and Wren to restore the Sunset Bowling Parlor.

Cassidy and Bentley moved out in the fall when she got a

West End job. She rented a place behind the Starlight Museum, so technically, she was an East Ender—but folks were using the terms less and less.

Bentley loved Valparaiso Middle School and was on the first-ever pickleball team, which meant Caleb now played pickleball three nights a week.

On this New Year's Eve, he'd just showered and dressed when he heard Cassidy calling from the kitchen. "Caleb? Mom said to put the New Year's ham in your fridge. Wow, do you ever grocery shop? How did my kid gain ten pounds living with you?" He walked in as she shoved the ham on the fridge's top shelf. "This thing could feed the neighborhood. So, what are you doing for New Year's?"

"Meeting Emery at the Sands. Then we're going to the Fantastic Carnival."

"What? You're taking the love of your life to a carnival on New Year's Eve?" She didn't bother to hide her incredulity as she propped against the counter. "You riding the Ferris wheel?"

"Never mind me and the Ferris wheel. What are you doing tonight? Playing Minecraft with Bentley and going to bed at ten thirty?"

"Please? Bent and I are way more hip." She'd cut her hair since coming home, wore normal clothes, and sometimes attended church. Her Etsy shop with feathers and fringe was still doing well. "He's skating at the Starlight, and I'm going to the guitar pull at the Sands' courtyard." She gripped his arm with both hands. "Why don't you and Emery stay? Forget the carnival. Please? Share a glass of wine with me."

"I'll talk to Emery," Caleb said. "Not a bad idea."

"Really?"

No, but it'd get her out the door. He had other plans for tonight, and they did not involve a guitar pull with the Sands' guests and strangers from the Beachwalk. What Cassidy didn't know was she'd be at the carnival too.

"Hey, I'm making a New Year's resolution for you." Cassidy gripped his face in her hands, then pointed to the living room. "Unpack those stupid boxes."

Happy New Year, Sea Blue Beach

By Emery Quinn
Editor-in-Chief

Happy New Year! Sitting in my creaky editor-in-chief chair, which I love, I'm filled with gratitude.

A year ago, when Elliot Kirby offered me a job in the town where I'd learned my mother was dying, my first response was no. It was not how I wanted to start the next year of my life. But as I watched my younger sister say yes to a new adventure— marriage—the slight competitor in me stepped up.

Not quite 365 days later, we've made it—you, me, the *Gazette*, and Sea Blue Beach. But not without our struggles. Newspapers without ads. Threats of the West End becoming its own municipality. Discussion of bulldozing the Org. Homestead. Then an incredible visit from the House of Blue, only to have it trashed by a long-standing East-West rivalry.

Yet, in the aftermath, we took a deeper look at ourselves. We asked questions. Why are we divided East versus West? Where does history end and progress begin? Where does prosperity destroy our past, our story?

Meanwhile, under Mayor Simon Caster's and architect Caleb Ransom's leadership, the Main Street initiative brought new businesses into town. Be sure to stop by Read It Again, Sam, a new and used bookstore, the Artist Corner, and Knit One, Pearl Two with Adele. Doyle's Auto Shop opened in the fall, serving craft beer and hosting live music. I love how the owners kept the name to preserve history.

Alderman's Pharmacy completed its restoration in time for the holidays and opened as a lunch and soda fountain the day after Thanksgiving. The upstairs recently rented to a restorative massage therapy practice.

A generous donation from the House of Blue brought restoration to the Org. Homestead. These homes will provide affordable housing to our citizens. Two are now occupied—one by a retired couple, another by a young family. More homes in the neighborhood will begin restoration in the new year. This week we learned of a very generous contribution to the royal foundation by the Nickle family.

On the west side of town, Mayor Caster cut the ribbon at the opening of the new recreation center, and the Sunset Bowling Parlor is once again in operation. Check their website for tickets to Neon Midnight Bowling this New Year's Eve.

Over the summer, there were whispers of the Midnight Theater being sold to hometown boy and A-list actor Matt Knight. Keep up with the *Gazette* for breaking news.

We should never give up on ourselves or as a town. Moving past pain and hurt requires fortitude, but we have Immanuel, God with us, to see us through.

The *Gazette* will continue its mission to be *your* microlocal news source. We're excited to welcome our new advertising director, Edwin, who brings thirty years of experience after retiring from the *Tallahassee Democrat*. Rex, Jane, Junie, Gayle, Tobias, and I are dedicated to bringing you stories and news about you and our town. *Stories from the Archives* will continue, as well as columns from middle and high school students.

On this New Year's Eve, reflect on the good. Set aside fear. Embrace love in whatever season you're traveling. If you get too blue, stop by the Sands Motor Motel, where Delilah Mead makes music every Thursday and Friday night. You can swing by the Starlight and strap on a pair of skates. Perhaps stroll past the town mural on the side of Doyle's Auto Shop and take a moment with our history. Take a moment with Immanuel.

We live by the sands of Sea Blue Beach. Aren't we blessed?

When she left the paper, she walked east, down Sea Blue Way toward Doyle's and the sounds and lights of the carnival.

She was late, and Caleb waited for her at the Sands. They were spending New Year's Eve at the carnival, dining on cheap pizza and funnel cake. But on this crisp, clear, starry night, she ached for a moment at the mural.

Sea Blue Way was unusually quiet. Lately, folks had started referring to it as Old Sea Blue Way. The success of the Main Street initiative introduced locals and tourists alike to the beauty of the old downtown. The decks of the Blue Plate and the Fish Hook were probably overflowing tonight. Christmas lights glowed down the street from Mr. Po's, One More Cup, and Sweet Conversations. Every one of them ran half-page New Years' Celebration ads in the *Gazette*.

Emery arrived at the mural, pausing to study the images, seeing herself fitting into the story of this seaside town. When she gazed up at Immanuel, she felt immediately satisfied. Her lingering questions dissipated.

"Look, I don't really know you," she said. "Delilah says you're the real deal. But I think you've wanted me here from the beginning. Especially the night I learned about Mom." Emery drew a long, contented breath. "Thank you."

The clang of the carnival caused her to look around. Then Caleb texted.

Caleb:
ETA?

Emery:
5 min.

"We'll be talking in the new year, Immanuel," she said as she started down Avenue C.

The confession she didn't write about in her New Years' column was that she loved Caleb Ransom. Kisses were no longer enough. She finally said the words "I love you."

After breaking down the wall between her and Joanna, she changed. She could love Mom and Joanna. She could love Ava, Elianna, and Blakely freely. So she let her fears go to love Caleb with every fiber of her being.

The Sands' courtyard came into view with its string of lights wafting in the breeze, the courtyard Christmas tree twinkling, the firepit crackling. Caleb sat in one of the Adirondacks.

"Hey, babe." Emery dropped her bag to the ground and slid over the arm of the chair into his lap. "I'm starved. Let's go eat some junk food."

"All done with your column?" He cupped his hand around her neck and drew her in for a kiss.

"Finally. Rex and his red pen, sheesh. I might have to fire him."

Caleb laughed. Everyone in Sea Blue Beach knew she'd *never* fire Rex. "What will you do in two weeks when he's on his honeymoon?"

"Oh, I plan to send him my articles anyway." She planted her smiling lips on Caleb's. "With my luck, they'll get the bug to start up his travel blog again, and he'll resign." Rex had proposed to the girl he'd known since middle school in July and would marry her later this month.

The players for the guitar pull began to circle up, chatting, plucking, and tuning.

Emery stood and grabbed Caleb's hand. "Come on, let's ride the Ferris wheel."

CALEB

Emery Quinn stole his thunder, suggesting the Ferris wheel and racing to the carnival, passing the ticket booth because he'd purchased tickets while she finished her column. Families, teens, and senior citizens mobbed the thoroughfare while Christmas lights joined the neon colors of the carnival rides.

They passed the Serendiporama and twice Caleb lost hold of her. Looming on the horizon was the enormous Ferris wheel— bigger than last year, he was sure of it.

He wasn't much of a romantic, but even he could see the carnival's swift return to town was sort of a divine opportunity. Nodding to Bill, the romantically and financially inclined ride jockey whom Caleb visited an hour ago, he drew Emery to the front of the line.

"Caleb, we can't cut." She tugged him backward.

"It's okay," Bill said. "We've, um, been saving, yeah, saving a seat for you." He stuck out his arm to make room at the front.

"Why would you save a seat for—"

"Thank you, Bill." Caleb stepped into the bucket. "Just lock us in."

As the wheel lifted them from the ground, Caleb tried not to grip the safety bar, but old habits die hard. Emery gently tucked her hand under his.

"You stepped onto this ride without a fight. What's going on, Ransom?"

"Nothing. Well, something." Why did he think this was a good idea? He shifted in the seat to face her. "Emery Quinn?"

"Yes, Caleb Ransom." She peered at him, waiting.

"I walked the thoroughfare earlier. Visited the old Serendip-orama, dropped in a few coins." He produced two white cards.

"You didn't." Emery eyed the cards, then Caleb. "That crazy-eyed turban guy looks more lifeless now than he did sixteen years ago."

"Do you remember what our cards said?"

"Yeah, the town motto. Immanuel, God with us."

Caleb handed over the first card. "Maybe he's not so far off."

Emery read the card. "Immanuel, God with us." When she looked at him, her eyes were glistening. "Can I keep this?"

"That's my card, but yeah, you can keep it."

"What do you mean it's your card? What does the second one say? Obviously not that I'll be a millionaire?" She grinned.

"No, but I think it says something better."

Emery took the card, read it, then shot a glance at Caleb. The wheel had just completed its first rotation and was heading back to the top.

"Will you marry me?" she said, soft and low. "This came from the Serendiporama?"

"No. But what do you say?" Caleb released his last grip on the safety bar to pull Emery into his arms. "You make me a better man, and I don't want to spend another day without you." He retrieved the ring box from his pocket. "Will you ride the Ferris wheel of life with me? Wow, that sounded way better in my head." He opened the box. "Marry me? Do you mind if I don't get down on one knee?"

"No, I don't mind." Emery breathed in, smiling, eyes glistening all the more. "Of course I'll ride the Ferris wheel of life with you. Yes, I'll marry you."

As their bucket circled to the top, Bill stopped the ride and Caleb slipped the ring on her finger. The entire town, maybe even the whole world, spread beneath them, a river of glowing, vibrant Sea Blue Beach lights.

"I love you, Caleb," she whispered.

"I know you do." He laced his arm around her back and holding her close, kissed her again and again. Then the wheel kicked into motion.

"Engagement selfie." Caleb raised his phone while she held up her ringed hand and snapped the photo, riding free on the wheel with Emery.

As they approached the ground, she pointed to a tight clan gathered just beyond Bill's station. "Your parents are here with Cassidy and Bentley. And wait, is that Ava and Jamie?" She turned back to him. "What'd you do?" He smiled with a shrug. "There's Dad and Mom. Elianna and Blakely." She waved wildly. "Everyone, I'm engaged!"

The whole Ransom-Quinn clan rang in the new year at the Sands' courtyard with the guitar pull in full swing, taking any and all requests.

Delilah poured champagne and set out what could only be classified as the world's largest charcuterie board. Friends and strangers wandered in off the beach to congratulate the couple and wish everyone a Happy New Year.

By one in the morning, Caleb was back in the Adirondack with the only girl he'd ever really loved curled in his lap, her head on his shoulder.

Mom and Dad had gone, taking Cassidy and beaming Bentley with them. *"I told you to marry her,"* he'd said.

The Quinns disappeared inside their cottages, and Delilah approached with a blanket.

"Happy New Year, you two." She added a more logs to the fire before disappearing into Cottage 1.

Emery's soft breathing turned to sounds of sleep, and Caleb gazed toward the firepit and beyond to the darkened beach.

"Rosie," Emery said so soft he wondered if she was dreaming. "When we have a girl, I want to name her Rosie."

"Rosie Quinn Ransom."

"Rosie Force Ransom," she said.

"Rosie Pearl Ransom."

"Okay," she said with a sleepy pat of his chest. "We'll figure it out."

He relished the feel of her against him as she drifted back to sleep.

It was in that moment Caleb saw a flicker at the end of the courtyard, by the stand of palm trees. Angling forward, he narrowed his gaze to see what, or who, was out there.

The man from the Starlight wall, from the mural, looked on, his vibrant eyes overcoming the surrounding darkness and warming Caleb with a pure, clean sensation.

Immanuel. God with us.

After a moment, He nodded and walked on, vanishing between the light and shadows of the beach.

"I'll be seeing you, Immanuel," Caleb whispered, then settled deeper into the chair, closed his eyes, and drifted away to the song of the waves rolling along the white sands of Sea Blue Beach.

AUTHOR'S NOTE

Readers, you're the reason I love being an author. Thank you for going on every story journey with me. It was fun to go back to Sea Blue Beach and see the town through the eyes of Caleb and Emery.

I started out with a *Then* and *Now* love story, but the journey for Emery with her stepmom and sister, and Caleb with his sister, also became a family love story. Love is always worth our effort—even if someone doesn't love us back. Loving anyway is such freedom.

Jesus loves those who don't love Him, and He is our marvelous example. By His grace, we can do the same.

I pray each one of us can experience His love and catch glimpses of Him throughout this story. He is Immanuel, God with us!

ACKNOWLEDGMENTS

Let's see, they're around here somewhere. The names of people I'd like to thank scribbled in notebooks and on sticky notes. I'll just have to go from memory.

Thank you to:

Sharon Migala, Doug Hogan, and Matthew Flores for advice on architecture. Any and all mistakes are mine.

Beth Vogt for reminding me about working in a newsroom, for the video chats and reading opening chapters.

C. J. Casner for the story about a newspaper's maintenance man unplugging the server to do cleaning, thus causing production problems. Then for talking out how to use it in my story.

Susan Warren for "condiment plotting" at our favorite Florida breakfast place, the Beachside Café. And for answering your phone when I call for help.

Dave Long, Jessica Sharpe, and Jennifer Veilleux for those first insightful editorial notes. Kate Jameson for the copy edit. Raela Schoenherr and Emily Vest for inspired marketing and promotion labor.

My agent Chip MacGregor for being on this journey with me for sixteen years.

My husband for the life we've built together. I am so grateful and blessed.

Mom for always cheering me on. My siblings and their families, my cousins and their families as well. I love you guys!

My church family for being a place where I know I'll encounter the love of God. And for occasionally asking, "What are you working on?" Then standing there smiling while I tell you more than you wanted to know.

DISCUSSION QUESTIONS

1. Emery faced a challenging time when her mother died and her father remarried. How would you have responded to a similar situation? Do you empathize with her?

2. Emery took a chance when she accepted the job at the *Sea Blue Beach Gazette*. Talk about chances or challenges you've taken. How did you fare?

3. Caleb's sister left her son in his care. Have you cared for children of siblings? How have you resolved conflict with family members?

4. In the flashback scenes, we follow sixteen-year-old Emery and Caleb as they fall in love. Take a moment to reminisce about your teens. Did you marry your high school sweetheart? Are you still in touch with old friends?

5. Delilah Mead found something greater than herself and her music career. Did you relate to her story?

6. Caleb didn't like the Ferris wheel, though he couldn't articulate if he was afraid of heights or safety. Usually fears don't make sense. How have you faced and overcome a fear of yours?

7. The big trashing events . . . Crazy, no? Every story has a bit of hyperbole, but can you think of any incidents that sound a lot like one of the trashing events? Who do you think trashed the royal brunch on the beach?

8. Emery was very protective of her mother's pearls, for good reason. Do you have a family heirloom you treasure? What role do heirlooms play in a family?

9. Emery finally embraces Joanna as mom. How do you feel about that? What about their pact to keep Rosie in the picture whenever possible?

10. When Cassidy finally tells Caleb her story, there's healing and cleansing. What did you think of what happened to Cassidy? Do you know someone who's gone through something similar?

11. Sea Blue Beach is a town of "Immanuel, God with us." Share moments you knew God was with you.

12. Both Emery and Caleb overcame their fears in this story. Love was a key factor. How has love helped you overcome your fears?

13. Share a takeaway from the book that impacted you, inspired you, or made you laugh or cry.

1

TUESDAY

June 1932
Sea Blue Beach, Florida

The sight of the Starlight just on the edge of her kitchen window eased her lingering regret over her fight with Leroy last week.

Even though she deserved an answer, she hated his pained expression as she called him a scallywag, declaring how he'd let her and their boys down. *"I've never been more disappointed. Where do you go each week? Tell me now."*

More disappointed? Those words were not true. Tuesday Knight had been disappointed plenty in her life. Leroy was least of them all.

Still, after three years of his clandestine activity, she had a right to know, didn't she? He must work hard at whatever he was getting up to because he brought home cash, enough to pay the grocer and keep the lights on. And in these lean times, that was saying something.

Ever since the Crash and the Depression sat down on everyone, Leroy Knight had changed. Her hero, her knight in shining armor, a Great War soldier with chest full of medals, had become *way* too friendly with the Memphis and Chicago gangsters passing through their beloved Sea Blue Beach.

Wiping her hands on a stained dish towel, she stepped onto the porch and into the humid evening heat of Florida summer. At six o'clock, the day remained summery bright, with a bit of the Starlight's neon light in its ribbons.

"It's been too long since I visited you with my skates." She'd been speaking to the rink as a friend ever since she was a girl. Shoot, the rink was her *family* before Lee and the boys.

The Starlight gave her comfort. Skating helped her think through things. And she needed to *roll* her way through this turmoil with Leroy.

"Why can't I know where you go every week? I'm your wife, the mother of your sons. Is that too much to ask?"

"Well it is, Tooz, so drop it. I'm here now, aren't I?" He'd pulled a few greenbacks from his pocket. *"This ought to square our account with Old Man Biggs at the grocery store. There's a bit more here to stock up on what you need."*

"I won't touch a penny of that until you tell me where it came from. 'Cause if it's blood money or from running booze—"

"It ain't blood money. Holy shamoly, Tooz, can't a man provide for his family without the third degree?"

That's when he'd left without a by-your-leave. Since they didn't have a phone, he couldn't call. And Leroy was not one for writing letters. So she had no idea if he'd return home as usual this Friday.

"Beg pardon, Tooz." She glanced around to see Drunk Dirk, as everyone called him, coming up the shell-and-sand driveway.

"Dirk. What can I do you for?"

Not much older than Leroy, Dirk was also a Great War veteran who played the Wurlitzer at the Starlight. It was a darn shame his reputation, lovely wife and two sons, along with his touted musical ability, was eclipsed by his drunkenness. Lord only knew where he got the hooch in the first place. Sea Blue Beach was a dry town.

"I's just wondering if Lee was around. You seen him lately?"

"Sure haven't." Giving Dirk the once-over, she wondered if it was her husband supplying Dirk's habit. Another second passed before she pointed to the kitchen's screen door. "Care for some dinner?"

"Naw, naw, Tooz, but thanky. I got a hankering for . . . something else." He sloughed off without another word, tripping as he entered the street, turning left, then right toward the Starlight.

That's it, Drunk Dirk, get to the Starlight. That'll soothe your soul. Maybe help you to stop drinking. Besides, the evening session started in an hour, and Dirk was scheduled to play.

Back in the warm kitchen, Tuesday removed the pork and beans from the old potbelly, which glowed with burning logs and turned the whole house into an oven. She set the table and stirred up a pitcher of iced tea, using the last bit of ice from the icebox. She'd have to make up a list, send Leroy Junior to Biggs tomorrow.

Speaking of LJ, where was he? And Dupree? Her old dinner bell had blown away during some storm or another. Back out on the porch, she looked toward the horizon for signs of her boys, thirteen and eleven, respectively. They'd probably lost track of time.

Well, she'd wait. Tuesday sat on the old stone step and faced the beautiful, beautiful Starlight—she would love that place till the day she died—and wondered if Dirk had made it to the organ.

He had to know, as she and everyone in Sea Blue Beach, that no town in all of America, maybe the world, had a skating rink as grand and lovely as the Starlight. After all, it was built by a prince—Prince Rein Titus Alexander Blue, or Prince Blue as they called him—from faraway Lauchtenland, a tiny North Sea nation.

Tuesday hoped to go there one day, see where Prince Blue had lived before he crashed on their north Florida shore. He'd built the Starlight on the very spot, on the bedrock that held everything together—the sand and shells, the dirt and grass, trees, maybe even the Gulf itself. Certainly all of Sea Blue Beach.

"Ma, Ma." LJ, tall and lanky, sprinted down the driveway. Trailing behind was Dupree, pumping his still-short legs to keep up. "Can we skate tonight at the Starlight? Mr. Hoboth ain't there, but Burt says we can skate for free if we help clean up."

"That was kind of him."

Jud Hoboth, along with Burt, had managed the rink ever since Prince Blue left to command a Lauchtenland regiment during the Great War. Hoboth was a nice man, if not temperamental, with one foot out the door, always talking about adventures out west or down Mexico way. But what would happen to the Starlight if he just took off?

"Go on inside, wash your hands. Dinner's on."

"Can we go, huh? All the kids are going tonight."

"When have I ever said no to the Starlight? I might go too."

The house rattled as the boys ran up the stairs and fought to be first at minuscule bathroom sink. When they came down, their faces were washed, their hair combed and slicked back, and their shirts soaking wet.

Tuesday loved her boys.

She served them bowls of pork and beans, corn bread slathered in butter, and cold milk. "What'd y'all do today?"

In the summer, she let them tear all over God's green earth after morning chores. Growing boys needed to use up their energy. They came home to dinner stained, filthy, and full of stories, then scampered back outside until dark. Then it was bath time, followed by popcorn and their radio program, Jack Benny or Eddie Cantor, ever since baseball banned broadcast of their games.

"We went fishing on the beach," LJ said, dipping his corn bread in his bowl.

"We helped Cap'n Tatum unload a fresh haul." Dup gulped down his milk. "He gave us fifty cents, so we went to Biggs for candy. Got a milkshake at Alderman's too." He handed Tuesday his bowl for seconds.

"Then we got up a game of kickball with the fellas," LJ said. "We lost, thanks to Dup."

"Did not."

"Did so."

Tuesday returned Dup's bowl, steamy and full. "I thought two young men in this house wanted to go to the Starlight tonight."

That shut them up. Worked every time. The forty-five-year-old rink was loved by the entire Knight family. Even Leroy.

"I'm going to skate on a racing team when I get bigger," Dup said.

"Ah, you're not fast enough." LJ reached around and yanked Dup's hat from his head. "You're at the table."

"I am too fast enough. Take it back. Ma—"

"You'll be fast when you need to be." Tuesday gave LJ a side glance. *Be nice.*

When they finished eating and the boys had washed the dishes—which always included flinging Super Suds at each other—Tuesday said, "Get your skates. Bring mine as well."

It had been a splurge, more than they could afford, to buy everyone Richardson boot skates for Christmas. But last year Leroy played the big shot, telling Tuesday to order whatever she wanted from the skate catalog. He brought home a money order from the bank, and she put the whole kit and caboodle in the mail the day after Halloween. The skates arrived a week before

Christmas. Lordy, how the boys shouted when they unwrapped their boxes.

While Tuesday loved her skates—which she'd not trade for anything—she remained a bit vexed that she still cooked on a wood-burning stove. Sakes alive, it was 1932, and no matter how many hints she dropped to Leroy, he never clued in. She might just have to take matters into her own hands. Or flat out say, *Lee, I need a new stove.* But he was stubborn. Sometimes the more a body wanted something from him, the more he resisted.

While the boys thumped around upstairs, Tuesday got to work on tomorrow morning's bread, then hurried to freshen up.

"Can we get some popcorn, Ma?" Dup dropped into his usual seat at the table, clutching his skates.

"Don't see why not." Tuesday set the dough aside, then reached for the cannister on the pantry's top shelf. "Maybe a soda pop too." The can contained the fun money she earned from helping Mr. Hoboth at the rink. "I can hear Dirk firing up the organ as we speak." She took her pocketbook off the hook by the door and stuffed two dollars inside. "LJ, what are you doing?" She called up the stairs. "Get a move on. Don't forget to bring my skates. Dup, go see what your brother is doing."

His skates clattered to the floor, and he started yelling before he left the kitchen, "LJ, Ma says hurry up."

Now where was her lipstick? Caught in the torn lining of her purse, that's where. Tuesday leaned toward the windowpane, using it as a mirror, when she heard, "Am I invited too?"

She whirled around to see Leroy at the door, his broad shoulders filling the frame. He gave her a sheepish grin, hat in his hand. Fifteen years together, and he still made her knees weak.

"Lee, what are you doing here? It's only Wednesday." She capped her lipstick and ran into his arms. "About the other day . . . I didn't mean what I said."

"Sure you did, and I deserved it." He pressed his lips to hers, drawing all the blood in her veins to her heart. "I'm sorry, Tooz. I didn't mean to pop off and leave without a word."

"I'm sorry too, and I'm so glad you're home." She brushed aside his dark bangs and searched his blue eyes. Too handsome for anyone's good, she'd fallen in love with him the moment he asked her to skate.

He'd just returned from the war, and her friends whispered, *"He's trouble."* But Tuesday Morrow did *not* care. If he was trouble, let her sink in deep. Beneath his cotton shirt beat the heart of a warrior.

"The boys and I took a run near here." He released her as he gazed toward the stove and tossed his hat onto the table. "I thought I'd pop in to see my favorite gal. My beautiful wife."

"Well, my *boys* and I were about to go skating." She took a step back. She hated that he referred to his crew as "the boys." LJ and Dupree were his boys. The others were junior thugs of some sort.

"Don't start, Tooz." He opened the icebox. "Can you heat up some supper?"

"Why don't you come with us and buy a hot dog?"

He frowned. "All I ever eat is diner fare. I'd like some home cooking."

"Home cooking? You think I made pot roast and potatoes, with an apple pie for dessert? We live on beans, corn bread, sourdough bread, eggs, cereal, and milk, Lee. If you want a bowl of beans, stir up the stove and grab a pot. And if you're tired of diner fare, well, that's all on you." Tuesday braced for his reply, but the boys—*their* boys—clambered down the stairs and into the kitchen.

"Pa!" LJ dropped his skates and fell against him. Dup clung to Lee's arm. "You're home. Golly gumdrops. Can you skate with us?"

LJ poised for a dash upstairs to retrieve Lee's Richardson skates, the ones he'd worn only once in the last six months.

"Um, well, I suppose." He glanced at Tuesday, longing in his eyes for something besides dinner, which made her burn through and through, wanting him more than the Starlight. At least for now. He tipped his head toward the ceiling. *Can't we . . . ?*

"Get your father's skates, LJ," Tuesday said. Lee would just have to wait. "We'll have a much-needed family outing."

LJ retrieved his pa's skates, then shot out the door after Dupree and raced down the drive to Sea Blue Way and the Starlight.

Tuesday was about to follow when Leroy spun her around for a kiss, moving his warm lips from hers down to her collarbone.

She refused to surrender, no matter how much she wanted to take his hand and head up the stairs. "The boys will expect us."

"Tooz, don't punish me."

"Punish you? Why would I when it means punishing myself? But your boys—your *sons*—need time with you. Now let's go so's you can put your skating talent on display."

He sighed and searched her eyes. "Look, I don't want to open the can of worms again, but I want you to know this is not the life I dreamed for us."

"Well, we have that in common." Tuesday clung to her skates. The stove fire had died, but the kitchen seemed warmer than ever. "Just what did you dream for us? And why aren't you doing it?"

"I sort of am, I reckon. Don't you see? I'm setting us up, giving LJ and Dupree a better future. You think I can buy you nice things, like those skates you're holding onto for dear life, or send the boys to college by working on a fishing vessel? Or breaking my back logging? I was a soldier, Tooz. A fighter. I earned medals. Do you see me clerking at the bank or stocking shelves for Biggs?" He pointed to water stains on the ceiling and the tired wallpaper curling away from the corners. "This place . . . it's a dump, and I aim to find a way to change our station."

"How? By doing what? Where does a soldier go for a job? Don't tell me you're back in the army."

"I tried the army," he said softly. "They thanked me for my service but didn't have anything for a man my age."

"Lee, I'm sorry." Tuesday pressed her hand on his. "Just so you know, I love this house. I gave birth to our sons in this house."

"Never mind the army. You wouldn't have wanted the army life anyway, Tooz. Can you see yourself leaving Sea Blue Beach or the Starlight?" Lee leaned out the door and gazed toward the changing horizon. "Don't you want to move across the street to one of the new cottages they're building on the beach? Three bedrooms, two baths, a sunroom, solid wood floors, and a roof that don't let in the rain. How about new furniture and a bed that don't creak when we . . ." Her man blushed. Sure enough.

"Not if it means you leaving every week to do God only knows what. Lee, I don't want much in life. I'm the unwanted child of an unmarried sixteen-year-old girl who was so delirious with pain that she named me Tuesday 'cause she thought the midwife asked what day it was."

"I still want to know why a midwife would ask a laboring mama to tell her the day of the week."

"I'd love to ask more than that, but since I've never even met her. . . ." Every now and then, if she spoke of her mama, the tears bubbled up. And she resented it. Margie Lou was a rebel who wanted nothing to do with her family or her newborn daughter. "Then Mamaw and Gramps raised me as a cousin, though everyone knew I was Margie Lou's daughter. I looked just like her. Then Gramps died, and Mamaw sold up and moved to Tampa with Aunt Marcy, leaving me here all by myself at fifteen." She gripped his shirt. "But you know all of this. You know this town and our family are everything to me. I want our boys to come home to a loving mother *and* father every night. But lately, they only have me."

"I want everything you want and more." He hooked a strong arm around her. "I *am* your family, Tooz, and I'm doing my job to provide and make a better life. Dream a little with me, will you?"

"You know what I'm dreaming, Lee?"

"Tell me."

"That I wake up one day to find an electric stove and refrigerator right here in this kitchen."

"Golly mo, Tooz, you dream of appliances?"

"I'm more practical these days. It's 1932, and I cook on an ol' potbelly and keep our food in an icebox." He laughed and hugged her close. "But, Leroy Knight, hear me now, I don't mind none of it if it means you hang your hat on that hook"—she pointed to the largest nail by the door—"every evening."

"One day, I promise, Tooz. I'll be home. We just got to get through this government mess. Ol' FDR and his henchman Hoover has messed us up something fierce, but—Oh, wait, I got a surprise for you. How could I forget? It's the reason I'm home. Shoot fire, your kisses got me all confused."

"Oh hush, now what are you talking about?"

"When I proposed, I promised one day I'd buy you the biggest, brightest diamond to wear on your finger."

"How could I forget? My warrior is also a big talker." She didn't want him to buy her a ring if it meant him running all over who-knows-where, but oh, wouldn't it be lovely to have a symbol of belonging? A sensation she'd never had growing up. Until Mamaw left and Prince Blue took her in, gave her a room at the Starlight along with a job.

"I mean to keep that promise, Tuesday. But for now, I wondered if this would do." Lee stepped onto the porch and took a rolled document from his worn travel bag and tossed it to the old, scarred table. "Read it." He puffed up like he'd done something extraordinary.

Tuesday set her skates on the floor and reached for a parchment-like document. "It's a deed . . . to the Starlight." She peered up at him. "Lee, what is this? I don't understand."

"I got you the Starlight, Tooz."

"You . . . you *bought* the Starlight?" She scanned the ornate deed with gilded edges and calligraphed inscriptions.

Prince Rein Titus Alexander Blue, of the House of Blue, to Miss Tuesday Morrow, on this day, the twelfth of June 1916 AD.

The prince's titled signature, in his lovely penmanship, stretched across the bottom of the parchment.

"It's signed by the prince."

"Yeah, ain't that something? Anyway, I'd heard Hoboth decided to scratch his itch to see the world. You know running a skating rink weren't his idea of a good time." Leroy shrugged, leaving Tuesday to figure out the rest of her husband's noble deed.

"Goodness, I figured he'd leave one day, but we were just talking last week about how Mrs. Elkins made me the most delicious silk cake for my birthday. He said, 'How old are you now?' I said thirty-two, and he got this smarmy expression and said he had something to do." She read the parchment again. "Leroy Knight, you best not be joshing me. This doesn't look like a county deed. And my married name isn't on it."

"Got me, Tooz. I handed him money and he handed me that-there deed. Maybe he forgot your married name."

"The date is 1916."

"Hoboth is missing a few, if you know what I mean." Lee tapped the bottom of the document. "But it says whoever's name is on this piece of paper is the pure and true owner of the Starlight.

That's good enough for me. But ask the boys at county records when you file the deed."

"Where did you get the money? How much did it cost?"

"Listen, doll, when a man gives his wife a gift, he doesn't tell her how much it cost. Do you like it? Are you happy?"

"Leroy Knight, you almost make me sorry I badgered you about never being home. This . . . this is the greatest thing anyone has ever done for me. I feel like. . . a princess. With her own little kingdom."

"I promised you a diamond ring, but—" Leroy tugged her curves against him. "How about a little starlight for now?"

2

HARLOW

March 1987
Manhattan, New York City

About a month ago, she'd started referring to herself in the third person. *Harlow Hayes should do something about her life. Harlow Hayes should take a shower. Harlow Hayes should get a haircut. Harlow Hayes, Harlow Hayes, Harlow Hayes.*

That's when she realized something had to change.

But how? She had become a joke. To the world. To herself. Friends pitied her. Comedians made her a punch line for their late monologues. Last month, *Saturday Night Live*'s Victoria Jackson played Harlow Hayes while wearing a ridiculous wig and some sort of fat suit.

But when the love of her life crushed her without so much as an "I'm sorry," Harlow Hayes gave up and gave in.

Maybe living in the third person wasn't so bad. And the dark "cave" in which she dwelt most of the time was comforting. Her small, narrow bedroom—which was probably once a Gilded Age butler's pantry—allowed no expectations and thus no failures. No letdowns. No feckless laughter from late-night audiences.

But it's all sticks and stones, right?

Harlow flicked an empty box of Cheez-Its to the floor, ignoring the few crumbs that scattered over the small rug. She'd clean it up later. On her twin bed, she tried to sleep while Jinx—make no mistake, this was her apartment—blasted the six o'clock news.

Chuck Scarborough's smooth news voice reminded America that presidential candidate Gary Hart withdrew from the race due to his affair with Donna Somebody, and then recapped the aftermath of a Belgium ferry capsizing, killing 193 passengers and crew.

She shivered with the cold of the news as well as her room. The old window in the exterior wall allowed in the heat and the cold. But Harlow didn't care as long as she had a place to escape, a place to sleep, and let's be honest, a place to eat.

When she moved in six months ago—her last landlord, also a friend and fellow model, had kicked her out to move her boyfriend in—Harlow had asked Jinx for a space heater.

"No, you'll asphyxiate yourself or wake up in a fiery blaze." She'd bent down to pick up the Hayes Cookie wrapper on the floor. *"And burn us all down."*

Not true, but just in case, Harlow didn't press the issue. Burrowing under the blanket she'd purchased in Egypt two years ago, she considered how *that* Harlow Hayes knew who she was, where she was going, and what she wanted.

Two years ago, her life of photo shoots, haute couture fashion shows, and one small part in a romantic comedy made sense, because every road led to Xander Cole, the gorgeous Gilded Age heir, financier, and almost billionaire. She'd been named the Most Beautiful Woman in the World and one of the first models to earn the moniker "super."

Muffled voices seeped through the thin apartment wall.

Mom?

Harlow pressed her ear to the wall. A door clicked. Muted footsteps struck the hardwood, then landed on the carpet. Glasses clinked.

"Thank you . . . darn plane was late . . . rain . . . Atlanta . . . should've hired a car . . . cab driver . . ."

What was Mom doing here? Did Jinx call her? Well, no surprise there. Those two were tight. Jinx, a former model turned Icon Agency scout turned executive for CCW Cosmetics, founded by the illustrious Charlotte Coral Winthrop.

But Jinx had discovered Harlow twelve years ago when she was barely seventeen—much to Mom's delight. Then Icon took a slow approach to Harlow's career—much to Mom's consternation—until a photographer friend asked her to pose for a poster. Kaboom!

"I think we do, Jinx. Get her going. Moving forward. Kick in . . . keister."

Mom. Such a southerner. No one said *keister* in Manhattan in 1987.

"I can prescribe something."

A third voice? Harlow slipped on her fuzzy slippers and, gathering the gaps in her too-tight pajama top, she schlepped from her dark hovel into the bright living room lights.

"Well, look who's up." Mom held Harlow by the shoulders and kissed her cheek. "Still wearing those same wool pajamas, I see." Her gaze swept Harlow up and down. "A bit tight but still rather darling."

"What are you doing here, Mom?" Harlow retrieved a glass and filled it with milk, which would be spectacular with a large squeeze of Hershey's chocolate syrup. But considering her current audience, she'd refrain. "You brought the shrink along?"

"We're here to help, Harlow." Dr. Tagg had a smooth and not quite but almost condescending tone.

"Help me do what?" Harlow worked her way through the crowd for the sofa. Jinx's apartment was a one bedroom, one bath, with a square living room and minuscule kitchen, along with Harlow's "closet." Two was a crowd. Four was a throng.

"Figure out your life, darling," Mom said.

"Well, if you don't mind . . ." Harlow sat on the sofa and reached for the VCR remote. "I fell asleep during *All My Children* today. Thank goodness I have it recorded. Angie and Jesse are in a real battle for their marriage."

"And you are in a battle for your life, Harlow Anne. We want to talk to you." If Mom added, "young lady," Harlow would be out. Literally. Through the door in her too-tight pajamas.

"Can't you berate me in the morning?" she said.

Mom grabbed the remote to shut off the TV, but a picture of Xander popped on the screen as Mary Hart opened *Entertainment Tonight*.

"We open with happy news. Xander Cole"—Harlow shrank back and cradled her milk—"and his ex-wife Davina will be tying the knot *again*, in style on the Coles' private Caribbean Island." A clip played of Xander and Davina standing on the sandy shore of the beach, their Frank Lloyd Wright–style home looming in the background.

"Did you know about this?" Harlow glanced at her guests as Mom shut off the TV. "Is that why you're here, Mom? Because they've announced their wedding?"

"Of course not. How would I have even known? If he called, I'd have given him a piece of my mind." Mom's disgusted tone was offset by her lilting southern charm.

"Oh please, you love him. If he came back to Harlow Hayes, you'd be buying bridal magazines."

"I beg your pardon. I would—"

"Anne, Harlow, let's talk about why we are all here." Jinx sat on Harlow's right, while Mom sat on her left. Dr. Tagg perched on the coffee table, clicking her pen in an annoying rhythm, prescription pad in hand.

"Are you committing me to a psych ward?" Harlow pointed to the prescription pad. "Don't even think about it. You're all aware of the Studio 54 scene. Drugs kill. Listen to Nancy Reagan, if not me. 'Just Say No.'"

"This is different," Mom said. "This will help you get over this slump . . . this depression."

"Is that what you call a broken heart?" Harlow set her glass on the coffee table next to the good doctor and tried to squeeze out from between Mom and Jinx.

"Let's review the last two years," Jinx said, holding onto Harlow's arm.

"Must we?" She'd been trying to forget the past two years. But when a supermodel gains something like forty pounds—she'd not stepped on the scale in a year—she loses her career.

"I'd like to point out *two* key words." Mom's lilt came with a verbal highlighter. "*Two. Years.* Harlow, it's been *two years* since Xander went back to Davina. It's time to move forward. Write a new future. Xander is getting married, yet you sit here—"

"Wallowing?" Harlow freed herself from the sofa's confinement. "News flash, Mom, Jinx, Dr. Tagg. I've loved every minute of it." Not true, but she had to fight back somehow. "The End. Film at eleven." She leaned over Dr. Tagg. "Don't you have something for these two? Help *them* leave me alone?"

"I really think losing your money sent you over the edge." Mom frowned.

No, losing the love of her life sent her over the edge. Discovering her financial advisor—recommended by Xander, of all people—absconded with her small fortune was the cherry on top.

All she had left after being Felix Unger'ed from the penthouse she'd shared with her fiancé and future husband was the savings Dad insisted she set aside for a rainy day. Or, in her case, a deluge.

All of her hard work—the early days of go-sees, of running from one catalog shoot after another, of sleepless nights in Milan during fashion week, and years of being primped and plucked—vanished in an FBI white-collar crime raid.

She imposed on the generosity of friends, sleeping on their couches and in their guest rooms. When her fellow models were on location, she fed their cats in exchange for living quarters. Somewhere in the madness, food became her solace. Maybe it was her first bite of Lombardi's Pizza, or that thick burger with a side of fries. Or maybe her first bag of Hayes Cookies—which she spotted at a Broadway tienda—that she'd consumed with a chocolate shake from a mom-and-pop diner.

Snap. Years of disciplined eating ended. Junk food was marvelous. Comforting. And something that was all hers.

Around her, Jinx, Mom, and Dr. Tagg talked as if she wasn't there. Mom mentioned something about Harlow's famous poster, the one that launched her career.

"If you had royalties from that thing, you'd be in better shape." Mom had never forgiven Jinx for letting Harlow go to the shoot without a contract in play.

"He was a friend," Jinx said. "Asking a favor. How was I to know it'd become a worldwide phenom?"

"In my view," Dr. Tagg weighed in, clicking her pen, "you've given Xander too much authority. What right does he have to kill your spirit because he went back to his ex?"

"Exactly. Where's our girl who wowed everyone on the set of *Talk to Me Sweetly*?" Mom switched from fretter to cheerleader. "Everyone thought you were amazing, and it was your first movie."

"HH got the stuffing kicked out of her." Harlow took a big

gulp of milk, then tugged on her pajama top where her middle pushed against the buttons.

She'd met Xander—he was one of the executive producers—on that movie set, where she'd also been given the nickname *HH* because she was so businesslike.

"I know, sweetie." When Jinx pulled Harlow down to the couch next to her, one of her pajama buttons popped off and landed on Dr. Tagg's prescription pad. Okay, that was embarrassing. "But it's time to get to work. Your mom is here because I have good news. Charlotte Winthrop wants you to be the new face of CCW Cosmetics."

Dr. Tagg discreetly set the button in the coffee table ashtray.

"Why me? Trace Sterling is their face."

"Her contract ends in August." Jinx's expression was bright, like a parent about to tell their kid he's getting a puppy or a pony. "And she asked me to get you." Ta-da. She spread her arms wide, smiling big. Expectant.

"Okay, but when? Not now." August was only five months away. She'd have to starve herself to get down to her modeling weight, and frankly, she didn't have the heart for it. Five-eleven, a hundred-and-thirty-two just didn't seem feasible for a grown woman.

"She wanted to meet right away, but I put her off until September. Charlotte likes to launch new faces over the holidays. So, do you think you could, well, pull yourself together by then?" Jinx squeezed her hand. "CCW is willing to shell out big bucks to get you, Harlow. Like *never*-before-seen money."

"Harlow, darling, isn't that marvelous?" Mom carried Harlow's glass of milk to the kitchen sink and dumped it out. "You've always wanted to work with CCW, and here they are coming for *you*."

"To be honest," Jinx said, "I think Charlotte hired me away from Icon for the express purpose of bringing you in one day."

"I don't know." Harlow gathered her pajama top, missing the popped button. "CCW *has* always been a goal. Harlow Hayes likes their brand, history, and products." She flipped to third person seamlessly. "Are you sure they don't want Kim Alexis or Christie Brinkley?"

"It's all you, sweetie. They believe your time away from the scene will make you all the more intriguing when they roll out their new campaign."

Hmmm, this put a wrinkle in her wallowing. If she couldn't have what she really wanted, had *always* wanted—a husband and kids with the house and sprawling yard, white fence, dogs and cats, a hamster on the wheel, and eventually the PTA and a mommy carpool—why not get back to work? Sign with CCW? She'd given her life to modeling. Trimmed the edges of her education, even friendships, to go along with Mom's grand scheme of creating *the* Harlow Hayes, *supermodel*.

In that moment, the clouds parted, and she realized if she let her hard work go to waste, continued to give Xander Cole power over her, she was denying her very being.

On the other hand, she'd become accustomed to sleeping in, eating whatever she wanted, whenever she wanted, and parking on the couch from one to four every afternoon for *All My Children*, *One Life to Live*, and *General Hospital*.

"I can prescribe diet pills." Dr. Tagg clicked her pen.

"No way, Dr. T." Harlow moved around the small space to think, to stretch.

"There's more," Mom said, nearly as expectant as Jinx had been. "Icon called and—"

"Icon fired me."

"They want you back. Designers are asking for you, missing your focus and work ethic."

"I'll go to Wilhelmina or Ford before Icon."

"I knew you still had some fight in you." A giddy Anne Hayes launched into full cheerleader mode. *S-u-c-c-e-s-s, that's the way we spell H-a-r-l-o-w.* "Darling, let all this with Xander go, and get back to work. You're Harlow Hayes, the Most Beautiful Woman in the World."

Yeah, about that . . . The title was almost four years old, and she'd been eclipsed by Jaclyn Smith, yet every time her name was mentioned, the moniker tagged along. And she was proud of it. She'd worked hard at her craft, and the world took notice.

"I don't know if I was ever the most beautiful, but I did work hard."

"Exactly," Jinx said. "So don't lose all your hard work over a *man.*"

Dr. Tagg nodded as she doodled faces on her prescription pad. She'd done that through most of Harlow's sessions last year. While she was grateful to talk to someone, Harlow never really gained any power over her troubles. The best part of each session was the subway ride afterward to Lombardi's for a slice or two. Food was more than her solace. It was her late-in-life rebellion.

"One last thing," Jinx said. "You can't keep living in my closet. I was fine when you landed here last fall, but that room is not safe for you physically or emotionally. Not to mention it's the only closet in the apartment."

Harlow sank down to the nearest chair. "I figured this day would come sooner or later."

"Darling, you're coming home with me," Mom said. "We can work on getting in shape together."

"I'm not going to Atlanta, Mom."

"Whyever not?"

"Because I'm not seventeen. I'm almost thirty. I'll find a place. A room to rent." It would deplete the last of her savings, but she was squandering her money anyway, one takeout at a time.

However, if she signed with CCW, she'd be in the black. "How big of a contract, Jinx?"

"Let's just say *I'll* be asking to room with *you* at your Park Avenue penthouse."

"That's it, you're coming home with me." Determination powered Mom's words. "We'll do this together, Harlow. It would make me *so happy* if you—"

"Anne, don't. Harlow is not responsible for your happiness." Dr. Tagg said what Harlow couldn't. What she wouldn't.

"I resent that, Dr. Tagg. I only have my daughter's best—"

"Harlow, you're right. You don't need a prescription." Dr. Tagg scooped up her Coco Chanel coat and matching bag. "You need to get off your duff, take control of your life, and stop letting someone else drag your heart around." She glared at Mom. "I'm sending you the bill for this one."

"Well, that was rude," Mom said when the door closed behind the good doctor. "And what was that look she gave me on her way out?"

"What look?" Harlow said, feigning ignorance. She may have mentioned once or twice during her sessions with Dr. Tagg how she lived to make her mother happy.

Still, through all the pain and humiliation, she'd managed *not* to tuck her tail and run to Atlanta. She saw no reason to give in now. Yet how many options did a broke, overweight supermodel have?

A firm knock rattled the quiet room.

"Dr. Tagg must've forgotten something." Jinx opened the door to find a messenger standing on the other side.

"Delivery for Harlow Hayes."

The plain white envelope had no markings, only the letter inside along with a deed to a property in Florida. "It-it's from Xander."

"What does he want?" Jinx leaned to read over Harlow's shoulder.

"Did he finally apologize?" Mom squeezed in for a look.

"No, he's, um, he's giving me the cottage we bought and renovated in Sea Blue Beach, Florida." She'd secretly wanted the cottage when they separated but never had the chance to ask.

"Now?" Mom said. "Where's this been the last two years? Read his note, Harlow."

"Can you back up?" Harlow shrugged off Mom and Jinx. "Give me a minute."

Harlow, see enclosed. Sincerely, Elmar, Assistant to Xander Cole. A second note fell to her lap, with a key taped to the plain, thick stationery.

Enjoy the house, H. I mean it. Please.—X.

"Well?" Mom hovered five feet away with Jinx.

"He said to enjoy the cottage." She reread the deed with her name and buzzed with a bit of excitement.

"Why now?" Jinx said. "Can you accept it? What if there's some sort of lien attached, or the police just discovered a murdered body?"

"Murdered body? Geez, Jinx, your one episode on *Kojak* really messed with you." She'd played a murder victim during her modeling days. Slept with a night-light ever since.

Harlow reread Xander's brief note. This was classic Xander Cole. He was equal parts scumbag and good guy.

"Tell him no thanks and come on home," Mom said. "I think that's best and—"

"Harlow Hayes is going to Sea Blue Beach." She headed for her room. "It may be two years late, but this is his apology. And I accept. Jinx, I'll write a check for my half of the utilities. Mom, thanks for coming."

"You're leaving now?" Mom said. "It's almost eight o'clock."

"Perfect. Traffic will have died down. I can drive all night."

"Don't you want to sleep? To think about it?"

"I've been sleeping for two years, and for the past hour, you've been telling me to get myself together, so here I go. This is it. Harlow Hayes is heading down the main line. Off to Margaritaville. I am woman, hear me roar."

"Any more song lyrics in there?" Jinx said, laughing, approval in her voice.

"So you'd rather live in a house your ex-fiancé bought for you than come home with me?"

"I renovated that house, Mom. It's all me—well, almost, except the ghastly chandelier Xander insisted on—and frankly, he owes me. One for recommending that lousy financial advisor, and two for . . . for *everything* else."

"Go get 'em, girl. The beach will do you good," Jinx said. "Fresh air, sunshine, and sand. You'll be in shape for CCW in no time."

Maybe. Maybe not. But for now, Harlow Hayes was *doing* something with her life.

3

SEA BLUE BEACH

Welcome to Sea Blue Beach. Founded by Prince Rein Titus Alexander Blue in 1882.

He landed on our dark shores with the pieces of his wrecked yacht as a storm raged in the Gulf. Malachi Nickle, a young, freed slave, found him alone, half drowned, and gave him shelter. Together, they built Sea Blue Beach. The prince built the Starlight so Sea Blue Beach would never be dark or lonely again.

We've quite a history, you see. Besides a prince and freed slaves, we've hosted rumrunners and gangsters, hobos and drifters, families looking for a warm meal, families on holiday, and kids on spring break, all the while nesting our hometown folks in sunbaked cottages on sunbaked streets.

Look, there's Harlow Hayes. We'd have put up a sign for her, but we didn't know the supermodel was coming. It's been a while since she graced our shores. Three years, perhaps, since she sailed down with Xander Cole on his fancy yacht.

So we whisper to Dale Cranston, owner of the Midnight Theater, to show *Talk to Me Sweetly*, Harlow's movie with our very own hometown boy, Matt Knight. Yes, sir, an A-list actor grew up here.

After a run of horror flicks and B-cop movies, Dale needs to change the marquee anyway. Folks on a beach holiday want a comedy or love stories.

Harlow parks in front of 321 Sea Blue Way. We've kept our eye on that place for years. It's special. The first and only home of our prince. When he left for the Great War, he sold it to Malachi and his wife, Ida, for a song. They passed it down to their son, Morris, and his wife, Harriet.

When the Beauty and the Billionaire bought the place and sent in men with hammers and saws, we hoped they wouldn't turn all of our memories to sawdust.

While things are peaceful in town, something is afoot. A contingent of men in fancy suits are gathering at the town hall with the mayor.

In the last year, we've heard whispers. Change is coming. But know this, every little town has a secret. Sea Blue Beach is no different.

Rachel Hauck is a *New York Times*, *USA Today*, and *Wall Street Journal* bestselling author. She is a double RITA finalist, and a Christy and Carol Award winner. Rachel was awarded the prestigious Career Achievement Award for her body of original work by *Romantic Times* Book Reviews. Her book *Once Upon a Prince*, first in the ROYAL WEDDING series, was filmed for an Original Hallmark movie. Two more of her titles are under film contract. A graduate of Ohio State University (Go Bucks!) with a degree in journalism, Rachel is a former sorority girl and a devoted Ohio State football fan. Her bucket list is to stand on the sidelines with Ryan Day. Rachel lives in sunny central Florida with her husband.

Sign Up for Rachel's Newsletter

Keep up to date with Rachel's latest news
on book releases and events by signing up
for her email list at the link below.

RachelHauck.com